---

# LOST FREQUENCIES

### BY CAITLIN LYNAGH

---

## THE SOUL PROPHECIES

First Edition 2019
Outlet Publishing. P.O. Box 1372 Blackpool. FY1 9NQ.. UK.
www.outletpublishinggroup.com

Requests to publish work from this book should be sent to:
info@outletpublishinggroup.com

This book is a work of fiction.
Any resemblance to actual events or persons, living or dead, is entirely coincidental.
Lost Frequencies (The Soul Prophecies)  copyright ©2019 Caitlin Lynagh



www.caitlinlynagh.com



Cover design by atrtink covers

ISBN: 978-1-9995965-4-5 eBook: 978-1-9995965-5-2

*To my cousin Staci, because we laughed at a cube*


Now I have to write at least ten more books to cover
the rest of the family.

Love you all.

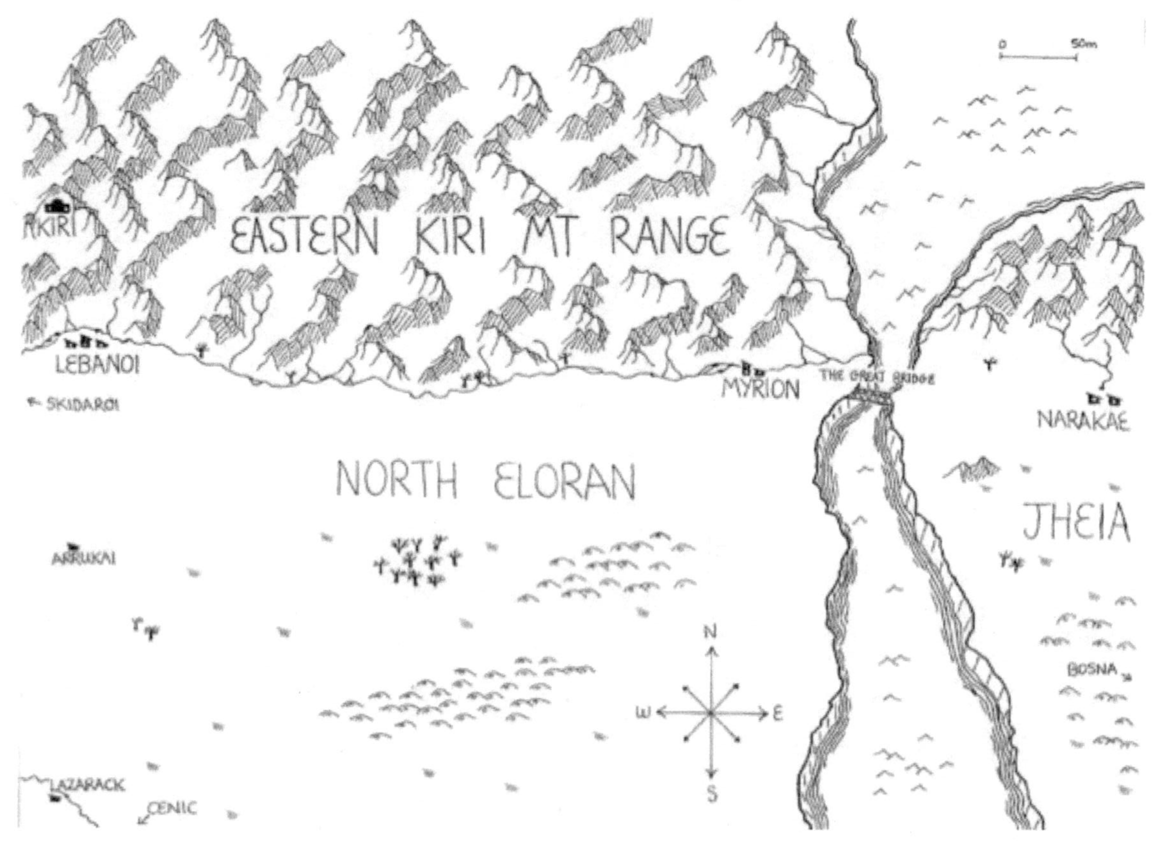

0  50m
EASTERN KIRI MT RANGE
KIRI
LEBANOI
SKIDAROI
MYRION
THE GREAT BRIDGE
NARAKAE
NORTH ELORAN
JHEIA
ARRUKAI
BOSNA
N
W
E
S
LAZARACK
CENIC

# PROLOGUE

*Seven hundred years earlier*

He had seen all the secrets of time. Every life, every death, every decision and every thought that could ever be, for hundreds of thousands of years. He had seen too much, and he knew that one day he would pay the price for it. Arkeenell gazed out across the land from the top of the outcrop where his house stood. Below him stretched the district of Bosna, swathes of greenery and little groves sprouting across the land. It was a very different place to the Jheia he had seen in the future. He watched as an eyeleetansy fluttered up from his garden, its purple wings flashing in the etansy-light. When he had moved to Bosna, he had had no house, and the garden was nothing more than a patch of dirt and grass. Now his garden was a wonderful splash of colour, with a little stone fountain at the centre holding a bronzed pool of water. A tiny blue nawushi flew down, chirped, and dipped its feet into the cool, clear water.

The Jheians of Bosna thought he was mad for living out here alone, but Arkeenell had two very good reasons for picking this spot. It was high up and would withstand most of what nature could throw at it. And here, he could be himself, without having to hide from prying eyes. The eyeleetansy hovered around his head and he held up his hand and watched as it settled on the tips of his fingers, resting its delicate wings. Arkeenell gazed at its purple iridescent hues and smiled.

'Your wings are like my eyes,' he said. The eyeleetansy's wings twitched and it flew away. He reached for a pen and a sealed envelope which he had placed at his side. 'My child,' Arkeenell said, 'I hope that this letter never finds you.' He smoothed the envelope down, and carefully wrote a name on the front. *Ehi.*

# ONE



*The present day*

'Tye, I can't go on,' Yabeesha said.

'Yes, you can. You must,' Tye said. He had his arm around his grandma's waist and his shoulders under her arm. The etansy shone high in the pale pink sky and beat down on them, probing the dry land for moisture.

'No, Tye, I must stop. I know my time has come.'

Tears welled in his eyes but the etansy stole them away before they could fall. 'No,' he said quietly to himself.

'Tye,' Yabeesha said softly. They stopped and Tye watched the air wavering above the ground as though it were rising from red hot embers.

'We must rest, I need to rest,' Yabeesha said. Tye gazed at the wrinkled face of his grandma. Her eyes were closed and shallow breaths escaped through her chapped lips. He cursed silently and scanned the horizon again; they were a couple of days from the nearest district, an abandoned one for sure, but it had a well, and it hadn't been completely empty the last time they had passed this way. He turned his head to the east and saw the O'ekma Mountains curving around the eastern edge of Jheia and stretching up high above them. They weren't far, half a day's travel at most, but dread pinched his heart as he stared at those mountains. Yabeesha was right.

There had been more who travelled with them at one stage;

their ancestors had crossed the southern sea from the volcanic island of Faroi to Jheia with thousands of others, but some had never been able to settle down in one place. Instead, they had travelled peacefully over the once bountiful land of Jheia, but as the land had dried up and the grass turned to dust, their group had dwindled and now it was only Tye and Yabeesha who remained. Tye reached for the water sack hanging across his chest and heard the sloshing sound of water inside. He had another full sack in his rucksack and enough food for several days.

'Hold on, just a little longer,' Tye said. He turned them towards the mountains and reluctantly placed one foot in front of the other.

The sky was a deep shade of purple by the time they reached the foot of the mountains. They found a small cave and Tye checked inside for animals, but it would have been a surprise to find anything more than bones. He helped his grandma inside, dumped his bags, unscrewed the top of his water sack and held it up to Yabeesha's lips. She drank sparingly and slowly.

'It's just as we foresaw,' she croaked.

'Don't be silly, Grandma,' Tye said. 'You've got years ahead of you yet. We can make this.'

'No, it's almost time.' Yabeesha smacked her lips together and gasped as she drank some more. She passed the water sack back to Tye with trembling hands, and let her arms drop like heavy weights at her sides. She turned her brown eyes on Tye and mustered as much strength as she could into that one stare. 'When I have joined our ancestors, you know you must go to Narakae, Tye.'

'You're not going anywhere,' Tye muttered, avoiding her gaze. He busied himself by unpacking their belongings.

'Tye,' Yabeesha said.

He didn't turn around.

'Tye.'

He looked at her.

'Come here.'

He stopped unpacking and went to her, his head hanging low.

'Tye, please don't be sad, I'm the lucky one here,' Yabeesha said. Tye felt the tears welling in his eyes again as he looked up at her.

'I need you here, Grandma, I can't do this alone.'

'Oh, you can, Tye.' Yabeesha stroked the back of his head. 'Go to Narakae and tell her everything we know.'

'What if she doesn't come?' Tye asked.

'She will, Tye. When have we ever been wrong before?'

Tye lowered his gaze; his grandma was right, she was always right.

'I wish it were different, Tye, I really do. I wouldn't wish your fate on anyone and I'm lucky that my life has been this long. But it will be quick when it comes; you don't need to be afraid.' Yabeesha brought his face closer to her own and then pressed her scorching forehead against his.

'I'm not afraid,' Tye said.

'I know.' Yabeesha released him from her grasp. Tye returned to his rucksack and unrolled a small thin mattress. His grandma groaned as she lay down, then she closed her eyes and clasped her hands lightly over her chest.

'Would you like something to eat, Grandma?'

'No, you should save the food for yourself.'

'Grandma…'

'Not another word. Let me rest.'

Tye clamped his mouth shut, it was no use pushing her further. He pulled out a carefully wrapped package, opened it and chewed on the hardened mixture of seeds, oats and dried fruits. Yabeesha lay still as though she was sleeping, but Tye knew that she was awake. He built a small fire and watched the stars appear by the mouth of the cave as the hours passed. Every so often he would cast his gaze over his grandma and, although she lay still, he noticed the lines of pain deepening across her face. Her breathing became louder and deeper and her brow glistened in the firelight. Tye watched her, unable to do or say anything to help her; even the medicinal herbs which had once grown at the foot of these mountains no longer existed. Yabeesha's eyes sprang open and Tye was by her side in seconds.

'Tye,' Yabeesha said.

'I'm here, Grandma,'

'It's time. Promise me… Promise me you will go to Narakae.' Yabeesha held out her hand and Tye clasped it between his own.

'I promise, Grandma, I will go,' Tye said. Yabeesha smiled. She took one final shuddery breath and then her body fell limp and silent. Tye rocked back and forth on his feet, sobbing as he grasped her hand. He didn't know exactly how long he stayed like this, but he became aware of the dawn light creeping into the cave. He gently lowered Yabeesha's cool hand and stood, despite the protests from his aching body. He dried his tears; death for Iyeekans was meant to be a subdued but happy occasion of remembrance. Tye had little time or strength for a ceremony or burial, so he stood in silence and recalled as many happy memories as he could, then began the task of packing his rucksack. He had always known this day would come, the day when he would have to either find another group or travel alone, yet despite how much he had thought he had prepared himself for it, the reality was harsher and more final than he could have imagined. Tye pulled out a lif gauntlet from his bag. It was made from solid metal plates lined with a thin black fabric; it wrapped around and under his thumb, but left his fingers free and open to the air. A thin transparent tube imbedded into the gauntlet on the back of his wrist carried a silvery liquid with a blue sheen which seemed to pulse ominously from within its transparent cage. It was a little too big for him.

He shouldered his rucksack and returned to his grandma's body one last time and removed her necklace. The little black shells, found on the treacherous shorelines, were strung onto a thin piece of rope. He fastened the necklace around his own neck and walked to the mouth of the cave. He took ten paces out, then turned and raised his right arm, the arm that bore the lif gauntlet.

'Goodbye, Grandma.' Tye focussed his mind on the lif; it began to glow brightly and then a thin line of silver shot out from the end of the tube and split into several liquid lines. He imagined these lines driving into the rock around the cave and a second later they did just that. That was the nature of lif – it reacted to thoughts, and Tye bent it to his bidding. He let the lif exploit the cracks in the rocks and then he sent a thought which solidified the lif and made it expand. He heard the rocks begin to crack and withdrew the lif; it became liquid once more and returned to the gauntlet. The mouth of the cave began to collapse, the rocks and rubble filling the entrance. When the last stone had fallen and the dust clouds had cleared, he said one last farewell and then turned and headed back out across the arid lands of Jheia.

# TWO

A pattern of high pitched clicks broke through the crackling sounds emitting through the kaelo's speakers. Varth stopped the yebon and reached forwards to the dashboard for a pencil, a notebook, and a small sound key which could be used to make coded clicks. He cranked up the volume on the kaelo sitting in the centre console and flicked a switch at the side. He pushed a button on the sound key in his hand and sent a series of clicks back through the yebon's kaelo. Once he was done he flicked the switch again and the crackling sounds came back. Varth waited, it wasn't long before another series of clicks sounded through the kaelo and he hurriedly jotted them down, translating the code into words as he went. The kaelo crackled louder and let out a shriek before the clicking stopped. It fell completely silent. Varth stared at it and cursed. He flicked the switch up and down but nothing happened. He pushed a few buttons and turned the dials but still the kaelo remained stubbornly silent. He hit the top of the console with his fist.

Varth felt the engine of the yebon vibrating and humming quietly beneath him. He checked the speedometer and energy levels but found nothing amiss; there was still plenty of energy left in the batteries, the yebon was still drivable, but the kaelo was dead. Varth sighed. *Syvvak is not going to be happy about this.*

He glanced down at the part of the message he had managed to decode.

*Varthrune.* Varth grimaced, no one called him by his full name except his estranged parents and Syvvak, leader of the Neo Iyeeka Liberation group. *I trust your trip has been uneventful so far. I want a full report once you have reached Lazarack. I have begun to...*

*Begun to what?* The partial sentence alone was enough to make Varth feel uneasy. He drew a hand over his tired face; he already knew that Syvvak wanted a report from Lazarack, Syvvak had repeated it many times before Varth had left. It wasn't enough that Syvvak had sent Varth back to the one place he had vowed never to return to, but he had also sent him on a near impossible mission, and now the kaelo was broken.

'Varthrune,' Syvvak had said. 'Recruit these brothers, particularly the youngest one, we need all the talented lif users we can get if our vision of Iyeeka is to become a reality.' Varth threw the notebook and sound key onto the seat beside him, released the handbrake and pushed his foot down lightly on the accelerator. The yebon moved forwards, slowly picking up speed across the dusty, dry land of Iyeeka's biggest continent, Eloran.

Once, this land had been fresh with green vegetation, now it was bare and barren, the unhappy result of centuries of ignorance. It wasn't that Iyeekans were stupid, far from it, they were incredibly bright and talented in certain areas, but their ancestors had never been curious enough to ask *why?* They had never dived deeper into the inner workings of their world, rather, they had been content to ignore and float above such questions as long as everything worked as it was supposed to. This type of happy-go-lucky existence had worked for a long time, and when peace was second nature and supplies plentiful, most problems they encountered didn't need vast amounts of understanding, they could be solved through trial and error, even if it meant multiple attempts to get things right. Now Iyeeka was a vastly different place; supplies were not plentiful and peace teetered on a fine edge. Even without resorting to violence, some Iyeekans had had to make difficult decisions in the past; building walls, taking yebons, rationing supplies. Varth understood this; it was why he had joined Syvvak and the N.I.L. in the first place; tough decisions had to be made sometimes, even if they were uncomfortable to deal with. You couldn't rely on peace when there wasn't enough food or water to go around.

The shapes of indistinguishable buildings began to appear on the horizon and Varth felt a pinching sensation in his chest. He eased his foot off the accelerator and let the yebon slow down a little. *Lazarack* he thought, *the district of suffering and injustice.* He grimaced and clenched the steering wheel tighter. It had been a long time, ten years to be exact, since he had lived in Lazarack, and he still felt the same red hot fury charging through his veins when he thought about those few fateful days. He skirted around the edge of the district; there was only one house he needed to go to, and he didn't want to be seen by any more eyes than necessary. *At least I won't have to deal with Mum and Dad.* The last thing he had heard of his parents after he had left was that they had abandoned Lazarack and travelled to a northern district; he hadn't seen them since. *They probably believed the council members when they said I couldn't be trusted and had evil intentions.* Varth snorted as he laughed. *It was so typical of the council members to see themselves as virtuous, even when they caused so much pain and suffering, even when they were wrong.* His sweaty palms squeaked as they tightened around the steering wheel.

'Focus, Varth, that's not why you're here,' he told himself. He let out a deep breath, eased his grip and forced his shoulders down, but every fibre of his being still felt as though it was tied up in knots. He could make out the familiar shapes of the buildings now; the homes, school buildings and warehouses all looked the same in Eloran. They all had four walls, square windows, tall doors and one, single, gently, sloping roof. Some buildings, like the bigger schools, warehouses and homes, had two storeys, but most buildings were single storey. Every home in every district was surrounded by a large patch of land which belonged to the family, it was where they grew and harvested their food. Though nowadays it was a miracle if any district could grow enough food to survive. Every district was situated either around or near to a freshwater lake or river, though many districts had also drilled wells to gain access to the underground freshwater aquifers.

Lazarack looked the same as it had when he had left; dry, brown and desolate. It was barely clinging onto survival. *Why haven't the council members moved the district already? The lake receded years ago, so surely the well must be almost empty by now?*

He caught sight of two figures working in the land behind a small building on the edge of the district. He parked the yebon and cut the engine. He got out and looked out over the small field; the leaves of a few root vegetables sprouted up from the ground, but they were shrivelled and yellow. It had been a long time since he had set foot onto the brother's land, but he recalled many fond memories of the place. He climbed over the fence and drew nearer to the two men. Varth noticed that the brothers had both cut their hair, their long brown locks were gone, and their hair was now short and stuck out around the tips of their pointed ears. His own hair hung down to his waist in the traditional Elorish style. The eldest brother, a tall, stocky man, dropped his shovel and approached Varth, at first cautiously, and then his face slackened as the shadows of questions and answers flashed across his eyes.

'Mother Iyeeka! Varth? Is that you?'

Varth felt his throat crack, he couldn't muster any words so he tried a small smile and a nod. The man grinned as he bounded over to Varth and hugged him fiercely.

'Varth! I can't believe it, it's really you.'

'Yeah, Roarn, it's me,' Varth said. Roarn relinquished his hug but held onto Varth's shoulders and peered into his face.

'It's been a long time,' Roarn said; his grin was infectious and for a moment Varth forgot the pain and fury he felt at being back in Lazarack and found himself grinning too. 'I didn't think you were ever going to come back,' Roarn said.

'Believe me, I didn't think I would ever be back myself,' Varth said. He caught a glimpse of Roarn's brother, smiling behind him. 'Zerren,' Varth said as he pulled away from Roarn.

'Hey, Varth,' Zerren said.

'Hey, it's good to see you,' Varth clasped Zerren's arm and patted him on the back.

'You too,' Zerren said.

'You've grown up a lot,' Varth said. 'You were still a kid when I left.'

'I was sixteen.'

'Barely walking then, by Iyeekan standards.'

Zerren grinned and shook his head. Varth cast a searching glance over the land and house.

'Where's Lucoe?' he asked. The grin instantly dropped from Zerren's face and his body became stiff. Varth glanced between the brothers. The smile had vanished from Roarn's face too and he stared at the ground. 'What? What's wrong?' Varth felt a familiar squeezing sensation, like string being wound too tightly around his chest.

'It's…' Roarn said glancing quickly up at Varth. 'Lucoe… he…'

Zerren turned his back on both of them and his shoulders began to tremble. Varth followed Roarn's gaze across their land to a line of statues near the entrance to their land. *No? It can't be?*

'Roarn?' Varth said.

'It happened eight years ago…' Roarn began but Varth was already hurrying across to the statues. He stopped in front of the nearest one. It was eight feet tall, carved in Lucoe's likeness, a true representation of the Iyeekan buried beneath it.

'No,' Varth said as he gazed at the statue. Lucoe, the middle brother, the compassionate and rational brother, the brother who always smiled when he talked to anyone, he was dead? Varth heard footsteps approach and stop beside him.

'What happened?' Varth asked.

'It was an accident,' Roarn said, placing a hand on Varth's shoulder and giving it a squeeze. 'There was a call for volunteers for the western sanitation team. We decided to go, we had heard they had seen fresh bellua prints on their last trip to the ocean; Zerren was desperate to see them and Lucoe wanted to go and see if there were any sea-nawushi. We broke away from the group and, well, we found a small herd of bellua.' Roarn's voice cracked. 'The herd bolted and Lucoe and Zerren got caught in their path; both of them were badly injured but Lucoe's injuries were far worse. I managed to get them both back to the group and then we made it to the nearest district. Lucoe died a couple of days later and Zerren was lucky to survive.' Varth nodded, he knew what bellua looked like, he had seen them himself when he had been sent to sanitation. The herd he had seen had been small and the beasts thin, but they were still the biggest land animals in Iyeeka. Varth watched as Zerren aggressively drove a shovel into the ground.

'When Zerren woke up and realised that Lucoe was gone he blamed himself,' said Roarn. 'He's never forgiven himself for it.'

'How did you manage to get them back to the group by yourself?' Varth asked.

'I used lif. I might not be the most competent lif user but I was pretty desperate. I knew it would be difficult to carry both of them and that it would potentially make their injuries worse, so I made a lif raft of sorts and dragged them both back to the group.' Varth eyed Roarn's broad shoulders and muscled arms; if anyone could accomplish such a feat it would be Roarn. Varth gazed at Lucoe's statue and felt the bitter taste of regret; it was another death he hadn't been around for, another friend's funeral he had missed.

'I'm sorry I wasn't here,' Varth said, brushing at his eyes before the tears could fall. 'I liked Lucoe a lot; he was a good friend.'

'I'm guessing you haven't been to Anorae's house?' Roarn asked.

'No. I came straight here. I don't want to come into contact with anyone else from the district, least of all those damned council members,' Varth said, gripping his hands into fists.

Roarn nodded. 'What happened to you? Where have you been all this time?'

'Just here and there.' Varth uncurled his fists. 'I was lucky. I made some friends who looked after me.'

'It's nice to know that there are still some Elorans out there who follow the Iyeekan code,' Roarn said. 'We look after each other; it's what our ancestors taught us.'

Varth bit back a snort of laughter. *I doubt you would still say that if you knew my friends were part of the N.I.L.*

'Is that your yebon?' Roarn asked.

'Yes, well, I borrowed it from a friend actually, why?'

'It's just…' Roarn drew his bottom lip between his teeth.

'Just what?'

'The district are making plans to move north,' Roarn said. 'The lake is dry and our well is nearly empty. We're planning to take the old laburnem carriage as we don't have enough Zirees to carry the entire district, and we have a number of children and elderly. The laburnem needs repairing and it's likely that the tracks will need repairs en route.'

'So?' Varth said.

'We've been talking about visiting the nearest ghost towns to search for resources, but we don't have any way of transporting anything. If we had a yebon though, we could do that.'

'I see.' Varth weighed this new information in his mind; the brothers needed him, it was the perfect opportunity to talk to them and to try and recruit them to the N.I.L. It wouldn't be easy though, most of the remaining districts distrusted the N.I.L. Roarn's high morals and principles would be difficult to overcome and Zerren was sure to agree with his older brother. Syvvak had only given Varth two weeks to recruit them but travelling south in the yebon would take much longer and he no longer had a kaelo to inform Syvvak of any change of plan. *Would Syvvak be pleased enough to let that go if I successfully recruit them?* Syvvak would be disappointed when he found out that Lucoe was dead, but he would be more disappointed if Varth didn't recruit the remaining brothers, particularly Zerren. The decision was easy.

'Ok, let's do it.'

'What? Really?'

'Yeah, I mean, you'd do the same for me if I needed help, and besides, Anorae loved this district and its residents. She would hate me if she knew I hadn't helped, no matter how I feel about certain individuals.'

'What about your friend though?' Roarn asked.

'I don't think he'll mind. He knows how difficult my past has been and he let me borrow his yebon specifically for this trip. I guess I just wanted to see the place where I grew up again, try and remember the good times, do you know what I mean?'

'I do,' Roarn said. He smiled and patted Varth's shoulder again and Varth smiled back. *Syvvak should congratulate me on using my initiative.*

'I want to take half of what we find,' Varth said.

'Half?'

'It's only fair, without the yebon you'd have none,' Varth said.

'That's true... I guess.'

'Deal,' Varth said, holding out a hand. Roarn shook it.

'The sooner we leave the better,' Varth said. 'I don't really want to hang around the district for any longer than necessary.'

'No, of course,' Roarn said. 'I'll tell Zerren. We can leave tomorrow at first light.'

'Good,' Varth said.

'It will be nice to spend some time together and catch up,'

Roarn said. 'I'm sure you've got lots of stories.'

'Maybe a few.'

# THREE

*What is this?* Zerren brushed his fingers over the smooth metal. Warped silvery lines decorated the curved, polished surface as it gleamed under the dim lights. His scalp prickled and the voices inside his head, the ones he had grown so accustomed to over the last eight years, all leapt out at once. *Fear, death, despair, anger, guilt,* they said in turn, man and woman, young and old. They spoke for his ears alone, clambering for his attention, speaking over each other in a cacophony of sound.

'Hey, what have you found down there?' Varth asked, breaking through the noise inside Zerren's mind; the voices began to fade. Varth's heavy footsteps descended the stairs behind Zerren and one last voice rang out from the deep, untouchable place inside his mind. *Hope,* a woman's voice said before fading with the rest. Zerren pulled his hand away from the curved metal.

'I don't know,' he murmured as he gazed up at the large metal cylinder. It was at least twelve feet tall and four feet wide, standing against the furthest wall in this little underground room. Attached to the right side was a tall rectangular metal box; it looked like a battery, but it was bigger, and covered with buttons and switches.

'Woah, you hit the jackpot,' Varth said. 'Look at all that metal.'

'It's metal, it's not lif,' Zerren said as he gazed down at the gauntlet strapped to his right wrist; both Varth and Roarn had one too. Zerren looked back up at the metallic cylinder. 'I don't know what this is.'

'No, but it's still metal.' Varth stopped beside him and gestured at the cylinder. It had taken them eighteen days to reach Cenic, the southernmost district they had agreed they would attempt to reach before heading back to Lazarack. Varth held up a glowing glass cube in one hand which lit up the bottom of his smooth, angled jaw and caught on the harsh lines of his cheek bones.

*Don't trust him,* an elderly man's voice yelled at the back of Zerren's mind. He pushed the voice back; he didn't need to be told, he was already wary of Varth. Varth had been nothing but friendly towards Zerren and Roarn, and he spoke highly of his western friend Zael, but there were details missing, inconsistencies in Varth's stories. Zerren glanced down at the floor where chunky wires protruded from the bottom of the cylinder and curved outwards into the cramped, windowless room. All of the wires except one led to tables where strange black boxes with dusty glass fronts sat. Zerren crouched and picked up the one odd end; a metal square with four short prongs; it looked like the miniature head of a deadly sheeka, beached on the sandy banks of the river, gasping for air. It seemed to be some sort of plug, but the plugs Zerren was used to had one or two prongs, not four.

'This is strange,' he said as he scanned the floor. 'Why would anyone build underground like this?' His gaze snagged on another wire with a black boxy end and he picked it up.

'To hide this, obviously,' Varth said. 'It's clever, if you ask me; no one would think to look for hidden, underground rooms, not with the tremors we have.' Varth moved his glowing, glass cube in a wide arc. 'Woah, even the walls, floor and ceiling are made of metal.' Zerren followed the yellow patch of light cast from Varth's torch as it drifted across the metallic grey walls. Every inch of smooth surface was covered by large, interlocking, rectangular metal plates.

'They're the same metal sliding plates we use for the bases of our buildings. A room made out of soil or bricks would crack and cave in on itself,' Zerren said. He went back to studying his new wire and found that the black boxy end had four metal holes about the same size and width apart as the end which looked like a miniature sheeka head. He pressed the two together gently and found that they slotted together easily.

'What is this? Zerren? Varth? Are you down there?' Roarn's voice boomed from above. Zerren glanced up to the rectangle of light at the top of the narrow stairwell.

'Yeah, we're down here,' he called, dropping the wire as he stood up.

'We should take the floor and walls apart,' Varth said.

'What is this place?' Roarn asked as he cautiously descended the stairs. Zerren gazed at his brother; they both stood at over seven feet, but Roarn had a couple of extra inches in height and width. They were both pale too, like the majority of their kind; their skin was as white as Iyeeka's two moons.

'Zerren found the mother lode of metal,' Varth said, fishing out a tool from his dusty brown rucksack and setting to work, unbolting the metal plates on the floor.

'Be careful, Varth,' Roarn said as he surveyed the room. 'What is that?' Roarn marched over to the cylinder.

'We don't know,' Zerren said.

'Hmm, it looks high-tech, but it must have some practical use,' Roarn said.

'Do you think some Elorans were experimenting down here?' Zerren asked. Roarn frowned.

'Probably. Those big boxy things on the tables remind me of the mathematical computers I once read about. They were used to help launch rockets into space decades ago when we mined our moons, but this…' Roarn gestured to the cylinder. 'I don't like it, this isn't natural,' he said. 'We should leave.'

'Are you kidding me?' Varth said. 'Use those eyeballs for a second and look around. We've found nothing of use to us in hundreds of miles and you want to leave?'

Roarn glanced at the metal around them. Over the centuries, because of the droughts, the famines, and the limited resources available, the population of Iyeeka had dwindled. And those who remained lacked both the relevant skills and the motivation to make much of anything. The metal around them was a valuable resource, not as valuable as lif, but still, any metal was highly sought after. Roarn bit his lower lip.

'Alright, but make it quick. Being this far south makes me nervous; the sooner we leave Cenic the better,' he said. Varth grinned, revealing a missing canine, and then began working to free the plates from the floor.

'This is hardly the far south,' Zerren said.

'You know what I mean,' Roarn replied. 'The far south of Eloran might as well not exist anymore since the desert claimed it.'

'Your brother's right,' Varth said, without looking up. 'If you think Cenic is hot then further south is much, much worse. Even the N.I.L. won't go there; there's no water, no food, and it's not worth even trying to salvage anything.'

'The N.I.L.?' Roarn said. Varth paused.

'It's just what I've heard,' Varth said. 'Cenic is about as far as anyone can go without being roasted to death, and there isn't any water or food there either.' Zerren watched as Varth continued to pry up the plates from the floor. He raised an eyebrow at Roarn.

'Come on,' Roarn said with a tight smile. 'Let's just get this lot out of here.' He began rooting around inside his bag. Zerren wandered over to the table where one of the strange boxes with the glass fronts stood. He tapped the glass, but nothing happened. He looked down at some dusty, abandoned paperwork on the table. He picked up a slim folder, brushed off the dust and opened it. Inside was a single sheet of paper, tinged yellow with age on which was a neat diagram of the cylinder and a jumble of hand written letters and numbers which made no sense to Zerren. At the top of the page someone had written, in the Elorish script, *The Usol Key*. Zerren picked up the page and walked back to the cylinder. He ran his fingertips over the polished, curved metal and then curled his hand into a fist and knocked on the surface, *bong*. The sound carried a faint ring that echoed back at him.

'We'll have to cut through that with lif,' Varth said, glancing briefly in Zerren's direction. Zerren looked at the rectangular metal box beside the cylinder. It reached up to his waist. There were wires protruding from the back. He pushed one of its silvery buttons and flicked a black switch, nothing happened.

'Quit messing around with that,' Roarn said.

'Alright.' Zerren turned to help Roarn and Varth but his ears popped and a tingling sensation charged over his scalp, settling silently behind his eyes. He froze as the voices came back, swamping over him like a wave of sound. *Check the back,* a familiar, melodic voice said, louder than the rest. Zerren's felt his guts twist, *Lucoe.* He gritted his teeth and focussed on pushing the voices away, and, slowly, they retreated back beyond the realms of his consciousness. Zerren sighed and rubbed the sweat from his brow; he felt his body trembling and gripped his arms to stop them from shaking. Lucoe's voice brought him both pain and comfort; he never ignored it. He turned back and leant behind the device to see if he could feel anything on the back. His fingers tripped over some switches and he heard a couple of clicks. Something hummed to life and, from somewhere within the cylinder, a faint whirring sound grew louder and louder. The boxes on the tables began to glow and a white light shone through tiny vertical seams on either side of the cylinder and two curved seams above and below it.

'What did you do?' Roarn snapped. He was beside his brother in three long strides.

'I… I don't know,' Zerren said, gazing at the cylinder.

'We need to get out of here,' Roarn said, standing back.

'Hang on a sec.' Varth grasped Roarn's arm. Roarn stared at his brother and reached out towards him.

The humming grew louder and louder until they could no longer hear their own thoughts. Roarn and Varth clasped their hands over their ears but Zerren stood tall before the cylinder and stared as the light pulsed from within. The ground trembled and the noise reached its peak. The light went out and everything fell, still, quiet and dark. Roarn and Varth lowered their hands slowly and the cylinder let out one final dry, spluttering sound. Something popped, and the front of the cylinger broke away and slid in one smooth movement to the right. A cloud of smoke erupted from the cylinder but Zerren barely had a moment to register the fact that it was hollow inside. As the smoke cleared, a woman fell forwards, straight into his arms. He knelt down slowly under the weight of her slight frame.

'What the…' Varth said.

'Zerren,' Roarn said, stepping up to his brother.

'Look at her hair,' Varth said. The woman's head lolled, and her body sagged as Zerren held her.

'Is she alive?' Roarn asked.

'I don't know,' Zerren said, glancing down at her. He moved two fingers up to her neck to check her pulse and noticed her chest rising and falling slightly. 'I think so.'

'Look at her freaking hair,' Varth said. It was a pale purple, so pale it was almost like starlight, not a natural colour found amongst Iyeekans. Her eyelashes and eyebrows were the same whitewashed colour and her pale pink lips were parted slightly; Zerren could just about hear her faint breathing. His gaze travelled down her body and snapped back up again as he realised she was naked. He held her tightly to his body, obscuring her from both Roarn and Varth's view.

'Roarn, get my cloak out of my bag,' Zerren said. Roarn quickly complied, handing over the garment. The brown fabric was thin, but it was durable and weatherproof.

'Who is she? How come her hair's like that?' Varth said.

'Who knows?' Zerren pulled the cloak around her.

'Who cares about that? What I want to know is, why was she inside that thing?' Roarn pointed to the open cylinder. Zerren twisted to face Roarn and Varth. 'No one has lived in Cenic for decades now. Has she been in there the entire time? How is she even alive?' Roarn asked.

'It must be a medical machine of some sort. Look, I found this.' Zerren handed Roarn the page he'd found.

'She's probably important,' Varth said. 'Why go to all that trouble to build that thing and put her in there?' His murky green gaze shot up to the cylinder and then back to the young woman. Zerren's brow tingled. *Don't trust him,* a man's voice warned from the back of his consciousness.

'The Usol Key?' Roarn said, as he studied the page.

'Or she's a criminal and this is some unique form of punishment,' Varth said. 'She could be dangerous.'

'I don't think so, no one would do something like this,' Roarn said.

'You'd be surprised,' Varth muttered.

'Here,' Roarn said handing the page back to Zerren. 'I don't understand it but keep hold of it for now.'

'What are we going to do about her?' Varth asked, eyeing the woman.

'I don't know, but we can't leave her,' Zerren said. He stood up, lifting the woman and cradling her to his chest.

'It'll be an extra mouth to feed,' Roarn said, rubbing his jaw.

'Your brother's right. We can't really spare the food or water,' Varth said.

'Only if she wakes up, and besides, if things had been different then there would have been an extra mouth to feed anyways,' Zerren said as he stared at his brother. Roarn let out a sigh and nodded.

'Take her back up to the yebon and see if you can wake her,' Roarn said. 'Varth and I will salvage as much metal as we can and meet you up there.'

'She'll stick out for sure,' Varth said.

'We can hide her,' Zerren said.

'You're going to hide a woman with purple hair?' Varth raised a dark brow.

'Yes,' Zerren said. Varth shrugged and set back to dismantling the floor as Zerren headed up to the surface.

# FOUR

Zerren held the woman in his lap like a young child as the yebon grumbled beneath them. Its chunky rubber wheels kicked up clouds of dust behind them and the etansy-light gleamed off of its oval, glass doors. Roarn wasn't pleased about the lack of space as he worked on trying to fix the kaelo lodged in the centre of the yebon's dashboard. It had been a rare sight to see a yebon in the past as there hadn't been much need to travel anywhere, it was even rarer now. Roarn muttered under his breath and cursed as he pulled out wires. Zerren studied the page he had salvaged from the strange underground room. The numbers and symbols seemed like a mess, the product of a mad Eloran's ravings, but there was a familiar symbol at the bottom of the page. In dark red ink there was a little logo depicting several mountain shapes.

'The Moribi of Kiri's symbol is on this page,' Zerren said.

'Ow,' Roarn said as a spark jumped between the wires and singed his fingers. He sucked on them and turned to Zerren.

'I told you you'd never fix it,' Varth said. Roarn rolled his eyes and took his fingers out of his mouth.

'It's from Kiri?' he said, taking the page from Zerren and scrutinising the symbol.

'Looks like it; someone must have taken it from their records,' Zerren said.

'Stolen it, you mean,' Varth said. The woman groaned and wriggled in Zerren's arms; he glanced down at her just as her pale eyelashes fluttered open like delicate eyeleetansy wings. Zerren felt his jaw drop; her irises were purple, a deep, vivid purple with lighter purple flecks around the outer edges. The yebon swerved sharply and Roarn yelled. Varth cursed, straightened the yebon and stopped abruptly.

'Varth!' Roarn growled.

'Her eyes,' Varth said. 'Her eyes are purple too!' The woman didn't speak but she looked up at Zerren and moved her lips.

'Roarn, do you have some water?' Zerren asked.

'I was hoping she'd stay asleep,' Roarn said, handing Zerren a water sack. Zerren helped the woman to sit up and held the water sack to her lips. She drank slowly and just as Zerren's arms began to cramp she stopped drinking and let out a small, satisfied sigh. She stared at the three of them with large round eyes.

'Well, what's your name?' Varth asked.

'We really should introduce ourselves first,' Roarn said. Varth frowned. 'Apologies,' Roarn said. 'My name is Roarn, this is Varth. And the one who won't let go of you is my younger brother, Zerren.' Zerren felt a rush of warmth shoot up the back of his neck and into his cheeks. The woman turned to look at him for a brief moment and then gazed back at Roarn and Varth.

'So what's your name?' Varth said, leaning forwards eagerly. The woman said nothing. 'Do you know where you are? Where are you from? How old are you? Do you speak? Why do you have strange eyes?' Varth plucked the page from Roarn's grasp, held it up and pointed to the picture. 'Do you know what this is?'

'Varth, give her a break, she's probably confused and disorientated,' Roarn said. Varth grumbled, dropped the page in Roarn's lap, folded his arms and sat back in his seat. The woman gazed up at Zerren again, staring into his eyes; there was no recognition in her gaze, but Zerren sensed a deeper intelligence lurking in those purple depths.

'I think she likes you,' Roarn said. 'It's not the way I envisioned you settling down but Mother will lose it when she hears about this.'

Zerren stared at his brother with disdain and Roarn laughed.

'I'm joking,' he said. He gazed out at the dry cracked land and up at the pink-tinged sky. 'Here, put this somewhere safe; I'm sure Father will want to see it.' Roarn gently folded the page and handed it back to Zerren. 'Alright, we should probably recharge the yebon's batteries since we've stopped now anyways.' The woman's body went rigid, as if she had somehow found a burst of energy; she pulled herself up and gazed out of the window. Her mouth fell open and she twisted violently as she searched the horizon.

'Hey,' Zerren said, struggling to hold her, and pulling the cloak back up as it slipped down her shoulders. The woman pushed her hands up against the glass and peered out at the world; she began to tremble.

'Is she ok?' Varth asked. She turned her gaze briefly on them and tears ran down her cheeks. She continued to stare out of the window and cry; there were no sobs, no sharp intakes of breath, just deathly silent tears. Roarn motioned for Varth to get out of the yebon. He flashed Zerren a helpless smile as they climbed out.

Roam and Varth opened the rear doors of the yebon. Roarn leant inside, avoiding the scrap metal that had been thrown in, and pulled on a little lever on the inner wall near the rear doors. There was a muted click from the front of the vehicle. Roarn picked up three chunky black cables hanging on a hook and headed back to the front.

'I don't think she's seen the outside before,' Varth said. 'And her eyes, no one has purple eyes.'

'I know,' Roarn said. 'Who knows how long she was in that weird machine or what it did to her.' Their steps crunched as they reached the front of the yebon where a curved metal hood had lifted to reveal three black batteries side by side. The batteries were two feet tall and one foot wide, shiny black with silver trims, the same batteries that were used to power their homes.

'It makes no sense,' Varth said as he helped Roarn plug one end of each cable into a battery and the other into a slot at the top of the front windscreen. Zerren opened his door, swung his legs round and stepped out, holding the woman as she clung to him weakly.

'She needs some clothes,' Zerren said.

'She'll have to wear your spare clothes,' Roarn replied. Zerren nodded and carried the woman to the back of the yebon. He set her down just inside, pulled out his bag and rooted for a top and trousers. The woman leant heavily on the side of the yebon, tears still falling down her cheeks and dripping onto the cloak she clutched around her.

'Here, you need to put this on,' Zerren said, offering her a top and trousers. She took the clothes but she made no move to put them on. 'I'll be round the front with Roarn and Varth, just, err, make a noise if you need help.' Zerren made his way to the front of the yebon.

'You know I've met some of the members of the N.I.L.,' Varth said. Roarn drew in a sharp breath and exhaled slowly.

'You shouldn't get close to them, Varth, they're dangerous,' he said.

'No, some of them are crazy, but most of them are just scared Elorans trying to protect their families,' Varth said.

'I find that hard to believe,' Roarn said. 'I've heard that it was the ancestors of the N.I.L., who convinced the northern districts to build their wall.'

'Yeah, but you can't really blame them,' Varth said. 'The signs were there just before the great famine. Elorans were beginning to move from the southern districts up to the north and the western districts knew that a sudden mass influx from the south would cause all sorts of problems. At first it was thought that the problems in the south were only temporary, but when it got worse and fighting broke out, they had to build the wall around the western districts, they were right to do so. Shortly after that the great famine hit and it was chaos. I mean, even Lazarack barely survived from what our grandparents told us and not everyone in Lazarack now is a true native. Farmland was raided, Elorans became violent, and as much as the northern districts tried to accommodate the southern districts, many districts were completely destroyed under the pressure. Thousands died, everywhere throughout Eloran, but no more than usual died behind the western walls. The Elorans there had done what they had set out to do; they protected their families and community.'

'Yes, at the expense of everyone else,' Roarn said.

'And would you have done anything differently had you been a council member with a family in the west at the time? Who would you choose?'

'I… I don't know,' Roarn said. 'There just had to be another way.'

'That's what I thought, but I spoke to some of the sensible N.I.L. members and their stories are interesting; there really wasn't another way.'

Zerren cleared his throat and they both turned to look at him.

'How's it going?' Roarn asked.

'I don't know. I left her to get dressed,' Zerren said.

'Did she speak?' Varth said.

'No.' Zerren shook his head.

'Do you think she can speak?' Roarn asked.

'I don't know; she might be a mute, or not understand Elorish.'

Roarn nodded. 'We're stuck here for a few hours; you might as well try and get some rest too.'

'What about you and Varth?'

'One of us will keep watch,' Roarn said. 'Let us know if anything changes.'

'Sure. I'll just give her a few minutes,' Zerren said. He waited until he couldn't stand the heat of the sun any longer and then he went back round to the back of the yebon. He found her, dressed, but collapsed in the back of the yebon with her legs hanging out between the doors. He pulled the scrap metal and the rest of their spoils out of the back, placing them in a pile on the ground. He hesitated as he watched the woman, but they had done this for the last four days; Roarn, Zerren and the woman sleeping in the back whilst Varth slept on the seats in the front. Zerren got in the back, and pulled the woman's legs inside before shutting the doors behind them; he lay down on the bumpy metal surface next to the woman and used his bag as a pillow. He stared up at the ridged metal roof of the yebon and flicked a switch on the side which sent a pleasant, cool stream of air over them.

Zerren thought about what Varth had said. He had grown up being told that the N.I.L. were selfish and cruel Elorans who didn't care about anyone but themselves, but Varth's question had thrown him. *What would I do?* Zerren wondered. He knew deep down that what the western districts had done was wrong, his guts twisted at the thought, but he couldn't say for sure whether or not he would have acted any differently. He shifted uncomfortably and turned his head to the side where the woman slept; her hair seemed to shine in the dim light. He wondered if perhaps they were wrong, perhaps whoever had put her in *The Usol Key* had just been trying to protect a member of their family too; perhaps there were no ill intentions behind her apparent confinement. He closed his eyes, but it was a while before his mind let him fall asleep.

# FIVE

Everywhere Ehi looked, her mind fought with the reality that was presented to her. She saw the dry land and a ghostly image tried to surface from the depths of her memory. The faint echo of a lush, green world painted itself over the barren brown landscape in her view but then it would disappear again before she could even blink or fully comprehend what she was seeing. That wasn't all though. There were other images, other things in her mind that were clearer and more terrifying, but there were thousands of them, all jumbled up together, desperately trying to push to the front of her jaded memory. It was too much; her skull ached, and her body was so tired. Every time she opened her eyes it seemed as though she had been teleported into a new place. Yet the disturbing images found her in her sleep too; there was no escape from them. She had re-awoken into this world like a new born baby; nothing made sense to her and all the sounds were too loud, all the colours too bright, even the etansy's rays and the night time breeze felt like fire and ice upon her skin.

She heard the name Borucree mentioned by her three companions and it was a word among many that teased her memory. The man who her companions called Zerren held her on his lap in the cramped metal box they had been travelling in. They had called it a yebon and she thought she had heard that word too somewhere before, but every time she tried to recall it, her head ached as though it was being squeezed from all sides. They spoke constantly to each other and sometimes to her; Zerren would speak the most to her but she could only stare at him in response. She sometimes understood what he said, but her mind was too busy sifting through the worrying pictures to form sentences or gestures in return.

Sometimes she would look at her three companions and her vision would waver and struggle to focus. She would blink a few times and sometimes it would stop, and her vision would be clear again, but at other times the world around her would change. When this happened, she saw little translucent spheres appear at the centre of her companions' bodies, glowing with multiple colours. She could also see what looked like black storm clouds with thin bands of golden light weaving their way through the air. The black clouds were enormous and stretched everywhere over the land; she could feel their heaviness on her skin and around her mind. The heaviness cast a chill and drew out intense feelings which made her want to curl up into a ball and hide. The thin golden bands were much smaller and fewer, but they felt much more pleasant. Sometimes she would see the world this way for a short time and other times for much longer, and she had no idea how to control it. When her vision returned to normal, the clouds and golden light disappeared, along with the little spheres.

The yebon stopped and Ehi watched Zerren open the passenger door; he swung them round and stepped out, gently setting Ehi onto her feet. The trousers she had been given slipped down her waist and hips and she grabbed at them to hold them up.

'I know,' Zerren said, 'they're too big for you.' He knelt down in front of her. 'I need you to hold still for me, ok?' Ehi didn't reply. He raised his right arm slightly and she gazed at the strange contraption around his wrist. She had seen it before and recognised it. Her vision began to waver again, and a familiar buzz grew around her mind; she tried to concentrate on it, to grab hold of it, but it wriggled and fought against her fragile state. She chased it around somewhere inside her head and then she had it; her focus sharpened and she felt a spark shoot from the top of her head to the tips of her feet. Her vision switched and the sphere inside Zerren's body bloomed into her sight. It was different from the others; she noticed what looked like a hairline crack running through the centre of his sphere and one half was brighter whilst the other half seemed to be hardly there at all. She stared at his many colours; they were beautifully hypnotising. Aqua and lilac hues twisted around one another, and a big band of deep red circled a tiny black, oval shaped core. This core didn't seem to be related to the black clouds she could see hovering all around them. All three of her companions shared the same core, but their colours were different. She looked down at her own body, but for some reason she didn't have the same colourful sphere; nothing appeared to her.

She gazed at Zerren's core and watched as he took a deep breath and closed his eyes. As he did this, a golden light seeped down from the top of his head and gravitated towards the sphere at his torso. A thin band of golden light leapt out from the sphere, travelled up through the right side of his chest and then down through his right arm to the strange gauntlet he wore. He opened his eyes and the golden light jumped into the tube with the silvery liquid, coating the blue sheen with a golden glow instead. She felt her vision slip away from her and the sphere; the colours, the golden light and black clouds all disappeared. She watched as the silvery liquid, now without its golden glow, shot out the top of the tube. It curved and then hardened into a small, solid blade and Zerren glanced up at her.

'Lif,' Zerren said, pointing to the newly formed blade. 'It's a rare, biological metal found in certain places, though the last known source ran out years ago. We can manipulate it with our thoughts with the right training, though most Iyeekans struggle with even the small amount I have here.' She stared at him and absorbed every word but uttered none in return. 'Anyways, I'm going to cut some of the material off your trousers so I can make you a belt.' Zerren pulled the baggy fabric taunt against her leg and carefully cut in a circle just below her right knee. The bottom of her trouser leg came free and he slid it off her leg before cutting it an inch wide in a spiral fashion, producing a long, single, length of cloth. She watched as the Lif turned back into a liquid and retracted into the tube on Zerren's arm. He stood and looped the cloth around her, securing it around her waist with a knot.

Her trousers felt secure now and she stepped gingerly across the hot ground. She wobbled and Zerren caught her, steadying her.

'We need to find you some shoes,' he said, gazing down at her feet. 'Here, hop on my back.' He knelt down in front of her again with his back to her. Ehi stared down at him, and a memory from some deep, dark recess in her mind leapt out at her. She could remember another man offering this to her, a man who she had loved and trusted. She remembered being smaller and the world seeming much bigger. She shook the memory aside, put her hands on Zerren's shoulders and leant forwards. He caught her weight, clamped his hands under her legs and lifted her up with ease.

'Zerren, let's go,' Roarn said as he shut the yebon's doors. His eyebrows shot up when he saw Zerren and Ehi. 'She's coming too?'

'Yeah, I thought it might be good for her,' Zerren said. 'It might help her speak if she sees something familiar. She also needs some shoes.'

'I'll look out for some,' Roarn said, his gaze dropping to her shortened trouser leg. 'It's a shame you cut up your trousers; eyeleetansy silk is hard to come by these days, but I suppose needs must. Let's go.' Ehi caught Varth's narrowed gaze for a few seconds, but he turned his head and followed Roarn.

They walked past square buildings almost identical to one another, each one set within a large and equal patch of brown dirt, fenced off with broken wooden fences. For a moment Ehi's memory painted a scene of unbroken fences and green shrubs, bushes and trees growing on the land around each building, and Elorans harvesting fruit and vegetables. She blinked and the memory retreated, leaving behind the brown, barren reality. She rested her forehead against the back of Zerren's head and he cleared his throat.

'There's an old story, you know, to do with how Elorans measure out their land. You've probably heard of it.' Ehi said nothing, instead she closed her eyes and focussed on the air passing into her nose and out through her mouth. 'There was a grandfather who had two children, who also had their own families, living on the same patch of land. The grandfather knew that one day he would no longer be around, and he was having trouble deciding how he should divide the land amongst his children and grandchildren. Fortunately, he lived near to two mountains which, from his viewpoint, were identical in height. When the etansy set and the two moons, Orleetan and Ariyeetan, rose up above the mountains, he noticed that a big rock on his land cast a long shadow. So he decided one evening that once each moon reached the tip of each mountain and stood side by side, that he would measure the length of the shadow cast by the rock. He did this and with this measurement he divided the land accordingly; that measurement became the accepted width and length for each individual family's land.'

'That's not how the story goes,' Varth said. 'It wasn't a rock, it was a tree, and I'm sure he had more than two children.'

'It was a rock,' Zerren said.

'It doesn't matter,' Roarn said. 'Every family has a home and enough land to be able to bury their dead, feed themselves and do their work, that is all.'

'Had,' Varth said.

'What?' Roarn said.

'*Had* a home,' Varth said with a sweeping gesture of his arms.

Roarn grunted in response. Ehi cracked open an eyelid as Zerren carried her towards a building with an opening in the fence. Several stone statues of Elorans stood on either side of this opening and Zerren set her down on the ground beside one of them.

'I won't be long. I'm just going to take a look inside that house and see if I can find anything useful,' Zerren said, pointing at the dwelling. Ehi stared at him and watched as he walked away. He stood in the little porch by the front door, took a quick look around, and then he kicked open the door and disappeared from sight.

Ehi leant heavily against one of the statues and looked up at the grey, carved stone. The statue was a lifelike depiction of an elderly woman with long flowing hair, dressed in a simple long dress. Ehi let her gaze wander over all the statues. Those furthest away depicted elderly Elorans, but she noticed that they seemed to get younger as they got closer to the house. There was even the statue of a child amongst the adults and young adults. *What are these? Why are they here?* Ehi turned to look across at the nearby homes. There were more statues, some lining the small barren plots, whilst others stood together in small groups. She searched her mind for an answer and a memory pushed forwards, a memory of a celebration marred by sadness, and she saw a large hole in the ground. *Graves, they're graves.* Her eyes welled and she bit back a cry as several more images passed through her mind, flickering behind her eyes.

She saw a blue and green planet floating amongst the stars; her mind dropped to the planet's surface and she found herself in a world that was both strange and oddly familiar. The creatures looked like Iyeekans, but were different - they were smaller, more fragile, and they walked around amongst towering stone and metal structures with glass windows. A word jumped out in her mind, *humans.* There were yebon-type vehicles of many sizes and shapes gliding by on rubber wheels, yet their occupants did not seem to be controlling these vehicles at all, they barely touched or even faced the wheels which Ehi assumed were for steering. These humans had a variety of hair, skin and eye colours, some even had hair on their faces or wore cloths over their heads. Where they were going or what they were doing, Ehi didn't know, but she sensed that the majority of these humans were happy and content with their lives. Metallic duplicates, loosely based on the human form, walked beside these humans, fulfilling the simplest chores and dealing with waste and infrastructure. Some of these metallic creatures looked almost exactly like their human counterparts and Ehi saw the light of awareness gleaming in their perfectly crafted eyes, but there was no ill intent from either humans or these metallic creatures. She felt a pleasant warmth wash over her and she gazed up at the sky to see a strange golden light over this world.

The sky darkened and she felt the warmth draining out of her. She dropped her gaze and found that the pleasant world she had just witnessed was gone, replaced with a charred and blackened planet. Fires dotted the land and smoke rose up to choke a blood red sky. She could hear almighty crashes as the ground shook violently and trembled beneath her feet. Humans clad in black armour raced across the earth with weapons in their hands which shot projectiles engulfed in their own little lightning storms at high speeds. She saw the humanoid creatures made of metal, moving with a deadly grace across the land, leaving a trail of destruction in their wake. The armour-clad humans fell beneath these metallic creatures as though they were nothing more than flowers being crushed into the ground. She could feel the sense of sadness, frustration, anger and fear emanating from the humans, but with the metallic creatures she felt nothing but the desire to kill. There was something wrong with these creatures, no matter how humanlike some of them appeared; when Ehi's mind reached out to them they felt empty and cold. Their intelligence and strength were obviously superior to that of the humans, but they lacked certain emotions, which left them far removed from humanity.

Her mind flickered rapidly back and forth between both worlds; one moment she would see the pleasant peaceful utopia where these creatures and humans existed side by side and the next she would see the burning, desolate world. *Why?* Ehi thought, but as soon as she thought the question the answer appeared in her mind. She saw one group of humans, followed by several others, developing these metallic creatures, and a world of peace, order and happiness seemed to be the outcome. Then she saw another group developing these same creatures and the outcome was very different; there was violence, death, and life on their planet seemed to end in a great ball of fire. Ehi tried to pull her mind away but another string of images painted their way across her vision; her head throbbed and her mind felt as though it was tearing itself in two. She clutched the sides of her head and tried to will the strange images away. But she knew that she had seen them before; she felt as though she had walked among these images for a long time, searching for something that had been of the utmost importance, but what that was, she had no idea.

# SIX

Zerren lifted the strange woman onto his back again and left the dwelling and its empty land. He had found nothing of use inside, just skeletons. The woman squeezed his shoulders and he wondered if she was ok; she had been gripping her head pretty tightly and grimacing when he had first come out of the house but now she seemed to be back to her usual vacant self. He walked into what would have been a main street and caught sight of Varth appearing from one of the other homes with a victorious smile, but then the strange voices rushed into his mind and he stopped in his tracks. *Death, fear, prey, kill,* they said in turn. The words echoed around his mind; he felt every muscle in his body tighten and then he heard a low rolling growl, punctuated with an intermittent rattling sound.

'Behind you, run!' Varth yelled. *Duck* a voice screamed at the back of his mind. Zerren heard the ground tearing behind him and he dropped to both knees as another growl ripped through the air and a mass of thick muscle, limbs and a greyish-green hide leapt over him. The beast skidded to a halt several metres before Zerren, and turned to glare at him.

'Bokhanya,' Zerren murmured under his breath. He stood slowly, willing his shaking limbs to be still as the woman clung to him. The bokhanya stood just under two metres tall on four powerful legs, and black spikes extended from its back. It had hooked claws and two long canines protruded from its upper jaw. The bokhanya pinned Zerren with its yellow eyes and narrow black pupils as it moved back and forth, and Zerren could see its scaly skin dipping into the hollows of its ribcage. Zerren gulped. *Death, fear, prey, kill, blood, death,* the voices in his mind yelled over one another. The bokhanya growled, raising its haunches and ripping the ground, before lunging straight at them again. Zerren barely had time to breathe, let alone think, as he felt the woman twist on his back. She wrenched herself free and Zerren felt his lif gauntlet grow almost unbearably hot as the woman grasped his shoulder. It happened all at once then; he felt the ripple of energy rip across his scalp and a burning smell stabbed at his nose. She pulled him down and thin lines of lif ran in the air just inches above them, coalescing into an oval-shaped mesh. They fell as the bokhanya leapt and the lif solidified into a shield. *Push up!* a voice yelled in the back of Zerren's mind and he thrust his arms up towards the underside of the shield. There was a muted thunk as the bokhanya hit the shield, glancing off the smooth surface as Zerren and the woman pushed upwards together, using the beast's momentum to send it flying behind them.

Zerren stared up at the silvery underside of the shield, blinked and then saw the pink sky. The woman had already spun away from him, holding her new-formed shield as she faced the bokhanya. He rolled to his feet to prepare for another attack but, in that instant, the lif shield disintegrated and split into five liquid lines. The woman sent the lif through the air straight at the bokhanya, wrapping one liquid lif line around each limb and another around its jaws. The lif solidified and the bokhanya fell to one side, thrashing against its new bonds. Zerren glanced down at the tube on the back of his gauntlet; sure enough, it was empty. No one in the history of Iyeeka had caught a bokhanya; no one had probably ever tried.

'What? How?' Zerren said, glancing between the woman and his lif gauntlet. She didn't react to him, she just stared as the bokhanya thrashed about on the ground.

'She stole my lif,' Varth said, running towards them. 'How the hell did she steal my lif?'

'Yeah, thanks for the help,' Zerren said.

'She took mine too,' Roarn said, approaching from the opposite direction. 'Are you alright, Zerren?'

'I'm fine,' Zerren said, turning to face his brother. 'She took my lif too.' He held up his empty gauntlet.

'How? How can she do that?' Varth asked.

'I've heard of it happening,' Roarn said. 'But it's rare.' They turned to the woman who was still staring at the bokhanya. 'I've never seen a bokhanya this close up before,' Roarn said.

'I've seen them,' Varth said.

'When?' Roarn said.

'I was sent to sanitation for six months, remember,' Varth said.

'It shouldn't be out here,' Roarn said with a frown.

'The fences have probably deteriorated,' Zerren said.

'Or someone let them in,' Roarn said. 'I bet Syvvak would…'

'Syvvak might talk big but he wouldn't do something like this,' Varth said.

'You've met him?' Roarn asked.

'Well,' Varth rubbed the back of his neck, 'I mean, I've seen him a couple of times.'

'You've spoken to him?' Roarn said.

'Only briefly,' Varth said, casting his gaze to the ground. 'He's pretty busy most of the time.'

'What's he like?' Zerren asked.

'Syvvak? He seems to be a difficult Eloran to get to know, but he does care. He has a son who's sick; it's said that he does everything for him.'

'Whilst letting the rest of Eloran suffer, no doubt,' Roarn said.

'You shouldn't judge him so quickly, Roarn. You haven't met him.'

'I don't wish to meet him.'

'Well he's a bit of a hero in the west, he looks after the vulnerable and the weak.'

'I'm surprised by that,' Zerren said.

'You're forgetting, brother, that he only looks after those behind his walls, he doesn't spare a thought for those outside of them,' Roarn said.

'It's not that simple.' Varth sighed.

'Hey, I wouldn't do that if I were you,' Roarn said, gazing at the woman. She ignored them as she slowly approached the bokhanya. She kept her arms out, with her palms facing up.

'She's mental,' Varth said. The bokhanya stopped thrashing and fell limp, breathing deeply as it lay on the ground. It kept a large eye on the woman as she knelt down by its head. The bokhanya growled quietly, snorting through its narrow nostrils as she placed a hand on top of its head. Zerren leapt forwards to stop her, only to feel a strong hand grasp his upper arm and yank him back.

'I think she might be the first to touch a living bokhanya,' Varth said.

'What's she doing?' Zerren said. 'She'll get herself killed.' Roarn held him as he tried to tug away.

'No,' Roarn said. 'The lif is strong.' They watched as the beast stiffened, its eyes bulged, and its pupils shrank into narrow lines for a brief moment. Then it relaxed and gazed up at the woman and she stroked its head as though it was nothing more than a child.

'What did she do to it?' Varth asked.

'I have no idea,' Roarn said. The woman's head snapped up and her gaze flew to Roarn. She stood up and marched over to them on shaky legs but with a fierce determination, reached for the bag on his back, pulled out the water sack and returned to the bokhanya. With no word or gesture, she released the bonds tying the creature and the liquid lif ran back into the tubes. Varth cursed as the bokhanya got to its feet and Zerren braced himself for another attack.

The woman didn't flinch away from the bokhanya; instead she held the water sack up and put her hand gently on the side of its neck as she tipped the water into its mouth. The bokhanya drank greedily and, once it had drained the entire sack, a forked tongue slipped out between its jaws as it licked up any moisture which had managed to escape from its deadly mouth. It fixed one eye on the woman, gazing at her for one long last time, before it turned and ran off across the desolate land. Varth let out a low whistle.

'I've never seen anyone do that before,' he said. The woman's shoulders shook and she turned slowly to face them, tears running down her cheeks. Roarn released his grasp on his brother and Zerren approached the woman cautiously, placing his hands on her narrow, shaking shoulders.

'Are you ok?' he asked. 'It's gone now.' She looked up at him as the tears continued to fall. There was a desperate abandonment in her gaze, a sadness that seemed unfixable.

'Here, I've got shoes,' Varth said. He tossed the boots to Zerren, who knelt down, brushed the dirt from the woman's soles and then fastened the boots to her feet. They were a little big, but they were better than nothing.

'How does that feel?' Zerren asked, gazing up at her. She didn't reply but the tears kept falling.

'Is she ok?' Varth asked.

'I don't know,' Zerren said, standing up again. 'I don't think she's hurt.' He cast his gaze over her, but he couldn't see any wounds or bruises. Her eyelids dropped and she swayed on unsteady feet. 'Are you…' Zerren said but the woman closed her eyes and fell straight into him.

'What happened?' Roarn said.

'I don't know, she's just…' Zerren held her gently by the shoulders. 'I think she's just tired.' He picked her up.

'Take her back to the yebon; we'll finish looking around, but I don't want to stay too long just in case there are more bokhanya nearby,' Roarn said.

'Ok,' Zerren said.

'I can't believe what I just witnessed,' said Varth. He eyed the woman with a mixture of awe and disgust.

'Come on,' Roarn said. 'Let's get this over with.' Varth grunted and the two of them resumed their search for supplies.

Zerren carried the woman back to the yebon and lay her down on the front seats. Her eyelids remained shut and she didn't stir; he checked her pulse to make sure she was alive. He pressed a button which drew a blind over the glass windows and doors, blocking out the light and heat. Then he shut the door and leant against the side of the yebon, keeping a watchful eye on the horizon while he waited for Roarn and Varth.

Roarn returned first with a length of rope curled around his shoulder.

'Find anything?' Zerren asked.

'Just a few pieces of clothing, some knives and this rope but no metal,' Roarn said. 'How is she?'

'Asleep.' Roarn sighed, dropped his bags and stood beside his brother.

'I don't know what she did with that bokhanya, but I've never seen anything or heard of anything like it,' he said. 'Bokhanyas are aggressive creatures, they've always been aggressive and they've always attacked Iyeekans; that's why our ancestors fenced them out of the fertile grounds in the first place.'

'It was like she managed to connect with it somehow,' Zerren said.

'She managed to manipulate three separate lif sources from three different distances; it takes years of practice to manipulate one small source of lif from just a couple of inches, and she did it, just like that,' Roarn said.

'She's powerful.'

'The way she moved whilst fending off that bokhanya; it was like her body was made of liquid lif the way she twisted and curved.'

'You saw it too?' Zerren asked.

'I was by the grave statues there. I was trying to think of what I could do to help you. The woman made the choice for me when she stole my lif, but Mother Iyeeka, Zerren,' Roarn clasped Zerren's shoulder, 'I thought I was going to lose you too. I thought you were going to die and I couldn't even make myself move to help you.' Roarn hung his head. 'I'm ashamed of myself. I'm sorry, brother, forgive me.'

'It's ok,' Zerren said, clasping Roarn's shoulder too. 'I didn't know what to do either. She saved us all.' Roarn lowered his gaze to the ground.

'I don't think Varth has told us everything,' Roarn said. 'I'm worried, he seems to know a lot about the N.I.L.'

'I know,' Zerren said. 'I want to believe him but…'

'He seems different,' Roarn said.

'It has been ten years and he didn't exactly leave Lazarack on pleasant terms.'

'No, I know. Anorae's death was hard for everyone, but it was harder for Varth given the circumstances. I just don't like it; he defends the N.I.L. and now he's talking about Syvvak, it's just, unsettling.'

'He's bound to have heard stuff about Syvvak, though,' Zerren said. 'His friend Zael lives in the western districts. They've probably been brought up with a different, kinder, vision of the N.I.L.'

'You sound like Lucoe,' Roarn said, flashing a weak smile. Zerren was taken aback; he glanced down and scuffed the top of his boot against the ground.

'No, I'm just trying to think things through. I've never been to the western districts before, it's impossible for me to comment on how they operate.'

'True, me neither,' Roarn said as he rubbed his jaw. 'Just keep your guard up. I don't think he's still the same Varth that we once knew.'

Zerren nodded.

'What are you two talking about?' Varth asked, as he rounded the corner of the yebon.

'The woman, she needs a name,' Roarn said quickly. 'Do you have any suggestions?'

'Yes, Freaking Weird.'

'We're not calling her that,' Zerren said.

'Why don't we just call her Cenic?' Varth said. 'It's where we found her.'

'It doesn't really suit her,' Roarn said, folding his arms. 'What about Aetulae?'

'The girl you liked back when we were in school?' Zerren asked.

'I did not.' Roarn's cheeks turned pink.

'Yes, you did,' Zerren said.

'We could call her our mother's name, but that doesn't seem right,' Roarn said. Zerren's skull tingled and a man's silvery voice leapt out from his consciousness, a voice which simultaneously brought a smile to his face and ripped out his heart. *Ehi, her name is Ehi,* Lucoe said, and then his voice sank back down to some dark corner of Zerren's awareness. 'Are you alright, Zerren?' asked Roarn. 'You look a bit grey.'

'I'm fine,' Zerren said, inhaling a shaky breath. 'I'm fine. Ehi, I think we should call her Ehi.'

'Ehi?' Roarn said. 'Where did you get that from?'

'I don't know,' Zerren said. 'It just popped into my mind.'

'Suits me,' Varth said with a shrug, as he carried his spoils to the back of the yebon.

'Fine, I guess we'll call her Ehi,' Roarn said.

# SEVEN

Ahrl approached the district of Skidaroi from the east. He had spent the last few months travelling through the Kiri Mountains and northern Eloran in his search for information and to establish fragile ties between the fractured districts. He had once been a teacher and council member in the district of Jhovire, now he was little more than a nomad. Being a teacher had been one of the most difficult and greatest professions anyone could hope to realize. At least, that had once been the case throughout all of Iyeeka; now there were only two landmasses left with surviving populations: Jheia across the sea to the east and Eloran, with Loenya over the Kiri Mountains to the north. He walked around the edges of the former great Skida lakes, where the water had once glistened in the etansy-light and stretched as far as the eye could see, but now the water lay low and was muddy brown. All the major districts had been situated next to freshwater lakes and rivers, but with the lakes drying up over the long years, only a few places remained. Dwindling resources, changing weather patterns, coastal erosion and dying species had greatly reduced the size of all the land masses in Iyeeka.

He came to the quiet outskirts of the district where few homes were occupied. A couple of trees and bushes bent low under the etansy rays, their few small leaves, once green, now yellow. Ahrl sighed, hefted his pack and gulped past the dry lump in his throat. He heard a commotion up ahead and the sound of bare feet scuffing the ground. He hurried towards the sound and came across two youngsters, a boy of Eloran origins and a girl of Faroi origins – she was small in stature and had deep, dark skin tones. The boy ripped a water sack from the girl's hands and pushed her onto the ground. She cried out and the boy turned to bolt, but Ahrl caught him by the arm.

'Drop it,' Ahrl said. The boy glared up at him and Ahrl felt as though weights had been strapped to his legs. There was so much anger in the boy's green eyes and so much fear. The boy dropped the water sack. 'Get out of here,' Ahrl said, releasing him. The boy paused briefly as if to argue, then ran off. Ahrl shook his head as he watched the boy disappear; he had seen this sort of incident many times before. Ahrl bent down, picked up the water sack and offered it to the girl.

'Are you hurt?'

'No,' the girl said in between gasps; she took the water sack back and sipped from it.

'What's your name?' Ahrl asked, as he helped her to her feet.

'Roe.'

'Nice to meet you, Roe. My name is Ahrl.'

'Thank you for helping me, Ahrl.'

'You should get going, your parents will be worried about you. I'll walk you home,' Ahrl said. Roe turned her gaze to the ground.

'My parents are dead.' He felt as though her words had stabbed him. Ahrl stood silently on the spot; it wasn't uncommon these days, there were many orphans in Eloran now.

'I'm sorry. What about your siblings?'

Roe shook her head and her knuckles whitened around her water sack.

'Don't you have any family?'

'No,' Roe said. A loud booming sound echoed through the air; the ground shook beneath their feet and the buildings closest to them quivered. 'What was that? Was that a tremor?' Roe asked. Ahrl turned and saw a column of dust and smoke rising up into the air over to the west, deeper into the Skidaroi district. Another boom sounded, and then another, and another, as more clouds spouted up into the air. The sounds of screaming and crying rose up and grew in volume and intensity. Another boom sounded, cracking the air like a whip just a few streets away from where they stood, and a fine shower of dust and grit fell down on them. Ahrl bent his knees as the ground shook and his ears rang, then he grabbed hold of Roe's arm and started to run.

Another series of booms sounded, growing ever closer as Ahrl pulled Roe through the streets. They passed a large, two-storey school, smoke drifting away from the front of the building, revealing ruptured walls and broken windows as though a massive beast had taken a bite out of the side. Bodies lay bloodied on the ground and Elorans wailed around them.

'It's the N.I.L.,' a man screamed as he ran past them. More Elorans appeared, running from the same direction, jumping over the bodies in their haste to get away. Another cracking sound echoed through the air, showering them with more fine dust and grit. The screams surged around them but Ahrl didn't loosen his hold on Roe's arm. He urged her onwards and felt a small measure of relief when the sounds of the explosions lessened behind them. They darted down another street and he spotted his cousin's home on the corner.

'Myaie! Myaie!' Ahrl called as they burst in through the front door.

'Ahrl,' Myaie said, appearing from one of the rooms. 'You're back. What's going on out there? Who's this?' Her gaze fell on Roe.

'This is Roe, we just met,' Ahrl said. 'I'm not certain, but I think the N.I.L. are using explosives to kill.'

'To kill?' Myaie said, placing a hand on her chest and blinking hard. 'I have to get to the school. The other council members will be there. We've got to evacuate the district.' She made her way to the door.

'We just passed what was left of the school,' Ahrl said, catching her by the arm. 'There were bodies.'

She placed a hand over her mouth and squeezed her eyes shut. 'Why?' Myaie said.

'I don't know, but it's probably because most council meetings and public meetings are held in schools,' Ahrl said, as he moved towards a window and peered outside.

'Those criminals have always hated council members,' Myaie said.

'Not all of them are criminals, Myaie,' Ahrl said.

Myaie shook her head. 'I just don't understand what their goal is. What do they gain by killing us and destroying Skidaroi, or any of the districts and putting children at risk?' Myaie said.

'I wish I knew. It's been a while since I've travelled to the far-western districts. I haven't been to Kubus since last year and there was a great deal of unrest back then. I was planning to head that way again after a brief stop here.' Another boom echoed through the air, closer this time. It rattled Myaie's house and sent debris scattering across the roof like hailstones. 'We need to get out of here, Myaie,' Ahrl said. 'Whatever the N.I.L. want, they're not here to negotiate with us. They're here to kill and they won't look favourably on your position as a council member.'

Myaie gulped and nodded. 'Where will we go?' she asked as she dried her eyes.

'We'll have to get a vadi and head down the rivers to Lebanoi,' Ahrl said. 'But we need to move quickly. The whole population of Skidaroi, what's left of it, will have the same idea.'

'Right,' Myaie said. 'I'll just pack a few things.'

'Be quick,' Ahrl said. Myaie nodded and dashed out of the room. She returned quickly with a bag on her back. 'Roe, you should come with us. Can you keep up?'

'Yes,' Roe said.

They left the house and ran through the streets, past abandonded homes, their gardens scattered with small, yellow-tinged shrubs and skinny fruit trees, that lay empty and abandoned. The air was heavy with the weight of its unnatural silence. There was no sign of anyone anywhere, but as they ran north towards the Skida lakes, the wails and shouts of hundreds of Elorans grew steadily louder and louder. They ran out onto the shoreline, the Kiri Mountains on the opposite side, protruding into the sky like the spines on a bokhanya's back. Elorans filled the pebble beaches and muddy banks as they clambered desperately onto the flat-bottomed vadis. Some of the vessels were small, and only meant for six passengers, whilst others could hold up to thirty.

'There are too many of us,' Myaie said, as her gaze swept across the dozen or so vadis bobbing in the low waters. Ahrl glanced up and down the lake and spotted a white vadi to the west, further down on a bend of one of the rivers.

'Come on, this way,' he said.

'Ahrl, that's heading towards the N.I.L., not away from them,' Myaie said, as she hurried to keep up with him.

'Exactly,' Ahrl said. 'Few will follow us.' A sudden booming sound from the centre of Skidaroi caused the Elorans on the shore to fall silent for a few seconds. A great cloud of dust and smoke rose up into the air just a few hundred yards from where they stood, and then the noise of hundreds of Elorans panicking erupted around them. 'Quickly, Myaie, Roe,' Ahrl said as he pushed forwards.

They left the chaos on the shoreline and drew nearer to the single vadi; a small group stood up to their knees in the water, weighed down with bags, children and personal belongings. One man stood on the vadi, brandishing a long stick and hitting at anyone who got too close, whilst several others blocked the path of his vessel.

'I said get back,' the man said. 'I won't let any of you take my vadi.'

'Kes, please,' a man standing in the water said. 'We have children among us. We don't want to take your vadi, we just want safe passage away from Skidaroi.'

'Lies, all lies,' Kes said, as he smacked his stick against the side of his vadi. 'How do I know you're not secretly with those thieving members of the N.I.L., they have spies everywhere you know.'

'We've already told you, we're not with the N.I.L.,' the man in the water said. 'Why would we be standing here in the water begging for safe passage if we were?'

'What's going on here, Estan?' Myaie said as they drew nearer. The man in the water turned to face her and Ahrl saw a flicker of hope and recognition light up across the gathered faces.

'Council Member Myaie,' Estan said inclining his head slightly. 'Kes refuses to help us.'

'It's my vadi,' Kes said, scowling. 'And I get to decide who rides on it and it won't be any of you.' Ahrl eyed the vadi; it was big enough for the small group assembled before it and more.

'Kes,' Myaie said. 'You seem to have forgotten your morals and values, and your responsibilities to your fellow Elorans.'

'Ah, you can keep your morals and values, council member,' Kes said. 'Morals and values don't matter anymore; they won't save you.'

'I demand that you let us on your vadi,' Myaie said.

'No,' Kes said, spitting into the muddy water.

'Kes, do you really want the blood of children on your hands?' Ahrl asked. Kes narrowed his gaze at Ahrl.

'I recognise you,' he said, pointing a wrinkled finger.

'Yes, we hail from the same district, you and I,' Ahrl said.

'I'd be damned.' Kes smacked his lips together. 'Former Council Member Ahrl of Jhovire.'

'Yes,' Ahrl said.

'I thought I recognised your voice, you sound like your father. I respected your father a lot, he was a great Eloran, forward-thinking and wise,' Kes said. 'That was until Loenya offered him sanctuary and he abandoned his district and fled, leaving all of us to rot. I thought you would be with him.'

'My father and I don't always see eye to eye and Myaie is my cousin, Kes,' Ahrl said. 'I wouldn't abandon her, and she wouldn't abandon her district.'

'Oh, but isn't that exactly what she is doing right now?'

'We both know she has no choice.'

'You always have a choice.'

'Kes, you know me, I grew up alongside you. If you can look me in the eye and honestly tell me that it is safe for us to stay then I will gladly stand on the shore and watch you sail away,' Ahrl said. Kes stared at Ahrl and twisted his stick in his hands.

'If I let you on here, then one of you will try and take my vadi from me, or I'll end up dead.'

'We already told you we wouldn't do that,' Estan said. He groaned and shook his head.

'Are you really saying that you would leave all these fellow civilians here when there is plenty of room on your vadi?' Ahrl said.

'Yes.'

'And if we do die, would you be ok with that on your conscience?' Ahrl asked. Kes opened his mouth and then clamped it shut as he glared at Ahrl. 'You don't need to take us far, just a little bit to the east. If you want us to get off at any time, we will, I'll make sure of that, and you have my word that no one will take your vadi from you. You know my power with lif; I can and will stay true to my word, and I am not my father.'

Kes leant on his stick and looked over the group as he ground his teeth. He stared at them for what felt like forever to Ahrl, and then finally he sighed and his shoulders slumped.

'Alright, fine then, but I'm only taking you a couple of districts down the river. If anything happens to my vadi, it'll be on your head, Ahrl.'

'I understand Kes, and thank you,' Ahrl said. He turned to the group. 'Alright, you heard him, board up one at a time please.' Ahrl lifted Roe onto the vadi and then helped several others - three women, two children and four men including Estan. 'Myaie, you next,' Ahrl said, helping her up onto the vadi before hoisting himself up beside her. Ahrl stood tall with his hands on his hips as he glanced over the sturdy wooden structure. It was a good-sized vadi, roughly ten-foot wide and forty feet in length with a small cabin.

The vadi began to move slowly towards the lake where all the other Eloran's stood. They would have to cross this lake and enter the river on the other side in order to head east towards Lebanoi. They hadn't travelled more than a few minutes before an ear piercing scream silenced the Elorans around him and Ahrl's head snapped up to the source as a chorus of screaming erupted from the lake before them. Ahrl felt the blood drain from his face; he could just make out the shapes of Elorans flailing in the water and darker, sleeker shapes lunging up at them. The vadis on the lake pulled away from the shoreline, abandoning the Elorans fleeing from the water and those who hadn't yet boarded.

'Sheeka!' Kes shouted, breaking through their silence. 'Sheeka!' He scrabbled to the controls at the back of the vadi.

'There shouldn't be any Sheeka this far inland,' Ahrl said. He couldn't take his eyes off the scene as the desperate cries echoed across to them. There was a thud on the bottom of the vadi, followed by another, and another.

'What the...?' Estan said. The thuds amplified and there were cracking noises like wood splitting as the vadi began to rock. Roe shrieked, and the other passengers cried out, dropping low to the deck and grabbing hold of anything firmly attached to the vadi.

'Kes, get us out of here,' Ahrl said.

'I'm working on it.' There was a splash from the side of the vadi, followed by a yell and several screams. The thudding stopped.

'Kes!' Estan said, lunging forwards. Ahrl caught the back of Estan's shirt and saw the end of a long scaly tail disappearing beneath the water, but Kes was nowhere to be seen.

'Where is he?' Ahrl said, as he pulled Estan back.

'A sheeka got him, he's gone!' Estan said. 'Mother Iyeeka, he's gone.' Estan drew his hands over his ashen face. Ahrl desperately scanned the water for any sign of movement, but then a terrible deep, murky red bloomed up to the surface, spreading like ink erupting from the riverbed.

'Ahrl?' Myaie said.

'Everyone stay back from the edges,' Ahrl said. 'Estan, can you get us out of here?' Estan said nothing, just stared blankly at the water. Ahrl gripped him by the shoulders and shook him. 'Estan?' Estan blinked, his dulls irises brightening with a small measure of awareness.

'I… I hope so,' he said as he made his way past the little cabin to the controls at the back of the vadi. There was a low rumbling noise as a motor fired up again and the vadi began to pick up speed. Ahrl almost gagged at the stench of death; he held a hand over his mouth as Estan manoeuvred the vadi further into the lake and Ahrl felt as though his body had been snared by the hundreds of sullen-eyed Elorans standing back from the edge of the bloody thrashing water, silently watching them go by. The passengers on the vadi eyed the water nervously and shrank back from the edges, huddling together in the middle of the vessel.

'We should stop and pick up more Elorans,' Myaie said, pulling the edge of her top over her mouth.

'There are too many,' Ahrl said through his fingers. 'They would swarm the vadi and even if they didn't, how could you choose?' Several dark shapes moved under the water, their scaly backs cresting the surface before disappearing once more. Myaie shuddered.

'I thought sheeka lived in seawater,' she said.

'They do,' Ahrl said. 'Sometimes they swim up the rivers into the freshwater lakes, but that hasn't happened for years since the dams and fisheries were put in place. They shouldn't be here, especially with the low-lying water levels; it should be impossible.'

'What are you suggesting? Do you think that someone put them here? The N.I.L.?'

'I hate to say it, but yes,'

'Damn them,' Myaie said, thumping the side of the vadi with her fist.

The vadi drifted on, trailing behind the other vadis that were filing into the rivers heading towards the east. As they entered the eastern rivers, Ahrl felt the tension in his body subside, his adrenaline crashed, and he felt as though his guts had dropped to his feet. He gripped the edge of the vadi for support and looked over to Myaie as tears fell down her cheeks.

'Myaie?' Ahrl said.

'Kes was right,' Myaie said. 'I had no right to demand passage on his vadi and now he is gone, just like he feared.'

'No Myaie, don't blame yourself for what just happened back there, I was the one who convinced Kes to let us board his vadi, not you,' Ahrl said.

Myaie clamped a hand over her mouth and bit back a cry and Ahrl placed a hand on her shoulder.

'It's ok, we're ok,' Ahrl said.

'But Kes…'

'I know. We lived on the same street in Jhovire. I used to go and help him with his land. I used to play futama with his son… There was nothing anyone could do. I need you to be strong Myaie, you're a council member and all of these Elorans here with us, they'll look to you for guidance.'

Myaie's lips trembled and she nodded.

'We will all remember what happened here, Myaie, but please

don't carry all this blame.' Ahrl hugged her.

'Myaie, can I talk to you for a moment,' Estan called from the back of the vadi. Ahrl released Myaie and then cast his gaze over the other passengers. Their faces were haunted, their eyes vacant; they hugged themselves and shivered even though the heat from the etansy was uncomfortable and the air constantly stole away the moisture from their bodies. Myaie dried her eyes, took a deep breath and gave him a small smile before she walked down to the end of the vadi.

# EIGHT

Her eyes watered as a strong and sharp fishy smell rose up from the little parcels wrapped in leaves cooking on top of their small fire. Her head ached as thousands of thoughts, feelings and memories passed through her mind. She could barely grasp the meaning of one foreign memory before another memory knocked it aside and commanded her attention. She huddled under a blanket and felt her brow crease as she stared across the flames, paying little attention to anything else but the sights and sounds inside her head.

'It smells revolting,' Zerren said.

'Yeah, but it's food and it's good for you,' Varth said. 'I bet Ehi won't complain.'

'Are they done yet?' asked Roarn.

'Nearly,' Varth said as a gust of wind blew the smoke in his direction. He coughed and spluttered as he tried to waft it away from his face.

'We're all going to smell like fish and smoke for weeks,' Zerren said.

'I don't know if you've realised,' said Varth, 'but none of us smell so good right now. They're done.' He deposited the parcels from the mesh onto a wooden plate and passed it around. 'Careful, they'll be hot.'

'Here, Ehi,' Zerren said. She blinked at the sound of the name they had given her; it sounded familiar, almost as though it really did belong to her. She concentrated and nudged the memories away for a few seconds and felt her body slump as though extra weights had been added to her limbs. She looked up to see Zerren offering her a plate with the fishy food parcels on it as the memories buzzed around her consciousness like flies. Ehi took the plate, picked up a parcel and blew on it before taking a bite. The memories swamped over her and she felt a sharp pinching sensation behind her eyes and nose. She passed the plate back to Varth and ate in a methodical fashion as a new stream of memories filtered through her mind.

'You know, you guys should really come back to Kubus with me,' Varth said.

'Kubus?' Roarn asked.

'That's where Zael lives,' said Varth.

'It's also where Syvvak's rumoured to live,' Roarn said.

'It's a pretty big district; there are six main districts surrounded by the wall,' Varth said.

'What's it like there?' Zerren asked as he gulped down his food.

'It's not easy by any means,' Varth said. 'They have rationing but it's nowhere near as bad as the rationing outside the districts. You can get three meals a day and four cups of water and pregnant women and children get more water.'

'Do they even realise how bad it is for everyone else?' Roarn asked.

'Yes,' Varth said. 'They know they're lucky.'

'We wouldn't be allowed in anyways,' Zerren said. 'Don't they have strict controls on who gets in and out?'

'They do,' Varth said. 'But you'll be with me. I can get you in.'

'The district and our parents need us, we can't waste our time going to the western districts now,' Roarn said.

'You don't have to stay, Roarn,' said Varth. 'I'm just saying you should come and visit.'

'Yes, but I'm sure the western districts don't just give their food and water away for free. What would they want in return?' Roarn asked.

'Nothing,' Varth said. 'You would be guests.'

'How do you know?'

'It's not an evil place, Roarn, just misunderstood,' Varth said. 'I mean, they accepted me as a citizen when I was homeless and desperate.'

'You didn't have to leave,' Roarn said.

'I couldn't stay.' Ehi momentarily pushed the memories aside again, glanced up and looked between Roarn and Varth.

'How did you get accepted?' Zerren asked.

'Just told them a bit about my past, showed them my abilities with lif, nothing much,' Varth said. 'They would probably accept you two right away.'

'What about our parents and the rest of the district?' Roarn said.

'I don't know,' Varth said. Roarn snorted and picked up another parcel of food.

'Where do they get all of their water from?' Zerren asked. Ehi felt a burning sensation in her chest, it spread out to her shoulders and up through her neck and into her head.

'The wall goes into the mountains,' Varth said. 'They built it around a big lake and placed a reflective cloth over the lake like a tent. It stops the lake from drying out and also allows water to pass through if it rains.'

'That's pretty clever,' Zerren said. The burning sensation began to tingle and itch beneath Ehi's skin, her vision wavered. She blinked to clear it, but something switched, the strange spheres she had seen before appeared again, hovering inside the bodies of her companions. The images which had intruded upon her every waking moment and even her dreams disappeared completely. She tilted her head and marvelled at the many glowing colours twisting inside the spheres.

'It is clever,' Varth said. 'It makes you wonder why no one thought to do it sooner, but then our ancestors were never that good with preventive solutions or even any solutions.' Ehi gazed at Varth's sphere; there was a great deal of grey at the centre and a brilliant golden band around the outer edges, but a burst of green broke through followed by orange.

'That's not exactly a fair comment, Varth,' Roarn said. Ehi's gaze turned Roarn and his sphere; he had thin bands of the brilliant gold and a smaller amount of grey, but he also had a deep red and dark blue band, though a pale, icy blue appeared, spreading out over his sphere before disappearing again.

'What? I'm just saying that maybe things might have been different had our ancestors been a little more aware and proactive,' Varth said. Ehi's gaze darted back to Varth and she watched as the grey at his centre engulfed his sphere for a few moments and orange flashed across the surface.

'Perhaps.' Roarn frowned.

'The N.I.L. want to change things for the better, or so I've heard. Syvvak makes a compelling argument and he has a growing number of loyal followers,' Varth said.

'Brain washed,' Roarn said.

'Why do so many follow him?' Zerren asked. Ehi turned her gaze to the sphere inside Zerren's body; it was by far the brightest, though like Varth's, it too had a large amount of grey at the centre. Multiple colours flashed on the outer edges of Zerren's sphere, icy blue, dark blue, red, gold, green, they changed as quickly as the images which haunted her mind.

'Syvvak wants to help Iyeeka; he wants to change Eloran so we don't make the same mistakes that our ancestors made. He wants to make our districts fairer and give Iyeekans control over their own lives,' Varth said. Ehi saw hues of green bleeding across Varth's sphere, contained within a band of dark blue and pink.

'Our districts are already fair,' Roarn said.

'No they're not. Syvvak wants to get rid of council members, so that decisions aren't left to just a few Iyeekans.'

'Varth, have you heard yourself?' Roarn said, as a flash of orange shot across the colours in his sphere. 'The big decisions are never made solely by council members, the entire district is involved.'

'Are you going to tell me then that what happened to Anorae was fair?' Varth said. 'She wasn't even allowed the dignity of her own choice.'

'That was different.' Roarn lowered his gaze and green quickly replaced the orange.

'How?' Varth said. 'I may have deserved my punishment but Anorae just wanted to die with dignity; the council members of Lazarack wouldn't even allow her that. They didn't send for me when she died, I wasn't granted the choice of attending her funeral, how is that fair?' Ehi gazed at the burning oranges and reds which engulfed Varth's sphere. The thick band of grey at the centre swelled and spread out amongst his other colours. Roarn couldn't even look at Varth.

'It may have been the wrong decision, but there's nothing we can do about it now,' Roarn said. 'The council members try their best to guide us and make decisions to preserve life, but sometimes those decisions are not always easy to make; they're only Iyeekan.'

'You still defend them, even now,' Varth said, throwing his hands up in the air. 'Lucoe was the only Eloran in our district who tried to stand up for me, everyone else just stayed silent. I bet if he was here now he would be willing to visit Kubus and at least listen to what Syvvak has to say.' More green hues spread out across Varth's sphere, almost entirely obscuring his other colours.

'It never sat well with Lucoe,' Zerren said, as his grey grew and stretched out across his sphere. 'He spoke about it a lot after you left. He said the ethical and philosophical arguments were complicated and he didn't know what was right or wrong.'

'This is the sort of thing that Syvvak wants to change, he wants the wishes of Iyeekans to be respected and properly considered before any decisions are made,' Varth said.

'Is that the argument he uses when he defends the choices his ancestors made when they built their wall and let everyone else starve?' Roarn asked. A burst of orange painted Varth's sphere again but Ehi watched as he took a deep breath and the orange subsided.

'It's as you said, Roarn, it may have been the wrong decision, but there is nothing we can do about it now,' Varth said.

'Thousands suffered,' Roarn said.

'Anorae suffered,' Varth said.

'Enough you two,' Zerren said. 'We shouldn't be arguing amongst ourselves. Anorae and Lucoe wouldn't like it.' They fell silent and Ehi heard the spitting sound of little embers jumping out of the fire. Her vision wavered again, the spheres disappeared from her view and the buzzing sensation grew around her mind as the images came back and swamped her awareness.

'Zerren's right,' Varth said. 'I'm sorry, Roarn.'

'No.' Roarn sighed. 'I'm sorry, I know how much Anorae meant to you.' Varth nodded. No one spoke for a while as Ehi grappled with the images inside her head. One moment she saw Earth and humans, the next Iyeeka and Iyeekans. Her mind bounced back and forth, following one human after the next and then trailing behind an Iyeekan instead. The scenes she saw didn't seem to be related, but her mind recalled thousands of different humans and Iyeekans as though she had lived among them all.

'I know you hate the N.I.L. but you should still come and hear them out before you judge them,' Varth said.

'You may be right, but it's not possible, Varth,' Roarn said. 'We don't have the time and our parents and district come first.'

'What about after your district moves?'

'We'll have to see,' Roarn said.

'What about you, Zerren, what do you think?' Varth said.

'I agree with Roarn,' Zerren said. 'I'd also like to help Ehi too; her parents may still be alive and looking for her.'

'I see,' Varth said. He stood and groaned loudly as he stretched. 'I'm going to get some sleep before we get moving again.'

'OK,' Roarn said. Varth trudged back to the yebon, climbed into the front and shut the door loudly behind him.

# NINE

'Varth, where are we going?' Roarn asked. He frowned at the tattered paper map in his hands.

'To Lazarack, of course,' Varth said, staring straight ahead.

'But we should have come to the Serca district by now,' Roarn said. Zerren sat up straighter and held Ehi as she slept heavily in his arms.

'It's just a little further,' Varth said.

'Varth?' Roarn said. No one spoke for several long heartbeats and then Varth sighed and slowed the yebon to a stop. He cut the engine and hung his head over the steering wheel. 'Varth?' Roarn said again. Without warning, Varth released the steering wheel, a static tingle charged the air and Zerren felt a familiar pressure ripple over his mind. A faint metallic smell burned the back of Zerren's nose and he heard a sharp hiss like a thin wire whip splitting the air. Zerren barely had time to blink. Varth grabbed Roarn's arm, twisted it behind his back and held Roarn between himself and Zerren like a shield. 'Varth, what the...' Roarn said.

'I didn't want to do this, but you left me no choice,' Varth said quietly. Tightly around Roarn's neck was a thin line of lif from Varth's gauntlet. 'No one make a move or a sound,' Varth said. Roarn remained as still as possible, but the lif wire still cut into the left side of his neck and blood began to trickle down to his collarbone. 'I really thought you would listen, I thought that you would see that Syvvak and the N.I.L. aren't the terrible monsters that the rest of Eloran make them out to be. I wanted both of you to come to Kubus with me, but since you've both declined I've decided that I'll just take Ehi instead. I've realised that Ehi is special; her skills and control over lif is something that Syvvak would appreciate.'

'You're working for Syvvak?' Roarn asked.

'Quiet now, I said no sound,' Varth said as he tightened the lif around Roarn's neck. 'Syvvak wanted me to recruit you, and I tried, but you two are not forthcoming. Ehi has no home, and her family are probably dead; she'll be well cared for and safe in Kubus.' Zerren gritted his teeth and was about to connect his mind to the lif around his wrist. 'Ah, I wouldn't do that if I were you,' Varth said. 'You know all lif users can feel when someone nearby makes a connection. If I even get the slightest hint of one of you trying to connect with it, I'll slice your brother's head off so fast you won't even have time to close your eyes.' Zerren let his mind go blank and glared at Varth. 'We could have all travelled to Kubus quite happily and Syvvak would have been pleased to meet you, but here's what we're going to do. Firstly, Zerren, you're going to remove your lif gauntlet, and your brother's, and you're going to put them carefully in the footwell, right now.'

Zerren stared at Varth and, as he opened his mouth to retaliate, he felt another warm tingling sensation across his scalp and then a voice leapt into his mind. *Do what he says but don't hate him for this, he has been misguided and manipulated,* Lucoe said. The tingling sensations stopped and Lucoe's voice disappeared. Zerren clamped his mouth shut.

'Good choice. Don't disturb Ehi now, Zerren, or you might end up with your brother's head in your lap too,' Varth said.

Zerren reluctantly and slowly undid his gauntlet and then Roarn's.

'Put them on the floor now,' Varth said. Roarn let out a muted hiss as the lif wire bit deeper into the side of his neck.

Zerren slid the gauntlets to the floor and heard them drop

with a soft thump. Varth glared at him but Ehi didn't stir.

'Now, Zerren, you're going to open your door and, without disturbing her, you're going to leave Ehi on the seat and you're going to get out and walk away with your back to the yebon, and you'll keep walking until I tell you to stop.' Zerren stiffened and stared at Roarn; his brother's eyes bulged at him. Zerren opened the door and gently slid Ehi onto the seat, whilst stepping out of the vehicle. He left the door open and prayed that the hot daytime air would rouse her. Zerren turned and, just as Varth had said, he kept his back to the yebon and walked away. He heard the door slide open on the other side of the yebon and two sets of feet step out and crunch quietly round to his side, but Zerren didn't turn around. The two sets of feet stopped behind him. 'Keep walking,' Varth said. Zerren ground his teeth and marched forwards. He kept his gaze on the murky copper horizon. To his left he thought he could just make out the jagged peaks of the Kiri mountains. Time seemed to drag, he didn't know how far away the yebon was behind him, but he heard a soft thud, then footsteps and the sound of wheels spinning over the loose dry land. Zerren whirled around and saw his brother a few dozen yards before him, face down on the ground, and the yebon speeding away. Zerren cursed and ran back to his brother, heaving him onto his back.

'Roarn? Roarn?' Zerren said, checking his brother's neck. Roarn groaned and coughed and reached for the back of his head. Roarn winced and groaned as he sat up. 'You're bleeding,' Zerren said, noting the thin red lines on the side of his brother's neck.

'Don't worry about that, we need to stop…' Roarn was cut off by the sound of screeching tyres. Their heads snapped up and they saw the yebon stop sharply in the near distance and then a body flew out on the driver's side.

'Ehi!' Zerren said, jumping to his feet. He ran towards the yebon. He saw Ehi step out on the passenger side and walk around to the driver's side with something which flashed in her right hand.

Zerren drew closer and saw Varth scrabbling backwards on the ground whilst Ehi walked towards him with her right fist encased in a thin layer of lif. She glared down at Varth and raised her right arm. 'Ehi!' Zerren said. She froze and turned her head slowly to look at him; relief flashed over her features and she smiled for the first time since they had found her. Zerren reached her just as tears began to spring from her eyes.

'May I borrow this?' Zerren said, pointing to the solid lif encasing her right fist. She glanced down at her hand and the lif melted off her fingers like wax before coalescing into a single liquid sphere in the air between them. Whilst watching Varth, Zerren focussed his attention on the lif and reached for it with a passing thought. It felt like an extension of his own mind stretching out beyond the confines of his physical body with its own unique energy signature. It was a strange sensation with a strange inner sight that was like bringing into focus a blurry picture deep within his memories. He could see and feel the energy patterns from his mind and he could see and feel the energy patterns belonging to the lif. He let his mind wrap around the lif and then adjusted its energy patterns to match his own. The familiar static tingle brushed over his mind, causing the hairs on the back of his neck to stand on end; the metallic, burning smell grew in intensity at the back of his nose. He had it, or so he thought, but the lif slipped from his mental grasp and disappeared. He drew back, letting his connection recoil slightly, and then he renewed his focus. It had been a long time since he had had to give this much attention in order to manipulate lif. He examined the lif and its energies and realised that another mind was still controlling it. He glanced at Ehi; her connection with the lif was strong and the patterns her mind gave off were unusual. There were no irregularities, no bursts of energy in her mental connection; it was as though she had been practising her focus and control nonstop for hundreds of years. He had never seen anything like it before, and he had only heard the odd stories about the Moribi of Kiri.

'You need to let go,' Zerren said. Ehi stared at him and then her gaze darted to Varth and back to Zerren. 'It's ok, let go,' Zerren said. He felt her mind cautiously relinquish its control, but he was ready for it; he reached out with his mind and bent the lif to his will. He turned to Varth and with a single thought stretched the lif into a sharp solid spike a hairsbreadth from Varth's neck.

'Zerren,' Varth said. 'I wasn't really going to kill your brother. You know me, I wouldn't do that.'

'Do I?' Zerren narrowed his gaze.

'It was just a joke.' Varth let out a choked snort of laughter. 'I was just kidding; I wasn't really going to leave you behind and drive to Kubus.' His voice wobbled as beads of sweat ran down his face.

'How can you still lie to us? I should kill you,' Zerren said.

'Why don't you then?' Varth said, his gaze hardening.

'Zerren, don't,' Roarn said, wheezing as he came up beside him. 'Don't dishonour yourself and our family.' Roarn glared at Varth. 'The council members were right to put you in sanitation with the rest of the criminals.'

'I'm sorry about your neck but that's cruel, Roarn, I'm no criminal and I've never actually killed anyone.' Varth cut a sideways glance at Zerren.

'Why Varth? Why have you joined the N.I.L.? Why are you so desperate to take us back there?' Roarn said.

'I told you last night. The N.I.L. aren't as terrible as you think they are. Syvvak wants to change things but he needs strong lif users; he promises to create a new and fairer Iyeeka, without council members who are too blind to see when someone is suffering. I hoped you would see that, I thought you might be willing to listen and see the N.I.L. for yourselves. You were Anorae's friends too.'

'Anorae would be disgusted if she knew you had joined the N.I.L.,' Roarn said.

'Perhaps, but I think she would be more understanding.'

'What is there to understand? You've joined a bunch of criminals,' Roarn said.

'Not everyone in the N.I.L. are criminals, and you asked for my help, so what does that make you? Criminals too? The real criminals are all those of past generations who let us rot away and turn into a furnace. Our grandparents, great grandparents and great, great, great, great, great grandparents, all of them. Do you know how many millions of Iyeekans have died because of them?'

'They didn't know what they were doing,' Roarn said.

'Oh, spare me. Ignorance is hardly an excuse. Our planet is almost dead because of them. We're all starving or dehydrating and the eyeleetansy populations have died out or flown north to Loenya.'

'You accuse our ancestors for what has happened to Iyeeka, yet how many have died because the western districts turned them away?' Roarn asked.

'They didn't have a choice, they would have died themselves if they had opened their doors to everyone,' Varth said.

'Of course they had a choice,' Roarn said. 'I thought about what you said but you're wrong; what if one of the Elorans from the south had been the key to saving Eloran and Iyeeka? What if one of those starving refugees, had they lived, had come up with a solution to our problems?'

'There's no way of knowing that. There were too many begging for food and water; the western districts barely had enough to feed themselves,' Varth said.

'There's no way of knowing it because the western districts wouldn't even give them a chance,' Roarn said.

'They did what they had to, and it was already too late by then.'

'Every other district tried to help, it was only the western districts who were selfish.'

'Most of the other districts collapsed under the pressure. The western districts had to make a difficult decision. The irony is, even when you don't kill someone, you're still apparently responsible for their death.'

'Don't even try and use that as an excuse,' Roarn said. 'The west abandoned their fellow Elorans.'

'Loenya did the same; they chose a few precious Iyeekans that they thought would be useful, but they shut everyone else out, yet they don't receive half the hate or anger that the west get,' Varth said.

'The Kiri mountains separate us from Loenya and at least Loenya tried to help; they sent food and water to Eloran for as long as they could which was more than the west ever did.'

'Loenya isn't as compassionate as you seem to think it is,' Varth said. 'They had more to part with and they still have more. Do you think Loenya will let anybody in if we're all suddenly forced to cross the mountains?'

'I don't know,' Roarn said, shaking his head.

'Yes, you do. They would make the tough choice and they would choose themselves over everyone else,' Varth said. 'I just want you to talk to Syvvak. You don't have to stay in Kubus forever, I just want you to listen.'

'Varth, are you kidding? You just threatened to kill me in your bid to please Syvvak. We would have probably perished too out here. We will never join the N.I.L,' Roarn said.

'That's precisely the problem, you're too stubborn and closed-minded. Lucoe would have at least considered all options first and I said I'm sorry, I wasn't really going to kill you.'

'Lucoe would have correctly concluded that joining the N.I.L. would be a bad idea,' Roarn said.

'You don't know that for sure. Tell me, Roarn, if you had one meal left to feed your family or another family, who would you feed, who would you save?'

'What are you talking about now?' Roarn said.

'Just answer the question.'

'I'd feed both,' Roarn said. 'Even if it meant we had to split everything and couldn't fill our stomachs.'

'And what about the next day? When you had even less food to go around, and the next day and the next day?'

'I would do it for as long as it takes; I wouldn't let anyone die.'

'And what if conditions never improved and there was only a limited supply of food? Would you let everyone grow weak and frail until they eventually all died?' Varth said. Roarn opened his mouth to speak and then clamped it shut again. 'You see, that's the decision the western districts had to face, that millions of others had to face, and what you will eventually have to face. Iyeeka is not what it once was, resources are not plentiful, and we have to make hard decisions in order to survive, but one thing is for certain, our ancestors got it wrong, they messed up, and we, the members of the N.I.L., refuse to go back to that.'

'I'd keep going. I'd keep everyone alive for as long as possible and wait for conditions to improve,' Roarn said.

'Roarn,' Varth said. 'They won't improve; we've already seen that fail to happen many times.'

'Roarn, stop,' Zerren said. 'This is pointless.'

'We won't go back to the ignorant ways and we won't let council members decide for us,' Varth said. Roarn turned his back on him and Zerren kept his eyes on Varth as he leant towards his brother.

'What are we going to do?' Zerren said.

'We can't just leave him here,' Roarn said. 'We would be no better than the western districts if we did.' Roarn sighed. 'Give the lif to Ehi. We'll use some rope to tie up Varth and we'll put him in the back of the yebon. Then we'll drive to Lazarack, take our part of the supplies and metal as agreed and send him back to Kubus.'

'We're going to let him go?'

'What choice do we have?' Roarn said. 'We're Iyeekans, we look after each other even if we don't always agree. He was our friend once and I won't betray Anorae or Lucoe.'

Varth snorted.

'Besides,' Roarn said, lowering his voice, 'there are no sanitation and disposal units anymore, and even if there were, he would probably break away and head back to the N.I.L. anyway.'

'You're making a big mistake, you should join the N.I.L.,' Varth said. 'If things get any worse, then every district this side of the Kiri mountains will head to Loenya, only they won't make it; most of them will die before they get there and those who do make it, Loenya will turn away.' Zerren handed the lif over to Ehi and went to the back of the yebon to retrieve some rope.

'I'm sorry about this, Varth,' Roarn said, as he pulled Varth to his feet and pinned his arms behind his back.

'No, you're not.'

'Yes I am, I don't want to do this, but we can't trust you anymore.'

'You're no better than those council members.'

'We won't hurt you, or leave you out here to die,' Roarn said. 'But once we get to Lazarack you'll leave in your yebon and you will never come back to our district.'

# TEN

Ehi enjoyed the new space in the yebon. Roarn drove and Zerren sat to her right whilst Varth travelled in the back. She held the lif gauntlets in her hands and felt the hum of energy from the lif vibrating through her fingertips. Over the last several nights she had watched and marvelled at Orleetan and Ariyeetan passing over the inky black skies, pregnant with stars, as a great sense of sadness weighed down on her shoulders. Her mind was still full of images and memories that didn't seem to belong to her or Iyeeka. She subconsciously reached up to the little point at the top of her right ear as she pictured humanity, the odd violent creatures with their curved ears and world with one moon. Her thoughts were short-lived; she sat up and leaned forward as buildings began to appear on the horizon.

'We're almost home,' Roarn said, flashing a grin at Ehi and Zerren.

'Good, I don't think I can take much more dried, mashed fruit, vegetables and fish, or the conversation,' Zerren said glancing towards the back of the yebon.

'I agree,' Roarn said. 'Give Ehi your cloak and pull up the hood; we need to keep her hidden for now. She stands out too much.'

'Ok,' Zerren said. He reached down to the rucksack by his feet and pulled out his cloak. He helped Ehi into it and pulled the hood up over her head. Roarn stopped the yebon on the outskirts of the district and Ehi strained to see more of the little dwellings sitting on the horizon.

'Stay here, Ehi,' Zerren said. The brothers got out of the yebon and headed to the back. She heard struggling and curses, then the ear-raking screeches of metal scraping against the bottom of the yebon.

'You're making a big mistake,' Varth said.

'That's your opinion,' Roarn said.

'I said I was sorry.'

'You're only sorry because Ehi stopped you,' Roarn said.

'Zerren?' Varth said. There was no answer. 'Jeez. Roarn, would you just hear me out?'

'We're done talking,' Roarn said. Ehi waited for what felt like forever but, finally, Zerren opened the passenger door. He had a big rucksack on his back with several sheets of scrap metal strapped to it.

'Come on,' Zerren said, as he offered his hand to Ehi and helped her out of the yebon. Roarn pushed Varth ahead of him and round to the driver's door.

'Get in,' Roarn said.

'My lif gauntlet,' Varth said, turning to glare at Roarn.

'I'm sorry, but that's something I'm not giving back to you.'

'You bokhanya,' Varth said. Roarn twisted Varth around so he could untie his bound hands. 'Syvvak will already be angry with me but he'll be furious if I lose that lif gauntlet. You have to give it back.'

'Your problem. I can't trust you,' Roarn said. Varth rubbed his wrists and glowered at him. 'Go, get out of here before I change my mind.' Varth cast a long glance at Ehi and Zerren before he scrambled into the yebon. The engine fired and grumbled and the yebon sped away to the west. Roarn sighed and turned to where his rucksack and a pile of metal lay on the ground. He shouldered his bag and carried as much metal as he could, balancing it on his shoulders.

'Are you ok with that?' Zerren said. 'I could use our lif…'

'No, save it,' Roarn said. 'I'm fine.'

'I can't believe Varth…' Zerren said.

'Let's discuss it when we get home.'

Ehi gazed at the approaching district. They passed a sign with the word *Lazarack* written on it. The land held the first sign of greenery that Ehi had seen since waking up. The odd tree tried in vain to grow but they were bent under the heat of the etansy. Shrubs and bushes held dry leaves in pale green and sickly yellow hues. Bleached blades of grass grew in loose wiry tuffs like little islands surrounded by a dirt sea.

'This isn't good,' Zerren said, as they passed the dwellings. The odd Eloran stood outside, unnaturally thin as they tended to their few crops. Ehi studied the new faces with interest, particularly the women and the few children. The clothes these Elorans wore were baggy on their frames, stained and full of holes. Shoes were falling apart on feet and the children often wore none. They stood as though it was a great effort to keep their bodies upright and their faces bore grim lines; even the children didn't smile.

'Quick, drop your bag and get her inside, Zerren,' Roarn said. Ehi heard Zerren's rucksack fall to the ground with a thud and a clatter. He placed an arm behind her back and guided her towards a house and Zerren opened the door and ushered her inside.

'Abener? Is that you?' a female voice called from inside.

'No, Mother, it's Zerren. We're back,' Zerren said. A woman with Zerren's eyes appeared in the narrow hallway. Her dark, grey streaked hair stretched down to her hips and lines creased the corners of her eyes.

'Zerren!' she said, pausing as she looked Ehi up and down. 'Ah, and who is this?'

'It's a long story. Her name is Ehi. Ehi, this is my mother, Clari.'

'Nice to meet you, Ehi.'

'Sorry, she doesn't speak,' Zerren said.

'Doesn't or can't?'

'I don't know, but she hasn't said a word since we found her.'

'The poor thing, who knows what she's seen. Let's get that old cloak off you and sit you down.'

'Oh, another thing…' Zerren said, as Clari pulled back Ehi's hood. Clari froze and stared at Ehi's hair and eyes.

'Zerren?' Clari said, without taking her gaze from Ehi.

'I'll explain, but don't tell anyone about her except Father,' Zerren said. 'I need to help Roarn; keep Ehi out of sight until I get back, we won't be long.' Zerren turned and left, closing the front door behind him. Ehi picked up a lock of her own hair and inspected it; somewhere in her hazy memories she knew her hair had once been a lot darker. Clari stood gaping at the door, but then she blinked and closed her mouth.

'Well, come on in, Ehi,' she said. She put an arm gently across Ehi's shoulders and guided her into a large open room with long padded chairs and cushions and a table on a soft rug in the middle. Clari pulled a thin fabric over the windows and then pressed a button on the wall. A glass, square light shaped like a cube lit the room from above. Ehi took off the cloak and sat down as she gazed around the room. There was a familiarity to the space, something that made her feel warm and safe. Clari stepped out of the room through an archway at the back and Ehi leaned to the side to look through the archway into a kitchen. Ehi heard the door open and close and then Zerren and Roarn appeared.

'Ma,' Roarn said.

'Roarn, is that you?' Clari said. She came back with a huge smile on her face and tears glistening in her eyes.

'Yeah, it's me, Ma,' Roarn said.

'I'm so glad that you're back and that you're safe.' Clari clasped Roarn's face between her hands and reached up to kiss his forehead before doing the same to Zerren.

'Come on, we told you we'd be back,' Roarn said.

'I know, I know, it's just… it's just been so long,' Clari said. 'Your father will be so happy; he should be back soon.'

'Where is he?' Roarn asked.

'The council members are holding another public meeting; they're discussing the details and plans for when we move north.'

'When do we move?' Roarn said.

'Soon.' They heard the front door open again. 'Abener! The boys are back,' Clari said. There was a pause, and then the door to the front room burst open.

'Roarn, Zerren,' Abener said, rushing forwards to embrace his sons. 'When did you get back?'

'A few minutes ago, Father,' Roarn said.

'Where's Varth?'

'He left already,' Roarn said.

'Oh, I was hoping he might stay.'

'No, he's still angry about what happened,' Roarn said.

'I see, I guess I shouldn't be so surprised, I just hoped that time might have eased things.'

'It's even worse,' Roarn said. 'He's joined the N.I.L. He spent the whole trip trying to convince Zerren and I to go back with him.'

'The N.I.L.?' The blood drained from Abener's face.

'Yes. Syvvak has promised to get rid of council members and he's trying to recruit lif users,' Roarn said.

'It makes sense now... Clari, have you told them?' Abener said, glancing at his wife.

'No.'

'Told us what?' Roarn said.

'You haven't heard the news, have you?' Abener said, turning back to Roarn and Zerren.

'What news?' Zerren asked. Abener hesitated and cast a sideways glance at Clari.

'The N.I.L. attacked Skidaroi; they destroyed the district with explosives, forcing everyone there to flee for their lives. We believe that many didn't make it.'

'That sheeka…' Roarn said.

'Roarn,' Clari said.

'I bet Varth knew; I bet he knew about this and didn't say anything.'

'When did this happen?' Zerren asked.

'Four days ago,' Abener said. 'We received word from Skidaroi's neighbouring districts over the kaelo; the first few refugees were just arriving in those districts. The neighbouring districts are nervous now; they're wary of what the N.I.L. will do next. The western districts have always been selfish, but they have never directly attacked another district before, not like this.'

'Why would they do this? What reason could they possibly have for killing their fellow Elorans? Is it not enough that we'll most likely starve to death?' Zerren asked.

'Food, water, supplies,' Abener said. 'It seems that even the western districts' supplies are running low now and they no longer feel they have enough, so they're taking what they can from the other districts by force.'

'Varth spent the entire trip trying to tell us that we were wrong about the N.I.L., but I was right,' Roarn said. 'He threated to cut my head off and then he tried to kidnap Ehi and now this.'

'Ehi? Who's Ehi?' Abener said. Roarn glanced over his shoulder and Zerren stepped to the side. Abener's jaw dropped. The room fell silent as everyone seemed to hold their breath. 'Where? How?' Abener said.

'We found her in Cenic,' Zerren said.

'Well, we've named her Ehi,' Roarn said. 'We think she's mute.'

'Ok,' Abener said. 'Forgive me for being rude, but why is her hair purple?'

'We don't know,' Roarn said, glancing sideways at Zerren.

They all sat down, Roarn and Zerren on either side of Ehi.

Roarn recounted the details of their trip and explained how they and Varth had found her. Ehi listened closely; she'd been curious about where she had been found and in what state. All she could remember was waking up in the yebon with three unfamiliar faces. Abener leant forward, his chin on his hands. No one said a word for a long time after Roarn finished his tale, but the brothers watched their father closely. Finally, Abener cleared his throat and lowered his hands.

'Let me see this page you found,' he said. Zerren retrieved the page from his bag and handed it to their father. 'Ah yes, this is definitely the Kiri symbol of the Moribi.'

'Do you know what it means, Father?' Zerren asked. Abener frowned.

'I can't make any sense out of these numbers and symbols, it looks like some complicated maths but I'm no mathematician,' Abener said, fixing his gaze on Ehi. Ehi noticed that Abener's long greying hair was tied back from his hairless face; this was another thing Ehi had noticed that was different between Iyeekans and the humans she saw in her mind. Iyeekans had smooth hairless faces, while some of the humans had very hairy faces.

'I think,' Abener said, placing the page on the table, 'I think you need to go to the Moribi of Kiri. They're the only ones likely to know anything and they have an extensive knowledge of Iyeeka's history.'

'It would take weeks to get there in a yebon, and we don't have a yebon anymore,' Zerren said.

'No, you would have to take the ziree,' Abener said.

'But we only have two ziree and they're not as strong as they should be.'

'Yes, but they would manage Ehi with either you or Roarn; you'll have to decide who would go between yourselves,' Abener said.

'Abener, is that really necessary?' Clari asked.

'The sooner the better,' Abener said. 'Varth has already tried to kidnap Ehi once and take her to the N.I.L., and we know that her lif abilities are unusually strong. Syvvak has already proven that he is willing to destroy districts to achieve his goals, he might be tempted to send N.I.L. members here.'

'Would they really travel this far? We're a long way from Kubus,' Roarn said.

'Depends on how talented Ehi really is, but Varth certainly believed she was worth the risk. It wouldn't take much, a small group of desperate Elorans who believe Syvvak can keep them and their families safe and fed, travelling by yebon,' Abener said.

'Ehi would never let them take her; I won't let them take her,' Zerren said.

'As talented as Ehi is, I don't think that she can overpower multiple lif users all at once. They will take her by force, Zerren. Syvvak has already shown that he will do just that. If we resisted, it would endanger everyone here. Lazarack isn't a big district, and we won't fight violence with more violence.'

'You would really send one of our boys away from us?' Clari said, as tears welled in her eyes. 'They've only just got back.'

'You've seen her hair and eyes, Clari. Even if Varth doesn't mention Ehi's existence to Syvvak, and even if we kept Ehi hidden, there is always the danger that she may be discovered. It wouldn't take long for a rumour about Ehi to spread across the few remaining districts. No, it's best if Ehi gets out of here as soon as possible.' Ehi watched Zerren out of the corner of her eye; he hadn't said much, and his gaze was distant, as though he were not just deep in his thoughts but lost in them. His eyes brightened and he straightened up.

'I'll go,' Zerren said. 'I'll take Ehi to Kiri.'

'Zerren,' Clari gasped.

'Roarn would be better here to help you and the district to move north,' Zerren said. 'It makes more sense for me to go.'

'Actually,' Abener said, 'I have to agree with Zerren on this one; you're both more than competent users with lif, but Zerren's control is better than yours, Roarn.'

'Which is why he should stay,' Roarn said.

'Which is why he should go,' Abener replied. 'If Syvvak is truly looking for talented lif users, then your brother is more of a potential target, and Zerren is right about your strength, Roarn, we will need all the able bodies we can get. How much life is left in your lif, Zerren?'

'Quite a bit, as long as I don't have to use it too often.'

'Good, good,' Abener said. 'That's the last of our lif supplies, so use it wisely.'

'I took Varth's lif gauntlet from him,' Roarn said. 'I didn't want him to come back and surprise us with it.'

'I understand, I would have done the same,' Abener said. 'Take the lif tube out of Varth's gauntlet, I'm sure Clari has a spare empty gauntlet it can go into. It should fit Ehi. For now, you should all rest. I'll prepare the ziree and supplies for Zerren and Ehi.'

'When should we leave?' Zerren asked.

'I wouldn't wait any longer than a couple of days,' Abener said. A strangled sob escaped Clari; she fled from the room.

'Mother,' Zerren said, standing up to follow her.

'She'll be ok,' Abener said. 'I'll talk to her.' Zerren hesitated and then sat back down.

'Has old Jhujin and his family agreed to the move?' Roarn asked. Abener's lips strained into a small smile for a brief moment.

'Stubborn as ever, but yes, even Jhujin has reluctantly agreed to travel north with the rest of us. The fisheries are all dried up now and our crops aren't growing; there are just too many mouths to feed. I think the reason we have survived this long out here is because we were one of the smaller districts with a lake and a river.' Abener sighed again and rubbed his face with his hands. 'No one wants to leave, we all grew up here and our ancestors lived here.

Every home has a family history which spans back hundreds of generations, but we have no choice now; the climate is too warm and harsh, there isn't enough water left for ourselves let alone our crops, and I haven't seen a single eyeleetansy here since you were born. Your mother and I feared that this day would come, but we've been preparing for it as best as we can.'

'How are the repairs going on the laburnem?' Roarn asked.

'Well so far,' Abener said. 'I'm hoping that you found things that will help us, then we'll start loading the necessities on board.'

Roarn nodded.

'Now,' Abener turned his gaze on Ehi. 'Does Ehi understand what we say?'

'I think so,' Zerren said.

'I wonder.' Abener stood and approached Ehi. She tilted her head to the side as she studied him. He reached out his hands and she took them and let him pull her to her feet. Abener looked over her and made her turn in a circle. 'She seems to be moving ok, physically speaking.' He looked at her hair. 'I've never seen a hair colour like this before, and her eyes…' He gazed straight into them and Ehi stared back until Abener looked away. 'Ehi, would you walk around the table a couple of times?' he said, standing back. Ehi glanced at the table; she took a step forward but stopped as she felt something tear through her mind. Her head felt like it was on fire and her vision flickered; the room before her disappeared and she found herself in another, similar-looking room. She saw herself as she appeared now but with dark brown hair and eyes, sitting on a seat with an older woman beside her. Across from them, on two smaller chairs, were two middle-aged men dressed in dark blue eyeleetansy tunics and grey trousers…

'And you say that you don't know if this will work, even if my daughter agrees?' the older woman said.

'That is correct,' the first man said. 'We're not certain.'

'I'll do it,' the dark-haired Ehi said.

'Ehi, no!'

'Mother, it's ok. It will be ok.'

'No, it's not ok,' her mother said.

'I know it's risky, but Hasree and Seffen will be there, monitoring everything,' the dark-haired Ehi said.

'That's right,' the second man said. 'We won't leave your daughter unattended; we will be monitoring and watching the entire situation.'

'I don't like it,' her mother said.

'It's too good an opportunity to miss, Mother.'

'This is just a pipe dream,' her mother said. 'There's no proof, there's no reason why their machine would work; it never worked with anyone else.'

'We believe that the answer is in your blood,' the first man said.

'And how long do you intend to take my daughter away from me?'

'A year at most. We will bring her back to you once we get the answers we need.'

'And if you don't get any answers?'

'We won't keep Ehi away from you, even if we don't get answers,' the second man said. Ehi's vision began to waver again, fading at the edges as the colours turned to grey and black. She felt hands gripping her arms and someone shaking her.

'Ehi, Ehi,' Abener said. She blinked several times and the front room of the brothers' home flooded back into her vision. 'Ehi?' Abener said again as he peered into her eyes. Zerren and Roarn were on their feet, standing on either side of her, looking worried. Ehi gently pushed Abener's hands away from her arms and sank back down. She hid her face in her hands and felt the warm tears seeping out between her fingers. She had had a mother once, but she had no idea where she was now or even if she was still alive. A deep sadness permeated into her bones and a coldness pinched her heart; something wasn't right about her situation. What had happened to Hasree and Seffen?

'What was that?' Roarn said. 'What just happened?'

'I don't know,' Abener said. 'It was as though her awareness just disappeared for a moment. Are you ok, Ehi? Did we upset you?' Ehi didn't respond.

'She seems to cry a lot,' Roarn said. Ehi felt the seat cushion sink down beside her.

'Ehi?' She felt a warm hand settle on her shoulder. She turned her face to Zerren, but the tears continued to fall and her eyes stung.

'You should show her to the guest room and get some rest,' Abener said. 'I'll go and talk to Clari now.'

# ELEVEN

He felt the sting of fine dust on his skin as his hair whipped about his face and the wind wailed in his ears. He squinted as he tried to peer through the storm and felt his muscles tense as his body was buffeted from all directions. There was a moment of reprieve, a small break in the storm's relentless battering. He looked up, and ahead of him, caught within the same storm, a woman like none he had ever seen before stood with her arms stretched wide. Her hair was almost white with an ethereal glow and her eyes were a deep, bright purple. She grimaced as the wind clawed at her hair and clothes, caking her pale skin in a fine layer of dust and grime.

*You must find me,* a female voice said inside his mind. A deep sense of sadness and loss permeated her words, binding his chest into knots of dread.

'Find you?' Ahrl said. 'Find you where?' But even as he spoke those words, he felt drawn to this woman, a compulsion to find her whatever the cost. The wind picked up, its roar deafening as the dust and dirt thickened in the air, obscuring everything from Ahrl's view. He felt his stomach lurch violently as though the ground had suddenly disappeared.

'Ahrl, Ahrl,' Myaie said. A hand gently shook his shoulder as he came to and he blinked as the pale pink morning skies of Eloran brightened above him. He felt the hard surface swaying gently beneath him and his thick blanket itched his chin. He groaned, and his body protested as he pulled himself upright on the edge of the vadi.

'How long was I asleep?' he asked, pressing the heel of his hand into his brow.

'Not long. A few hours. Here.' Myaie handed him a steaming cup.

'Laluta?' Ahrl asked, cupping the clay cup between his hands. 'Where did you get this?'

'It seems that Kes had a tin of dried laluta leaves on board,' Myaie said.

Ahrl brought the cup up to his lips, but then hesitated and glanced up at his cousin.

'Don't worry, there's enough for everyone,' Myaie said. Ahrl took a sip and cast his gaze about the vadi; a couple of bodies lay huddled under blankets but most had squeezed into the cabin below. Estan stood at the back of the vadi, and a fine mist rose up from the shallow river in the morning light. 'We'll be approaching the Garakeeish district soon; I think we should stop and speak with their council members, though I'm sure they would have already heard the news by now,' Myaie said.

'Has there been any word about Skidaroi from the western districts?' Ahrl said.

'No, only speculation from the outer districts. The western districts refuse to comment.'

'I'm not surprised.'

'Many are calling for a united council, like the one they had when our ancestors built the great bridge; they want the western districts to be held accountable for the attack.'

'What will they do? What can they do? Sentence thousands to work in sanitation without the power to enforce it?' Ahrl said. 'No, the majority of those who live in the western districts are innocent; the N.I.L. only represent a small percentage.'

'The N.I.L. are deeply rooted in Kubus, everyone knows that, and are the other western districts really so innocent when they just stand by and watch?' Myaie asked. 'Our communities weren't built so that only a few have their voices heard.'

'No, but they will be afraid.' Ahrl stood and stretched and watched as the Garakeeish district slowly came into view. As the etansy rose and the mist dwindled, dwellings appeared, curving around the edges of a small lake and up along the river. Several vadis were already moored to a wooden pier and a small group of Elorans stood watching their arrival from the shore. Estan guided the vadi to a space near the end of the pier, cut the engine and let a small anchor drop.

'Are you from Skidaroi too?' a man said, stepping onto the pier.

'Yes, we are. I am Council Member Myaie of Skidaroi.'

'Well, I am Council Member Malaki of Garakeeish. There are more from your district here.'

'Are they safe and well?'

'Yes,' Malaki said. 'Though many wish to travel as far as Lebanoi.'

'We're headed that way too,' Myaie said.

'Then you will have to leave your vadi and go by foot,' Malaki said. Myaie glanced at Ahrl and raised an eyebrow before turning back to Malaki.

'Why is that?'

'I'm afraid the river dries up just ahead; you can't get through by vadi,' Malaki said.

'I see.' A deep crease formed on her brow.

'You are welcome, all of you, to take refuge here in the Garakeeish district,' Malaki said.

'Thank you, Malaki.' Myaie nodded at the Elorans on their vadi and then went into the cabin below to wake those still asleep. She appeared again with Roe by her side. A wooden plank was put between their vadi and the pier. Ahrl followed as the Elorans from their vadi disembarked and were led by Malaki deeper into the Garakeeish district.

'We heard about the attack a couple of days ago,' Malaki said. 'We couldn't believe it until the first refugees turned up and told us their stories. Is it really true that the N.I.L. attacked Skidaroi?'

'Yes, as far as we know,' Myaie said.

'They must be stopped,' Malaki said. 'The western districts can no longer turn a blind eye and harbour such violence amongst them.'

'I agree. I'm grateful that you've taken care of my fellow Elorans,' Myaie said.

'We have offered homes, and what little food and water we can spare, but there isn't much.'

'How have your harvests been?'

'Terrible. We had hoped that it would pick up this year, last year seemed a little better but it still wasn't enough, it seems our hopes were misplaced this year. We've had to increase our rationing. I'm sorry, there isn't much food here for you.'

'I appreciate what you share. Has word of the attack reached Lebanoi?'

'I believe so,' Malaki said. 'Though I doubt Ruick or the other council members there will be able to help you much. Lebanoi is already at several times its capacity; they have built walls to stop the district from being completely overrun by every Eloran this side of the Kiri Mountains. Though I daresay they are temporary walls and nothing like the walls of the western districts.'

'They have food and water though?'

'Yes, some, though how long it will last is anyone's guess,' Malaki said.

'They already have strict rationing too,' Ahrl said, quickening his pace to join Myaie and Malaki. 'I passed through there four months ago; they can feed their district, but it is barely enough.'

'Peace is hard to maintain when Elorans are hungry; we lost so many during the last great famine,' Malaki said.

'You mentioned that the river has dried up? Did this happen recently?'

'Yes, we've been keeping an eye on one particular bend because the water was lying very low and seemed to be dropping; vadis were just about managing to scrape through a couple of weeks ago but now it's impassable.'

'Is there no other river we can take?'

'No,' Malaki said. 'The other rivers are far too narrow; you would struggle to steer even a small vadi down them. It never used to be like this. Back in my great grandfather's day there were still several rivers that could take you east and, before his time, dozens. The etansy, as beautiful as it is, has stripped our rivers back one by one over the centuries.'

'It's not just the etansy,' Ahrl said. 'The whole atmosphere has changed and the weather patterns, mainly because of our ancestors' lack of foresight.'

'True, apparently, and we still have no real solutions,' Malaki said. He led the way inside a school and ushered their small group into an empty classroom. Ahrl could feel the temperature rising outside as the air inside the classroom began to grow thick and heavy.

'Here, I have a map that shows all the rivers from here to the eastern districts,' Malaki said. He smoothed out a large map on a small table at the front of the room. 'This was our last way through.' He pointed at a wiggly blue line. 'And here is where this river has dried up.' Malaki moved his finger to one of the bends closer to the Garakeeish district.

'How long would it take to travel on foot to Lebanoi?' Myaie asked.

'Three weeks at a good, strong pace. But with the elderly and children, maybe four or five.'

'Are the rivers clear past this point?' Myaie said, pointing at the bend and running her finger eastwards towards Lebanoi.

'I assume so,' Malaki said.

'So it may be possible to gain passage on another vadi at the next district?'

'Yes, but you may find it difficult to persuade them to take you all the way to Lebanoi.'

'Even if they were to take us part of the way, we could find passage on another vadi later; it will be quicker and safer than walking,' Myaie said. Ahrl felt a sharp tug on his sleeve and turned to see Roe standing beside him.

'What is it, Roe?' Ahrl asked quietly. Roe looked up at him and motioned her head towards the door. Ahrl nodded; they stepped into the corridor.

'What's wrong?' Ahrl asked.

'Sorry, there's something bothering me and I don't know who I can talk to about it,' Roe said.

'You can tell me, Roe, what is it?'

'I had a strange dream this morning,' Roe said. 'It's bugging me; it seemed more than just a dream.' Ahrl peered at Roe and noted for the first time the dark circles under her eyes.

'Yes, I think most of us have had unsettled nights,' Ahrl said. 'It's to be expected. Dreams are just dreams, Roe, they don't mean anything.'

Roe shook her head. 'No, this was different. I saw a strange-looking woman with pale purple hair and bright purple eyes.' Ahrl fought to keep the surprise away from his face.

'Ok. Why is this bothering you? What did she say?' Ahrl dropped down to Roe's level, clasping her shoulders gently.

'She told me to find her, but I don't know who she is.'

'Interesting. She said the same thing in my dream.'

'You dreamt about her too?' Roe said, her eyes wide.

'Yes, I dreamt about her this morning. There was a great storm going on around us and it seemed dark.'

'And she seemed really sad, even heartbroken.'

'Yes, this is strange,' Ahrl said.

'How is it possible to have the same dream?'

'I don't know.' Ahrl glanced up and down the corridor. 'Keep this to yourself for now, Roe. I'll talk to the others and see if anyone else has shared our dream.'

'It seemed more like a nightmare.'

'Yes, you're right. It was more like a nightmare.'

'I've never heard of anyone sharing dreams before. What if it's not just a dream? What if it's real?'

'I highly doubt that; have you ever seen or heard of a woman who looked like the one in our dreams?'

Roe shook her head.

'See, so how can it be real? No one looks like that.'

'Yes, I guess you're right.'

'It's probably nothing, just a spooky coincidence,' Ahrl said, giving Roe's shoulder a small squeeze. He stood up. 'Don't worry about it for now. Come on, let's get back to Myaie and the others.'

Roe nodded and smiled hesitantly.

'If you do dream about her again, you will tell me, won't you?' Ahrl said as they approached the classroom door.

'Yes,' Roe said. Ahrl smiled and held the door open for Roe, but he felt his smile quickly slip away once she'd passed him. Doubts were already troubling his brain as Roe's words played repeatedly at the back of his mind *What if it's not just a dream?* Ahrl pinched his lips together and stepped into the classroom; there was no way their dreams could be real, and from what he had seen, he sincerely hoped they weren't.

# TWELVE

Varth drove the yebon to Kubus, only stopping briefly to recharge the batteries. On the sixth day, the walls of the western district came into view, and by the afternoon, Varth could make out the details on the walls. It had taken thousands of Elorans just over two years to build the eleven-hundred-mile-wall around the six largest western districts. During the early days of the great famine, the council members at the time, along with the former I.L., had unanimously agreed that it was a necessary measure to keep themselves and their families safe. The wall was twenty-five feet high and was made from stone from the Kiri Mountains. It stretched around the districts, around the lakes, and into the mountains where a combination of walls and the steep sides of the mountains closed off the districts from the rest of Eloran. Most of the rivers had been built over, but two of the largest rivers, one each on the western and eastern sides, had small guarded arches to allow vadis access to the districts.

It was a fortress, and at the heart of this fortress was the district of Kubus where Syvvak awaited. Varth felt his hands tighten around the yebon's steering wheel. The mere thought of Roarn and Zerren caused profanities to spring from his lips. He had reluctantly admitted to himself that he may have taken things too far with the lif around Roarn's neck, but he had been desperate. He drew up to a break in the wall where several Elorans stood. They wore grim expressions and every one had a lif gauntlet strapped to their wrists. Varth stopped and opened his window slightly.

'State your name and business,' one of the men said.

'You know who I am, Zael. It's me, Varth.'

'Oh, who is this Varth? I don't think I've heard of him.'

'Stop being a ziree's behind. I'm back from Lazarack with supplies for Syvvak,' Varth said. Zael peered at Varth and grinned.

'You're late. Syvvak has been expecting you.'

'I know.'

'He was in a good mood earlier, don't ruin it.' Zael nodded to the other guards and waved Varth through. Varth slowly navigated his way through to Kubus. Inside the walls, western Eloran appeared to be a pleasant and populous place. Healthy-looking Elorans moved freely about the streets and harvested crops, but even Varth could see that the crops were small and not as plentiful as they should have been. The Elorans behind the walls were not skin and bone like they were in the other districts, but there was a hardness to their eyes and a sourness to their expressions. Their clothes were clean but threadbare. The western districts were managing well enough, better than anywhere else, but they were hardly thriving.

Varth eventually passed a sign announcing the district of Kubus. He wound his way through the streets, aware of the gazes following him as he approached the larger warehouses. He stopped beside several other yebons in an open space just in front of one of these large warehouses, and caught a glimpse of Syvvak and a male council member from one of the other districts; they appeared to be having a heated discussion. *Why are there so many yebons here?* Varth reluctantly stepped out of his yebon and made his way over to them.

'Syvvak, you have gone too far,' the council member said. 'We do not condone your actions.'

'If I had waited around for the western districts to agree then there would never be any action,' Syvvak said.

'We would never have agreed,' the council member said. 'Our

ancestors taught us to…'

'To do whatever is necessary, or have you forgotten that?' Syvvak asked. 'When our ancestors built the wall around our great districts they knew they were signing the death warrants for thousands of Elorans on the outside.'

'That was different and you know it.'

'Was it?' Syvvak said. 'I don't see much difference, and besides, I think it's more merciful my way.'

'There is a difference, Syvvak.'

'Enough, you're taking up too much of my time. The deed has been done, we can't go back and change the past now, can we?' Syvvak said.

'You could do the right thing Syvvak, beg for forgiveness and atone…' Syvvak's upper lip curled and his eyes narrowed. Varth felt a ripple of cold energy tingle across his scalp and a burning sensation in his nose that made his eyes water. A flash of silver erupted from the gauntlet strapped to Syvvak's right wrist and before the council member could react, a curved blade solidified just millimetres from his neck.

'I don't think so,' Syvvak said, his eyes fixed on the curved lif blade. 'You forget, council member, the Elorans here are loyal to me, not you, and I really think you might start to change your tune in a couple of months when you realise that, without these supplies, our own food resources won't be enough.'

'Syvvak, I meant no offence,' the council member said, as his skin turned unnaturally pale. 'I was only saying that you… you… should have consulted the other districts. I know that you do these things with the best intentions for…'

'Shut up and get out of my sight,' Syvvak said. The lif blade liquefied, condensing into a little sphere before returning to Syvvak's gauntlet.

'Yes, Syvvak.' The council member inclined his head and then turned and hurried away as quickly as he could without breaking into a run.

'What was that about?' Varth asked.

'Ah, Varthrune, It is nice to finally see you again. I trust your journey went smoothly. Though, wait, I wouldn't know, would I? Someone didn't even bother to contact me, even on a kaelo.' Varth remained silent and gazed down at his shoes. 'Where were you? You've been away for over a month. I gave you two weeks and I see that you've brought me no brothers,' Syvvak said.

'There was a problem, a couple of problems actually.'

'Go on…' Syvvak narrowed his gaze.

'Firstly the yebon's kaelo broke, so I couldn't contact you. Then I discovered that one of the brothers, the middle brother,' Varth felt his throat constrict, 'Lucoe. He's dead. He died shortly after I left Lazarack.'

'That doesn't explain why you're so late. Where are the other two? Why aren't they here?'

'Roarn was difficult, just as I suspected,' Varth said. 'I made a deal with him. I agreed to go with him and Zerren in the yebon to search the southern districts for supplies. I thought that the extra time would allow me to convince them both to come back to Kubus with me.'

'And?'

'It didn't go quite as planned,' Varth said. Syvvak shook his head and began to pace up and down. He stopped and frowned as his gaze dropped to Varth's bare wrist.

'Where is your lif gauntlet?'

'The brothers took it from me.'

'Varthrune,' Syvvak said, pinching the bridge of his nose. 'Did you do anything useful apart from waste time and resources?'

'I managed to find some metal, but there's something else that you should know,' Varth said.

'What is it?'

'The brothers and I found a woman in the district of Cenic.'

'A woman? Was she dead?' Syvvak said.

'No,' Varth said. 'We found her inside some sort of machine; it was as though she'd been asleep and we had woken her up.'

'But no one has lived in Cenic for decades,' Syvvak said. 'Was she alone?'

'Completely alone, and exceptionally healthy given the famines and droughts,' Varth said. 'But that's not even the strangest thing; her hair was a pale purple colour, almost white, and her eyes were a deep, vivid purple.'

'So you found an unusual woman?'

'She is an exceptionally talented lif user, more talented than Zerren and Roarn put together, more talented than the Moribi of Kiri,' Varth said.

'Really?'

'Yes, I saw her power with my own eyes. We stopped in the district of Borucree and we were attacked by a bokhanya. Ehi fended off the bokhanya by manipulating all of our lif; she captured the bokhanya and then she somehow communicated with it and it ran off; it didn't attack any of us.'

'Now that is interesting,' Syvvak said. 'How many lif sources did she use?'

'Three, from three different distances, but I have a feeling she can manipulate more,' Varth said.

'Hmm, to manipulate that much lif would require a lot of talent and practice. You have three different energy signatures to command and dividing your attention amongst three different sources, well… that's more than impressive.' Syvvak rubbed his jaw. 'You say she communicated with a bokhanya too?'

'Yes,' Varth said. 'She captured it with lif and then released it, but it didn't attack her.'

'And this machine you found her in, where was it?'

'In an underground room in Cenic.'

'An underground room?'

'It was made from interlocking plates of metal. Someone went to great lengths to keep her hidden. This machine was like nothing I've seen before; I don't know what it was used for. Zerren found a page with a diagram of the machine and a bunch of numbers and symbols; it had the Moribi or Kiri's logo on it.'

'Do you have this page?'

'No.'

'Where is this Ehi now?'

'She's with the brothers,' Varth said.

'You didn't bring her here?'

'I tried, but she was too strong with her lif.'

'Why didn't you knock her out then? Better yet, you should have knocked them all out,' Syvvak said, shaking his head. 'Never mind, I have a better idea. If she's really as strong as you say, then I want to keep a close eye on her.' Syvvak smiled like a bokhanya.

'Who will you send?' Varth said.

'Oh, just you,' Syvvak said.

'What? Me? You're not going to send a group to get her?'

'No, not yet. I want you to follow her and report back to me for now. Think of it this way, Varthrune, you can make amends for failing to bring the brothers back.'

'But Ehi and the brothers will recognise me.'

'Then change your look, cut your hair, wear a scarf around your face. I don't care what you have to do, just get it done,' Syvvak said. 'I want to know where this Ehi is and exactly what she's capable of. If she is of value to us, then she will join us or we will get rid of her.'

'Get rid of her?'

'Yes, Varthrune, I can't have powerful lif users against me when I take control of northern Eloran,' Syvvak said. 'I plan to increase pressure on Lebanoi; they're the last biggest district in my way, but they're struggling. Ruick is trying to find solutions to their problems and the more time he has, the more he can do. I do not wish for his success; he will only restore Eloran back to its old ways and we all know what that did to us. I vowed to all the members of the N.I.L. that I would not let that happen.'

'Increase pressure? How?' Varth said.

'Father!' A young boy ran out from the warehouse behind them, straight at Syvvak.

'Jhuka,' Syvvak said. A grin stretched across his face, and he picked the boy up. 'What are you doing here? I told you to stay at home.' Jhuka fought to catch his breath as he clung to Syvvak, who waited patiently, stroking Jhuka's dark hair and rocking him gently from side to side, but the flush in the boy's cheeks did not abate.

'I wanted to see you, Father,' Jhuka said finally, through his wheezes.

'The medics told you to be careful; you shouldn't be running around like this, Jhuka.'

'I'm not so bad today.'

'No, you need to rest, little one,' Syvvak said. 'And I'm busy making plans to help keep you safe and well.'

'When will you be home?'

'Later, Jhuka, I promise. I'll be back before it gets dark.'

Jhuka frowned.

'Where's your mother?' Syvvak asked.

'In the warehouse.'

'Go, Jhuka, and tell your mother that I wish to speak with her,' Syvvak said, setting the child down. Jhuka began to run. 'Walk, Jhuka,' Syvvak said. Jhuka slowed his pace. 'Varthrune, get ready, you can leave tomorrow, and for Iyeeka's sake, make sure you take a kaelo with you that works this time.'

'As you wish,' Varth said.

# THIRTEEN

Ehi stepped out into the hot daytime air. It had been another restless night, riddled with strange dreams filled with the same peculiar and frustrating creatures called humans. She didn't know them or their world; she was certain that she had never been there before, but she was also certain that she had. Statues framed the entrance to the rest of the family's land and she spied Zerren standing, head bowed, before one, rubbing his eyes. She walked out towards him and he looked up at her as she drew nearer, rubbing his eyes harder.

'Oh, Ehi, did you sleep well?' A smile trembled on his lips and he blinked his red-rimmed eyes a few times. Ehi turned her gaze to the statue; it was a young male Iyeekan around eighteen years of age with Zerren's angled jawline and Roarn's nose. She reached out and touched the smooth white stone and wondered why it brought Zerren to tears. 'It's my older brother, Lucoe,' Zerren said. 'He died many years ago.' Zerren straightened up and took a deep breath. 'I just came to say goodbye, again, but hopefully I won't be gone for too long. I hope we can all return to these lands one day.' Zerren stared hard at the statue and then turned and walked towards a small wooden building. Ehi followed him, passing by rows and rows of lines carved into the soil where the odd little shrub pushed through, but mostly the land remained bare. She heard a deep, groaning, hoarse sound and then a snort of air coming from inside the little wooden building, and then she caught a whiff of something foul-smelling and she covered her nose with her hands.

'Yeah, the ziree do smell pretty bad in their pen but you get used to it and it won't be so bad when we're travelling,' Zerren said. They rounded the corner and Ehi saw two large animals tethered by a rope. The ziree were tall creatures with elongated faces and long curved necks. They had thick lips, deep set eyes and pointy ears with darker tuffs of hair at their tips. One of the ziree nudged its head through the gap and Ehi immediately drew away from it.

'It's alright,' Zerren said patting the ziree's neck and stroking its head. 'This one's called Kana and the other is called Keno. She won't bite you, she's just curious.' Zerren looked at Ehi and motioned for her to come closer. Ehi approached cautiously and extended her hand towards Kana. She put her hand just above the ziree's nose and stroked the coarse brown hair there. The ziree jerked its head and a greyish pink tongue shot out between its teeth and licked Ehi's hand. Ehi jumped back and examined the wet saliva dripping from her fingers. Zerren gawked at her for a moment. A chuckle escaped his lips and he pressed his hand to his mouth; he snorted and then burst into laughter, holding his stomach. 'You should see your face,' Zerren said, in between gasps. Ehi wrinkled her nose, walked over to Zerren and wiped her hand on his sleeve. 'Hey, that's not fair,' Zerren said, twisting away from her. He rubbed his eyes and contained his laughter. 'I needed that, thanks, Ehi.'

'Ehi, Zerren,' Roarn called as he approached them. He rounded the corner with two saddlebags in his arms.

'Ah, I was just about to get those,' Zerren said.

'They're all done and packed with everything we can spare, but there isn't much,' Roarn said.

'We'll manage somehow.' Zerren took a saddle from a hook on the wall and placed it on Kana.

'I hope so. I really wish I was going with you.'

'If we had another ziree then it may have been possible,'

Zerren said. 'But Mother and Father need you.'

'I know,' Roarn said, hanging his head. 'It's a nightmare. The planning will take several days and many sleepless nights to complete.'

'I don't envy you.'

'Ah, I'm not sure who has it worse.' Roarn grinned. 'At least you'll have someone interesting to travel with, even if she isn't much of a talker.'

'If you mean bokhanya-type interesting then I'd rather the journey be uninteresting,' Zerren said. He tightened the saddle around Kana's middle and then did the same to Keno. Roarn helped Zerren to secure the saddle bags to the back of the zirees' saddles.

'Ma has found a cloak and gauntlet for Ehi,' Roarn said.

'That's good, though it'll be warm and uncomfortable to wear one.'

'It's better than Ehi being spotted; there's no telling what some Elorans would do if they saw her now.'

Ehi patted Keno's head and smiled when the ziree didn't try to lick her. Zerren untied the ziree and they led them to the back of the house where Abener and Clari stood waiting for them.

'All set?' Abener asked.

'Pretty much,' Zerren said, taking another bag from his father and attaching it to the back of Keno's saddle. Clari placed a brown cloak around Ehi's shoulders and helped her to attach a lif gauntlet to her wrist.

'There,' Clari said, pulling the hood of Ehi's cloak up over her head. Ehi frowned as the air around her face and head grew stuffy and hot.

'I won't say goodbye as I hope this will be temporary. We will see you soon, son.' Abener clasped the back of Zerren's head and touched his forehead with his own. Clari hugged Zerren, tears in her eyes, and Roarn patted him on the back before embracing him in a hug. Abener turned to Ehi.

'I know that we haven't been together for long, but I hope that you will be safe, and keep Zerren safe for me.' He placed a hand on Ehi's shoulder and gave it a gentle squeeze. Ehi held Abener's gaze; his eyes glistened, and she felt as though he had more to say but he averted his gaze and looked at Zerren. 'Travel swiftly and remember you are an Eloran of Lazarack,' Abener said. Clari hugged Ehi gently and Ehi relished the brief soft, warmth and the sweet smells which emanated from Clari's body.

'Here, you should ride Kana,' Zerren said as he guided the ziree to Ehi's side. Ehi eyed Kana, particularly her mouth. 'You just need to put your foot here and…' Ehi grabbed the saddle between her hands, jumped and launched herself into the saddle in one swift movement. 'You've ridden before,' Zerren said, blinking at her in amazement. He turned to Keno, placed a foot into a stirrup and swung himself up into the saddle. Ehi picked up Kana's reigns and Zerren guided Keno in a small circle before halting the ziree beside Ehi.

'We'll see you in Lebanoi,' Zerren said, as he gazed down at his family. 'And if not, I'll leave a message and hope that we'll not be parted for long.'

'I'll hold you to that, brother,' Roarn said.

'Don't miss me too much,' Zerren said, as he flashed a grin.

'Go now, before the district fully wakes,' Abener said.

'Mother, Father,' Zerren said, as he inclined his head to them. 'Come on, Ehi, let's go.' Zerren nudged his heels into Keno's sides and the ziree moved forwards at a gentle pace, moving both legs on one side first and then both legs on the opposite side. Kana needed no instruction; she followed Zerren and Keno. Ehi glanced back at Zerren's family one last time as the ziree carried her away, and she felt a deep pang of sadness in her guts. Her vision became blurry and tears fell down her cheeks. She looked away and faced forwards, watching the back of Zerren's head as they made their way out of Lazarack. She let her tears fall unhindered onto the inside of her cloak and somehow, somewhere deep inside, she knew that she and Zerren would never return.

# FOURTEEN

Three days after they had first arrived in Garakeeish, Myaie, Ahrl and a small group of Elorans had reached the district of Rashna and boarded their second vadi to Lebanoi. Ahrl sat at the front of this larger vadi, keeping a wary eye on the low-lying rivers. Every night since they had arrived in Garakeeish he had had the same dream, and he didn't even have to ask Roe if she had shared it; he knew it from the wide-eyed look she woke up with. He heard footsteps approaching and glanced up to see Myaie with a kaelo tucked under one arm.

'So, will Terrian take us to Lebanoi?' Ahrl asked.

'Yes,' Myaie said. 'He has agreed to take us.' She set down the kaelo and sat down beside Ahrl.

'What did you give him?'

'Nothing,' Myaie said. 'He didn't want anything, he only wished to help in whichever way he could and hoped that if he ever needed it, then someone would do the same in return. Terrian is not from around these parts, he's from Myrion.'

'That explains it then,' Ahrl said. 'He would have to pass by Lebanoi on his way to Myrion anyway.'

'Precisely,' Myaie said. 'We were lucky to find him; had we been delayed by a day or two then it's quite likely that he would have already left Rashna before we got there.' Myaie flicked a switch on the kaelo and turned a dial back and forth. The kaelo emitted a crackling, squeaky sound. As Myaie turned the dial, voices leapt out from the crackling and then disappeared again. She frowned and turned the dial slowly with her fingers; the crackling subsided and a voice spoke out from the kaelo's speakers.

*'There have been reports of tremors and landslides throughout the Kiri Mountains. The northern districts are warning all Elorans to approach the Kiri trail with extreme caution. A landslide at the foot of the Kiri Mountains near Tuskeean has entered the lakes and caused high waves, but there has been no damage reported to the district.'*

'I guess there's a plus side to the low-lying water levels. In the past those waves would have been much bigger and could have wiped out the entire district,' Ahrl said.

'That's true. I've heard horrific stories about that from my grandfather. He said that many districts chose to move a few miles away from the lakes because of the threat.'

*'The first Elorans returned to Skidaroi yesterday and have confirmed that little remains, many homes have been destroyed along with all the schools and warehouses. Calls for a united council have increased as refugees who have fled to other districts have begun to share their stories. Reports of yebons moving between Kubus and Skidaroi have been confirmed by outlying districts. So far the western districts refuse to comment.'*

'It's as I feared,' Myaie said. 'There's obviously nothing left of Skidaroi.'

'It will be rebuilt in time,' Ahrl said, placing a comforting hand on Myaie's shoulder.

'Yes, but that won't bring back the lives we've lost.' Myaie turned the kaelo off and sighed. 'I haven't really had a chance to ask you about your travels, and you've been unusually quiet since we left Garakeeish.'

'I haven't been sleeping well, that's all.'

'I understand. I haven't really slept much since we left Skidaroi, I've been… stressed.'

'I think we all are; even my dreams are strange.'

'If I slept long enough then I'd probably have nightmares,'

Myaie said. 'I imagine many here are suffering from their own nightmares at the moment. It's barely been a week since their whole lives were turned upside down.'

'Yes, I guess you're right.'

'I take it you have been having nightmares?'

'You could say that.'

A small smile tugged at Myaie's lips.

'What's so amusing?'

'Nothing, I've just never seen this side of you before. Ahrl disturbed by nightmares. It's refreshing actually; since your father left you've been a little too cold.'

'Cold?'

'Maybe that's the wrong word, but you've seemed, distant, I guess,' Myaie said.

'I'm just a little confused.'

'Don't worry. I expect your nightmares will ease with time. I think all of us will feel some relief when we reach Lebanoi.'

They drifted on down the river and gazed at the Kiri mountains stretching up into the sky. As the vadi rounded the next bend they heard gasps. They looked up at the sound, and the laluta rainbow fields slowly came into view on the lower edges of the mountains. It was as though a giant had taken a paintbrush and painted the gentle slopes in many colours, though the colours appeared to be fading and brown patches of land dotted the fields.

'They're dying out,' Myaie said. 'I can see very few eyeleetansy.' No one on the boat said a word as they passed by; there was a sadness in their awe. Ahrl could see the little leaves of the nearest laluta plants bleached yellow and shrivelling under the hot afternoon rays. He gazed down at the river and noted the low-lying muddy water and the exposed ends of riverbed plants that would have once been fully submerged. The rainbow fields stretched as far as the eye could see, but the large exposed areas of land dotted throughout made Ahrl's guts twist.

'They won't last much longer,' Ahrl said. 'Things seemed to be improving after the great famine, but it has been up and down for decades now and there have been no vast improvements. It's the same everywhere; I saw it during my travels.'

'I fear you're right. We won't have any choice but to move north at this rate,' Myaie said.

'To Loenya?'

'It's the only place we can go.'

'The pass through the mountains is dangerous, and there are too many Elorans in northern Eloran and northern Jheia. Loenya would never be able to take all of us.'

'I know. I just hope that conditions improve soon, because if they don't…' Myaie didn't finish her sentence. They stood in silence for a few moments under the weight of the words they had spoken and those they had left unspoken.

# FIFTEEN

Ehi heard feet patting against the ground, soft thuds and children laughing and shouting. She opened her eyes and pushed back her blanket. Zerren lay asleep on another thin mattress on the floor just a few feet away. They had stopped after several long days in the Arrukai district, just five days south of the district of Lebanoi. Ehi stretched and slipped out of bed quietly; the last few days had been nothing but rocky riding plagued with the strange images which tried to take over her mind. She hurried to the door, her bare feet padding quietly across the floor. She pushed it open a crack and gazed outside; a group of young children were kicking a dusty ball across the ground. Several faded memories skimmed her awareness; she remembered this game. She watched them beaming despite their baggy clothes and skinny limbs. Ehi glanced back at Zerren and the cloak she had left on the floor next to her lif gauntlet. She bit her lower lip, then stepped outside without them.

The children paused in their game and looked up at her in silence as she approached. They stared at her hair and her eyes but Ehi stopped, pointed at the ball and smiled. The children grinned and the game began again. They ran and weaved around one another in an attempt to gain sole control of the ball and Ehi snagged it with her foot, bouncing it up onto her knee and using her body to keep the ball aloft for a few moments before it hit the ground between her feet. She hadn't realised before, but compared to the children, her body seemed to move like water.

Her movements were more refined; she could bend in what seemed almost impossible gravity-defying ways. It was as though her muscles remembered these strange positions and movements but the memories of them were just out of reach.

The children laughed and shouted as she whisked the ball away and twisted around them. She stopped. A tingling sensation sparked around her mind and a child snatched the ball from her feet. Her vision swayed as she felt a pressure rising around her head and her ears rang. The Elorans of the Arrukai district disappeared around her, a room opened up before her and four humans stood there, two women and two men. Ehi gazed around, she was sure she had never seen a room quite like it before, yet it felt familiar. There were box-like machines which glowed around them and before Ehi could even wonder what they were, the answer appeared in her mind. The four individuals gazed at these computer screens with smiles on their faces. They had learnt something new and momentous, something both life-changing and dangerous. Ehi felt the enormity of the discovery, the excitement emanating from these humans, but she didn't understand it. She felt a sharp tug on her mind and the room slipped away as though it was nothing more than smoke on the wind.

A new scene formed around her and she found herself outside, standing on a strange smooth stone surface with curved stone structures like waves stretching up around her. The area was enclosed by some sort of fence but beyond that she saw green grass stretching out towards a lake where strange little animals floated upon the surface. Ehi felt her jaw drop; there was so much greenery here, so much flourishing life compared to the barren lands of Eloran. She turned, and at the top of one of the stone waves she saw a boy and a girl sitting side by side. The boy held a small curved piece of wood on his lap with what looked like little yebon wheels attached to it. Ehi gazed at their faces. She recognised them; they were two of the four individuals she had seen moments before, but they were younger, their faces were softer and more curved. Ehi looked closer and watched as two colourful spheres seemed to bloom at the centre of their torsos. *They have the same spheres as Iyeekans?* She marvelled as colours grew and twisted about their little spheres. Deep blue and red radiated outwards from the boy whilst lighter blues and purples danced within the girl. Brilliant bursts of gold eclipsed their spheres frequently like the etansy in their blue sky.

The scene faded and her mind was wrenched again as though someone had shoved her to the side. She became aware of all of the boy and the girl's potential futures, all the different pathways twisting and splitting through a labyrinth of possibilities. They glowed and pulsed with energy as though they were lines of shooting stars. She saw the lives of other humans twisting and wrapping around their pathways like the branches of many trees, coming together in a great, tangled mess. Some of these branches thrived, and other dwindled into nothing, but they all reached towards a single point, a point where there were only two options. Either all the pathways ended, or all the pathways survived. Another torrent of information flooded into Ehi's mind as she struggled to comprehend what she'd just seen. The pathways faded, shrinking away from her and out of view.

Iyeeka appeared around her with its dry, brown landscape, yet she was both there and not there at the same time. She looked down at her body and saw nothing, no legs, no stomach and no arms. A shadow grew across the land and she looked up to see a colossal planet, its rocky surface covered with craters, looming above her, blocking out the sky. The wind picked up around her, throwing the dust and sand into the air. In the distance a giant wall of debris and dirt sped towards her, stretching out and upwards as it ripped up Iyeeka and engulfed all that lay in its path. *Why? Why is this happening?* She turned to see Zerren standing beside her. In the next moment her view was obscured by the dust-clogged wind and she felt herself, whatever she was, being snatched up into the air as the wind roared around her. Silence. It was dark, she felt nothing, and she saw no more.

# SIXTEEN

Zerren opened his eyes and stretched underneath his blanket. He blinked a few times and turned to check on Ehi. He felt his body go cold. She wasn't there. He sat up quickly and was on his feet in a heartbeat. His gaze tore around the room; her cloak and gauntlet were there, but there was no sign of Ehi herself. *Outside!* a female voice said from the back of his mind, just before hundreds of other voices raced into the forefront of his awareness. *There's no time,* a male voice said. *I miss my daughter,* another voice said. Zerren cursed as he pushed the tide of voices back. He burst through the door to the outside and threw up a hand as the morning light temporarily blinded him.

'Ehi!' Zerren yelled. His eyes adjusted and his gaze snagged on a group of children and adults standing around something as they looked down at the ground. He ran and pushed his way through to the middle of the group and there he found her. 'Ehi!' Zerren said, dropping to his knees and clasping her shoulders. Her hair spilled out in a halo around her head and he could see that her eyes were moving relentlessly behind her closed eyelids. 'Ehi, wake up, come on, please.' He touched her cheek and placed the back of his hand gently against her forehead. Her skin was scorching and her breathing was heavy and irregular. Zerren felt the constant hum and buzz of voices latching onto his thoughts and echoing around his mind. *Lost, everything is lost,* a voice said. He gritted his teeth and squeezed his eyelids shut as he felt a pinching sensation behind his nose.

'What's going on here? What is this?' Zerren glanced up and saw the crowd part as a woman strode forward. She wore a light blue tunic with beige trousers and her dark long hair was in a twisted braid, circled many times around her head. She planted her hands on her hips as she gazed down at Zerren and Ehi.

'Council Member Deyelnorae,' a man said. 'The children say that she just collapsed.'

'They're travellers,' another said. 'They stayed last night at the guest house.'

'Someone get Nari,' Deyelnorae said. 'You there, what is your name?' She pointed at Zerren.

'Zerren, I'm from the district of Lazarack. And this is Ehi.'

'Where are you travelling to?'

'Lebanoi,' Zerren said. Deyelnorae seemed to churn this over in her mind for a moment.

'Ok, can we take Ehi back to the guest house?' Deyelnorae said.

'I think so, and thank you,' Zerren said as he stood and lifted Ehi from the ground.

'Don't thank me yet,' Deyelnorae said. 'I have some questions for you and I expect answers.' Zerren nodded and then carried Ehi back to the guest house with Deyelnorae walking beside him. He placed Ehi down on a mattress and then turned to face Deyelnorae.

'What did you want to ask?'

'Firstly, you can tell me why Ehi has such strange-coloured hair and why you didn't state her district.'

*Time. All Time. There is no time,* three voices said from the recesses of Zerren's mind. He blinked and pushed them back. 'I don't know the answers to those questions. We met recently and Ehi doesn't speak.'

'Can she not speak at all?'

'I don't know,' Zerren said. 'But she hasn't said a word since we first met.'

'And where did you first meet?'

'Cenic.'

'Cenic? But no one has lived that far south for years,' Deyelnorae said.

'My brother and I travelled there, looking for any resources that had been left behind in the ghost districts. We found Ehi, very much in the same state as you see her now.'

'I see, so you're telling me that you're just as uninformed as I am? Is there anything else that you do know?'

'There is something else you should know,' Zerren said.

'Oh?' Deyelnorae raised a slender brow.

'Another man was travelling with us when we found Ehi, his name was Varth, he is part of the N.I.L.,' Zerren said. 'He tried to kidnap Ehi.'

'And why would he do that?'

'Ehi has skills,' Zerren said. 'Skills that Varth thought the N.I.L. would like to acquire.'

'And I'm guessing you're not going to tell me what these skills are now?'

'I think it's better if I don't say.'

'Hmm, so we may have to keep an eye out for the N.I.L. now as word will get about.'

'I'm sorry,' Zerren said. 'Ehi usually wears a cloak with a hood so no one sees her hair or eyes. I don't know why she went out without it.'

'Her eyes?'

'Her eyes are purple,' Zerren said.

'Purple?' Deyelnorae cast her gaze over Ehi.

'Norae, I'm so sorry, Norae, I ran here as fast I could.' A young woman appeared in the doorway, her cheeks flushed.

'I told you not to call me that, Nari.' Deyelnorae frowned.

'I know, sis, but Council Member Deyelnorae of Arrukai is way too long to say every time,' Nari said. She dropped down to her knees beside Ehi. 'Wow, I love her hair colour.'

'Nari, please check to see if she's ok,' Deyelnorae said.

'Sure,' Nari said. She raised her hands above Ehi's body with her palms facing down and closed her eyes. Zerren watched closely; it wasn't often that you got to see a medic work. Medics used a similar mental control that the majority of Iyeekans used with lif, but it was directed at the biological body. They could sense where problems were and even accelerate the body's natural healing abilities with the right focus. This worked best with minor injuries; major injuries usually required other medical techniques too. After a few moments, Nari opened her eyes.

'Well?' Deyelnorae said.

'She's not hurt, at least, not physically,' Nari said. 'However, her physical symptoms suggest that her body has gone into a state of shock and exhaustion. Has she been eating and drinking enough?'

'Define enough,' Zerren said. 'It's not like any of us have plenty of food and water to go around.'

'Let me rephrase that, has she been eating and drinking regularly?'

'Yes,' Zerren said. 'We ate last night.'

'Hmm.' Nari hooked a finger under her chin and gazed down at Ehi.

'Will she be ok?' Zerren asked.

'It's hard to say,' Nari said. 'Physically speaking yes, but I don't know why she's unconscious.'

'Could it be heat stroke?' Deyelnorae asked.

'It could be, but we've not even reached the hottest part of the day yet,' Nari said. 'And the children I spoke to on the way here told me that she hadn't been playing with them for long.'

'She was playing with the children?' Zerren asked.

'Yes, they were playing futama,' Nari said. 'Apparently she was good at it, but then she just stopped and fell to the ground.'

Zerren shook his head.

'Thanks, Nari, I'll call you if anything changes,' Deyelnorae said.

'No problem, Norae.' Nari grinned as she got to her feet. 'I'll see you back at the house.'

'I'm sorry to cause you so much trouble, Deyelnorae,' Zerren said. 'We'll leave as soon as Ehi wakes up.'

'No need to apologise. We're all growing more agitated by the day. Our food supplies and water are running low and we're rationing what we have. I don't want the others to become desperate and do something foolish; that's why I wanted to know more about you and Ehi. I have to know if we're likely to be open to threats from other desperate and foolish Elorans.'

'I understand,' Zerren said.

'I'll ask you again, is there anything I should know?'

'Only that we ran into a bokhanya on the way back from Cenic to Lazarack,' Zerren said.

'A bokhanya? You're lucky to be alive.'

'I know,' Zerren said.

'Is that all?'

'Yes.'

'Good, I'll be going now, but I'll check in with Nari later.'

'Thank you.'

A small smile flickered across Deyelnorae's lips before she left.

Zerren propped himself up against the nearest wall, closed his eyes and let the tide of voices, which he had been keeping at bay, wash over him. It was a clamour of noise inside his mind, just like standing in a crowded room where everyone spoke at the same time, and no one made sense. He cracked open an eye and watched over Ehi as she lay on the mattress. Her fingers twitched from time to time, but she didn't wake. He wondered what was happening to her inside her mind and hoped that whatever she was going through wasn't more suited for nightmares. He sat there for hours; there was no use in wasting energy or doing anything until the voices in his mind quietened down and Ehi woke up. Yet there was a terrible thought gnawing at his brain; what if she never woke up again? He had deliberately left out the fact they had found Ehi in a strange machine, but she had been unconscious the first time he had seen her, and he couldn't dismiss the idea that this sudden collapse might be related. He watched a square patch of light stream in though one of the windows and drift slowly down the wall and across the floor as one by one the voices died off.

# SEVENTEEN

'Go on, get going,' Zerren heard, followed by the sound of children laughing and the patter of feet retreating into the distance. 'Zerren?' Zerren cracked open his eyes, his body ached and his mouth felt like a ziree's armpit. 'You finally got some sleep, did you?' Deyelnorae said as she crouched down before him. 'Here, I've brought you some water.' Zerren rubbed his stiff neck.

'Morning,' he said.

'It's hardly morning. More like afternoon.'

Zerren gulped down the water and looked past Deyelnorae; Ehi was still unconscious, lying on the thin mattress on the floor.

'She's still asleep,' Deyelnorae said. 'Nari said there's still no visible change. She gave Ehi a hydration pack but she's worried about the lack of nutrients.' Deyelnorae stood up and moved back so Zerren could stand and stretch his stiff limbs. A small groan escaped from Ehi and Zerren forgot his protesting muscles as he knelt beside her.

'Ehi? Are you awake?' He picked up her hand and clasped it gently between his own. Ehi's eyes raced back and forth behind her eyelids and then all of a sudden her eyes flew open and she bolted upright.

'Zerren!' Ehi gasped. Her gaze locked onto Zerren and she grabbed his shirt, pulling him sharply towards her as she bent her head towards his chest. Her shoulders trembled and he felt the moisture from her tears soaking into his clothes. Zerren froze, the sound of Ehi's voice had been so wonderfully strange and yet so beautiful. He had never heard a voice quite like it before; it held so much emotion and depth as though she had experienced the highs and lows of a thousand lives. Zerren blinked and placed his arms around Ehi's quivering frame.

'Did she just speak?' Deyelnorae said, with wide eyes. 'I thought you said she didn't speak?'

'It's the first time she's ever spoken,' Zerren said. He felt Ehi's body grow slack in his arms and she leant heavily on him as her breathing fell into a regular pattern. Zerren gently clasped Ehi's shoulders and lowered her back down onto the mattress.

'Well, I don't think I'll be forgetting that voice in a hurry,' Deyelnorae said. 'It sent shivers right down my spine. Can you lift her? We really should move her to the medical building; it will be easier for Nari to treat her there and Ehi needs to eat and drink to regain her strength.'

'Ok,' Zerren said. He picked Ehi up and followed Deyelnorae out of the guest house and towards Arrukai's school.

'Have you heard any news yet over the kaelo?' Deyelnorae said.

'No,' Zerren said.

'Then you should know, the N.I.L. have attacked three more districts; it seems like they're heading to Lebanoi.'

'What?' Zerren said.

'The western districts are in a complete mess over it, Syvvak has many supporters and those who have spoken out against his actions have been quickly silenced,' Deyelnorae said. Zerren opened his mouth to speak but quickly shut it again; he didn't know what to say, there was nothing to say. 'I know you wish to travel to Lebanoi but I think you should reconsider your plans.'

'We're going to Kiri,' Zerren said.

'Kiri? Why are you going there?'

'To try and find answers about Ehi,' Zerren said.

'I see,' Deyelnorae said. 'I guess it is the only place where you're likely to find answers. If you must go, then you should travel as soon as possible. It would be wise to travel through Lebanoi before the N.I.L. get there.'

'I know,' Zerren said.

'That's not all. I'm concerned about the Elorans here, many have heard the news and they are unsettled by it. I think the sooner you can leave the better.'

Zerren nodded.

'The medical building is just up ahead between the school and the warehouses,' Deyelnorae said. As they rounded the corner, the one-storey medical building came into view; it was smaller than the school and the warehouses but larger than a family home. 'It might be a bit busy in here; the older and younger Elorans struggle the most with the rations and hot temperatures,' Deyelnorae said. They entered the building and Zerren immediately regretted not covering Ehi's hair. There were dozens of Elorans in the cramped waiting room, many were children and the elderly as Deyelnorae had warned. Deyelnorae strode past and pushed open a door and ushered Zerren into the hallway beyond.

'Wait, shouldn't they be seen to first?' Zerren asked.

'You're anxious to continue on your journey, aren't you?' Deyelnorae said.

'Yes, but…'

'Ehi's condition is more serious for the time being,' Deyelnorae said. They passed many rooms with closed doors before Deyelnorae stopped and opened a door to a small room in which was a single bed. 'Put Ehi on the bed and I'll go and find Nari,' Deyelnorae said. Zerren did as he was told. Deyelnorae returned moments later with Nari who checked over Ehi and left some food and water on the little table beside the bed.

'She seems to be ok, just exhausted,' Nari said. 'If she eats then she should be alright after a couple of days rest, though ideally I would leave it a little longer before you start travelling again.'

'I would prefer to get on the road again as soon as possible,'

Zerren said.

'Two days minimum then,' Nari said, as she glanced over Ehi.

***

As soon as daylight began to show on the morning of the third day, Zerren woke Ehi. They ate, dressed and packed their belongings and went outside to fetch the ziree. He watched Ehi closely; she hadn't spoken again and, although she had eaten, her expression echoed that of a confused and lost child. Every so often she would clutch her head and wince, and as soon as they stepped outside she looked up at the sky as though she was searching for something.

'I see you're leaving early then,' Deyelnorae said. She approached with her sister as the rest of the Arrukai district still slept.

'I really don't think it's a good idea for Ehi to be travelling so soon,' Nari said. She placed her hands on Ehi's shoulders. She stared at Ehi and Ehi stared back.

'We have to go,' Zerren said.

'There doesn't seem to be any major changes,' Nari said. She sighed and let go of Ehi.

'Well, I wish you a safe journey,' Deyelnorae said. 'I wish I could spare you some more food, but you should have enough water.'

'No, it's ok,' Zerren said. 'You've done more than enough for the both of us, thank you.'

'Alright then, I hope when we meet again it's a happier time,' Deyelnorae said.

'Let's hope.' Zerren gave her a curt nod and then nudged Keno forwards. He heard Kana's hooves clip the dirt close behind him, but he didn't look back. He held in a sigh of relief as they left the borders of the Arrukai district. He pulled gently on Keno's reigns and travelled abreast with Ehi as she gazed up at the sky.

'So, you said my name three days ago,' Zerren said. 'Was that just a one-time thing or can you talk now?' Ehi lowered her chin and turned to look at him for a moment, and then she tilted her head back and gazed back up at the sky. 'I guess it was just a one-time thing.' Zerren sighed. 'What are you looking at? Are you looking for nawushi?' Ehi's gaze swept back and forth across the sky. 'If you're looking for nawushi you'll have a hard time finding them; the ones that have survived have flown north with the eyeleetansy.' Ehi winced and clutched her head again. 'Are you ok?' Zerren asked. He pulled out a water sack from his saddle bags and offered it to Ehi. 'Here, you need to drink more water.' Ehi accepted the water and took several long gulps, and then she went back to searching the sky. Zerren put the water sack back in his saddlebags. 'We should arrive in Lebanoi in five, maybe four days,' Zerren said. 'If I see any nawushi I'll point them out.' Ehi didn't reply. Zerren shook his head and nudged Keno forwards, He was growing accustomed to her strange behaviour, but sometimes it was as though she lived on another planet. Zerren glanced up quickly and then let his gaze roam around them. *What is she looking for?*

# EIGHTEEN

It hadn't been difficult to find them, but it had been difficult to remain hidden. Varth kept his yebon well away from the Arrukai district, tucked within the dips of the land. He lay flat on the ground at the top of a small rise with a pair of binoculars and a portable kaelo at his side. He had watched Zerren and Ehi enter the district four days ago, but neither one of them had left and their zirees were still resting inside a ziree shelter. *Where are they? What are they doing?* Varth held the binoculars up to his eyes and searched the district. *There!* He saw both Zerren and Ehi emerge from one of the buildings with their bags. They spoke to a couple of women for a few minutes and then they retrieved their zirees, saddled them up and rode out to the north in the direction of Lebanoi. Varth lowered his binoculars and rolled onto his back. There was no point following them immediately; the yebon was much faster than their zirees.

He had barely slept for days and the reports coming through the kaelo from the various remaining districts had been troubling. The N.I.L. had attacked Skidaroi, Garakeeish and two other districts in the space of three weeks, yet the first thing he had heard about the Skidaroi attack was from the whisperings of frightened Elorans living in Kubus. Syvvak hadn't said a word to him; he had acted as if nothing had happened at all. It unsettled him; he could recall the look on Roarn's face and his words of warning: *'You shouldn't get close to them Varth, they're dangerous.'* Varth frowned and rubbed his tired face. *Why, Syvvak? Why are you attacking the districts? You said you wanted to change things but you never said you were going to kill innocent Elorans.* Varth tasted bile at the back of his throat; was this what Syvvak meant when he said that tough decisions had to be made? It made sense now why the council member had been so angry with Syvvak when Varth had arrived back in Kubus, and why Syvvak had been so evasive of his questions. Roarn's words came back to him again: *'They built their wall and let everyone else starve.'*

Varth gazed up at the pale pink and purple morning sky. In the stillness of the hot morning air, his thoughts were free to trail back through his memories. He felt his nostrils flare and his fingers curling into fists. Varth remembered a day very much like today, a day that had occurred ten years ago…

Not a single cloud graced the sky and the etansy stared down on Eloran like a giant fiery eye. Varth made his way across the district of Lazarack to a home he had visited every day since he had been a young Eloran, only now he approached Anorae's home with a heavy heart. He passed the grave statues of Anorae's ancestors, their stone faces and smiles nothing more than frozen memories lost in time. He pushed open the front door but didn't announce his arrival, and he heard hushed voices drifting down the short hallways.

'I'm afraid it's not good, she is dying,' a voice said. Varth stood frozen by the front door.

'Surely you can do something?' Anorae's mother said.

'Anorae's condition cannot be cured,' the first voice said. 'I can give her something for the pain, but she hasn't got long…' Varth heard a muffled sobbing sound.

'How long?' Anorae's father said.

'Six months, a year, maybe two,' the first voice said. 'It's impossible to say for sure. I'm sorry, but her condition can only worsen rapidly with time. I wish I could give you better news.'

'I know. Thank you for being honest with us,' Anorae's father said. There was a moment of silence and muffled sobbing then the sound of footsteps grew louder. Three Elorans appeared from around a bend at the top of the hallway where Varth stood.

'Varth,' Anorae's mother said as she dried her red-rimmed eyes and forced a smile. 'Anorae has been looking forward to your visit.'

'Is she ok?' Varth asked, the words sticking in his throat.

'No better and no worse really,' Anorae's mother said. *No worse? How can you say that?*

Varth nodded and made his way down the hallway; he glanced back over his shoulder to see Anorae's father and mother saying goodbye to the medic at the front door. He turned left around the corner and then stopped outside a pale, wooden door. He took a deep breath, knocked and then opened the door. Anorae smiled as he walked in; she was sitting up in bed, propped up by several cushions and covered by a blanket of blue eyeleetansy silk.

'Varth, I'm so glad you're here.'

'Hello, Anorae,' Varth said. 'How are you feeling?'

'Not too bad at the moment. I can only feel a little bit of pain; the medic gave me some really strong painkillers.' Anorae smiled again but Varth could see the lines of distress etched into her forehead. 'Would you take me outside? I'm so sick of staring at these four walls.'

'Will your parents be ok with that?'

'I don't want to go far, just to the swing seat behind the house.'

'Ok, sure,' Varth said. He stood up and leant towards her, placing an arm behind her back and another under her knees. Anorae reached up and wrapped her thin arms around his neck and, when he lifted her up, he noted the lightness of her frame. It seemed that every time he carried her she weighed less and less. He took her outside and across her family's land, where few crops grew amongst patches of brown, dry soil, wilting away just like the rest of the Lazarack district. The swing seat stood in the furthest corner, its wooden slats bleached by the etansy. He put her down gently, sat beside her, and let her rest her head upon his shoulder.

'Did you manage to eat today?'

'A little.' Anorae sighed as she cast her gaze about the land. 'I so hoped this land would improve, even as a child I kept hoping, but now…'

'It will get better, it has to, you'll see,' Varth said. 'It can't last forever.'

'I won't be around to see it,' Anorae said. Varth felt his blood turn cold.

'Nonsense, you don't know that.'

'Varth, I know I haven't got much longer.'

'You might have years,' Varth said. 'The medics don't know everything; you might make a miraculous recovery and see the Eloran we've always been told about, and grow old, with me.'

'No,' Anorae said softly. She shook her head as tears began to fall slowly down her cheeks. 'I can feel my body growing weaker; I feel the pain of my illness burning through my veins. I don't want to deteriorate any more, I don't want to become bedbound and crippled for the last few months, maybe the last few years of my life. I don't want you to remember me that way, or for that to be my family's, and my, last memory.'

'What are you saying, Anorae?'

'I wanted you to take me out here because I wanted to ask you something, Varth, away from my family's ears.'

'What? What is it?'

'Varth, I want you to end my life,' Anorae said. Varth's mouth dropped and his heart froze for a couple of beats. 'Varth?' Anorae said, lifting her head from his shoulder to look at him.

'You don't mean it.'

'I do,' Anorae said. 'I do.'

'How could you ask me to do such a thing?'

'I know it's selfish, but I'm asking you because you're the

only one I can trust,' Anorae said. 'We grew up together, played together, we've spent almost every day in each other's company. You know everything about me and you're my closest friend.'

'I can't.'

'Varth, I wouldn't ask anyone to do this if I felt I had a chance, but all I see are endless days of pain as my body grows weaker and weaker. I see the despair and misery on my parents' faces, on your face. I don't want there to be any more pain, for anyone. Can you tell me that if you were in my shoes you wouldn't wish the same?' Varth lowered his gaze.

'I cannot.'

'Please then, Varth, please do this for me,' Anorae said. 'If I must die, then let me choose how I go and when.' Varth didn't say anything for a long time; his mind was racing through all the possibilities, all the words he could say to convince her to change her mind.

'Anorae, I need to think about this,' Varth said. 'This is too big, too much to digest right now. You need to think about this.'

'I have thought about it,' Anorae said. 'I've been thinking about it for a long time.' Varth stared into her eyes and searched her gaze for a flicker of uncertainty, anything that would suggest she didn't really want to go through with it, but he found none. He sighed sadly.

'I'll ask you again tomorrow, if you are sure, then…' He gulped. 'I'll do it. But please think about it again, Anorae.'

'I will, and thank you, Varth,' Anorae said.

'You will do no such thing,' Anorae's father said. Varth and Anorae jumped and turned round to see her father standing behind them. His face was bleached white with rage.

'Father…' Anorae said.

'Get away from her, Varth,' Anorae's father said.

'Father, please, don't blame Varth,' Anorae said as tears sprung from her eyes.

Varth didn't move.

'I said get away from her!' Anorae's father marched over to them and hauled Varth to his feet. 'How could you do this? How dare you even consider?' Anorae's father shook his head as he dragged Varth away.

'Father!' Anorae said.

'Anorae, we will talk later,' Anorae's father said.

'Where are you going? Stop,' Anorae said. She struggled to her feet but fell straight down onto her knees and burst into tears.

'Anorae,' Varth said. He struggled but Anorae's father tightened his grip and marched him back to the house. Anorae's mother ran out the back door towards them.

'What's going on? What are you doing?' Anorae's mother said. 'Anorae!'

'Get Anorae back into her bed, I'm taking Varth to the council,' Anorae's father said.

'What? Why?'

'Because he was planning to do the unthinkable, he was planning to kill our daughter.'

'Varth?' Anorae's mother said. Varth saw the hurt and dismay flash over Anorae's mother's face and that cut him deeply. He opened his mouth to speak but Anorae's father pulled him away.

Varth let the memory roll forward and recalled the moment he had stood before the council. Most of the district had been packed into the school hall and in the middle was a small circle where Varth stood facing the six council members of Lazarack. Varth's wrists were bound with lif and he could sense the hum of energy from the council members who kept it there.

'Varthrune do you understand the severity of your plans with Anorae?' an elderly council member named Jinhiro said.

'Yes, I understand,' Varth said. 'But I will not apologise for it, Anorae is dying and she wants to choose to die with dignity on her own terms.' He could hardly look at his parents who stood on the edges of the circle, he knew his father was furious and that his mother was quietly sobbing.

'Varthrune, I sympathise but you know that this goes against our laws and customs. We do not and must not kill our fellow Elorans or assist with suicide. It is not for you to decide,' Jinhiro said.

'It is not for you to decide either,' Varth said.

'May I speak?' Varth recognised the sound of Lucoe's voice and saw him push his way through thr crowd. A small measure of relief flooded through him, Lucoe was both practical and logical with his arguments and the Elorans of Lazarack respected him for it.

'You may speak, Lucoe,' Jinhiro said.

'I know our laws and customs forbid us from killing fellow Elorans, and for good reason, though few of us would ever dream of commiting such an act,' Lucoe said. 'But I believe Varth and Anorae's situation is unique.'

'Unique as it may be it is still against the law, we cannot allow such decisions to become normalised. We do not kill any living creature unless it is in self defence,' Jinhiro said.

'True,' Lucoe said. 'However, here is a question for all of you, for everyone who is gathered here today. If you were suffering and in a great deal of pain and knew that your life was coming to an end soon. Would you really want to go on suffering?' There were a few murmurs and grumbles from the gathered crowd and Varth felt a flutter of hope for a second.

'I must object,' Anorae's father said. 'Anorae's mother and I just wish to be able to spend as much time as we can with our daughter. We don't know how long she has left and we know our time together is precious.'

'You're only seeing it from your side,' Lucoe said. 'Think about being Anorae, think about how she feels and the amount of pain she is in. Imagine being your daughter for a second.'

'Imagine it?' Anorae's father said. 'I live it. I see it every day, and don't think for a second I wouldn't do everything I could to see my daughter fit and healthy again.'

'But that isn't possible,' Lucoe said.

'We don't know that Anorae is going to die for sure,' a voice said from the crowd. 'There have been miraculous recoveries before.'

Lucoe shook his head. 'Two medics have told us that Anorae doesn't have very long.'

'They might still be wrong,' another voice said.

Lucoe frowned.

'You can't know for certain,' a third voice said.

'Alright settle down, quiet please,' Jinhiro said. 'The usual punishment for killing an Eloran is forty years in sanitation along with banishment from the district.'

'That punishment is too severe, Varth hasn't carried out the act and Anorae asked him to do it,' Lucoe said.

'Yes Lucoe, we know,' Jinhiro said. 'I propose an alternative punishment given the circumstances. Varthrune will be sentenced to six months in sanitation and he will be allowed to return to the district once he has completed his sentence.'

'No,' Varth said. *Away for six months? I don't want to be away for even a day.*

'That is too lenient,' Anorae's father said. 'What if he tries to end my daughter's life when he returns?'

'Once Varthrune returns and if Anorae is still with us, which I sincerely hope she is, he will be prohibited from seeing or contacting her. Varthrune will also be banned from using lif,' Jinhiro said.

'That isn't fair! You can't be serious?' Varth said.

'I'm sorry, Varthrune,' Jinhiro said. 'We will allow the public to vote now. If you agree with our sentence then please raise your hand.' Varth turned to look at the gathered crowd and saw a number of Eloran's raising their hands. He could guess that about forty percent of the room agreed with the council members. 'Ok, if you disagree please raise your hand,' Jinhiro said. Those who had agreed dropped their hands and now a number of Elorans raised their hands. Lucoe raised his hand too but Varth could already tell that it wasn't enough, there were too many who hadn't chosen to vote at all and who looked uncomfortably at the ground.

'The public have voted. If all the council members agree then we will make the preparations and you will leave immediately,' Jinhiro said.

'Immediately?' Varth said. *Can't I even say goodbye?*

'Do all council members agree with the sentence I have decreed?' Jinhiro looked at his fellow council members and each council member nodded and affirmed their support. 'Varthrune, with the agreement of the Lazarack council I hereby sentence you to six months in sanitation with your immediate departure and all other restrictions effective on your return.'

'I would ask that you reconsider your sentence,' Lucoe said.

'Lucoe, our decision is final,' Jinhiro said.

The radio crackled beside Varth and he let the memories go back to the deepest recesses of his mind. He uncurled his fists and blinked back the tears. It had been a while since he had remembered that dreadful day. He wondered what Anorae would have been doing now had she lived, but he already knew the answer. She would have been helping the district move north, she would have kept him in Lazarack, he would have never ended up in Kubus. Roarn's words came back to torment him again: *Anorae would be disgusted if she knew you had joined the N.I.L.*

Varth sat up and wiped away his tears. He remembered meeting Syvvak for the first time. Syvvak had spoken to a crowd gathered outside one of the schools in Kubus promising a better Eloran, a better Iyeeka. He had condemned the decisions of their earlier ancestors and council members, and highlighted how the voices of the few were often correct yet ignored by their current system. It was an injustice Varth was familiar with, a pain which had moved him to speak to Syvvak and join the N.I.L., but he had never imagined that Syvvak would attack a district. The radio crackled again, and a series of irregular clicks began to sound through the speaker. Varth got up, picked up his belongings and hurried back to the yebon. He found his notebook and sent a series of clicks back before waiting for Syvvak's message. The clicks came and Varth translated them into words.

*Varthrune, head towards Lebanoi and stop at the populated districts on the way. Pose as the concerned older brother and ask questions, use an alias. Find out where the targets have been and where they are heading. Respond as soon as you learn anything.*

Varth sent back a reply and turned off the kaelo. He had a few days to spare before he needed to head to Lebanoi and catch up with Ehi and Zerren. He drew down the blinds, lay across the seats and shut his eyes. He didn't want to think, or feel, or remember; he just wanted his mind to be still and silent. It was a while before sleep found him, but when it did, his mind was not silent. He dreamt of Ehi. And a storm.

# NINETEEN

Ahrl sat near the front of the vadi with Roe as they approached the outer districts surrounding Lebanoi.

'I dreamt about her again,' Roe said.

'Me too.'

'What does it mean, Ahrl?'

'I don't know. Nothing, I hope.'

'What happens if we do find her?'

'I'm not sure,' Ahrl said. He hadn't really considered the possibility that the woman in their dreams actually existed. He had travelled all over northern Eloran and northern Jheia and he hadn't seen or heard anything about anyone with pale purple hair and purple eyes.

'I hope she's nice,' Roe said. The vadi continued to drift on the gentle currents and soon they could see the district of Lebanoi stretching out across the horizon. Terrian stopped the vadi on a crowded pier by the outer districts. Myaie thanked him for the safe passage and then she, Ahrl, Roe and their group of Elorans from Skidaroi disembarked.

They continued on their way, the Lebanoi district growing upwards and outwards on the horizon as they approached. There were Elorans everywhere as they passed through the districts bordering Lebanoi. Every home seemed full and many Elorans sat on the sides of the road or helped to farm whatever little food and produce they could. The stench of waste and the sound of a thousand conversations hit Ahrl first. Zirees almost trampled over limbs and children ran about, darting through the crowds. Masses gathered around those who handed out rationed fish, vegetables, fruit and water. They pushed and yelled whilst the few infants they had wailed, and the elderly sat in any shady spot they could find, looking glumly at the ground.

'This is unbelievable,' Roe said. 'There are so many of them.'

'Yes,' Myaie said. 'So many districts have become uninhabitable in the south and middle regions, families have had to move further and further north. Lebanoi is the last district before the pass through the Kiri Mountains to Loenya. Thousands of Eloran families have either travelled through here or settled here recently.' They moved onwards, and when they reached the edge of Lebanoi, they found that the district had closed itself off with a patchy wall made of metal and stone that looked as though it had been thrown together overnight. Elorans with blue sashes around their arms stood at a small gap in this wall, shaking their heads and turning refugees away from the central district.

'What's going on?' Roe asked.

'Lebanoi is a closed district now, only certain Elorans are allowed in and out,' Myaie said. She pushed her way to the front of the small crowd. 'I'm Council Member Myaie of Skidaroi and I wish to speak with Council Member Ruick.' The two guards glanced at one another and then they nodded, and one ran off inside. They waited silently for a few minutes and then Ahrl turned to the remaining guard.

'Is it really so bad inside Lebanoi?' Ahrl asked.

'Yes, we're bursting at the seams and many are starting to get sick. We can't keep up with hygiene and food demands, though Ruick has been working closely with the council members of Myrion and we…'

'Council Member Myaie.' The second guard had returned, panting. 'Ruick said he will see you, but he can't come to the gate as he is busy.'

'What about my group?' Myaie said, motioning to the dozens of Skidaroi Iyeekans who had come with them to Lebanoi.

'You're all permitted entrance to Lebanoi, for now,' the guard said.

'Ahrl, Roe, keep close,' Myaie said.

'Please, come this way,' the guard said. Ahrl followed Myaie and Roe into Lebanoi, glancing backwards as he followed the guard to make sure the rest of their party were also being allowed in. The guard at the gate had been telling the truth, much to Ahrl's dismay. Desperate Elorans were everywhere, occupying every space that the Lebanoi district had to offer which wasn't being used as farmland. There were tents propped up on the side of the roads, in the narrow spaces in front of homes, and some of the houses had been extended upwards, adding floors for more space. Gaunt faces stared at them as they weaved through the crowds. They passed one of Lebanoi's school buildings and Ahrl saw Elorans of all ages looking out of the open windows. 'Council Member Ruick had to repurpose the school for accommodation,' the guard said, following Ahrl's gaze.

'Where are you taking us?' Myaie asked.

'To Lebanoi's school for technological research,' the guard said. 'It used to be a general school, but Ruick deemed that we needed a school that could advance our technology and facilitate our understanding of our world in order to combat the global climate issues.'

'What does this school teach?' Myaie said.

'The school teaches students not so much how to do things but why things happen the way they do. Ruick believes that the whys are just as crucial as the hows and that you cannot really have one without the other.'

'Interesting,' Myaie said.

'Then the students, who are of all ages, come up with and test out solutions and theories based on their detailed understanding;

it's quite fascinating really.'

'Do you still have general schools where Elorans learn how to do things?' Myaie asked.

'Yes, of course,' the guard said. 'But Ruick is adding more detailed understanding to the curriculum in all fields of study, or at least making the students aware that there is more knowledge about their preferred work that they can learn.'

'I see,' Myaie said.

'Not all students want to learn all the details or the whys, you see, but Ruick feels it's important that they are made aware that there are details to be learnt.'

They walked past hundreds of faces and dozens of ziree as they came to another two-storey building on the edge of the street. A large black roof sloped at a slight angle towards the back of the building and large rectangular windows had been placed at regular intervals along the walls. The daylight cast a pinkish hue on the pale brickwork. Two more guards with blue sashes stood at the front of this building and two travel-weary ziree were tied to a post outside.

'Are they Ruick's ziree?' Ahrl asked.

'Oh no,' the guard said. 'They just arrived today.' The guard led the way into the building and Ahrl followed him down a long corridor to one end of the school. The guard knocked on a door before opening it into a large spacious room. Ahrl stopped in his tracks and gawped. Standing inside the room behind a desk was Ruick, dressed in white eyeleetansy robes, and before him were two Elorans: a man with short dark hair and a woman, no, the woman, from his dreams. She turned to look at him with her deep purple eyes as her long pale purple hair swished about her shoulders. Ahrl glanced at Roe and saw that she too had stopped and was staring with her mouth open.

'Council Member, Myaie of Skidaroi,' Ruick said. 'Sorry that we have to meet like this, but my time is limited.'

'Council Member, Ruick.' Myaie inclined her head slightly. 'This is my cousin Ahrl and our friend, Roe.'

'Ahrl? Is that really you? Mother Iyeeka, I thought you were in Loenya with your father,' Ruick said.

'Council Member, Ruick,' Ahrl said, briefly taking his eyes away from the purple-haired woman. The guard smirked at Ahrl's expression and then left, closing the door behind him.

'I haven't seen you in years and, Myaie, when did you become a council member?' Ruick asked.

'Last year, though I've always worked closely with the council of Skidaroi,' Myaie said.

'Of course. Come in, come in,' Ruick said. 'I know her appearance is quite a shock but Ehi doesn't bite.'

'It's not that,' Ahrl said stepping forwards. 'It's just Roe and I have had strange dreams about her.' Ehi's companion groaned and clasped a hand to his head.

'Not you too,' he said.

'Dreams? What dreams?' Myaie said, turning to face Ahrl and raising an eyebrow.

'It seems we have a lot to discuss,' Ruick said.

'So it does,' Myaie said.

'This is Zerren from the district of Lazarack and his companion Ehi from an unknown district,' Ruick said. 'Zerren, Ehi, this is Ahrl, an old acquaintance and his cousin Myaie, one of the council members of Skidaroi.'

'Though not anymore, I'm afraid,' Myaie said.

'No, of course,' Ruick said with a sad smile. 'We heard the news but you're the first physical refugees to turn up here. So it's true then? The N.I.L. really did attack Skidaroi?'

'Yes,' Myaie said.

'We've just received reports that Rashna has been attacked too,' Ruick said.

'Oh no. We passed through there,' Myaie said, raising a hand to her mouth.

'I'm so sorry, Myaie,' Ruick said. 'My deepest sympathies and condolences. I guess Syvvak has learnt of my plans, or if he hasn't, he will know soon enough.'

'What plans?' Myaie asked.

'We've finally perfected our methods for desalinating seawater; we're pumping new freshwater back into the Myri lakes around Myrion as we speak. We've also been working on ways to pollinate the laluta plants without eyeleetansy, and we've been cross pollinating crops in order to produce hardier crops which can withstand the hot weather. We've been working on new ways to produce clothing as well as keeping fish to populate the lakes and rivers we replenish. If all goes well, it means we will be able to restore some stability and security across northern Eloran.'

'I'm impressed,' Myaie said. 'I didn't think it would be possible.'

'Oh it's possible, but it's difficult, especially with our limited resources. Syvvak must have caught wind of our plans; he doesn't want the security and stability because he doesn't want society to go back to the old ways. I'm sure you've heard by now, the members of the N.I.L. blame our ancestors for the rising temperatures, and they are correct in many ways,' Ruick said. 'But Syvvak wants to use that to stamp out any resemblance of our former societies in order to carve a new one where he will name himself and a select few as council members of all of Eloran. My sources say that he sees himself as some sort of head councillor, above all other council members and above all Elorans. It's a ridiculous notion; council members are not above anyone; we are there to guide and use our knowledge to help the entire district make decisions; we're not here to control or amass power.'

'That's outrageous; there's no way that Elorans will support him,' Myaie said.

'It's true though,' Zerren said. 'I spent some time with a member of the N.I.L. and he had similar ideas and opinions. With so many starving, they might gain more support than you think. This chaos helps.'

'I know,' Ruick said. 'We've learnt a great deal in our quest to desalinate and purify seawater, most of it has been bad news. Our bright students determined that we needed to measure the toxicity of our oceans in order to understand its contents and be able to convert it to freshwater. So they came up with a few simple machines and tested different water samples. Our seawater is very corrosive and can dissolve rock easily and is partly the reason why our coastlines are eroding at such a trememdous rate. We can prove now that our ancestors' methods of disposal destabilised the ecosystem and increased the toxicity of our oceans and that it directly correlates with the rising temperatures. Our old methods of just shoving everything that we didn't want into the ocean had disastrous effects, killing important plants and releasing gases which have become trapped in our atmosphere, which we believe caused Iyeeka to heat up. Our ancestors didn't notice or even think to look into it because, before temperatures skyrocketed, we had a few extreme cold periods too, so our ancestors thought the rise was an anomaly and that the planet wasn't really heating up at all. The majority of our lakes are so massive that the evaporation from them was tiny at first. The rise in temperatures were gradual to begin with but caused disasters in small pockets all over Iyeeka, and then things escalated and the southern lakes and rivers dried up and no one knew why or how.'

'Can we stop it?' Ahrl asked.

'Straight to the point, just like your father,' Ruick said. 'Yes, we think so. Though we aren't sure how much damage has been done just yet, what we do know is that we need to rethink our methods of disposal and we will need to keep pumping desalinated water into the lakes and rivers until temperatures drop, if they ever do. But it could take many generations.' The room fell silent, they all had the same question but they weren't sure they wanted to know the answer, would there be enough time to fix things before it was too late?

'What did you mean when you said not you too?' Ahrl said breaking the silence, he looked directly at Zerren.

'You're not the only one who's dreamt about Ehi,' Zerren said. 'Ashta has dreamt about Ehi too.'

'Ashta?' Myaie said.

'Ashta is my partner,' Ruick said. 'She started having strange dreams about a month ago. She would wake up screaming in the middle of night and kept talking about a woman with pale purple hair and purple eyes. I thought nothing of it at first, but as time went on and her dreams were so frequent, I began to wonder. So I mentioned it to my newly appointed Peace Enforcement Group and asked them to look out for anyone who matched Ehi's description.'

'Oh, so that's who the guards are with the blue sashes on their arms?' Ahrl said.

'Yes,' Ruick said. 'We had hundreds of refugees coming here every day and many have settled here, but it got to the point where our supplies and produce couldn't meet the demands of feeding so many. Fights broke out and conditions were so poor that many of us were becoming ill. So we did the only thing we could; with heavy hearts, we built a wall and turned all other refugees away from the inner district. We didn't want to, but we had no choice; they were claiming the little productive farmland we had. It was a difficult decision and many have settled in the outer districts. We're stretching our supplies as much as possible to cater for everyone; I regularly send out Elorans to help our neighbouring districts. I'm hopeful that once we get the new freshwater across from Myrion that things will start looking up. Now, tell us, Ahrl and Roe, what did you dream exactly? I'm curious.'

'Yes, I'm curious too,' Myaie said, glancing at Ahrl.

Ahrl recounted his dream and told them how Roe claimed to

have had an identical dream. A small satisfied smile appeared on Ruick's narrow lips.

'I don't think we can call it a strange coincidence now, can we, Zerren?' he said. Ahrl glanced at Zerren who folded his arms and shook his head. 'Ahrl. You, Ashta and Roe have had exactly the same dream,' Ruick said.

'That's so odd,' Roe said.

'What about Ehi?' Ahrl said, as he turned to face her. 'Ehi, have you had any of these strange dreams?' Ehi blinked at him.

'I'm told she doesn't speak, or can't,' Ruick said.

'Council Member, Ruick of Lebanoi, Ehi and I must take our leave now; we still have a long journey ahead of us,' Zerren said.

'Where are you going?' Ahrl asked.

'We're going to seek answers about Ehi from the Moribi of Kiri.'

'Aren't you going to tell them why?' Ruick asked. Zerren glared at him.

'I met Ehi under some unusual circumstances,' Zerren said. 'She had a page with her which had the Moribi of Kiri's symbol on the bottom of it.'

'That's not all though, is it?' Ruick stared at Zerren and then turned to Ahrl. 'Zerren found Ehi in some sort of machine; this page he speaks of contains a diagram of this machine and what looks to be some complicated mathematics. Go on, show them.' Zerren reluctantly slid his rucksack to the floor and took out a folded page. He handed it over to Ahrl. Myaie stood by Ahrl's shoulder as Ahrl studied the page. Sure enough, the Moribi of Kiri's symbol was at the bottom of the page, but the diagram was of something that he had never seen or heard of before. Surely it was nothing more than a picture? He glanced at Ehi; up until the last few minutes he hadn't thought her existence was possible either.

'What is a Usol Key?' Myaie asked.

'No idea,' Ruick said. Roe reached for the page; Ahrl let her have it and she bent over it with a studious expression.

'You really think the Moribi will have answers?' Ahrl asked.

'There's only one way to find out,' Zerren said.

'We should contact them on the kaelo,' said Myaie.

'No,' Zerren said. 'I don't want anyone to know where Ehi is, let alone the N.I.L.'

'I don't need to warn you, the pass through the mountains is treacherous,' Ruick said. 'The mountains are steep and high; the temperatures drop rapidly and the air is thin. Not to mention the frequent landslides and rock falls due to the ground tremors.'

'I set off on this journey aware of all of that,' Zerren said.

'If you must go, will you at least join my parents, Ashta and I for our evening meal before you leave?' Ruick said. Zerren opened his mouth to reply but Ehi stepped forwards and nodded.

'Ehi?' Zerren said. Ehi nodded again.

'Looks like it's settled then. You can put your ziree in my family's ziree shelters; they will be protected and able to rest there,' Ruick said.

'Thank you,' Zerren said, inclining his head. 'Come on, Ehi.' Zerren took the page back from Roe. As soon as the door closed behind them, Ahrl turned to Ruick.

'What do you think of Ehi?'

'She has unusual hair and eyes, and apparently her lif control is exceptional,' Ruick said. 'I'm more interested in the author of that page though. That technology looks to be more advanced than anything I've seen or heard of in Eloran; if there are more pages in Kiri then I want to find them.'

'I wonder why you've dreamt about Ehi,' Myaie said. 'Why is it only you, Roe and Ashta? Why haven't I or Ruick dreamt about her?'

'It is strange, I don't know,' Ahrl said. 'But if anyone would know then surely it would be the Moribi of Kiri.'

'Yes, those were my thoughts too,' Ruick said. 'Myaie, Ahrl and Roe, I extend my invitation to you too; please come and eat with my family this evening.'

'Thank you, we accept,' Myaie said. 'We're exhausted from travelling and have been through a terrible experience.'

'Yes, of course.' Ruick leant back in his chair and sighed. 'I'm sorry for your loss; if there was anything I could do to fix this devastation then I would do it. My position as a council member makes things difficult for me. I can't leave Lebanoi to travel in good conscience when times are so troubled right now. There is too much to be done still with Myrion and the desalination efforts, and I fear that Syvvak will bring the N.I.L. to my doorstep, but…'

'But?' Ahrl asked.

'I'm curious, I must admit. I feel there's a lot we can learn that might help us,' Ruick said. The door burst open and an Eloran with a blue sash appeared.

'Ruick,' the Eloran said. 'We've got trouble.'

'What's wrong, Addeus?'

'There are thousands of Elorans approaching Lebanoi from the West.'

'Syvvak…' Ruick said, jumping to his feet and hurrying out of the room. Myaie rushed after him and Ahrl and Roe followed. Ahrl felt the eyes of hundreds of Elorans watching them as they were led back towards the gate. They entered a narrow three-storey building on the edges of the Lebanoi district and climbed up to the roof, which was surrounded by a low barrier. From their vantage point they could easily see across the districts bordering Lebanoi. The full scale and the amount of refugees already in the area astounded Ahrl. Another guard with a blue sash handed Ruick a telescope.

'This isn't good,' Ruick said, as he looked through the telescope.

'What? What is it?' Myaie asked. Ruick handed her the telescope and then disappeared back down through the building.

Myaie raised the telescope up to her eye just like Ruick had and looked through it. Myaie shook her head and lowered the telescope and Ahrl took it from her.

'What do you see?' Roe said.

'Lots of refugees,' Ahrl said. Myaie tore her gaze away from the horizon. Ahrl handed the telescope back to its owner and followed Myaie and Roe as they descended a ladder and two flights of stairs to the ground. They found Ruick with a group of Elorans a few feet away, standing at the gate. They made their way over to him just as a ziree carrying a guard pulled up to the opening.

'Ruick,' the guard said. 'It's the N.I.L.. They've attacked more districts. Those who've survived or escaped have fled here.'

'Damn Syvvak,' Ruick said.

'Are we going to be attacked?' Addeus asked.

'No, I don't think so.' Ruick shook his head. 'Syvvak wouldn't be foolish enough to do that now, there are too many here who oppose him. No, he's trying to put more strain on our already strained districts. He'll be hoping that the influx of thousands of Elorans will lead to desperate fighting and chaos in a bid to overturn the council members here and put a stop with our technological advances with Myrion.'

'The new arrivals could go to Loenya,' Addeus said.

'No,' Ruick said. 'The passes through the mountains are too few and treacherous and it's likely Loenya would turn them away. No, I'm sure Syvvak is using this to test our already overpopulated districts; he's hoping that the population will grow tired, frustrated and angry.'

'We'll have to inform everyone here about Syvvak's plans then,' Addeus said.

'We will,' Ruick said. 'But I don't know how much good it will do. Our supplies are already stretched to their limits; refugees are likely to have little patience, and with so many in one area, it would only take something small to cause trouble… I suspect Syvvak has hidden members of the N.I.L. in with the fleeing refugees to do just that.'

'You're quite the imaginative strategist,' Myaie said.

'I wish I wasn't, but I went to school with Syvvak. I know how he thinks,' Ruick said.

'Do you need our help?' Myaie asked.

'The offer is very kind, but I'm aware you've travelled far and will need to rest,' Ruick said. 'Addeus, guide Myaie and her companions to my home.'

'Yes, council member,' Addeus said.

'Are you sure?' asked Myaie.

'Yes. I'll sort out this mess and hopefully we'll be able to talk more later. I need to make contact with the Myrion district to assess their progress. Maybe they can send aid.'

'Ok, thank you, Council Member Ruick of Lebanoi, I wish you well,' Myaie said. Ruick gave her a tight smile and Myaie and her companions reluctantly followed Addeus into the heart of the Lebanoi district.

# TWENTY

Zerren watched as an elderly man called Tenar rose with effort from his spot by the table and embraced Myaie and Ahrl and greeted their young companion, Roe.

'Ahrl, it's good to see you, how's your father?' Tenar asked.

'Good, I think,' Ahrl said.

'And who is this you've brought with you?'

'My cousin, Myaie, council member of Skidaroi, and this is Roe.'

'Ah, it's nice to meet you both. This is Ashta.' Tenar gestured to a tall woman with deep red hair. 'And my wife Yuka, and I believe you've already met Zerren and Ehi.'

'Hello,' Ashta said clasping Myaie's and Ahrl's arms briefly just above the wrist in the traditional Elorish greeting.

'I hope you managed to get some rest before dinner,' Yuka said.

'Yes, your home and hospitality has been much appreciated,' Ahrl said.

'Come sit down with us, I'm afraid there isn't much of a feast but we have prepared some soup,' Tenar said, motioning to the low table. He knelt down on a small cushion at the head of the table with Yuka and Ahrl; Myaie and Roe knelt down across the table from Ashta, Ehi and Zerren. 'Ashta has informed me that you've shared some rather strange dreams about Ehi?'

'Some of us have,' Ahrl said. 'Roe and I have shared dreams, Myaie has not.'

'Interesting, and what about you, Zerren?'

'No,' Zerren said. He felt as though someone was squeezing his heart and lungs. He discretely rubbed his chest.

'What are your thoughts on these dreams?' Ahrl asked.

'Given the current situation and state of Iyeeka, I would say that dreams are hardly important, but…' Tenar said.

'Dreams are just dreams,' Myaie said. 'How can they possibly have any importance?'

'So we have always believed,' Tenar said. 'But with Ehi here before us, I have been forced to rethink.'

'What are you suggesting?' Ahrl asked.

'Ehi, as I've been told, has exceptional control with lif, and I wonder if perhaps there is a link between her abilities and these dreams,' Tenar said.

'Surely that's ridiculous,' Myaie said, shaking her head.

'Oh, I would usually agree with you, Myaie,' Tenar said. 'But what does Ehi think about these dreams?' All eyes turned to Ehi, and Zerren held his breath. Ehi shrugged and then a loud rumbling noise echoed out from her stomach. The others laughed.

'I think someone is hungry,' Tenar said with a chuckle. 'Let's dish up, Yuka. Ruick can join us when he's ready.' They heard the front door swing open and the sound of boots on the floor. Ruick appeared and smiled wearily. 'Ruick, just in time,' Tenar said, letting out a groan as he tried to push himself to his feet once more. The weariness fled from Ruick's face and he dashed over to his father and bent down to hug him before he could stand.

'How was it out there?' Myaie asked.

'Exhausting, but I think we can manage temporarily,' Ruick said, sitting down next to Ashta.

'Are the N.I.L. responsible?' Tenar asked.

'Yes, we're getting the same story from all the refugees,' Ruick said. Tenar lifted the lid off a big red pot in the middle of the table. Steam rose up from the simmering mixture inside and Tenar and

Yuka evenly scooped the soup into bowls and passed them around the table.

'This smells lovely,' Myaie said, as she accepted a bowl.

'Thank you. It's not much but we did manage to collect a few vegetables and enough water to stretch them out. The rest is just in the preparation, spices and cooking time,' Tenar said. Ehi's stomach grumbled again and she picked up her spoon and dove straight into the soup. Tenar smiled and the others quickly followed suit.

'So,' Tenar said, in between mouthfuls, 'Ruick, how many western districts have travelled to Lebanoi?'

'Nine so far,' Ruick said.

'You're expecting more?'

'Yes, unfortunately. Syvvak has been using the same method with all the districts from Skidaroi through to Aelodai. We believe he's using the same type of explosives that were used to dig up the ground and build the great bridge, but he's using them on buildings and Elorans instead.' Zerren worried the inside of his cheek with his teeth as he listened.

'Monstrous,' Tenar said, shaking his head.

'He doesn't behave like an Iyeekan,' Myaie said.

'True,' Tenar said. 'How could he even think to use explosives for such a purpose; it's malicious and evil.'

'Syvvak always had a disturbing imagination,' Ruick said.

'Can we cope with the new arrivals?' Tenar asked.

'Not really,' Ruick said. 'With the current harvest we can probably cope for another few months but after that we'll be struggling. I'm hoping that we'll have an influx of freshwater from Myrion soon.'

'Hmm, you should go to Myrion and evaluate their progress,' Tenar said. 'We've built the tubes here to carry water over many miles, but it is a long way to Myrion and our resources for infrastructure are few and precious.'

'I know,' Ruick said.

'Where have the new arrivals settled?' Tenar asked.

'Most have settled around Lebanoi, but we've allowed particularly gifted lif users and bright minds to settle in Lebanoi with their families to help in our technical schools. Many are using it as a resting point before heading to Kiri and up into Loenya.'

'I thought as much,' Tenar said.

'Which reminds me.' Ruick turned to look at Zerren and Ehi. 'Are you still insistent on traveling to Kiri?'

'Yes, we'll leave tomorrow,' Zerren said.

'Tomorrow?' Ashta asked.

'I think it would be for the best,' Zerren said.

'I should travel with you,' Ruick said.

'Is that wise, Ruick?' Tenar asked.

'Not under the current circumstances, no, but I've been considering it,' Ruick said. 'I wish to know more about the author of the page Zerren found with Ehi. The mathematics is complicated, but if I can find something to help me understand it, then it could be valuable to all of us.'

'Where is this page? May I see it?' Tenar asked.

'Here,' Zerren said, pulling the page from a pocket in his trousers and handing it over to Tenar.

'Ah, this is interesting,' Tenar said. The room fell silent as Tenar studied the page whilst the others ate. 'This is the machine you were talking about earlier?' Tenar glanced up at Zerren.

'Yes.'

'The machine is clearly advanced, as is the mathematics behind it. If the author wrote more, then it could be helpful to us now as we're advancing technology for our own survival.'

'Those were my thoughts too,' Ruick said.

'I agree with you, Ruick, but I don't think you should personally go; you're needed here with your position as council member,' Tenar said.

'Then I'll go,' Ashta said. 'If I find anything, I can bring the information back here to Lebanoi.'

'Ashta, it's dangerous,' Ruick said.

'I know the Lebanoi council as well as you do, and I've seen the plans with Myrion, I'm the perfect candidate to go. Besides, it would be nice to spend some more time with Ehi.'

'I hate to say it, but I agree with Ashta on this one,' Tenar said.

'We'll travel with you too,' Ahrl said. 'Myaie, Roe and I have talked about it. We're homeless for now and Myaie's and my parents are in Loenya. It makes sense for us to go through the Kiri pass and potentially onto Loenya.'

'They might not let you into Loenya,' Ruick said.

'Yes, but Myaie and I have a better chance than most, with family there.'

'There will likely be hundreds travelling along the pass to Kiri by tomorrow,' Tenar said.

Zerren felt a faint tingling across the back of his head; he was about to open his mouth to object but Lucoe's voice rang out from the back of his mind. *Let them come,* Lucoe said, and then a wave of voices crashed about his mind. Zerren closed his eyes and pushed the voices back beyond the edges of his awareness.

'The Moribi of Kiri's records are large and numerous; it's likely that they don't even know of everything their halls hold,' Tenar said.

'Ashta, are you really sure about this?' Ruick asked.

'Yes.'

'Then it has been decided,' Tenar said. 'Ruick will stay here, Ashta, Myaie, Ahrl and Roe will travel with Zerren and Ehi to Kiri. We will look after your ziree for you, Zerren, they won't cope with the high altitudes.'

'I'm worried about this, Ashta,' Ruick said. 'But I won't stop you from going, if that's what you really feel you should do.'

'It's ok, it won't be for long, and Ahrl, Myaie and Roe will be with me,' Ashta said.

'And what about when you come back?' Ruick said.

'I'm sure I will find someone to travel back with,' Ashta said.

'Ok.' Ruick sighed. 'Ok.'

The room fell into an uneasy silence and Zerren concentrated on pushing the last of the voices out of his head. *It's hopeless, utterly hopeless,* a female voice said. *Follow them, Zerren, follow Ehi,* Lucoe's voice said.

'Are you ok, Zerren? You've barely touched your food,' Tenar said. Zerren glanced down at the bowl before him and then pushed it across to Ehi who gladly accepted.

'Just a headache,' Zerren said.

'You should rest then, take as long as you need,' Tenar said. Ehi lifted Zerren's bowl to her lips and swallowed the food in several long gulps.

'Thank you for inviting us and for the meal, we should go now and rest, we have another long journey ahead of us tomorrow,' Zerren said as he rose from the table and helped Ehi to her feet.

'We will meet you here in the morning,' Ahrl said. Zerren paused at the door. *Let them come,* Lucoe's voice said faintly at the back of his mind, removing the last traces of any fight Zerren had left.

'Ok,' he said. He felt Ehi loop her arm through his, his chest tightened again and he felt a fluttering sensation in his stomach. *What is this?* He gazed at Ehi and caught her gaze for a second before she tugged him out the door and under the deepening purple skies.

# TWENTY-ONE

The steep sides of the Kiri Mountains stretched up around them as their narrow path stretched and disappeared before and behind them. It had been several days now and many of the refugees who had followed them around the dry banks of the Lebanoi Lakes and into the narrow pass had dropped back behind them over the long climb. Ahrl kept pace with Myaie, Ashta and Roe, and watched Zerren and Ehi who walked several paces ahead. There had been hundreds travelling along the same route, stretching in a wavy line, but now the line was thin and broken. At night they camped in tents, and every night Ahrl's, Ashta's and Roe's sleep had been tormented by dreams of Ehi.

At first light they awoke, but Zerren kept his distance from the others and Ehi never left Zerren's side. From the moment they had left Ruick's home, Ehi had worn a cloak with a hood covering her head and shadowing her face.

'I wonder what caused Ehi to have such unique characteristics,' Myaie said as she stared at the back of her head.

'Yes, I wonder that too,' Ashta said.

'I've heard of a few rare Iyeekans with white hair and pink eyes, but they're unusually sensitive to sunlight and they definitely don't have purple hair or eyes,' Roe said.

'I've come across a couple like that on my travels,' Ahrl said.

'Really?' Roe said.

Ahrl nodded.

'You've travelled a lot, or so Myaie tells me,' Ashta said. 'Why is that?'

'When the district of Jhovire was abandoned, the Elorans from Jhovire spread themselves out across other populated districts. My position as council member became redundant, so I decided to travel and observe.'

'But you were a teacher too?' Ashta said. 'A hard to come by profession and an admirable profession too; your father must have been proud.'

'I was, but no, my father was never proud of it. He would have preferred it if I had taken more interest in his line of work.'

'Ahrl's father was one of the last Elorans to mine the moons for resources. Ahrl and I come from a line of engineers and mechanics; our many great grandfather was the first Eloran to successfully launch an occupied vessel into space and make it back to Iyeeka in one piece,' Myaie said.

'Ah, no wonder Loenya opened their doors to your family then,' Ashta said.

'Yes, but I refused to go immediately, so he and my mother left without me,' Ahrl said.

'Why did you refuse?'

'Loenya only granted my family residence but not the rest of our district; there were many Elorans in our district who had helped my father. I felt that is was unjust and unfair.'

'And what about you, Myaie?'

'I didn't want to leave Skidaroi; there was someone close to me there at the time, but my father and mother were anxious to go,' Myaie said. They walked in silence for a while with heavy breaths as they climbed higher into the mountains.

'Do you think we'll find anything in Kiri?' Ashta asked.

'Who knows,' Ahrl said. 'It's the only place we can look for answers though. I'm going to try and talk with Zerren. Shout if you need me.'

'Good luck,' Myaie said. Ahrl hurried to catch up with Zerren and Ehi.

'Good morning,' he said as he fell into an easy pace beside them.

'Morning,' Zerren said. Ehi tilted her hood back briefly and flashed Ahrl a smile.

'I've been meaning to ask you more about when you found Ehi,' Ahrl said. Zerren didn't respond or even glance in Ahrl's direction. 'How long do you think she had been in Cenic for?'

'Your guess is as good as mine,' Zerren said. Ehi skipped ahead to where a family walked with two young Elorans; she summoned the lif from her gauntlet and Zerren felt the ripple of energy across the top of his head and shoulders, along with the burning sensation at the back of his nose. She began to change the lif into different shapes of various animals and the young Elorans laughed. Zerren clasped a hand to his forehead. 'I wish she wouldn't do that; she doesn't seem to understand that lif only has a temporary lifespan and I don't want others to see her using it.'

'You worry about her, don't you?'

'It's hard not to,' Zerren said. 'We live in uncertain times, when standing out isn't necessarily a good thing.'

'Your feelings are more than just concern though,' Ahrl said.

He opened his mouth to protest but a loud splitting, cracking sound ripped through the air before he could speak. There was a brief silence where no one dared to move or even breathe. Ahrl glanced up and down the slope and saw heads turning from left to right, gazing up at the lofty peaks. The ground began to tremble beneath their feet and there was a loud *thunk* followed by several grating cracking sounds as though someone was grinding rocks between their back teeth. Ahrl caught movement out of the corner of his eye as a few small rocks rolled down and hit the side of his shoe. He looked up at the steep slope and felt a cold numbness seep down to his feet. High above them a large chunk of the mountain looked as though it was peeling away.

'Run,' Ahrl said. He glanced at the faces of the others around them, all of them captivated by the moving wall of rock. 'Run!' he yelled. The gravity of the situation seemed to wake them up from their trance and then the screams and yells rang out down the side of the mountain. Elorans fled in both directions, many picking up children as they raced up and down the pass. Zerren ran towards Ehi and Ahrl waited for Myaie, Ashta and Roe to catch up before urging them to follow Zerren. Rocks began to fall across their path, small at first but steadily growing larger as they raced up the mountain pass. Someone ahead of Ahrl stumbled and he pulled them to their feet, and pushed them onwards as the ground shook and the mountains roared as though they were rocky giants waking from a deep slumber. He could see Zerren and Ehi just slightly ahead with Ehi holding the hands of the little girl and her brother, pulling them both along. A man scooped up the boy when they seemed to slow down and Ehi hauled the girl over the shaking ground. The path rose up steeply a couple of hundred feet ahead of them.

'Get to the top of that rise,' Ahrl said, pointing to the crest of the hill in front of them. Larger boulders bounced across the path and there were more screams as the travellers were forced to dodge them or be flattened.

'We're not going to make it,' Myaie said, panting beside Ahrl as they scrabbled over the loose rocks and soil rolling across their path. Roe shrieked as she slipped and Ahrl felt her hand wrench free from his grasp. A man who was running beside them quickly scooped her up from the floor and charged on. He wore a wide hat which shadowed his face and a thin scarf around the lower half of his face and neck.

'Keep going,' he said.

'Ehi!' Zerren yelled. Ahrl glanced up and saw Ehi had stopped up ahead to help the little girl to her feet. The ground roiled and shook as the mountains thundered around them. 'Ehi!' Zerren yelled again and Ahrl saw him leap over a bolder as he ran back down the pass. The ground shook again, and another violent crack rang through the air above their heads. He felt a warm rush of energy and a sparking sensation around his mind. If he had not been running for his life he would have stopped in awe at the sheer power he could feel. His lif gauntlet burned briefly around his right wrist and then everything went dark and the sky disappeared. He could hear cracks and thumps echoing around them, but nothing seemed to move in the immediate vicinity around them. Ahrl's eyes adjusted as a dull blue glow lit up the darkness and he saw a dome of lif had been placed above them; it stretched around them, meeting the uneven ground with a perfect seal.

'What the?' Ahrl said. Ehi stood before them with her arms above her head and her eyes fixated on the lif around them. Her hood had fallen back exposing her pale purple hair which shone like a pale moon in the darkness. The thumps and crashes echoed around them, ringing faintly as rocks and debris hit the outside of the lif dome. Ahrl cast his gaze over the lif and looked at his lif gauntlet, it was empty. He noticed several other Iyeekans raising their arms and inspecting their own gauntlets with perplexed looks. *She can control that much lif?* The man who had scooped up Roe set her on the ground and stared at Ehi in wonder. They waited for what seemed like forever until the thuds outside stopped and the mountains fell silent once more.

'Ehi,' Zerren said as he came to a halt beside her. She trembled beside him as beads of sweat sprouted from her brow, but she didn't take her eyes off the lif.

'Zerren… push…' Ehi said; her words were forced and slow as though her tongue wouldn't cooperate with her brain or vocal chords.

'Quick, she won't last much longer,' Ahrl said scrambling over to them. Ahrl cast his mind out to the hardened lif around them and felt the familiar rush of energy as a dozen other minds did the same. They latched onto the lif, their minds twisting around one another in a mesh-like pattern and then they focussed on pushing the lif upwards and out. 'Slowly,' Ahrl said. They heard the rumbling, crunching and cracking sounds of rocks and debris shifting above them as the lif dome expanded. Ahrl gritted his teeth; he heard a couple of Elorans groan and then Ehi let out a cry and the dome shot outwards in all directions, shifting the rocks above them and dispersing the lif into many tiny, fragments hovering in the air. Daylight flooded in around them and some of the lif fragments turned into liquid and coalesced into dozens of separate parts before returning to the gauntlets of their original owners; other fragments simply turned black and disintegrated, showering down on them as a fine ash. Dust rose up in great clouds from the mountains around them as the Elorans scrambled out of the mini crater Ehi had created. Her eyes rolled into the back of her head and Zerren caught her just before she hit the ground.

***

'Can you take my bag?' Zerren said.

'Of course,' Ahrl said. Zerren pulled Ehi's hood back over her hair and carried her to the top of the rise. Ahrl helped Roe, Ashta and Myaie up and over the debris and followed Zerren and the other Elorans. The rockslide had filled the dip in the pass where they had just been standing moments before and stretched down the pass as far as the eye could see.

'Do you think anyone got trapped further down?' Ashta asked.

'I hope not,' Ahrl said. They turned and looked at Zerren who cradled an unconscious Ehi to his chest.

'What have you done with my lif?' an angry voice yelled. Zerren turned to see another man with short, clipped, dark hair approaching them, holding an empty lif gauntlet and shaking it like a fish in his hand. 'I didn't give you permission to use my lif,' the man said. 'Now look, it's spent and there's none left.'

'I would drop that tone,' Myaie said.

'Who's going to replace my stolen lif?'

'No one,' Ahrl said. 'You're alive, you should be grateful for that. Look at the pass behind you.' Ahrl pointed back down the way they had just travelled. The man stopped shaking his lif gauntlet and looked back over the pass. The redness in his face bleached to white and he shook his head, muttered a couple of curses under his breath and shuffled away.

'We should get going,' Zerren said. 'We're already attracting way too much attention.'

'Will you be able to carry her?' Ahrl asked.

'Yes, but not with our bags too.'

'We'll take them,' Ahrl said.

'Do you think there will be aftershocks?' Myaie asked.

'I'm almost certain of it,' Ahrl said. They redistributed their bags and Zerren shifted Ehi's weight and carried her across his shoulders. He trudged on ahead at a quick pace.

'How can he move so quickly and carry another?' Myaie said, shaking her head.

'Stubborn willpower,' Ahrl said, though he did wonder how long Zerren would last. As their group set off, Ahrl noticed that Roe dropped way back to where her saviour in the hat walked. Ahrl slowed his pace and let dozens of Elorans pass him as he waited for Roe and her saviour to catch up. The man kept his gaze to the ground, hiding his face beneath his hat and scarf as he walked slowly beside them.

'Thank you,' Ahrl said, 'for helping Roe earlier.'

'It was nothing.'

'It wasn't nothing,' Ahrl said. 'You saved her.' The man nodded. 'My name's Ahrl, by the way.' The man nodded again and Ahrl frowned. He seemed to be just like the rest of the refugees trying to find a safe place with food and water; he carried a rucksack on his back and his clothes were loose and travel-stained. He even wore a lif gauntlet, partially obscured by the sleeve of his top. There was nothing unusual about a solo male traveller, but Ahrl couldn't help but feel a little uneasy.

'Come along, Roe, let this man travel in peace,' Ahrl said. Roe frowned but she didn't object. 'Thank you again,' Ahrl said. He led Roe back to the others but he made sure to keep a watchful eye on the solo traveller.

# TWENTY-TWO

She saw a man standing before a huge building made of white stone, speaking of dreams to a crowd of people that stretched back to where a single, white stone pillar pointed up to the sky. She saw a woman wearing a white apron and a hat as she moved amongst injured men on raised beds. She saw another man serving soup to a ragged, rough group of people. A mother who whispered encouragement into her children's ears. A medic who cared for the elderly. A traveller who helped aid reach impoverished areas. A friend who reached out to another, and a stranger who stood between a victim and their tormentor.

They were young, old, male, female, dark-skinned, fair and every shade in between. They had blue eyes, brown eyes, green eyes, dark hair, light hair, curly hair and straight; it didn't matter what they looked like, they were all the same. All of them had spheres glowing like their own internal etansy and whatever they did and wherever they went they seemed to draw people of all creeds and backgrounds towards them. There was an understanding, an acceptance and happiness. It was as though these few extraordinary individuals drew out all the good that humanity had to offer.

There were many more faces, some who stood out with obvious roles and others who worked behind the scenes. There was an artist with one ear. A scientist with crazy hair. A pilot in a fighter plane. A wife, a husband, sister, brother, father, daughter, mother, son and so on. All this Ehi saw and understood deeply and intimately, feeling every emotion and following every thought as though each individual life had been her own. Yet despite the golden spheres these people contained, Ehi saw black clouds twisting through the air and golden bands of light desperately punching through like the etansy breaking through a storm. They grew, surrounding the earth and feeding off all the decisions made by mankind. They were polar opposites, she realised, annihilating each other and tangled with human lives, no, all life. *But why? Why am I here?*

Ehi opened her eyes and blinked the fogginess away as dim shapes came into view. She found herself in a small room with a floor to ceiling open window to her right and dark orange drapes rustling in the cool breeze. Her gaze drifted to the corner of the room and she found Zerren in a chair, fast asleep with his arms crossed. She looked around; the room was made from blocks of grey stone, many with exposed mineral veins, and the ceiling had been carved into geometric patterns. She felt something pinching the back of her right hand, so she sat up and found a sharp instrument protruding from the back of her hand secured with some white tape. Zerren stirred.

'Ehi?' Zerren said. He stretched and rubbed his eyes and then he stood up and walked over to her. 'How are you feeling?' Ehi didn't reply but she cast her gaze around the room and then looked at Zerren again. 'Oh, we're at Kiri,' Zerren said. 'You passed out and I had to carry you here. The next time you decide to fall unconscious I'd prefer some warning.' A faint smile appeared on his lips. Ehi touched the instrument sticking out of the back of her hand and felt a dull pain shoot up her wrist. 'Don't touch that,' Zerren said gently, pulling her hand away. 'It's a needle; they had to pump you with nutrients and fluids. We were lucky, some of the Moribi were out on patrol and they found us. You've been asleep for seven days.'

There was a knock, and the door swung open. An elderly man with short grey hair, wearing dark orange robes, strode into the room followed by two others.

'Moribi Ioel,' Zerren said, inclining his head towards the elderly Eloran.

'Please, just Ioel. I see that Ehi is awake. How is she?'

'Ok, I think.'

'That's a relief,' Ioel said. 'When you first arrived on our doorstep I feared the worst.' Ioel turned to Ehi and smiled. 'It's nice to finally meet you properly, Ehi, rather than seeing you unconscious or in my dreams.' Ehi looked up into Ioel's kindly face and she let her mind slip free from the confines of her body and explore the sensations around her. The smile on Ioel's face faltered for a moment and the two Elorans beside him gasped. 'Amazing,' Ioel said. 'Can you feel her mind?' Ioel looked at Zerren.

'Yes,' Zerren said. Ehi pushed the invisible projections of her mind towards Ioel and she sensed a wall that would not easily be broken, but warmth and kindness seeped through this wall, she felt no ill intent. Ehi tilted her head as she scrutinised Ioel, his mind and presence felt familiar to her.

'You did a very brave thing, Ehi, I believe you saved many Elorans in the pass,' Ioel said.

'Have you found anyone who…' Zerren hesitated, 'who didn't make it?'

'No, not yet,' Ioel said. 'Rockslides happen quite frequently throughout the Kiri Mountains unfortunately. So we always have a team on standby ready to help those who may have become trapped and to clear the pass so that we and others can get through. It's a difficult task, but a necessary one. Our team should have the pass cleared enough for travellers by the end of next week.'

'Hirokai,' Ioel said. One of the male Eloran's behind him stepped forwards. 'Please check over Ehi and remove the needle from her hand, and Yue,' the other Eloran stepped forward. 'Please can you get some food and water for Ehi and Zerren.' Yue inclined his head and left.

'Please hold still, this will only take a moment,' Hirokai said.

He raised his hands so they hovered either side of Ehi's head and closed his eyes. She expected to feel something and at least be aware of Hirokai's mind, but she felt nothing at all. 'She's fine.' He opened his eyes. He moved to a little cabinet by the bed and pulled out a white strip of eyeleetansy silk and a small cushioned pad. 'This might sting a little bit.' Hirokai held Ehi's right hand. Ehi hissed as he removed the needle and Hirokai placed the pad firmly over the wound.

'I've been talking to the others about their dreams,' Ioel said, as Hirokai tied the silk strip tightly around Ehi's hand. 'It is a curious thing. I've heard of Iyeekans having strange dreams that did in fact become reality but whether or not that was a mere coincidence no one could ever truly know. However, I've never heard of several Iyeekans sharing exactly the same dream before.'

'Not all of us have dreamt about Ehi,' Zerren said.

'No, but most of you have, myself included.'

'If I'm honest, I'm not sure what to make of them. If your dreams didn't feature Ehi then I probably would have said it was just a strange coincidence,' Zerren said.

'Yes, many would,' Ioel said.

'Why do you think you've all dreamt about Ehi, when Myaie and I haven't?'

'Myaie has now,' Ioel said.

'What? When?'

'Last night, I'm told,' Ioel said.

'Then I'm the only one?' Zerren said as he raked his fingers through his hair.

'I'm not sure why you haven't. I've spoken to all the others and we've all had the same overwhelming feeling that we should be close to Ehi. If we are planets, then she would be our etansy. Maybe the only way we will find out if our dreams have any meaning is if we remain close to Ehi.'

'Ahrl told me that your dreams are set somewhere dry and

barren and that there's an extreme wind kicking up dust clouds around you,' Zerren said.

'Yes, that is true.'

'But that could be anywhere in Eloran or Jheia.'

'Potentially, yes,' Ioel said. 'I've asked some of our younger Moribi to search through records for anything that mentions a woman with Ehi's characteristics or strange dreams. It may take some time though; we have hundreds of thousands of records in many different forms. I have also studied the page you brought with you. I'm not sure where it came from within our records, but I have charged others with the task of finding its origins.'

'Thank you. I'll help with the search as soon as I can.'

'No rush,' Ioel said. 'Ashta and the others are already helping scour our records as we speak.'

There was a knock at the door and Yue entered holding a small, wooden tray of food.

'Ah, good,' Ioel said. 'Ehi, you should eat as much as you can and rest; when you're both ready come to the records hall, hopefully we'll be able to find some answers for you.' Yue set down the tray on the small cabinet beside Ehi's bed and followed Ioel and Hirokai to the door. 'Oh, and one more thing, Zerren,' said Ioel. 'At some time I'd like you to meet me and describe exactly what you found in Cenic. It seems important and should be added to our records.'

# TWENTY-THREE

Ehi washed, dressed and then left the small room she had slept in for several days. She stopped when she found Ioel in the hallway outside.

'I thought you might wish to take a walk today,' he said. 'Zerren is currently looking through our record books.' Ehi touched her exposed hair and glanced back at the door to her room. 'You don't have to cover your hair if you don't want to; I believe many have already seen your hair in the pass and rumours spread quickly.' Ehi bit her lip. 'Do you want to go and find Zerren?'

Ehi nodded.

'Follow me,' Ioel said. Ehi walked behind him and admired the carved star patterns on the ceiling and the mosaic tiles on the floor that were shaped into large white flowers. She ran her fingertips along the smooth stone walls and felt the polished surfaces of glittering mineral veins. Ioel paused and Ehi almost ran into him. 'The Moribi usually cherish function over beauty, but we place great importance and appreciation on artistic skill and ability,' Ioel said as he glanced over his shoulder. 'The Moribi believe any creative skill is important for the wellbeing of the mind as it is the only thing we can logically take with us when we die.'

Ehi continued to follow Ioel down to the end of the corridor, passing many doors on either side. They turned right onto another corridor and passed several Moribi, some of whom wore robes like Ioel. They finally stopped before a pair of dark wooden arched doors and Ioel pushed one open. Ehi felt her mouth drop; the room before her was a huge two-storey space lined with windows and filled with bookshelves running in rows down the centre of the room. The walls were covered in artwork - paintings, sculptures, embroidery and more. Carved wooden stairs at the sides of the room curved up to suspended balconies where more artwork, bookshelves and cabinets with clear protective cases lined the walls. But what held Ehi's attention was a curved dome in the centre of the ceiling made from different coloured glass. It had a single large circle at the centre and six smaller circles and six oval shapes alternating around it. The circles consisted of both clear and pastel-coloured glass and the ovals were made from different hues of dark blue. The light bounced around the dome and cast a mesmerising light about the centre of the room.

'Amazing, isn't it?' Ioel said. 'This room never used to have the glass dome, but about two thousand years ago Kiri had a particularly gifted glassworker who proposed the idea and the Moribi back then agreed, but I don't think anyone imagined it would be this spectacular.' Ehi let her gaze wander around the room; it was busy, some were reading at desks, others admiring the art and dozens browsing the shelves. 'It's always busy in here now; a thousand or so years ago and you would have been lucky to catch a glimpse of someone between the shelves. I can't say I dislike it, I just wish our growing visitors were due to better circumstances. This is our main and biggest records hall, but we have six smaller rooms which connect to this room.'

Ehi ignored the stares and walked over to a big stone slab which had been fixed to the right-hand wall. There was a carving on the stone, depicting an Iyeekan at the centre with their arms spread out. A small circle had been carved at the centre of their torso and radial lines had been carved spreading outwards in all directions.

'I'm not surprised this carving has captured your attention,' Ioel said, stopping beside her. 'This is an artistic representation of the idea of the usol, or more specifically, the circle at the Iyeekan's centre is the usol. It represents the essence of who you really are and not just your physical body or characteristics. Your eyes and mind are too easily deceived whilst you are alive; the usol is how you truly feel and think. Of course, not everyone is nice, even at the usol level. It is really chance; where you are born, what you look like and what your eyes and mind will have you believe. Some are born unlucky because of circumstances and it can wear them down after a while. They start to believe and do things that are completely horrifying to others, but these Iyeekans still believe they are doing the right thing, no matter who gets hurt, angry, silenced or pushed away in the process. It affects their usol so badly that even their true thoughts and feelings start to echo the misguided beliefs and thoughts they have picked up through life. Some say that if that happens then you have no hope of existence beyond death, but no one really knows if there is anything beyond death.'

'Ehi,' Zerren said. Ehi and Ioel both looked up at the sound of Zerren's voice.

'Ah, there he is,' Ioel said.

'Ehi? Why haven't you covered your hair?'

'I told her it wasn't necessary,' Ioel said.

'Not necessary?'

'Too many have already seen her hair when you brought her here,' Ioel said. 'If the N.I.L. are going to find out about her then it's probably already too late. Refugees arrive and leave Kiri all the time and rumours spread. Besides, from what you've told me, Syvvak is no match for Ehi.'

'I wouldn't wish to test that,' Zerren said. 'What happens if the N.I.L. come to Kiri?'

'They would be foolish to try,' Ioel said. 'The Moribi are some of Iyeeka's most gifted lif users; we will not take kindly to an attack and we will immobilise and capture every N.I.L. member that dares to cause any harm.'

'Then what?'

'Detain them. We have rooms here at Kiri with windows which look out over sheer drops. I can assign Moribi as guards if necessary.'

'You don't understand,' Zerren said. 'The N.I.L. members won't hesitate to kill you if they get the opportunity. They've used explosives.'

'Then I won't give them the opportunity.'

'They could be out there right now.' Zerren pointed towards a set of double doors at the far end of the hall.

'No one here wishes to cause us harm, Zerren; believe me I would sense it, and I would appreciate it if you would lower your voice,' Ioel said. Zerren paused and his gaze circled the hall; every Eloran had fallen silent and was staring at them.

'Fine.' Zerren sighed and his shoulders slumped. 'Have you found anything out about Ehi yet?'

'No, not yet,' Ioel said as the murmurings of conversations picked up around them again. 'As you already know, we have thousands of books, pages and other pieces here collected over tens of thousands of years; our record books are large and numerous. I've put as many Moribi as I can spare to the task, but Ehi is unique and finding information about her or others like her is like trying to find a single eyeleetansy cocoon in Eloran's largest laluta fields.'

'I feared as much,' Zerren said.

'Patience. It will take some time but I'm hoping I can at least help Ehi to talk whilst you are here.'

'You think she can?'

'Well, I know she can say words from what you've told me, so I don't think she has a physical problem. I believe whatever is stopping her may be more mind or memory related, which, if that's the case, then teaching her our language again may help.'

'I see.'

'I think having a Moribi monitor Ehi's mind during the process may also be helpful. No medics have picked up on any physical issues with Ehi, but then most medics are trained in the physical body alone. Everyone can recognise the lif connection to the mind, but few study the mind itself like the Moribi do,' Ioel said. 'If Ehi's memories are suppressed or her thoughts behave in illogical patterns, then that may be the reason why she doesn't talk very much.'

'And you have someone in mind?'

'Of course,' Ioel said. 'My trusted friend and Moribi, Naehanuoi. I'll go and fetch her now, if you like?'

'Please do, if that's alright with you.'

'I thought you might agree. Please feel free to have a look around; the last time I checked your friends were browsing Kiri's records too.' Ioel left and Ehi studied the stone usol carving again. The edges had been carved into a border containing many different plants and animals; one in particular held her interest. It was a small creature with large wings and it had been carved above a plant. Ehi ran her finger tips over the carving.

'Eyeleetansy,' Zerren said. 'Though they're much bigger in reality, about the size of my palms.' He held up his hands side by side. 'They're the lifeblood of Iyeeka; the silk from their cocoons are used to make clothes and they pollinate the laluta plants which provide food. There's a painting of one over there.' Zerren pointed to a framed painting a little further down. Ehi headed straight for it. She studied the eyeleetansy. It was a large insect-type creature with a small, furry, slender black body and big, iridescent blue wings. The wings looked extremely delicate, like thin cloth, and each wing seemed to be made up of three pieces.

Ehi's mind hummed and she lightly brushed her fingertips over the painting. A warm tingling sensation ran over her skull and a childlike laugh echoed between her ears. Her vision rippled and blurred around the edges; she blinked to try and clear it but the room around her disappeared. She found herself outside, amongst leafy plants which came up to her waist. Each plant held dozens of different coloured cocoons, a couple of inches long and a half an inch wide. She looked at her arms and hands, but they were smaller. She looked down at her small feet, clad in sandals, and her short, exposed calves. A childish laugh rippled out through her lips and she stretched out her arms and spun on one foot. Her purple tunic billowed out around her, lifting away from her white trousers, and a loud rustling sound charged into the air. Hundreds of eyeleetansy in multiple colours fluttered in the air around her, their wings glimmering like gems in the etansy-light.

'Ehi?' a familiar female voice called. 'Ehi?' Ehi turned to the sound of the voice and saw her mother standing at the edges of the laluta field, waving at her.

'Ehi?' Zerren said. Ehi blinked, the memory of her mother and the laluta field faded and the Kiri records hall came back to her. She removed her hand from the painting.

'Ah, there she is,' Ioel said. Ehi looked up and saw the Moribi approaching with a woman dressed in the same dark orange robes. 'Ehi, Zerren, this is Moribi Naehanuoi.'

'A pleasure to meet the both of you,' Naehanuoi said. Her long dark hair slipped over her shoulders as she inclined her head.

'Thanks for coming so quickly; I'm sure you're very busy.'

'Everyone is busy, but it's not a problem,' Naehanuoi said. 'I've been wishing to meet Ehi since the moment you arrived. I just hope I can help.'

'Naehanuoi spent some time as a teacher before becoming a Moribi,' Ioel said.

'Come, Ehi,' Naehanuoi said as she extended her arm and offered her hand. 'Let's find somewhere quieter where we won't be disturbed.' Ehi glanced at Zerren; he nodded and Ehi took Naehanuoi's hand and let the Moribi lead her out and away from the hall.

'You trust Zerren a lot, don't you?' Naehanuoi said.

Ehi nodded.

'Like a brother?'

Ehi felt her brow crease and shook her head.

'Ah, I see, something more than a brother?'

Ehi tilted her head as she thought about it and Naehanuoi laughed. She opened a door and ushered Ehi inside a small room. There was a little open balcony, bookshelves, a table and a couple of chairs. 'Ok, take a seat, Ehi. First, I'll teach you the common Iyeekan sounds to try, then we'll see what you can recall from your own memories.'

Ehi bit her lip.

'Don't worry, we'll just start with words for now. Later, I'll ask you to close your eyes and think back to your earliest memory. You'll feel the presence of my mind, but it won't hurt, ok?'

Ehi nodded.

Naehanuoi pulled a clean piece of paper from one of the shelves and took out a pen, then sat down beside Ehi and began to write in big sweeping letters. 'This isn't how we write our language in reality, but this should help you with the sounds,' she said. Ehi watched Naehanuoi write and felt a stirring of familiarity somewhere at the back of her mind.

# TWENTY-FOUR

Ahrl sat at a table in one of the six smaller, but still large, rooms branching off from the main records hall. Ashta was scrutinising the spines of the books and documents on one of the many bookshelves.

'I doubt we're going to find anything here,' she muttered.

'Don't give up yet,' Ahrl said, as he shut the heavy book in front of him.

'I won't, but I can see why many others before us have.' Ashta sighed. Ahrl rubbed his eyes and blinked a few times as he stretched in his chair. He let his gaze wander around the room where it inevitably lingered on a dark wooden door at the back of the room.

'What do you think is behind that door?' he said. Ashta glanced at him and then peered around the bookshelf before her to get a better look at the door.

'It's locked, I already tried. I think it's some sort of storage room.' She shrugged. Ahrl stood and walked over to the door.

'If I was trying to hide something, I would put it in a room that Iyeekans seldom visit.'

'The Moribi would know about this room, and why would such a book be hidden?' Ashta said.

'I know, but how useful is this room to them now with Iyeeka in its current state? What I mean is, when was the last time anyone would have looked in here?' Ahrl tried the handle; the door didn't budge.

"

'One of the Moribi would have a key; we should ask Ioel,' Ashta said. Ahrl focussed his mind on the lif gauntlet around his wrist and, with the barest of thought, the lif sprang free from its container and straight into the lock. He could feel the lock mechanism with his mind as though his body and brain were now housed within the tiny space made for a key. He sensed the shape and right pressure points and gave a mental shove; the lock clicked open.

'Or you could just do that,' Ashta said. Ahrl pulled the lif back to his gauntlet and pushed open the door. It was dark inside, with a small, narrow window letting in a tiny amount of daylight. Ahrl fumbled for a light switch and found one; a glass cube lit up in the centre of the ceiling and cast a golden glow around the room. There were boxes and bookshelves piled high with papers and books which looked like they hadn't been touched in years.

Ashta groaned. 'Great. Now there's even more stuff to look at.'

'Yes, but I'm willing to bet that what we're looking for is probably in this room,' Ahrl said. He stepped inside and let his gaze wander over the objects, before turning back to the door and scrutinising the items closest to it.

'What are you doing?' Ashta asked.

'If I start on this side of the door and work my way around the walls and you do the same on the other side, then we should meet in the middle and we won't cover the same area twice.'

'I see,' Ashta said. 'Ok.' She turned to the other side of the door and plucked a book from the nearest bookshelf on the wall.

They worked quietly; only the ruffling sound of paper and the odd muffled cough escaped them. Minutes turned into hours as they moved around the walls and Ahrl was beginning to wonder if Ashta might be right. They had been searching nonstop for weeks and they had found nothing, not even the Moribi had managed to find anything of any use. The only good thing that had happened was that Ehi's lessons with Naehanuoi had enabled her to speak, albeit simply and sparingly.

'Ahrl, I think I've found something,' Ashta said. Ahrl shelved the book he held in his hands and hurried over to her.

'What is it?'

'Look,' Ashta said, thrusting a battered book into his hands. He opened it and found that most of the pages were loose and falling out, but every page had been stamped with the Moribi of Kiri's symbol. In an instant, Ahrl recognised the handwriting and the ink and he realised that the page that Zerren had found with Ehi belonged in this book.

'This is it,' Ahrl said. 'I can't believe it. This is...' A scream shattered the air and rolled throughout the hallways to the little back room where they stood. Ahrl held his breath.

'That was Ehi,' Ashta said as she gripped Ahrl's arm. Another scream sounded and Ahrl shut the book, clamped it under one arm and ran towards the sound. They ran through the records hall where bewildered Elorans stood or sat frozen in place. Ahrl hurried past them and entered a narrow hallway and saw Zerren up ahead, running towards Naehanuoi's room.

'No, no, no, no, no,' Ehi yelled as Ahrl and Ashta burst through the door, seconds behind Zerren. Naehanuoi stood helplessly in the middle of the small room and Ehi cowered in the corner, her hands clutching the sides of her head. Her eyelids were scrunched shut as tears leaked out from the corner of her eyes.

'Ehi? What's wrong?' Zerren said as he knelt in front of her.

'What happened?' Ahrl asked.

'I don't know,' Naehanuoi said. 'I was just trying to get Ehi to remember her most recent years. It was going well, but then she just started screaming.

'No, no, no, no,' Ehi said, more to herself than anybody else. She shook her head from side to side as her body trembled.

'Ehi,' Zerren said gently.

'Zerren, I... I'm sorry,' Ehi said. Tears spilled down her cheeks.

'Sorry?' Zerren frowned.

'Is she hurt?' Ahrl asked. Ehi looked up and caught Ahrl's gaze. A pressure rose above his head as though he were sitting at the bottom of a lake with the weight of the water pressing down on his shoulders. The air felt heavy and difficult to breathe and his head throbbed, and for a moment he felt as though he was drowning in those purple pools of despair. She lowered her gaze, releasing Ahrl from his overwhelming feelings.

'I'm ok,' Ehi said. 'I'm ok.'

'Are you sure?' Zerren asked.

Ehi nodded.

'What were the screams for then?' Zerren said.

'Just… remembering,' Ehi said. 'It's… hard.' Relief washed over Naehanuoi's face but Ahrl gazed at Ehi; the strange feelings were vivid in his mind and his heart had only just about recovered. Zerren helped Ehi to her feet.

'Zerren, we think we've found something,' Ashta said.

'You have?'

'Yes, we believe we found the book the page was taken from.'

'What? Really?'

'Ahrl,' Ashta said, nudging him with her elbow. Ahrl blinked.

'Yes,' he said, taking the book out from under his arm and offering it to Zerren.

'Where did you find it?' Zerren asked, taking the book.

'In a little backroom behind one of the smaller record rooms,' Ashta said. 'We had just found it when we heard the… screams.' Zerren nodded and studied the book, turning the pages carefully.

'I think you're right, this looks like work by the same author. It even has a name written at the front,' he said. 'Arkeenell of the district Bosna, Jheia. We'll have to take this to Moribi Ioel to be one hundred percent certain, he has the page now.' He glanced between Ehi and Ahrl. 'Ahrl, Ashta, could you, would you take this to Ioel?' Zerren said. 'I don't want to leave Ehi alone right now.'

'Of course,' Ashta said, taking the book back. 'Ahrl and I will go and verify its authenticity with Ioel.'

'Thank you,' Zerren said.

Ahrl glanced at Ehi one last time and then followed Ashta out of Naehanuoi's room.

***

A knock at Ioel's door drew their attention away from the page Zerren had found and the book lying open on Ioel's desk.

'Come in,' Ioel said. The door opened and this time Zerren and Ehi appeared. 'I was just coming to find you,' Ioel said.

'Are you alright, Ehi?' Ashta said.

'Yes, thank you,' Ehi said.

'Ehi wanted to see the book you found,' Zerren said, as they drew closer to the desk.

'By all means, take a look,' Ioel said. Ehi turned the pages as though they were delicate laluta petals.

'The author was a man called Arkeenell who lived in the district of Bosna, Jheia, several hundred years ago,' Ioel said. 'Ashta has already found something of great value and interest.'

'There's a page written by Arkeenell which details the plans for the desalination machines being built at Myrion,' Ashta said. 'I'm sure they're exactly the same.'

'How is that possible?' Zerren asked.

'We don't know. I believe this Arkeenell may have been a scientist,' Ioel said. 'His book seems to be a collection of ideas with complicated mathematics and diagrams; he was clearly a great thinker for both his time and ours.'

'Is there anything about Ehi?' Zerren asked.

'We haven't had a chance to look through it all yet, but I wouldn't be surprised if we find more useful information,' Ioel said.

'Bosna?' Ehi said.

'Yes, he lived in Bosna,' Ioel said.

'I go,' Ehi said.

'To Bosna?' Zerren asked.

'Yes,' Ehi said.

'We can't go to Bosna. It's too dangerous,' Zerren said. 'It will take weeks, no months, to get there, and no one has lived in that part of Jheia for well over three centuries now.'

'I go,' Ehi said, as a crease formed between her eyebrows.

'No…' Zerren said.

'Let's not make any rash decisions right now,' Ioel said. 'I think we should all study Arkeenell's work first and then we can decide how to proceed.'

'Agreed, though if Ehi must go to Bosna then I will go too,' Ahrl said.

'It's potentially not a bad idea,' Ashta said. 'Especially if this Arkeenell has left more of his work behind in Jheia.'

'There's no guarantee that we would find anything there, or anything intact after all this time,' Zerren said.

'We didn't really think we would find anything in Kiri either,' Ashta said.

'Ahrl, you should find Myaie and Roe and update them on the situation,' Ioel said. 'I must go now and attend to matters here in Kiri, but you're all welcome to use this room for as long as you like. I must warn you though, don't speak about this book to others just yet.' The group nodded and Ahrl left with Ioel.

'Do you think this Arkeenell was really a scientist?' Ahrl said.

'Yes, why? Are you sceptical of science?'

'No, but many are.'

'Many are foolish and many before us just accepted things worked because they worked. Our ancestors would drop an object on the ground, but they wouldn't question why it fell, only that they knew it would fall because everything always falls. Tell me, Ahrl, how many Elorans died whilst your ancestors tried and failed to launch their rockets to Orleetan?'

'Hundreds, sadly,' Ahrl said. 'Though every time something went wrong my ancestors and others learned and tried something new until they found a way that worked.'

'Yes, but with a great waste of life and time,' Ioel said. 'I've read about your family in our records.'

'They didn't understand every little detail; it was the consequences of their actions that helped develop the technology needed. It's worked before for our ancestors. It's how the districts came together to build the great bridge to Jheia.'

'Yes, but building a bridge and launching an Iyeekan into space are two very different things. Science is a way of thinking and understanding the details of our lives and Iyeeka,' Ioel said. 'Something that is very important now that Iyeeka has changed.'

'I know, and I would have done things differently.'

'It's what happened when our repetitive lives were relatively easy; no one was curious. No one ever considered changing or doing anything differently,' Ioel said. 'It's when life becomes hard that real change is forced, and not necessarily for the better.'

'I wonder what the Jheians thought of Arkeenell. I wonder if they ignored him or supported him.'

'As a scientist, he probably didn't say very much and, if the Jheians knew, they were probably wary of him. As you will no doubt know, scientists back then were often associated with having big and crazy ideas of little importance and little use. As I said before, when life is relatively easy and old methods work just fine, then why bother changing anything?'

'Ruick has been changing that; there has been a gradual shift in opinions over the last century,' Ahrl said.

'Yes, we need more like him.'

'Do you really think we can heal Iyeeka by understanding Arkeenell's work?'

'Who knows,' Ioel said. 'I've watched Iyeeka change. I

heard the accounts from my parents and grandparents. We've lost millions over these long, dry years and now we are few in number and clinging on to life as desperately as our cliff edges cling to the land. Things have to change; we have to heal Iyeeka and we must learn from our ancestors' mistakes and build on their good accomplishments. It's no use rejecting everything that our ancestors have taught us in a bid to burden them with all the blame and distance ourselves from them. Just as there is no guarantee that heading solely in the opposite direction will lead to our salvation. Ruick has made some good headway and Myrion will be the start, but it does feel like we're searching for answers in the dark. If this Arkeenell can shed some light in this darkness, then it's worth going to Bosna. One thing is for certain though, Ehi is unlike any Iyeekan I've ever seen or heard of and I don't think her presence now is something we should ignore.'

'Your words put a lot of pressure on Ehi and Arkeenell,' Ahrl said.

'That's not my intention. I'm not foolish enough to think with absolute certainty that they have all or even some of the answers we seek. They may have no answers at all, but that doesn't mean we shouldn't try. Ehi may just be finding her voice again now, but when she speaks, I believe she'll be worth listening to. Whether it will help Iyeeka, well, that is yet to be seen.'

# TWENTY-FIVE

Varth sat with his legs dangling over the precipice. The mountains stretched out before him and their steep slopes stood like pointed blades around him. Behind him, Kiri sat with its great stone buildings and curved rooves surrounded by a plateau of flat land. They were up and away from the rest of Eloran; it felt like nothing and no one could touch him here. He had come to this one spot many times now; it was the furthest place from all the tents surrounding Kiri and it was partially hidden by a large rock. He had left his yebon behind in Lebanoi with Nerrox, a secret member of the N.I.L.

Varth pulled his kaelo from his pocket, turned it on and winced at the fuzzing crackling sound it emitted. Syvvak would be furious; he hadn't updated him in days, not since the rockslide in the Kiri pass. He didn't regret saving Roe, she was a kind young girl who didn't press or ask for his name, but she still came to talk to him. In fact he had found their recent conversations most enlightening, but it was a delicate and dangerous arrangement - he knew that he would be recognised if he got too close to Zerren or Ehi. That wasn't his only concern though; every night since he had watched Zerren and Ehi leave Arrukai, he had dreamt the same dream. There was always a storm and Ehi was always standing at the centre, asking him to find her. Now Ehi had saved his life; it was a debt he couldn't even begin to repay.

He tuned the kaelo to a different station and heard a male voice say...

*'Fourteen districts have been destroyed by the N.I.L. since the first attack in Skidaroi just five weeks ago. Refugees have been making their way to the eastern districts and many are attempting the difficult journey north to Loenya.'*

Varth turned the station off. The planned and deliberate destruction and devastation caused by the N.I.L. made his stomach lurch. This wasn't what he had signed up for; he hadn't signed up to join a group of mass murderers. But then he thought about the former I.L. and the western walls; they too had killed thousands with their choice, wasn't it the same? *It's not the same.* Varth shook his head. *It's different. They didn't go out and purposefully kill Iyeekans.* He looked down at the kaelo and felt the cool metal and plastic pressing into his skin. *I should be dead, no, I would be dead if it wasn't for her,* Varth thought. *But Syvvak is expecting an update, I can't… Maybe I can give him a small update. I could tell him that we have all arrived in Kiri. I don't have to mention what happened in the pass.* He pushed the button and began to send the message. Once he had finished, he pocketed the device, pulled out a notebook and a pencil and waited for a reply. Several long minutes passed and then his kaelo crackled; there was a short series of clicks. He quickly jotted down the message.

*Keep following target.*

Varth gulped. Three words. Syvvak was definitely angry. He switched off the kaelo and slid it and the notebook into a pocket in his cloak.

'There you are!' Roe said. He looked up at the sound of her voice and saw her approaching. His body tensed. *Did she see me? Did she hear anything?* She smiled easily at him though, so he forced a smile back.

'Roe, are you ok?'

'I'm fine. The others have found where Ehi's page came from.'

'Page?' Varth said. Roe put her hands over mouth.

'Oh, I probably shouldn't have told you that,' she said from between her fingers.

'It's ok, I won't tell anyone,' Varth said. *I can't believe they actually found something.* He smiled again. Roe lowered her hands.

'Zerren found Ehi in Cenic with this page; it's got these weird numbers and symbols on it and a strange diagram.'

'Oh?'

'Anyways, they think it's important; they think it's why Ehi looks the way that she does. They also think that the author was incredibly smart, and they wanted to see if they could find more work written by him.'

'That is strange,' Varth said.

'Yes but they did find something, they found a whole book written by the same author. Ashta is really excited about one of the new pages they found. Apparently it's got the same methods and diagrams for the desalination machines they've been working on in Myrion.'

'Oh yes, I've heard about that,' Varth said, rubbing the back of his neck. *Syvvak will want to know about that.*

'Well, this Arkeenell, the author I mean, he wrote these pages seven hundred years ago.'

'That long ago?'

'Yup, the others are looking over it now. I got bored and wanted to get some fresh air.' She sat down beside him and swung her legs over the precipice.

'I don't blame you. It's nice out here. The record halls must be a bit crowded and stuffy. I'm not really much of a book Iyeekan either.'

'Some of the artwork is pretty, but I've seen it all now a dozen times.'

'Hmm,' Varth said. Guilt wormed its way through his guts so he quickly changed tact. 'You know, I've been wondering about what happened in the pass. Ehi is pretty incredible, don't you think?'

'Yes, she is. Ahrl says she has a lot of power, too much really. I think that's why we have all dreamt about her, well, apart from Zerren.' Varth stiffened, this was the first time Roe had mentioned anything about dreams.

'Who are we?'

'A few of us. Me, Ahrl, Myaie, Ashta and Moribi Ioel,' Roe said. 'We've all had the same dream featuring Ehi.' *It can't be.*

'Oh, and what do you dream?' Varth said. Roe bit her lip.

'I shouldn't really be talking about this, Ahrl would be mad.'

'It's ok, you can trust me. I won't tell anyone.' Roe stared up at him and for a moment he thought she wouldn't say anything, but then she nodded.

'It always starts the same way, a big storm is going on around you and the air is so thick with dust it's almost impossible to see through it, but Ehi is standing there, right in front of you. She reaches out her hand and you just feel this overwhelming desire to follow her, to grab hold of her hand and never let it go, and then she says, you must find me.' Varth felt as though he'd been struck by lightning. *It's impossible, we can't... we can't have had the same dream?*

'Find me?' Varth said. 'Well, I guess you've already found her then.'

'Ehi doesn't know why we have these dreams,' Roe said. 'I've had them every night for a month now, and the others, apart from Myaie, have too.'

'The same dream?'

'Yes, the exact same dream, even before we had ever met her. I sort of wish that we all had different dreams, then there would at least be some variety.'

'And you say Zerren hasn't had these dreams at all?'

'Nope.'

*Interesting, Zerren was technically the one who found her.* Varth rubbed his jaw as he stared out across the valley.

'I'm bored,' Roe said.

'How about you find someone who will lend you a game of obimna,' Varth said.

'I've never played obimna.'

'I'll teach you; it's fun and it's easy.'

'You promise?'

'Promise.'

'Ok, but where will I find one?'

'I don't know, you'll have to ask around, but someone will have one somewhere, I'm sure of it.'

'I better get back, before they all worry where I am,' Roe said.

'Yes, you better,' Varth said with a smile, and he waved her off.

Roe stood and skipped away and Varth withdrew the kaelo and the sound key from his pockets as soon as she was at a safe distance. He turned the kaelo on again and was greeted by its constant low buzzing sound. *Should I really tell Syvvak about the page and the dreams?* He thought about the recent districts the N.I.L. had destroyed, all the Iyeekans who were now homeless and who had lost loved ones. It wasn't right; this wasn't the better Iyeeka that Syvvak had promised. Tough decisions had to be made, yes, but you couldn't make decisions about someone else's life, someone you didn't even know.

Varth lifted the devices above his head and swung his arm back; he almost felt as though Anorae was there with him, willing him to throw them over the edge of the precipice. *What if Syvvak does take Lebanoi? What if he really does create his vision of Iyeeka? Will I be a traitor?* He stopped and lowered the kaelo and sound key into his lap. He leaned over the edge of the precipice and the urge to jump grew greater with every second. He could just escape from it all. Maybe he could be with Anorae again; he could be free from all of his thoughts and feelings and the hurt he carried with him. The idea was so tantalising and sweet, the promise of a release from the burden of his mind. But then he remembered

Roe. He remembered her kind face and smile, and he remembered promising to teach her how to play obimna. Varth's shoulders slumped he leant away from the edge of the precipice and stared at the kaelo in his hands. He quickly reached a compromise in his mind and then he sent a coded message to Syvvak.

*Origins of page has been found. There is more information. Author is Arkeenell.*

He waited for a reply. It didn't take long.

*Keep watching, Varthrune. I'm pleased.*

Varth switched off the kaelo and pocketed his belongings. He looked around to check that no one was watching him, before heading back to Kiri.

# TWENTY-SIX

*B*osna... Zerren stared at the flames leaping from the bonfire at the centre of the courtyard as dusk slowly gave way to night. One by one the stars emerged above as though some cosmic beings were lighting their own distant fires, but Zerren continued to stare at the flames before him. He watched them twist and turn and his skin almost seemed to sigh contentedly in the halo of warmth they cast. Dozens of Elorans had gathered around the flames and hundreds more clustered around smaller fires dotted throughout Kiri. As much as the cold was welcomed, there was something magical about the warmth of a bonfire. Moribi wandered around the groups with large pots, distributing steaming bowls of soup and spoons to the many hungry faces. At the other end of the courtyard on the other side of the fire, someone began to tap a beat on a small drum and Zerren was aware that Ehi was swaying from side to side beside him. Naehanuoi and two other Moribi stopped before them; they hefted a large pot between two wooden slats and Naehanuoi carried dozens of stacked wooden bowls and spoons. The two Moribi set down the pot and Naehanuoi used a large bronze ladle to scoop out bowls of soup for both Ehi and Zerren and the other Elorans who were sat nearby.

'I'm glad to see that you're looking better, Ehi,' Naehanuoi said. Ehi stopped swaying and smiled.

'Thank you,' she said, accepting the soup.

'Ioel tells me you plan to travel to Bosna,' Naehanuoi said, turning to Zerren as she handed him a bowl.

'I haven't made up my mind yet,' Zerren said.

'But surely you will go with Ehi?' Naehanuoi said. Zerren glanced at Ehi, who raised the soup bowl to her lips.

'I have my family to consider,' Zerren said. 'They should be arriving in Lebanoi soon.'

'I see,' Naehanuoi said. Ehi upended her bowl and let out a satisfied sigh. Naehanuoi and the two Moribi picked up the pot as they moved on to the next group of Elorans. Someone across the courtyard had picked up a lyre and had begun plucking on the strings in time with the drum beat and Ehi began to sway again and tap her feet on the ground. Two more Moribi came round with big baskets filled with bread which they handed out. Ehi quickly demolished her piece and gulped down some water as another flute began. She sprang to her feet and was off towards the fire and music before Zerren could stop her. Zerren continued to stare at the flames as someone began to sing. He wasn't sure what he was going to do; everything had become rather complicated since they had arrived in Lebanoi. His plan had been simple up until that point. Take Ehi to Kiri, find some information about her past and then, after that, meet his family in Lebanoi and try and build a new life again. But these dreams, the Elorans who had ended up travelling with them, it was all so strange. Strange and unwelcome. Times were already hard enough without the extra added confusion, yet wherever Ehi went, chaos seemed to follow. *Perhaps I should leave Ehi here and travel back to Lebanoi alone.* Ahrl had already offered to accompany her to Bosna, if she still insisted on going. It would be one less problem and headache for Zerren. *Ehi could travel with Ahrl and the others; maybe Ahrl will be able to take her to Loenya eventually, she would be safe there.* He felt a familiar buzz growing around his mind, pinching between his ears and tingling the back of his nose. He put his head in his hands and lowered his gaze to the ground as his entire body tensed.

*Go with Ehi,* Lucoe's voice said.

'Why?' Zerren whispered. 'Tell me why?'

*Go to Bosna.*

'Why won't you answer me? Where are you, Lucoe?' Zerren twisted his fingers through the roots of his hair and gripped his skull. A barrage of voices flooded into his mind, sweeping Lucoe's voice away with a tide of desperate pleas and apologies. *It's over,* a female voice said. *We've lost, we've lost everything,* another voice said. Zerren gritted his teeth and shoved the voices to the back of his mind where they dwindled and died like the ashy embers on the breeze.

'I see we have learnt something new about Ehi,' Ioel said. Zerren glanced up to see the Moribi standing behind him and searched for Ehi. He found her quickly enough, standing on her tiptoes by the flames. All of a sudden, she dipped and twisted her body, moving as though she was nothing more than a piece of fabric in the breeze. Her arms curved upwards and outwards and her whole body swayed and moved in time with the music. She twirled on the spot and several children danced around her, trying in vain to copy her moves. Zerren heard Ioel settle down on the cushions beside him.

'I've never seen anyone move like that,' Zerren said.

'She's a dancer, probably one of the last of her kind.'

'I thought that skillset had died out centuries ago.'

'It did,' Ioel said. 'Though there were some who tried to keep it alive, it wasn't seen as a necessary skillset for the Iyeeka we live with now, so many dropped it in favour of more practical skills. It's a shame; dancing has always been very good for both the mind and body. It helps us to relax, laugh and have fun, which is important, especially when times are tough. It also brings Iyeekans together.' Zerren's eyes darted across to a young couple who had also joined the dance. He heard laughter as Ehi held a child's hand and helped her to spin on her feet.

'My grandparents used to tell my brothers and me stories

of the old days,' said Zerren. 'They spoke of a time when all the continents had been populated. There had been many dancers back then and theatrical groups, musicians and artists, and there was always plenty of food to go around, and the eyeleetansy were so numerous that when they flew together in their air they looked like great rainbow clouds. There was no fighting, no arguments and no despair. The N.I.L. didn't exist and the very few Iyeekans who did cause trouble were sent to work in sanitation for a period of time.'

'Yes, it was a better time, a utopia in part,' Ioel said. 'Things rarely went wrong; there was the occasional natural disaster, but communities pulled together as they always had done, and life continued on.'

Zerren didn't reply, his gaze was fixed on Ehi.

'I've spoken to the others,' Ioel said. 'It seems that Ahrl, Myaie, Ashta and Roe will travel with us to Bosna.'

'Us?'

'Yes, I'm coming too.'

'Moribi Ioel, I don't think this is wise,' Zerren said. 'The journey will be difficult and I beg for your pardon, but you're not as young as the rest of us.'

Ioel laughed.

'The others all have different reasons for wishing to go and yes, I'm aware of my age, but I will still travel with you. I have my own questions and answers to find.'

'Is this because of the dreams that you all share?'

'Partly.'

'I'm still not sure if I'll go,' Zerren said. 'I don't think there will be any answers in Bosna. Ehi hasn't remembered much about her past and she speaks little of it. I don't think she'll find the answers she seeks or any sense of closure in Bosna.'

'Maybe, maybe not,' Ioel said. 'We won't know until we try. And I think Ehi remembers more than she lets on.'

'What do you mean?'

'Zerren, have you looked at her? I mean truly looked at her?'

'I… I don't follow.'

'Look into her eyes, Zerren. If I know one thing from being a Moribi all these years, it's that Elorans can hide emotions from their faces, but they can't hide them completely in their eyes.' Ioel got up and motioned to Zerren to stand. The courtyard had become alive with bodies and their shadows dancing, and more Elorans had added their voices, instruments and whatever they could find to the melody and beat.

'Moribi Ioel, I must ask you to reconsider your plans. The Elorans here need you and northern Eloran has become a dangerous place. You're old and frail. I fear you would never make it.'

'Zerren, I have already thought it through and I have a plan,' Ioel said. 'So stop worrying and let an old Eloran make his own decisions.'

'But what if there is nothing to find in Bosna?'

'Then I will not be left wondering what if because I didn't go,' Ioel said. He placed a hand on Zerren's shoulder and gave him a gentle push. Zerren felt a small pair of warm hands slip into his own and then he was pulled into the mass of smiling and laughing Elorans, swaying and twisting to the music. He caught a glimpse of Myaie, Roe, Ahrl, and Ashta moving among the bodies. Zerren looked up to see who had taken his hand, and Ehi turned to face him with tears falling down her cheeks and a big smile on her face. He wondered for a brief moment how one Eloran could display so much despair and happiness so openly like she did, but then she was moving, and his body seemed to mirror her on its own. He couldn't dance well, he hadn't danced since he had been a child, but somehow, with her, he knew that wouldn't matter.

# TWENTY-SEVEN

An explosion ripped up the ground, showering the area with mud whilst inhumane shrieks sounded, and flashes erupted on the smoke-clogged battlegrounds. Twisted wires with wicked points and wooden stakes formed unnatural bushes on the ground. Ehi could hear an infrequent and sometimes constant rat-ta-tat-tat sound, followed by more cries, more yelling, and more chaos. She looked around and saw human bodies, swollen and bloody, lying in icy puddles. Another explosion followed several others and the earth trembled beneath her.

'Take cover,' a male voice cried.

'Man down,' another voice yelled. Ehi looked around but all she could see were small rises and mounds of dirt and the ground jumping up where an explosion occurred.

'Up, up, up, over the top,' a voice yelled. Ehi saw men clad in green uniforms, wearing helmets, crawling up and over the small mounds of dirt. They ran straight for her, but then the rat-ta-tat-tat sound came back, and she caught a glimpse of something metal streaking past the corners of her vision. The men stopped as though their bodies had crashed into invisible walls and then they fell to the ground. Ehi turned her gaze to the sky; black clouds loomed above, growing and crackling with a corrupted energy. She stood in a field of slaughter.

Ehi's stomach turned. Nausea gripped her, and an icy cold sensation swept through her. The fields of death disappeared, blurring away as the colours faded and twisted into new forms.

As she moved forwards, images of more senseless violence were presented to her. The bodies of children, clutching guns, lay in the streets. Buildings were toppled, and people were fleeing. *Why?* Ehi thought, and, just as before, the answers appeared in her mind. *Fear, greed, corruption, power.* She had asked these questions before; she had learnt these truths before. *But how?* She saw more visions of battlefields and large groups of men wearing metal clothes in different colours and waving sticks with patterned rectangular cloths attached to the ends. They stamped their feet, beat drums and then ran at each other screaming, any fear being hammered out into cruel, maddening gazes. They stained the ground red with their blood, bent on destruction only, and never collaboration.

The field gave way to gentle, golden sandy slopes, and the Earth became like much of the Iyeeka Ehi was used to. She saw soldiers who bore red crosses on their armour charging at more soldiers who wore cloth over their heads and spikes on the top of their metal helmets. Both sides brandished long metal blades, sticks with metal spikes and shields flashing in the sunlight. Some rode on the backs of fast animals and others ran on foot; they collided in a clash of angry yells and shouts. Many men fell, their blood spilling out onto the earth. Ehi turned her head from side to side but everywhere she looked, all she saw was death and destruction. The sand dunes were stripped back. Ehi's mind left the battle but more images flickered past her vision in quick succession, one after the other. They spoke of God, Allah, Jesus, Moses and many others as they gazed up at the sky or bent low to the ground, and all the while death seemed to follow these groups as assuredly as the light of day.

Ehi felt the weight of the violence and despair as though metal chains were being tightened around her chest. *What was the point? Where was the sense in any of it?* These humans had a beautiful world, a world with so much life, promise and prosperity, yet they fought as though their world meant nothing to them.

*Why?* Ehi asked again.

A hot breeze brushed past her face and then a furry sensation tickled her cheek. Her vision waned and faded, carrying the images of humans and their violence away from her awareness. Ehi groaned; she heard a snort by her ear and then something warm and soft nudged her cheek. She opened her eyes and felt every bump and stone in the ground beneath her. Her eyes and cheeks were wet, and her body felt heavy and cold. Hovering just a few inches from her face, a gopa breathed on her. Ehi smiled at the creature and reached up to stroke its head between its long oval ears.

'Sorry,' she said as she wiped her tears away with the cuff of her sleeve. Despite the disagreements over Bosna, their group with the addition of Ioel and some of the Moribi, had spent the last several days travelling down the pass back to Lebanoi. Each day Ehi was finding it harder to pull herself out of her makeshift bed. With everything she saw in her dreams or when the images took over her mind, she learnt much more than she wished about Earth, humans, and Iyeeka. A sense of hopelessness and despair had taken root in her heart and it grew every day. She stood, stretched and looked up at the pink skies, but she saw no signs of the rocky planet. It worried her, no one else had seen the planet in their dreams and she hadn't said a word about it. She knew Bosna was a long shot; she felt strongly that whoever had designed the Usol Key and whatever reason she had been put in there, the answers would still be found in Bosna. Perhaps they would find a warning, or a solution, should the planet from her dream ever appear. Though Ehi would have been happy with anything, her parent's names or even the name of her home district.

She scanned the group and saw that the others were rousing themselves from their slumber. Zerren caught her gaze; he was already awake, and he was staring directly at her with an intensity which unnerved her. *Doesn't he ever sleep?* She felt a tingling sensation run across her scalp, behind her eyes and nose. Zerren's usol appeared at the centre of his torso, the strange ghostly sphere with its many colours. She saw again the split down the centre, and the half which seemed brighter and more tangible than the other. She tore her gaze from Zerren and turned to the gopa that had woken her and stroked its long neck. The gopa didn't have usols, or at least, not the sort of usols Ehi could sometimes see. The gopa were slightly smaller than ziree and lived in the mountainous regions. They had shorter tails and shaggy beige and white coats. They also had two small horns at the top of their heads, auburn eyes and flat faces which were covered in white fur with greyish-blue patches.

'Good morning,' Ioel said. Ehi turned to face him, he smiled at her and she smiled back, though she knew her smile lacked Ioel's warmth.

'Good morning,' Ehi said with difficulty. Words were hard and uncomfortable; it felt like she was juggling rocks in her mouth, but some were easier than others. She looked up and caught Zerren's gaze; he was still watching her with a guarded expression.

'Did you sleep well?' Ioel asked.

'Yes.'

'Good.' Ioel moved over to the other members of their group and bid them good morning. Ehi turned to check the straps and fastenings on the nearest gopa's saddle and reigns, but she felt Zerren's gaze boring into her. She heard his footsteps, but she didn't turn around.

'Ehi,' Zerren said, 'I know you dreamt last night.' Ehi turned to face him. 'It's ok if you don't want to talk about it, but if it's something that upsets you, something from your past, then you can tell me, if you want to.' Ehi stared into his blue-green eyes; his concern caused her stomach to squeeze but he was so wrong. The past concerned her very little; it was the future that bothered her. She nodded though; and her gaze darted down to his usol, she could see the split in his usol more clearly now. The colours ran like layers of smoky bands around his little black core; they were bright on the left side of his soul but as soon as they hit the split which ran through the centre, they became diluted and almost disappeared entirely on his right side.

'What are you looking at?' Zerren asked.

'Your usol is split.' The words were out of her mouth before she could stop to think about it.

'My what?' Zerren said, taking a step back from her.

'I see…' Ehi shifted uncomfortably. 'I see usol.'

'What do you mean, you see usol?'

'Colours,' Ehi said. 'Usol.' Ehi searched the narrow pass around them as though something might be able to offer her a better way of explaining. She threw her hands up, frowned and licked her lips. 'Your usol is different than others.'

'Ehi, normal Iyeekans can't see usols, we don't even know if they exist,' Zerren said.

'What is this?' Ioel said. She had barely noticed him approach.

'Usol,' Ehi said, placing her hand on Zerren's chest. She felt Zerren's heartbeat speed up slightly; he gulped and averted his gaze up to the sky.

'Ehi thinks she can see my usol.'

'Does she?' Ioel said. 'Interesting.'

'You have usol too,' Ehi said, pointing at Ioel. 'And you, you, you…' She pointed at everyone in their group.

'What do they look like?' Ioel asked.

'Round,' Ehi said, forming a rough spherical shape with her hands. 'There but not there.'

'Invisible?' Ahrl asked.

Ehi shook her head.

'Translucent?' Ioel said.

'Yes,' Ehi said. 'They all different but Zerren's…'

'Zerren's is different from everyone else's?' Ioel said.

'Yes,' Ehi said. Zerren stepped away from her, leaving her hand hovering in mid-air. He looked uncomfortable and distant again, as though a private conversation was happening somewhere deep inside his mind. 'You all have different colours,' Ehi said.

'What does mine look like?' Roe asked, skipping forwards and stopping in front of Ehi. Ehi gazed at Roe's usol and watched its colours tumble over one another; they changed frequently on the outer edges as though they were transitioning like the sky through from dawn to midday to dusk and night.

'Colours change,' Ehi said. 'Mainly yellow, blue and white…'

'What do the colours mean?' Roe asked.

'I don't know,' Ehi said. She let her gaze wander across the rest of the group. 'Every usol has different amounts.' She winced as a sharp pulsing sensation began to make its presence known behind her right eye. Her vision wobbled and the usols began to fade one by one. She blinked and her eyes stung; the morning light had become too bright and the details around her too sharp. 'Can't see anymore,' she said.

'The usols are gone now?' Ioel asked.

Ehi nodded but even that felt like her head was being rattled around inside a box.

'Are you ok?' Zerren said.

'I think Ehi needs some space,' Ioel said. Ehi heard the murmurings of agreement, but she could still feel their gazes upon her, searching for answers that she wasn't sure she could give.

'Here, Ehi, you should eat,' Zerren said. He offered her a mixture of fruit, nuts and other things, squashed together in an oval shape, the same thing they had eaten for the last few days. She nibbled on it whilst the others ate and prepared the gopa for travel.

They reached the end of the Kiri pass just after the etansy reached its peak point in the sky and then they made their way slowly around Lebanoi's lakes. A couple of hours later they stopped on the outskirts of one of the outer districts. Ehi gazed at the bodies moving in and out of the district before them; there were Elorans everywhere. She held onto her hood and hopped down from the saddle and stroked her gopa's neck. The gopa made a strange groaning noise and then dipped its head to chew at the dry grass on the ground. The others dismounted around her, shouldering their packs, and Ehi went round to the gopa's saddle and unclipped and shouldered her own pack. Two Moribi helped Ioel down from his gopa and handed him a long stick to help him walk. The Moribi then said their goodbyes, rounded up the gopa and made their way back up the pass to Kiri.

'Will they be alright?' Ahrl said as they watched the Moribi go.

'They will be fine, I'm not worried. Naehanuoi will make a fine leader for the Moribi of Kiri,' Ioel said. Zerren placed himself by Ehi's side and their group headed through the outer districts towards Lebanoi. Elorans with thin faces looked up at their group warily.

They moved through the crowds, but made slow progress. Many recognised Ioel's orange robes and stopped to incline their heads towards the Moribi. Shouts and yells up ahead drew their attention and Ehi could see a large crowd gathering around a yebon.

'This way,' Zerren said as he tried to lead their group around the large crowd. Ehi caught a glimpse of two Lebanoi Elorans with blue sashes on their arms handing out packages and sacks of water to the swarming crowds. She felt a buzzing sensation ripple across her skull and a ringing noise sounded faintly between her ears. Her vision wobbled and then the strange balls of light appeared one by one at the centre of every Elorans' chest.

'Usol,' Ehi whispered as she gazed at the spheres and the various colours contained within.

'Please don't push, we have plenty for everyone,' one of the

Lebanoi Elorans yelled at the crowd. She noticed a man with a wicked grin on his face, the colours of his usol smothered by a dark, lightless energy which then expanded outwards from his body in great black clouds.

'He's lying, there isn't enough food, the yebon is almost empty,' the man yelled. The mood shifted across the crowd; the other Elorans' usols dimmed and their colours vanished to be replaced with hues of grey, orange and brown.

'There's not enough?' a female voice cried from the crowd. The black clouds grew outwards and Ehi shivered as the temperature around her seemed to drop.

'But we hardly ate anything yesterday,' another voice shouted. Murmurings of discontent ran through the crowd and these strange black clouds dived in and out, charging into every centre, leaving their usols a little darker than before. Ehi had learned that this darkness, this absence of colour and light, was bad, but now she could see exactly how it fed and grew.

'I'm not starving again tonight, I've got children to feed,' another voice yelled. The black clouds stretched overhead and continued to grow.

'Please...' the Lebanoi Eloran said.

'They're almost out!' another voice screeched. The crowd began to surge forwards and the Elorans yelled, screamed and shoved as they tried to get to the narrow space at the back of the yebon. Ehi felt Elorans shove past her and knock her as she tried to keep Zerren in her sights.

'Ehi,' Zerren said. She saw his arm reach out for her but several Elorans rushed towards her and swept her away into the crowd. Ehi twisted and caught sight of Myaie being swept up by the crowd too and then Ehi was pinned between bodies, her face squashed against another Eloran's back. The stench of body odour hit the back of her airways and she felt her chest constricting tighter and tighter. She tried to move to her left and then to her right, but no one would give and there seemed to be no end to the tangle of bodies, faces and arms.

Ehi looked up at a gap between the black clouds and caught a glimpse of the pale pink sky. Her head throbbed, and the tingling sensation renewed itself with extra vigour and spread throughout her body as the ringing noise grew louder between her ears. The edges of her vision began to fade and the screams and cries of the Elorans around her merged into a faint echo. The sights and sounds of the crowd and Iyeeka disappeared from around her and she found herself in a windowless room, standing before a hollow metal cylinder, no, a machine, the Usol Key. *Hasree, Seffen.* Ehi watched the two male Iyeekans dart around the Usol Key, plugging in wires, tapping on devices and looking at thin screens that were not too dissimilar to the computers of Earth. Seffen and Hasree looked away and kept their eyes up as Ehi moved forwards and climbed into the cylinder.

'Good luck,' Hasree said. 'Our screens should show us everything that you see, and we will wake you up if we see solutions before the year is up.'

'Ok,' Ehi heard herself say, though she was sure she had never opened her mouth.

'This might not work,' Seffen said. 'If it doesn't, we'll wake you up straight away.'

'Ok, just relax, Ehi, we're going to close the door now,' Hasree said. There was a whirring noise and the machine lit up around her as the door slid shut. Ehi thought of her mother as the machine continued to hum and she felt a rush of sweet smelling air rise up from her feet. She took a deep breath and then she felt her chest grow uncomfortably tight. She tried to breathe again but there seemed to be no air inside the cylinder. Her heart began to race, and her muscles squeezed painfully. She thrust out her arms and banged her hands and fists against the inside of the cylinder.

'I can't breathe,' she cried. She choked and spluttered, and her lungs burned. Her vision began to fade and blur; she felt as though she were falling backwards into nothingness as the last of the memories slipped from her mind. Something hard hit her in the face and she heard her nose crack. The sights and sounds of Iyeeka came back with a pop and Ehi gasped and blinked several times as the ringing in her ears subsided and the yells and screams of the crowd rushed back to her. Her skull ached, her nose hurt, and she could feel the blood pounding between her ears as her chest and body were being crushed.

'Stop! My child is on the ground, stop!' a woman cried but the crowd ignored her and continued to force its way forwards. Ehi closed her eyes and reached for her frazzled mind. She connected to the lif on her right wrist and sent it up and above the crowd in minute silver droplets. She imagined the back of the yebon and the packages of food and water sacks inside. With a thought she willed the liquid lif to coalesce at the back of the yebon, underneath all the food and water, and then, with another thought, she commanded the lif to become a solid ball and grow outwards exponentially in a single burst. There was a muted bang and gasps from the crowds as food packages and water sacks flew out the back of the yebon and were scattered around. The crowd broke, Elorans darting off in all directions, scrambling to pick up the food and water.

Ehi gasped and choked as she dropped to her knees and wrapped her arms around her heaving chest. Zerren was by her side in seconds; he pulled her hood back over her head and hauled her to her feet. Ehi stumbled, each footstep jarred her head and she touched the end of her sensitive nose and pulled back her fingers to see that they were coated in blood. She glanced backwards over her shoulder and felt a small measure of relief when she saw Ahrl guiding Myaie away from the chaos.

They reached the others and quickly made their way to Lebanoi, whilst the crowd ran in the opposite direction towards the yebon.

'Come on, we've got to find Ruick,' Ashta said.

# TWENTY-EIGHT

'This is incredible,' Ruick said. 'Absolutely incredible.' He marvelled at the pages from Arkeenell's book, which, under Ioel's protection, they had brought with them.

'It's the same, isn't it? The plans are the same?' Ashta said.

'Yes, yes,' Ruick said. He nodded, his eyes wide, and continued to turn the pages. 'I just… I just can't believe this really exists. If only we had had this earlier…'

'We were just as amazed as you are,' Ahrl said. Ruick lowered the page he held in his hands.

'Quite,' he said. He cast his amber gaze over the group and lingered on Myaie. 'It seems like we've all shared the same dream, apart from Zerren of course. I wonder if there will be more of us out there.'

'Us?' Ashta said.

'Yes. Between the troubles outside and your arrival, you hardly gave me time to update you before you came here with Arkeenell's work,' Ruick said. 'I've also had the dream; I've dreamt it nearly every night since you left for Kiri.' Zerren felt his guts twist. 'There's more information here, not only about the desalination machines but details about which cross-pollinated crops are best for our current climate and the mention of use of electricity without wires and even a theory on how to create more lif,' Ruick said.

Yes, I've studied Arkeenell's notes every night we stopped in the Kiri Pass,' Ioel said. 'There also seems to be detailed information about how our connection with lif manifests. Arkeenell uses terms

I've never heard of before; he talks of things called particles.'

'Yes, I'm intrigued by this too,' Ruick said. 'It seems that this Arkeenell had a more detailed understanding of Iyeeka, though the terms he uses are not the terms the students of Lebanoi would use.'

'Perhaps the students here would be able to help more if they could see Arkeenell's work?' Ashta said.

'Yes, Ioel, would that be acceptable?' Ruick asked.

'A thousand years ago the Moribi would have allowed you to copy the work, but I know time is short so yes, it is acceptable. However, I suggest that we keep hold of the page with the Usol Key; if Ehi still plans to travel to Bosna then we may need to use the handwriting as a reference.'

'Bosna? That's a long way, Ehi,' Ruick said.

'I go,' Ehi said.

'And the rest of you?' Ruick asked.

'I've offered to accompany Ehi,' Ahrl said.

'I think it's a good idea,' Ashta said. 'If this Arkeenell did truly live in Bosna and left more information behind, then it could be of great use to us now.'

'What about you, Zerren?' Ruick asked.

'I haven't decided yet. I need to see my family first before I do anything.'

'I'm afraid the Lazarack district has yet to arrive,' Ruick said. 'I imagine they've stopped for more repairs on the laburnem tracks than they originally anticipated. It would have been quicker if they had walked, but with that many Elorans, including the young and old, the laburnem would be safer.'

'They've not arrived?' Zerren said. His stomach dropped as images of bokhanya and the N.I.L. flooded into his mind.

'No,' Ruick said. 'I'm going to send Elorans out in yebons to look for them as soon as I can, but the troubles here have required all of our resources. I'm confident they're safe; they've probably just been delayed.'

'I hope so,' Zerren said.

'When are you going to Bosna?' Ruick asked.

'Tomorrow,' Ehi said. Zerren looked at her. She couldn't be serious?

'That doesn't leave us with much time to prepare,' Ruick said with an amused smile. Zerren gulped and his palms grew hot and sweaty. *Bosna? Why must she go to Bosna?* The questions nagged at him as his heart stuttered in his chest. *I can't go to Bosna… I can't…* He felt a pressure ripple up and over his head and he resisted the urge to wince as his ears popped. A warm tingling sensation skittered across his scalp and buzzed behind his eyes and nose; he knew what was coming next.

*Go to Bosna with Ehi,* Lucoe's voice said. Zerren almost opened his mouth to speak and then his gaze darted to the others; their conversation about travel plans and possible routes felt a million miles away from him now. He thought of his parents and Roarn.

*They are fine. You must go to Bosna, Zerren,* Lucoe said.

*Why?* There was no reply. The pressure lifted suddenly, and the tingling sensation stopped. Zerren's body sagged and he just about managed to prevent himself from stumbling backwards. He pinched the bridge of his nose and blinked hard a couple of times.

'I'll travel with you as far as Myrion. I have matters to discuss with council members Arvita and Shousukei in Myrion, and it wouldn't be a bad idea to travel onto Narakae to see how the Jheian's fair, but I will have to speak to the other council members and my father first,' Ruick said. 'Are you sure you're not going to travel to Jheia, Zerren?'

'I don't know.'

'Come,' Ehi said. He looked up and was snagged by her gaze; it was that look again, the one which betrayed both equal measures of happiness and despair. It was tortured, certain, but fleeting. She masked it with a small, sad smile.

'I'll think about it,' Zerren said, tearing his gaze away from her.

# TWENTY-NINE

The wind raged around him and the dust stung his eyes. He held up his hands as he tried to shield himself from the storm but it was no use. He stepped forwards and tried to peer through the clouds of dirt and dust, but he couldn't see anything; he didn't even know where he was or which direction he was heading.

'*You must find me,*' a female voice said loud and clear from within his mind. He recognised Ehi's voice; he had heard her broken speech in Kiri.

'Why? Where are you?' Varth yelled.

'*Find me,*' the voice said again. The clouds of dust and dirt briefly parted before him and he saw her standing there. Her pale purple hair twisted like flames on her head and she smiled sadly at him. The wind howled louder, he felt his feet leave the ground and then everything went dark.

Varth awoke with a start. His gaze travelled wildly about the small tent. He felt his racing heart slowly calm down. *It was that dream again, surely the same dream that Roe and the others have had.* Every night since he had left the Arrukai district he had dreamt of Ehi, and every night it was the same dream. *Why is this happening to me? What does it mean?* Varth frowned. *It's just a dream Varth, a really strange and realistic dream.* He shook his head. *Don't be stupid, others have dreamt it too, it's not just a dream.* He rested his chin in his hands. *I should tell Syvvak about these dreams,* but even as the thought passed through his mind he felt his chest constrict. He tapped a finger against his lips and then he yawned and rubbed the sleep from his eyes. He opened the tent and looked up at the early morning sky and then he got up, packed up his belongings and made his way through the outer districts surrounding Lebanoi whilst the majority still slept.

His footsteps crunched against the ground, the streets were unnaturally silent. He made his way down the streets, avoiding the guards patrolling the districts. Roe had told him that Ehi planned to go to Bosna, but keeping out of sight and following their group as they rode gopas down the Kiri pass hadn't been easy. He had lost Zerren, Ehi and their group when they had entered Lebanoi, but he was sure that they were still inside. He wound his way through the district to Nerrox's home and he stopped before the small dwelling and knocked. He heard footsteps approaching, then the door opened a fraction and Nerrox's face appeared in the gap. He gazed at Varth for half a second and then the door swung open. Nerrox grabbed Varth, pulled him inside and shut the door again before Varth could blink.

'Varthrune!' Syvvak strode down the narrow hallway and embraced Varth, giving him a smile which seemed oddly out of place. 'I'm so glad you're back, I've been worried about you,' Syvvak said.

'Syvvak?' Varth said. *What is he doing here?*

'You don't need to sound so surprised,' Syvvak said. Syvvak clasped an arm around Varth's shoulders and guided him into Nerrox's front room.

'I didn't know you would be here,' Varth said.

'Ah, well, I thought I would stop by and check on things. The kaelo's are good, but they're a little impersonal at times. My plans are slowly coming together now,' Syvvak said. A cold heaviness settled on Varth, pulling at his internal organs, begging his body to cave and slouch. 'Please, sit down, tell us everything that you've learnt,' Syvvak said. They sat down on the padded brown chairs and Varth felt as though he was just sinking into the seat, into the ground and deep inside Iyeeka with the dirt and rocks piling on top of him. Nerrox poured water into four cups.

'There's not much I can say,' Varth said as he picked up a cup and twisted it between his fingers. 'I believe they're still inside Lebanoi and I think they're planning to travel to Bosna.'

'Come now, Varthrune, you must have more than that,' Syvvak said, reclining in his seat and putting his feet up on the low table before him.

'No,' Varth said, shaking his head. 'Ehi and the others are excited about this Arkeenell and they're hoping to find more of his work in Bosna, but that's all I know.'

'And what about Ehi's abilities? Did you see her use lif?' Syvvak said. Varth stared down at his cup.

'Only when she was making animal shapes for the kids, but she was only using one source of lif for that,' Varth said. 'You know, maybe I was mistaken. I don't think Ehi really is as strong as I thought she was. It's probably not even worth following her anymore.' Syvvak frowned.

'I have men inside Lebanoi; apparently Ruick is joining them, they're planning to go to Myrion, and then I presume some of them will go on to Jheia,' Syvvak said. 'This Arkeenell must have written some fascinating notes to get Ruick's attention. He surely knows that leaving Lebanoi unattended is a bad idea right now.'

'Ruick isn't the only council member here,' Varth said.

'No, but he has the most influence from pure popularity,' Syvvak said. 'My men tell me that Ruick has given these notes to the students and teachers inside Lebanoi. If these notes are as valuable as Ruick believes and they find more in Bosna, it could be disastrous for the cause. It'll be easy enough to destroy the notes inside Lebanoi, but as soon as they get out they'll be hard to track down.'

'Do you know what these notes contain?' Varth asked.

'Not exactly. I'm almost tempted to take Lebanoi now, but

there are far too many refugees alive who will oppose me, not that they'll last long. I will send men to follow Ehi and her companions east but we'll have to be careful about which districts we target next.' Varth tried to imagine himself on the other side, he tried to imagine himself as one of the Elorans who had just lost their home and loved ones. An Eloran who would be so scared that they wouldn't dare to speak against Syvvak or the N.I.L. It was wrong, he could feel it in every ounce of his being, it was all wrong.

'Is that really necessary?' Varth said. 'I mean, haven't you caused enough chaos? Surely we can just wait now?'

'Varthrune, this is all necessary. Sometimes we have to do things which aren't very pleasant. We can't make a better Iyeeka and show the Elorans the error of their ways unless we get rid of the old one. You understand that don't you?' Syvvak said.

'Yes, it's just…'

'Just what?' Syvvak frowned.

'It just seems a bit extreme,' Varth said. 'Destroying districts and,' Varth gulped, 'killing Elorans. How can you change Iyeeka if everyone hates you?' Syvvak tilted his head and stared at Varth for a long time before he straightened up and spoke.

'You've got it wrong, Varthrune.' Syvvak sighed. 'I don't care if everyone hates me, as long as they fear me. Anger and hatred are directly related to fear. When Iyeekans hate you it's usually because they are afraid of you. Fear is easy to manipulate, it gives me control.'

'And what about the Elorans who die?'

'Unfortunate causalities. They probably would have died soon anyways given the current state of Iyeeka,' Syvvak said. Varth's knuckles whitened around his cup. 'Varthrune, Iyeeka is like a lump of clay at the moment, it can be moulded into anything, but it needs hands to shape it. If we are not those hands then others will use their hands instead. You don't really want Eloran to go back to the way it was before, do you?'

'I have only known a time with food and water shortages, but the councils have conducted their business in the same way they have always done.'

'And they treated you unfairly, did they not?'

'Yes,' Varth said. 'But…'

'But nothing, we cannot allow Eloran to go back to its old ways. I thought you understood that,' Syvvak said. 'If the western districts had followed the traditional council methods and shared all of our resources with the rest of Eloran, then my son would not be alive today. Not to mention it was our ancestors and their old ways which led to this mess, they're the ones to blame.'

*Yes, but they're not blowing up districts and purposefully killing Elorans.*

'We will stick to the plan for now, it won't take long for Lebanoi to collapse. Ruick would be horrified if he knew just how extensive my little network is. I even have members in Myrion who can report back, as it happens. I need to speak with them.' Syvvak rose from his seat. 'As for you, Varthrune, I want you to continue trailing Ehi and Zerren and I want you to report back to me.'

'Yes Syvvak.'

'Is there anything else you need to tell me?'

'No.' Varth shook his head.

'I would be most upset if I found out you were keeping something from me. I'm sure that I don't need to remind you what happens to those who disappoint me.'

'No, I know.' Varth could feel the weight of Syvvak's scrutinising stare.

'You should get going,' Syvvak said. 'The rest of the districts will be waking up soon.'

'Yes Syvvak.' Varth stood and hurried to the door.

'Remember what I said, Varthrune,' Syvvak said, following him. 'I'll be expecting your reports.'

'Yes, Syvvak,' Varth said again. He opened the door and as soon as he stepped into the morning light, away from Syvvak, the cold heavy feeling which had pressed so hard on his chest, lifted. Varth headed back towards his tent and when he felt he was far enough away from Nerrox's home, he removed the kaelo from his bag, threw it on the ground and crushed it beneath his boot.

# THIRTY

Zerren had left a note for his family with Tenar but Ehi kept a close eye on him as their vadi sailed towards Myrion. She was glad he had decided to join them but she knew that he was unhappy. With any luck, the Elorans from Lazarack would be arriving in Lebanoi soon and Zerren would stop pacing around. They were waiting for word of their arrival over the kaelo which Ruick had brought with him, and Ehi's group had sent word ahead to the council members of Myrion. Their travel preparations had taken longer than Ehi had hoped but Ruick had managed, with the help of his students, to copy some of the pages from Arkeenell's work. The remaining council members of Lebanoi had been against Ruick's departure, but after many long discussions, they agreed and felt they could cope with the refugees in his absence. Myrion had made much progress replenishing their lakes and Ruick had promised to use a kaelo to keep in contact with Lebanoi. If there were any problems, he would turn around and head back with Ashta right away. A strange mixture of happiness and sadness had consumed Ehi when, one by one, the others had decided to join her. It felt as though they were going on one final adventure together before... she frowned, *before what?*

Another vadi slowly sailed past them and the Elorans and their young children on board called out and waved. Ehi tilted her hood back slightly, smiled and waved back. Once they had passed, Ehi dropped her gaze to the water and thought about the things she had seen whilst she had been caught up in the desperate crowd. She still wasn't sure why she had agreed to step into Hasree's and Seffen's machine, but she knew it was important. *Why do I have memories of these humans and their Earth? Are they the reason I stepped into the Usol Key? What are they to us?* She looked up and searched the sky again; her gaze kept returning to one spot. She wasn't certain, but she thought she could see a tiny dirt coloured smudge, an imperfect blemish against the pale pink skies. She raised up her hand and blocked the smudge from her sight with her thumb.

'Ehi, how are you today?' Ioel asked. Ehi dropped her arm and turned to Ioel as he sat down beside her.

'Good,' she said.

'That's good, you look like you're deep in thought.'

'Yes.' Ehi nodded. 'What...' Ehi frowned. 'What are memories?'

'A difficult question to answer,' Ioel said with a smile. 'Are you trying to remember things about your past?'

Ehi shook her head.

'Then why do you ask about memories?'

'Things… in my head,' Ehi said, pointing to her forehead. 'I don't… understand.'

'Well,' Ioel said. 'Memories are usually events that we experience directly using some or all of our senses, and then our brain remembers them.'

'What are senses?'

'Iyeekans have six senses,' Ioel said. 'Sight, smell, touch, hearing, taste and mind. The first five are easy to test and explain, the sixth sense is recognised through our connection with lif and some Iyeekans' medical abilities.'

'Do we remember everything?'

'No,' Ioel said. 'We don't remember everything; our brain usually picks out the most unusual things, and the events or knowledge that seem most important to us. We don't remember the ordinary day to day things as much as we remember when something extremely good or bad happens.'

'Oh,' Ehi said. She turned to gaze at the water again. *Am I remembering all the good and bad of these humans then?*

'Are your memories confusing?' Ioel asked.

Ehi nodded. 'What are dreams?'

'Dreams are usually figments of our imagination, often mixed with our memories that we have when we sleep. Sometimes we remember them when we wake. The dreams that I and the others have shared are strange and seem more than just dreams. For instance, none of us had met you or knew about you before but we still managed to dream about you and recognise you in the flesh.'

'Why?' Ehi said.

'I don't know why,' Ioel said. 'Some questions are harder to find answers to, and some just don't have answers at all.'

Ehi didn't reply.

'We should be arriving at Myrion's outer districts soon,' Ioel said.

***

'Oh, you lose again!' Roe laughed. Ehi turned towards her voice and saw Roe and Ahrl sat on either side of a circular wooden board.

'I can't believe you keep winning,' Ahrl said. 'Where did you learn to play Obimna?'

'The man who saved me taught me how to play in Kiri whilst you were looking through all the records,' Roe said.

'Oh?' Ahrl raised an eyebrow.

'He was really nice, but I don't think he liked being around so many refugees,' Roe said. Ehi stood and wandered over to them.

'How do you play?' she asked as she looked down at their game. There was a circular board divided into four concentric circles. In each circle there were different amounts of equally spaced black marks and on top of these marks there were little discs.

'The aim of the game is to collect as many discs as possible, the one with the most discs at the end is the winner. They're all identical on one side, on the other side they have either a number or a picture which equates to a number,' Ahrl said. He picked up a disc and turned it over, revealing a yellow number four. 'You have to start from the centre circle, select a disc and turn it over and work your way to the outer circle,' Ahrl said.

'The only way you can move is if you select a disc from either side of your previous disc in the same circle, and it must have the same value or lower. Or if you wish to go forwards to the next circle then you must select the disc that is directly in line with your previous disc and it must have a higher value,' Roe said.

'It's a game which relies on memory and luck,' Zerren said as he walked over to them.

'Why don't you two play?' Ahrl said, gesturing to the board.

'That's hardly fair, I don't think Ehi has ever played before,' Zerren said.

'I'll play,' Ehi said.

'Are you sure? I used to play this all the time with Roarn and he never beat me,' Zerren said. The first hint of a smile crossed Zerren's lips since they had left Lebanoi.

'Yes,' Ehi said.

'I'll help you, Ehi, because there are times when you can intercept your opponent's path. It's a little complicated to begin with but you'll pick up the rules quickly,' Ahrl said.

'I'll mix up the discs and place them,' Roe said. She sat down and worked through the discs before placing them at random on the marked spots.

'Ok, Ehi, turn over a disc from the circle in the middle.' Ehi did, it was a blue three.

'Zerren,' Ahrl said. Zerren selected a disc on the opposite side to Ehi; it was a red six.

'Aha, see Ehi has the advantage with a smaller number,' Roe said.

'Ok, Ehi, you can either select a disc from either side of your disc in the middle circle, but it has to have a value lower or equal to your disc. Or you can go for the disc in the next ring that is directly in front of your disc and the value must be higher,' Ahrl said. Ehi turned over the disc in the next ring and revealed a yellow disc with the picture of an eyeleetansy.

'Oh shoot, that one is twelve,' Roe said. Zerren turned over a disc in the next ring too and revealed a green eight. Ehi studied the board.

'You're going to have to stay in the same ring,' Zerren said. Ehi moved her fingers to the disc to the left of her eyeleetansy disc but paused; somehow she just knew it was wrong. She moved her hand up to the next ring and heard a muted squeak escape from Roe. She hovered over the disc directly in line with her eyeleetansy disc and felt a warm tingling sensation growing in her chest. She turned over the disc.

'I can't believe it, that's an Iyeeka disc, it's thirteen,' Roe said. The disc was blue with a little picture of their planet on it.

'Lucky,' Zerren said. He paused and once again she noticed his eyes dimming as though he were far away, somewhere inside his own thoughts. He blinked, and his eyes brightened again, then he turned over the disc to the left of his green eight and revealed a black four.

'Look,' Myaie said. They turned to where Myaie stood near the front of the vadi, pointing at something in the distance. Ahrl got up and walked over to her and the rest of them followed. Something glistened on the horizon and twinkled like thousands of clusters of stars in the etansy-light; it didn't take long for Ehi to realise what it was.

'Shousukei said that their machines were working and that they were filling their lakes, but I couldn't imagine this,' Ruick said.

'This is great news,' Myaie said.

'It's half the problem solved,' Ruick said. 'We have a real chance now.'

They stood for a while marvelling at the lakes and then one by one they turned away. Ehi returned to her game with Zerren and Ashta continued to steer the vadi down the river towards the Myri Lakes. A little while later they passed through the first lake and continued on to a second, larger lake.

Just before they found a place to stop, Ehi and Zerren's game was down to the last two rings; after their next turns there wouldn't be enough counters left to make up the second ring. Ehi's hand hovered over the five discs at the centre; she stopped when she felt the familiar warm sensation and turned over a disc. It was a four, she moved outwards to the second ring and found a six, she picked up the two discs and the last two discs in the pile were put in to replace them.

'Ah,' Zerren said. 'I need at least four to beat you.' His hand hovered over the five discs at the centre. He was about to pick one but then his eyes went distant again, he frowned, moved to the left and turned over a disc with the value of ten. He moved to the next disc to the left in the inside ring and flipped over a three. He bit his lip, moved his hand once more to the left and then snatched it back and frowned. Ehi gazed at him and watched as he struggled with his decision; would he go left in the same ring and try to win another disc, or did he go up to the second ring and end the game? Eventually he sighed and moved his hand up to the second ring and turned over the disc, it was an eight and he picked up three discs, ending the game. Out of curiosity Ehi flipped over the other disc Zerren could have chosen and found a five; if he had chosen it, he would have lost. 'That was a good game,' Zerren said. 'I've never lost or had a draw before.' He looked puzzled.

'Never?' Roe said.

'Ok, maybe when I was little, but not since I left school.'

'How many times have you played?' Roe asked.

'Hundreds, Roarn and I used to play all the time,' Zerren said as he helped Roe fold the board and scoop the discs into a bag. Ehi scrutinised his face; it seemed odd that with a game reliant on so much luck that Zerren should win so many times, apparently undefeated. She had watched his moves too; he hadn't messed up once, but then again neither had she. Ehi had been relying on the tingly warm feelings but Zerren, every move he had made he had seemed to retreat privately into his own little world.

'Where do you go?' Ehi said.

'Where do I go? What do you mean?'

'Your eyes,' Ehi said. 'It's like you go somewhere inside.' She pointed at her head. She saw the first signs of shock on Zerren's face and then he frowned and looked away from her.

'It's nothing, Ehi,' Zerren said. 'I was just lucky.' He hurried across the deck and busied himself by putting on his rucksack and helping the others. Ehi stood up and stretched her legs, then collected her rucksack and disembarked with the group. There were dozens of vadis and hundreds of Elorans around, hauling up fishing nets or collecting water. Zerren avoided her, heading to the front of the group with Ruick and Ashta whilst she walked with Roe behind Myaie and Ahrl. Ahrl paused and glanced uneasily at their surroundings.

'What's wrong?' Myaie asked.

'Nothing,' Ahrl said as he hefted his rucksack and pressed forwards. Ehi pulled her hood lower over her eyes.

The scenes at Myrion and the surrounding districts were very different from the scenes they had faced at Lebanoi. The Elorans here smiled more and seemed happier; they were still thin but there was a purpose in their stride and a glow to their eyes. Their small group entered Myrion unhindered and Ruick stopped to ask a young Eloran where they would find Shousukei and Arvita.

'They're at the northern school,' the young Eloran said and pointed. 'Just continue that way for a few minutes, you can't miss it.'

'Thank you,' Ruick said. They continued onwards and Ehi noticed the many hopeful faces carrying wooden buckets of water back to their homes and land.

They found the school and were ushered inside. Ehi took great interest in the classrooms as they passed; each room was packed with students of various ages, even adults, and there were lessons taking place that were unfamiliar to her. They stopped before a door; Ruick knocked and then they entered the room beyond.

Seated around a curved wooden table were fifteen Elorans. Two of these Elorans, a woman and a man, smiled and stood.

'Ruick, Ashta,' the man said. His hair was dark and long with a deep blue sheen to it. He strode over to them followed by the woman.

'Shousukei, Arvita,' Ruick said embracing the man and woman in turn. 'I'm sorry to disturb your meeting.'

'Not at all, we have been expecting you,' Shousukei said.

'You said over the kaelo that you had some interesting new information for us?' Arvita said.

'Yes, so interesting that it couldn't be shared over the kaelo,' Shousukei said, laughing. 'We have been deeply curious.'

'It's a long story,' Ruick said. 'We have a book with handwritten notes from a Jheian known as Arkeenell…'

'Arkeenell?' another woman said. She sat at the table with her hands clasped in front of her and her long chestnut hair hung down to her waist.

'Do you recognise the name, Dilaria?' Shousukei asked.

'Yes, I've heard stories about an Arkeenell,' Dilaria said with a frown. 'My grandmother said he was a deranged individual who claimed he could time travel. But it was just an old story, a folk tale.' Ehi listened intently.

'I don't know about that,' Ruick said. 'Though the notes we found are extraordinary for their age.'

'Why is that?' Shousukei asked. Ruick unshouldered his rucksack and then pulled out a folder containing a dozen or so clean, freshly-written pages.

'We left the book behind in Lebanoi for our students and teachers to study, but I had some students help me copy some of the pages,' Ruick said. He handed the pages to Shousukei and Arvita. Shousukei scanned the pages and it wasn't long before his eyes widened and his mouth fell open.

'This, this is the plan for our desalination machines.' He glanced up at Ruick briefly.

'Yes,' Ruick said.

'This is incredible, the maths is all here, the measurements, and the supplies we used… what is this? What are atoms?'

'I believe Arkeenell is talking about the transition from our seawater to freshwater,' Ruick said.

'It took us years to get fresh clean water; we tried so many different things and many became ill from drinking our attempts, yet here it all is,' Shousukei pointed at the page, 'exactly as it needs to be.'

'You said that these pages were copied, when were the original pages written?' Arvita asked.

'These pages are copied from a book which is seven hundred years old,' Ruick said.

'That can't be,' Shousukei said.

'That would make sense,' Dilaria said. 'My grandmother said that Arkeenell lived hundreds of years ago.'

'What else did your grandmother say?' Arvita asked.

'There were all sorts of stories; I think she said that he was originally from Eloran and claimed that one of her relatives had lived in the same district where this Arkeenell grew up.'

'Then how did he end up in Jheia?' Ahrl asked.

'My grandmother told me that he just disappeared one day, vanished into thin air and appeared in Jheia,' Dilaria said.

'He must have crossed the great bridge,' Shousukei said.

'No, the story is that he literally vanished one day and appeared in Jheia on the same day,' Dilaria said. 'It's impossible, I know. I used to laugh at my grandmother's tales.'

'Yes, it is impossible. Well, it's just a story from the past, and stories are often changed with every retelling,' Shousukei said.

'Yes, you may be right,' Dilaria said.

'So then, apart from these notes and our water situation, what brings you all here to Myrion?' asked Shousukei.

'We plan to stay for a couple of days,' Ruick said. 'But after that some of our party will continue onto Bosna.'

'Bosna?' Shousukei said.

'Yes, it's where this Arkeenell lived in his later years and we hope to find more work that he may have left behind,' Ruick said.

'I see.'

'What is the situation in Narakae?'

'The Jheian's are growing anxious. No one is sure how long the great bridge will last and their supplies are running dangerously low. They have two choices really, they either evacuate Jheia and move over to northern Eloran, or they build their own desalination machines and refill their lakes as we have done.'

'Do they have the resources for that?' Ruick asked.

'The Jheians seem to think so. It's been a heavily debated over there, many don't want to leave their homes, but I honestly believe it would be easier and safer for the Jheians to move over to Eloran.'

'We're planning to travel to Narakae. I want to speak with their council members and check on their plans.'

'That is a good idea.'

'I'm sure you've already heard the news about the N.I.L.'

'Oh yes. We've been paying close attention to all the kaelo broadcasts from various districts. We think they're using kaelo to communicate in code. There's a kaelo station that has puzzled us.'

'Why's that?'

'Well, whoever is using it doesn't speak, they just send clicking noises but someone else is responding with more clicking noises; we think it's a code of some sort and that has made us suspicious,' Shousukei said.

'The N.I.L.?' Ruick asked.

'It's possible, more than possible. The problem with kaelo is that as long as you can pick up the station then you can hear every noise and spoken word that station broadcasts. I thought that someone was using this clicking code so that others wouldn't understand it.'

'Well, only those who had something to hide would do such a thing; this must be the N.I.L.' Ruick shook his head. He caught Ashta's gaze and smiled sadly.

'How long do you think it will be before we'll receive water in Lebanoi? Our resources were already stretched thin before the refugees arrived, now there is desperation,' Ashta said.

'We've been constructing tubes which will be able to pump the new freshwater back to Lebanoi and we've been building water storage units and bigger vadis to carry the water down the rivers and distribute it along the way, but it's a long process with such limited resources,' Shousukei said. 'I will send yebons with water right away, but our food supplies are limited for now; it takes time for crops to grow. The more volunteers we have the better, but if the Jheians do decide to evacuate, then there will be little land here for other refugees.'

'We understand and thank you. I'll arrange for volunteers and see what we can arrange in Lebanoi to bring them here,' Ruick said.

'I just wish we could do more,' Shousukei said.

'We've been building tubes in Lebanoi and placing them in the ground, but I'm worried about the tremors; we've built them to be as flexible as possible and with extendable give, but a major tremor could still break them.'

'Yes, we've been doing the same. We'll just have to make repairs if that should happen.'

'I'm also worried that Syvvak will come here and attempt to destroy all of your efforts. He is making his move, I just don't know if he'll stop before reaching Myrion.'

'It's hard for me to control my rage when I think of him,' said Shousukei. 'The explosives he plants inside the districts aren't easy to spot. If he attacked directly then it would be a matter of protecting against their attack, we could use lif as shields. The explosives are indirect but deadly and their attacks are sporadic. They seem to choose districts at random, but once they've attacked they scatter and regroup at a later stage. It's virtually impossible to predict where they're hiding or where they will strike next. At best we can check all yebons but it's impossible to know who belongs to the N.I.L. and who doesn't.'

'I know, and I'm sure he has members hiding inside Lebanoi and probably inside Myrion too,' said Ruick. 'We are going to have to be extra vigilant and randomly question newcomers.'

'That's hardly right or fair, the majority are innocent,' Shousukei said.

'I know, but what other choice do we have?' Ruick said. Shousukei sighed.

'I have Elorans on the lookout for Syvvak and any signs of the N.I.L. If they come, they will not find a warm welcome here.'

'I'm glad to hear it,' Ruick said. Shousukei nodded and forced a small smile.

'Well, we can discuss this later, I'm sure you would all like to rest and eat. You're invited to use our home for as long as you like. Arvita, would you mind showing them the way?' Shousukei said.

'Not at all,' Arvita said.

'Ruick, Myaie and Ioel, you may stay and join our meeting if you like,' Shousukei said.

'I will stay,' Ruick said.

'Me too,' Myaie said.

'I will politely decline,' Ioel said. 'My old bones are weary and could do with a rest.'

'Of course,' Shousukei said, inclining his head.

'Follow me,' Arvita said, smiling at the rest of the group. She led the way back out of the school and headed towards the western part of Myrion. Roe hurried ahead and fell into step beside her.

'I'm Roe,' she said.

'Nice to meet you, Roe.'

'I've been dying to ask, how do you desalinate the sea water?'

'Ah well, the idea is quite simple actually, but it took many trial and error approaches to get it right on an industrial scale,' Arvita said. 'We basically make a hollow cylindrical shape with a closed bottom, about five feet in diameter and ten feet long. Then we have another, slightly smaller cylindrical shape with a curved closed bottom, like the bottom of a bowl. We drill lots of small holes about half way up this smaller cylinder. Then we partially fill the first cylinder with seawater and we heat up the second cylinder and place it inside the first cylinder. The water rushes into this second cylinder through the holes, but because the entire thing is hot, the water turns into steam. The steam rises, and we collect it and cool it, and it condenses into a less toxic form of the original seawater. That's the basic method but we do have to add certain things to the water at various stages. We have to repeat this process over and over until we get freshwater that we can actually drink and use.'

'What are these cylinders made of?'

'Carbon fibre and metal,' Arvita said. 'The same carbon fibre that is used to make the large vadis which can traverse our oceans.'

'Like the ones that were made when my ancestors escaped from the volcanoes in Faroi?' Roe said.

'Exactly,' Arvita said. They came to a modest single-storey dwelling which had little trees and bushes decorating its front. Arvita opened a wooden gate and ushered them inside her home. 'I will show you to the guest rooms; we have three rooms, so you will have to decide who you want to share with,' Arvita said. Ehi wrapped an arm around Zerren's and Arvita led the way up a small flight of stairs. 'The bathroom is downstairs next to the kitchen; you will be pleased to know that we now have a working shower and a tub.'

'Oh, I haven't had a long bath in forever, I can't wait,' Ashta said as she stroked her auburn hair. 'The vadi only had a bucket.'

'Here are the rooms,' Arvita said, stopping in a small hallway where three doors stood open.

'Ioel, you should have a room of your own, the rest of us can just split by gender,' Ashta said. Ehi reluctantly let go of Zerren's arm.

'That's very kind of you and, in that case, I will take the smallest room,' Ioel said.

'Alright,' Ashta said, taking the largest room. 'Roe, Ehi, this way.' Ehi smiled at Zerren, followed Ashta and shut the door behind them. They heard Zerren and Ahrl entering the other room across the hall. Ehi dumped her rucksack and rubbed her shoulders.

'It must be so hot and stuffy under that hood, Ehi,' Ashta said. 'You should be safe to take it off now for a bit.' Ehi lowered her hood just as the door reopened behind her.

'I just… Mother Iyeeka,' Arvita said. Ehi twisted to face her.

'Oh no,' Ashta said. Arvita leant around the partially open door with her mouth gaping like a fish and the colour draining rapidly from her face. 'It's ok, we can explain, Ehi is…' Ashta said.

'It's you,' Arvita said. 'It's really you.'

# THIRTY-ONE

A young woman and man stood before her with skin tones similar to Roe's and clothing wrapped around their bodies and heads. They held a baby in their arms and she watched as this baby grew into a young boy before her eyes. Two more brothers were born into the family, but it was the first child who held Ehi's attention. There was something about him, something she inherently recognised as pure and good which pulled at her being. She gazed at the usol at the little boy's chest and all she could see was the same golden light which Zerren had, and that the others had too, to varying degrees, emanating outwards from his core. She watched the boy grow into a man as crowds began to gather around him and everywhere he went people followed him and listened as he spoke. She felt a warm tingling sensation, an invisible power rippling from this man throughout the crowds. Hovering in the air, a golden fog grew and shimmered as though it contained scattered fragment of light. It thrived within these crowds, yet on the edges of these gatherings she saw individuals with spheres as dark as bottomless wells. There was something cold about them, something that chilled Ehi as though her nerves had been frozen and severed. They watched and waited, their eyes gleaming whilst small black clouds grew above them. *This is not why I'm here, this is not what I'm looking for.*

A flood of images with hundreds of faces began to flash before her eyes. All of them had usols glowing like their own internal etansy and whatever they did and wherever they went they seemed to draw people of all creeds and backgrounds towards them. There was no violence with these crowds, no anger or hatred, no fighting or bloody fields like Ehi had witnessed before. There was an understanding, an acceptance and happiness; it was as though these few extraordinary individuals drew out all the good humanity had to offer.

The scene around her changed, blurring into a mass of colour before refocussing again on another place, another time. A hairy creature stood on two feet like the humans she had seen before, but not. *What?* Before she could even think the rest of the question she had the answer. This creature was a human, but a much earlier form, similar to, but much more primitive than the Jheians who had lived in the south thousands of years ago, who had moved on their hands and feet before finally just moving onto their feet. There was another hairy creature and Ehi could see white usols at the centre of both creatures' torsos. They had no other colours, not even the tiny black core. The first creature shrieked at the second and beat its hands against its chest. The second creature growled and then they lunged at each other and fell to the floor in a clash of limbs and angry cries. It was over in seconds, but it had felt much longer. The first creature held the limp body of the second creature in its lap. It threw back its head and screamed at the sky and in that moment a tiny black core appeared, and a deep green colour bloomed outwards into its usol. A pale blue appeared next, followed by a dark blue, grey and a thin band of deep red. *What? What did I just witness?* And then she knew – she had just seen the birth of the first human usol, no, they called them souls. The creature and the scene slowly began to drift away from her. *No, not yet, I have more questions.* She reached out, but the scene faded, Earth and its humans slipped from her grasp and the visions left her dreams.

***

A few days later their group stood beside the laburnem track on the eastern side of Myrion. Two streamlined, silver laburnem carriages with curved glass windows sat on the single metal track, waiting to depart. Shousukei and Arvita had agreed to travel with them as far as Narakae as they had promised supplies to the northern Jheian district. After they reached Narakae, Shousukei, Arvita, Ruick and Ashta would head back to Eloran while the others travelled to Bosna. The carriages were several feet wide and about twenty feet long with glass doors which slid to the side. Ehi studied the laburnem; there were similar looking carriages in her mind from what she had seen of Earth. Humans called them trains and they had two tracks instead of one. She realised that the laburnem were superior to trains, yet other things she had seen about Earth and humanity seemed much more advanced. She watched as two Iyeekans carried a wooden box filled with water sacks onto the second carriage and returned to collect another box. Ehi walked up to the head of the laburnem where Ahrl stood with his hand shielding his eyes as he gazed out towards the horizon.

'I was trying to catch a glimpse of the bridge where we are so high here, but you can't, it's still quite far,' Ahrl said as Ehi stopped beside him.

'How far?' Ehi said.

'Over a hundred miles away,' Ahrl said. 'I've travelled across it several times; eventually the bridge will crash into the ocean as the continents drift apart, unless we somehow manage to save it. It's the sort of thing my father should be working on instead of hiding in Loenya, though if he were here he would probably tell me to work out a solution.'

'Ahrl, Ehi, we're ready to go,' Myaie said. They turned to see the rest of the group boarding the first carriage just a few feet behind them. There were a lot of Elorans from Myrion watching the laburnem and helping to load the supplies. Ahrl strode on ahead of her and Ehi turned her gaze upwards at the sky. She found the brown smudge in the sky; it was more like a spot now and it was growing, she was sure of it.

'Ehi?' Zerren said. She reluctantly tore her gaze away from the spot and looked at him. He waited by the laburnem's open door and watched her; although he had seemed in better spirits recently after hearing that the Lazarack district had finally arrived safely in Lebanoi, today his skin seemed to lack its usual glow. She noted the tension in his shoulders, neck and jaw and the wide-eyed look he tried so hard to control. She walked over to him, put her hand into his and watched as the tension ebbed away slightly. She pulled him gently onto the laburnem.

Arvita and Shousukei stood at the front by a control panel. The back of this carriage and the second carriage had been filled with boxes of food and water. A few seats bolted to the floor had been left free in the front of the first carriage for their group of eleven and four more Elorans. The rest of the supplies had been packed into the back of the carriage and any available space.

'Alright, find a seat,' Shousukei said. Ehi sat down on the left side next to the window and Zerren sat next to her whilst the others took their seats. Shousukei began to push buttons and flick switches; the door slid shut and a whirring sound rippled through the carriage. The sound grew louder and the laburnem groaned and gradually began to pull forwards. Ehi pressed her face up against the glass as she watched the land moving behind them as the laburnem sped up. The Kiri Mountains stood tall over to the north and seemed to drift by slowly like clouds. Within a few minutes they had left the district far behind.

It seemed like hardly any time had passed before the track began to descend and the laburnem disappeared into a tunnel.

'We should see the bridge any minute now,' Zerren said. Square lights lit up the dark tunnel and then a shock of bright light grew in front of them; in the next moment the laburnem had passed through the tunnel and Ehi's eyes adjusted to the outside.

She saw a huge cage-like structure around her, made from wound metal cables and interlocking metal tubes. She gazed out and back to see the steep cliffs of the Eloran eastern coast diving straight down into the ocean below.

'Wow, it's amazing,' Roe said as she peered up at the bridge.

'The great bridge was built by our ancestors one thousand years ago,' Ioel said. 'It was designed so that no part of it stands in the ocean. It was also designed to extend with the continental drift and coastal erosion, and withstand the tremors. It's ten miles long and it took decades of cooperation between all the thousands of districts in Eloran and Jheia to complete it.'

'Yes, but it is getting to the point now where soon it will be unsafe to use unless we add our own extensions,' Shousukei said. 'The problem is the bridge is made from interlinking metal tubes and rods which are housed inside of each other, and there are the metal wound cables which loop back into the tunnels. As you know, our resources are limited and there are only just over one hundred districts left. We don't have the metal or the engineers and builders to complete such a project.'

Ehi felt Zerren shift beside her and she turned to face him. He sat hunched in his seat with his head in his hands and his gaze fixed on the floor.

'The erosion is getting worse and we know that something bad is happening to our oceans without needing to test them,' Shousukei said.

'Why's that?' Roe asked.

'We have found all manner of sea beasts and creatures washing up dead on the shores. If they can't survive in the ocean, the place that has been their home for all these years, then something must be wrong,'

'Our waste disposal,' Ruick said.

'Unfortunately so,' Shousukei said. 'When we get freshwater back throughout the land and manage our waste disposal better, then we should see the populations grow again and then, who knows, maybe we will go on to build great things like our ancestors once again, only this time we will do it the right way.'

'We're over halfway across,' Arvita said. 'I haven't seen any foot passengers yet.'

'No, they're probably waiting for this laburnem,' Shousukei said. A loud boom echoed behind them, quickly followed by another and a deafening cracking sound. The laburnem jolted forwards violently and Ehi felt a whump hit her in the chest, almost launching her onto the floor. The bridge creaked and trembled.

'What was that?' Zerren said. Ehi straightened up and looked back towards Eloran and the tunnel they had left only a few minutes ago. A column of smoke and dust rose up behind them like a mighty fist punching through the air. Ehi watched in horror as the bridge began to list to the side, twisting unnaturally as it ripped away from the land.

'The bridge, it's falling, it's falling!' one of the Elorans cried.

'An explosion,' Ahrl said with a furrowed brow. The bridge let out a grating metallic sound, and a deep, low moan reverberated through the air. The laburnem trembled and then the bridge began to tilt to the left behind them, twisting and curving before crashing onto the shore and into the sea, disappearing beneath the waves. Shousukei rushed back to the front of the train and began frantically pushing buttons.

'Faster!' Ehi said.

'I'm trying,' Shousukei said. Ehi looked back at the rapidly disappearing bridge as it buckled and twisted like a giant serpent; it was gaining on them. She leapt to her feet and Zerren was up beside her without a word. The laburnem groaned painfully and began to slow.

'Shousukei!' Zerren said.

'We're losing speed,' he replied.

'The carriages,' Arvita said. 'They're not built for steep ascents.'

'We're going to die,' Roe wailed, as the metal cables cracked and snapped above them. Ehi grabbed Zerren and pulled him to the door.

'Open door,' Ehi said.

'Are you nuts?'

'Open!' Ehi shouted.

'Shousukei, open the door,' Zerren said.

'What?'

'Just do it,' Zerren said. Shousukei hit a button and the door slid open with a woosh.

'Hold me,' Ehi said, locking her left hand around Zerren's wrist as she placed her feet by the edge of the door and leant out of the carriage. She felt Zerren brace himself as he held onto her arm. Ehi could see the second carriage straining and pulling against the first, slowing their acceleration as the bridge twisted and plunged down behind it. Ehi took a deep breath, closed her eyes as the sea breeze whipped about her face, she summoned the lif from the gauntlet on her right arm. She felt the gauntlet grow hot and she opened her eyes to see a small ball of liquid lif hovering before her. She sent the lif between the two carriages with a quick thought and then solidified it and severed the link between the first and second carriage. The first carriage leapt forwards violently and Ehi felt her body crash against the side of the laburnem. She gritted her teeth and sent a thought out to the lif and called it back to her gauntlet.

'Ehi!' Zerren said as he held tightly to the door frame and hauled her back inside the carriage. She let her aching body sink into Zerren's and for a moment she clung to him tightly and breathed in his soothing scent.

'We're gaining speed again, what did she do?' Shousukei said, as a grin stretched across his face.

'The only thing she could,' Ioel said as he gazed off towards the back of the carriage. The grin disappeared from Shousukei's face and Ehi watched as the second carriage slid down the sharp twisted slope of the bridge and disappeared into the water below. Shousukei cursed and slammed a fist against the control panel.

'We're not out of this yet,' Ioel said as he turned his gaze back to the front of the laburnem. The bridge groaned and creaked like a huge wounded beast as their carriage picked up along the track. Cables snapped and twisted around them as the western Jheia cliffs grew before them.

'Are we going to make it?' Arvita asked, pressing her fist against her mouth as she gazed out the front window.

'I don't know,' Shousukei said. Ehi stared straight ahead at where the bridge and track disappeared into the tunnel before them. Her gaze travelled upwards to the metal cables and tubes as they strained and pulled at the cliff, tearing out chunks of rock.

'Need everyone,' Ehi said, as she stepped forwards.

'You heard her,' Ioel said. Ehi became aware of their minds and felt them hovering around the edges of her consciousness; one by one she connected with them. The faint burning smell stung the back of her nose and she felt the ripple of their combined energy like a blast of hot air against her face. Ehi directed the separate lif sources together and sent them out the window and over to the cables and tubes by the tunnel. She wrapped the lif around them and let it solidify as she tried to fortify their strained hold. The laburnem rattled over the track as the bridge continued to twist and fall behind them. The bridge swayed and Ehi gritted her teeth. She could feel the lif slipping from their mental grasp.

'The track!' Roe said. Ehi saw that the track bending and breaking apart just at the entrance to the tunnel. Ehi gritted her teeth; she split the lif, letting half of it drop to the tracks and solidify. The bridge wailed loudly.

'It's not going to hold,' Shousukei said. Ehi could see that the lif was stretching and cracking under the strain of the bridge.

'Ehi,' Zerren said. She suddenly felt another mind jump into her awareness, a mind she recognised. A small amount of lif shot past her, bursting through the front windscreen and shattering the glass. She didn't question it; she tugged on this new mind and used the extra lif, dropping it to the tracks just moments before the laburnem wobbled violently over the new track and into the tunnel.

She felt the mind connections around her drop and she tried to call the lif back but there was nothing to call back; the lif had been spent and it had already disintegrated. Shousukei hurriedly pressed buttons and flicked switches and the laburnem began to slow down to a much calmer pace as it rose out of the tunnel.

'Is everyone ok?' Myaie asked.

'I think so,' Ashta said. There was a chorus of grunts and affirmations. Ehi cast her gaze over the group; apart from the odd bump and bruise no one seemed to be severely hurt. She caught their worried smiles and nods in her direction. She was exhausted. She turned to Zerren and saw the colour draining from his face and his hands curling into fists as he stared towards the back of the laburnem; she followed his gaze. Standing at the back was a face she recognised. He had cut his hair and wore a scarf around the lower part of his face, but there was no mistaking him. It was Varth.

# THIRTY-TWO

Ehi watched as Zerren launched himself at Varth, knocking him to the floor and grabbing him by the front of his shirt.

'What are you doing here? Were you responsible for that explosion? Did you lead the N.I.L. to us? Well? Answer me!' Zerren said.

'Don't hurt him,' Roe said. 'He's the man who saved me.'

'Him?' Zerren said, shaking his head in disbelief.

'Yes.'

'You lying, manipulative, little sheeka; we should have left you out in the south to rot.'

'Zerren, stop,' Shousukei said.

'No, this is the man who joined the N.I.L., threatened to cut off my brother's head and tried to kidnap Ehi.'

'Yes, well, that was a stupid decision on my part,' Varth said.

'A stupid decision?'

'Ok, a terrible decision and I'm sorry. If I could take it back, I would.'

'You…' Zerren punched him. There was a crack, and Varth moaned.

'Ok, I might have deserved that,' Varth said.

'Alright, that's enough,' Ahrl said. He gripped Zerren under his arms and pulled him off Varth.

'Let me go, I'm not done with him yet. If Ehi hadn't have stopped you we would have been left for dead.'

'OK. I think you're done,' Ahrl said.

'He's with the N.I.L. You need to restrain him, not me, and following us incognito, he can only be reporting back to them,' Zerren said. Ehi felt the tingling sensation of several minds trying to reach for their lif, but there wasn't any.

'Listen, I'm not with the N.I.L., not anymore,' Varth said, getting to his feet and wiping the blood from his nose with the back of his hand.

'How did you get on here?' Ruick said.

'It was surprisingly easy actually,' Varth said. 'I posed as a volunteer and helped load these boxes and crates onto the laburnem last night. I kept my distance from anyone who might recognise me and made a spot for myself right at the back there behind the supplies.' Varth pointed towards the back of the laburnem. 'No one seemed to notice or question my presence.'

'I guess I'll have to have words with certain Elorans when I get back,' Shousukei said, shaking his head.

'Why are you here?' asked Ruick.

'A number of reasons, but mainly because of her,' Varth said, pointing at Ehi.

'What do you want with Ehi?' asked Zerren.

'I don't want anything from Ehi,' Varth said. 'I've been dreaming about her. I've dreamt about her every night since I started following you when you left the Arrukai district.'

'You've dreamt about Ehi?' Ruick said. 'Would you mind describing your dreams?'

'From what Roe's told me they're the same dreams you've all had. There's a storm, like nothing I've ever seen before. The wind is really loud, it howls in your ears and rips up the land. You can't see anything at first but then there's a break in the clouds of dirt and Ehi is standing there. Her voice sounds in your mind and she says, "You must find me."'

'He's lying,' Zerren said. 'He's just trying to save his own skin; he probably got all of that from Roe.'

'It's true that Roe told me about your dreams but I'm not lying,' Varth said. 'Ehi has been in my dreams for weeks now and I resisted coming to you. I knew I wouldn't be welcomed.'

'Why did you leave the N.I.L.?' asked Shousukei.

'Syvvak, he's gone crazy,' Varth said. 'I joined the N.I.L. because Syvvak promised he would make Eloran a better place, he promised he would create a fairer Iyeeka. I didn't know that he planned to destroy districts. When he attacked Skidaroi I was with Zerren, Roarn and Ehi and the kaelo in my yebon was broken. I only found out about the attack and the rest of Syvvak's plans when I got back to Kubus.'

'Is that true?' Ruick said, glancing at Zerren,

'Yes, but he could have known about it before he came back to Lazarack, and he could have stopped at any district on the way to Kubus and borrowed a kaelo,' Zerren said.

'I didn't know before I travelled to Lazarack, and no, I didn't stop to borrow a kaelo, I was in too much of a rush to get back to Kubus. Syvvak had given me a two week time frame and I had been away for over a month.'

'Why were you in Lazarack?' asked Ashta.

'I was supposed to recruit the brothers to the N.I.L. Syvvak wanted to recruit strong lif users. Only, I didn't know that Lucoe was dead and I didn't know why he wanted them but I do now; he wants to have strong lif users so that when he takes over northern Eloran the Elorans won't be able to oppose him.'

'As if anyone would use their lif to do that,' Ashta said.

'He's already recruited many strong lif users.'

'Damn, we need to get back to Eloran,' Shousukei said.

'The only way back now is by vadi,' said Myaie.

'Vadi? We can't go by vadi. It's far too dangerous.'

'I hate to remind you, but the bridge is gone.'

'I know. I know I said the beasts in the sea seem to be dying but there are still beasts lurking beneath those waves. And what about the Jheians? Mother Iyeeka, I hope Narakae have lots of big vadis,' Shousukei said, as he paced up and down.

'It's unlikely,' Ahrl said. 'They haven't built many big vadis for centuries since most Jheian's used the great bridge.'

'You can't seriously believe him?' Zerren said. 'He's a perpetual liar and he's probably still with the N.I.L. Don't you think it's a little suspicious that the bridge just happened to blow up when we were on it?'

'I didn't know about that,' Varth said. 'I left the N.I.L. three weeks ago, just before Syvvak attacked Jaas. Syvvak ordered me to follow you to Myrion and report back, but I didn't report back. I don't know anything else about Syvvak's plans and I was on the train too, don't forget. I would have also been killed.'

'You seem woefully uniformed, being a former member of the N.I.L. and having direct contact with Syvvak,' Ahrl said.

'Syvvak doesn't tell anyone any more than what he feels is necessary,' Varth said.

'He's right,' Ruick said. 'Syvvak has always been like that. He likes to withhold information and watch others become agitated with their confusion, particularly when it makes him feel powerful.'

'Zerren, if I let you go will you promise to remain calm?' asked Ahrl.

'Only if that sheeka over there doesn't do anything stupid,' Zerren said. Ahrl released him.

'I am sorry, Zerren, genuinely so,' Varth said. 'I should have listened to you and Roarn but I was too caught up in my grief and the past; it clouded my vision and thoughts. I really believed that Syvvak would help to heal Eloran and Iyeeka. I didn't see his flaws or consider he might resort to this violence.'

'You're lucky Roarn isn't here,' Zerren said and turned his back on him.

'What are we going to do about him?' Myaie asked, gesturing to Varth.

'There's nothing much we can do right now. He's as trapped as we are,' Ruick said.

'Roe, I'm sorry,' Varth said. Ehi glanced at Roe and saw that tears were streaming down her cheeks as she stared at Varth. Roe turned her back on him and flung herself in a seat at the front of the laburnem.

'Keep an eye on him,' Ahrl said to Ruick.

'Of course,' Ruick said. Ahrl headed over to Roe.

Ehi caught Varth's gaze but he quickly lowered his eyes to the floor. The adrenaline which had been charging through her body disappeared and she felt the energy draining out through the soles of her feet. She turned to Zerren and tugged on his arm. They sat down and she leant heavily on Zerren's shoulder. Manipulating the lif had drained her and she fought hard to keep her eye open. The air felt cold around her despite the searing heat outside; it bit into her skin and itched at her nerves. She curled closer to Zerren and felt the heat rising from his chest. The laburnem swayed gently on the track and Ehi could hear Zerren's steady soft breaths. Her eyes closed and she felt a warm, tingling sensation, a peaceful feeling, as sleep tugged at her mind. She opened her eyes for a second and caught the glimpse of a golden glow shining out from Zerren's body before sleep finally claimed her.

# THIRTY-THREE

'Ehi, wake up,' Zerren said as he shook her gently. Ehi frowned but her eyes opened and she sat up, yawned and stretched. 'Here, you should probably put on your cloak,' Zerren said, offering it to her. She took it from him, slipped into the garment and pulled the hood over her head.

'Alright, we're here,' Shousukei said. The laburnem drew to a halt on the outskirts of Jheia's largest district, Narakae. The group disembarked and were met by a crowd of eager faces, some of whom stood on their tiptoes to get a better view. Zerren resisted the urge to glare at Varth; if it hadn't been for Lucoe's voice begging him to do nothing in his head earlier, he would have thrown him off the laburnem hours ago. He felt Ehi's warm, small hand slip into his and a sudden sense of calm smothered his anger a little. Shousukei and Arvita embraced a group of council members dressed in dusty white robes.

'Council Member Carvosc of Narakae, it's good to see you,' Shousukei said, as he embraced an elderly male Jheian.

'It's a relief to see you too,' Carvosc said.

'I'm afraid we bring terrible news,' Shousukei said. The smile dropped from Carvosc's face and the lines deepened in his forehead.

'Yes, we've heard,' Carvosc said. 'Myrion contacted us over the kaelo, the great bridge… we thought you might have perished.'

'Yes, the great bridge has been destroyed,' Shousukei said. 'We barely made it over with our lives and we lost our second carriage.'

Gasps erupted from the crowds.

'It's true,' Ahrl said. 'There were two explosions on the Eloran side. We think the N.I.L. are responsible.' Murmurings of discontent ran through the crowd.

'This is outrageous,' Carvosc said. 'I can't believe they would do such a thing. Do they wish for our deaths?'

'I don't think Syvvak cares if we die,' Ahrl said.

'Do you have vadis capable of crossing the ocean?' Shousukei asked.

'No, not here in Narakae,' Carvosc said.

'Are there any in Jheia at all?'

Carvosc hesitated.

'There are,' a female Jheian said. She stepped forwards and Carvosc scowled.

'Fera,' Carvosc said, 'we have already discussed this. Those vadis are out of reach; there's no point in reclaiming them if it means our deaths in the process.'

'Tye knows how to get to them,' Fera said.

'Tye is just a boy.'

'Where are these vadis?' Shousukei asked.

'They're by the coast, just past the abandoned Jalshee district,' Fera said. 'I don't know if they're still there. The last time Tye checked he said they were in pretty bad shape.'

'He went back?' Carvosc said.

'He went to collect stones and shells from the beach, you know how he is,' Fera said.

'And what about the bellua and bokhanya?' Carvosc said. 'Do I need to remind you how many Jheians lost their lives to them last year trying to get to those vadis?'

'He mentioned bellua but there were no bokhanya,' Fera said. Zerren's blood turned cold as a memory tore through his mind, leaving a trail of destructive emotions in its wake. He remembered Lucoe's bloody and battered body lying on the ground as he struggled to breathe. He heard his own, younger voice, panicked and crying out Lucoe's name. Zerren pushed the memories away and dug his fingernails into his palm.

'How many vadis are there?' Shousukei asked.

'Three large vadis but they need repairing, Tye saw holes the last time he checked,' Fera said.

'They're old,' Carvosc said. 'They could be over a thousand years old; no one has travelled by vadi since the great bridge was built, it was always too dangerous with the sea creatures. Some are massive, several times larger than the biggest vadis.'

'We need to contact Myrion right away; they have vadis, they can send them across,' Shousukei said.

'Certainly, would you like to use one of our kaelos?' Carvosc asked.

'If you wouldn't mind,' said Shousukei. A Jheian stepped forward and handed him a kaelo.

'Council members of Myrion, this is Shousukei, is anyone there?' Shousukei said. He tapped his foot on the ground but stopped when the kaelo crackled and beeped in his hand.

'Shousukei,' Dilaria's voice crackled through his kaelo.

'Dilaria!'

'So happy that you're ok, we've been trying to contact you.'

'It was a little difficult to contact you earlier,' Shousukei said as his gaze darted to Varth.

'We have good news; we have caught the members of the N.I.L. responsible for destroying the bridge,' Dilaria said.

'That is good news. Did you get Syvvak?'

'No, I'm afraid not.'

'Keep them locked up until I get back and put extra Elorans out on guard. Syvvak may attack at any moment,' Shousukei said.

'Done and done,' Dilaria said.

'We also need vadis that can cross the oceans to Jheia.'

'How many?' Dilaria asked. Shousukei glanced at Carvosc

and Carvosc nodded.

'Enough to pick us up and eventually the rest of the party after they return from Bosna.'

'I'll get right to it then,' Dilaria said. 'It could take a while though, all of our sea vadis need repair work and it's a long journey from here.'

'How long will it take?'

'A couple of weeks at best, I would think,' Dilaria said. Shousukei sighed.

'Ok. I guess our plans will change. As we have time, we might as well travel with Ahrl's group now.'

'Understood. I'll keep you updated.'

'Thank you, Dilaria.' The kaelo hissed quietly once more and Shousukei turned it off.

'Shousukei, why do you travel with so many companions?' Carvosc asked. 'Usually there are only four or five of you.'

'I travel with a group of friends this time, though we do have one amongst us who is still questionable,' Shousukei said, glancing at Varth.

'Some of our friends were hoping to travel to Bosna and, I think, Arvita and I will be joining them after all. What are your plans Ruick?'

'Since we are here and have no way of immediately travelling back to Eloran, then Ashta and I will join you too,' Ruick said.

'Bosna? But why? No one has lived there in centuries,' Carvosc said.

'We're looking for something which could be of great value to Iyeeka,' Ruick said.

'I guess there's no need to be so vague about it now,' Shousukei said.

'True,' Ruick said. 'We recently found a set of notes in Kiri written by a Jheian called Arkeenell several centuries ago; his notes are extremely valuable. They contain written instructions, mathematics and measurements for ideas which could help us today. One of his pages was identical to the plans Myrion and Lebanoi drew up for the desalination machines. Arkeenell's last known location was in Bosna, so we're hoping we might find more of his notes there.'

'I see,' Carvosc said. 'Though I don't think it's a good idea. Is there any way I can dissuade you from your course?'

'I go,' Ehi said. Carvosc gazed at Ehi.

'Forgive me for being rude, but who are you and why do you hide your face from us?'

'Ehi, you probably don't need to cover your hair or eyes now,' Ioel said. 'If the N.I.L. truly wanted to recruit you to their cause then they wouldn't have destroyed the bridge.' Ehi lowered her hood and more gasps erupted from the crowd.

'Ehi is unique,' Ahrl said. 'She is the reason we are here.' Carvosc hushed the crowd.

'This looks like it might take a while to explain,' Carvosc said. 'We better take this conversation indoors or we'll be standing here all afternoon underneath the etansy.'

'We have some supplies with us but there isn't very much since we lost our other carriage on the bridge,' Shousukei said.

'Thank you, we're grateful that you managed to bring anything at all,' Carvosc said. He turned to the crowd and instructed them to unload the laburnem. 'Follow me,' Carvosc said to their group as he turned on his heel and marched deeper into the Narakae district. The crowd dispersed, leaving Fera standing alone, staring at Ehi with her mouth open. She blinked, closed her mouth and did a double take.

'It's…' Fera said.

'Fera,' Carvosc called. 'Do not hold up our guests.'

'Yes, Father,' Fera called back. 'This way,' she said to Ehi, then she turned and headed after Carvosc.

They were led to a large home near the centre of the Narakae district. The walls were cracked, and paint peeled away from the doors and windows. Fera held the door open as their group stepped inside; they dropped their bags in a large hallway and then joined Carvosc and Fera in their spacious but sparsely decorated front room.

'You have a lovely, large home,' Ashta said as they sat down on whatever seat or cushion they could find.

'Our family used to be a lot bigger,' Carvosc said, as he picked up a jug of water and poured out a small amount into cups for everyone.

'Father, I need to speak to you,' Fera said.

'What is it, Fera?'

'Privately, Father.'

'Fera, if whatever you have to say is important then you can speak here, or it can wait until later,' Carvosc said wearily.

'Father, Ehi is the Eloran from my dreams, the one I told you about.'

'Nonsense, Fera, I'm growing tired of your…'

'You've dreamt about Ehi too?' Ahrl said. Carvosc paused and lowered the jug.

'Yes, I've dreamt about Ehi,' Fera said. 'So has Tye, but father said I had just put the idea into his head.'

'What do you mean, too?' Carvosc asked.

'Fera and Tye aren't the only ones who have dreamt about Ehi,' Ahrl said. 'Everyone gathered here apart from you and Zerren has dreamt about Ehi.'

'What? All of you?'

'Yes,' Ruick said. 'Please, Fera, tell us about your dream.' Fera sat down and described almost perfectly word for word what the others had described. Zerren counted the number of Elorans and Jheians who had dreamt about Ehi. There were eleven, excluding himself and Ehi.

'We have all had the same dream,' Myaie said.

'The same?' Carvosc said. 'That's impossible.'

'It's true,' Shousukei said.

'But why?' Carvosc said. 'How can this be?'

'We don't know,' said Ahrl.

'Ehi, this dream is about you, you must know what it means, surely?' Carvosc said. They heard footsteps pounding down the stairs and a boy appeared in the doorway. He was of Faroi origins with his dark hair, eyes and skin. His clothing was simple and hung from his frame; he wore a necklace made from shiny black shells and he had an oversized lif gauntlet strapped to his right wrist.

'Tye,' Fera said.

'I felt her presence,' Tye said as he gazed directly at Ehi. He glanced at the others. 'Good, you're all here.'

'Tye, not now,' Carvosc said, shaking his head.

'What do you mean, we're all here?' asked Ahrl.

'We're all going to Bosna,' said Tye.

'If we're going to Bosna then he is definitely not coming,' Zerren said, pointing at Varth.

Tye rolled his eyes. 'You're the catalyst and the significant other. Anger will only hold you down though. Yes, he is coming too.'

'Tye has had more strange dreams,' Fera said. 'He often mentions dreams where he is invisible amongst the stars, and there are others who are also invisible with him.'

'How does he know that if they're invisible?' Ashta asked.

'I just know, I can feel them,' Tye said, pointing to his head. He turned his gaze to Ehi again. 'I've been waiting for you.'

'Waiting, what?' Zerren said, jumping to his feet. 'How do you know Ehi? You've only just met.'

'Yes, this is the first time we've met, but Ehi has stood on Iyeeka longer than all of us.'

'What are you talking about?' Zerren said.

'Tye, that's enough, please do not aggravate our guests,' Carvosc said. 'My apologies, Shousukei and friends. I'm sure you are tired and have much to discuss after your horrendous journey. There are several spare rooms in this house that you may use; I hope that you will join us for our evening meal.'

'That would be much appreciated,' Shousukei said. 'Please do not stretch your own supplies though; I know that northern Jheia has been struggling more than most areas. Use what we managed to bring with us.'

Carvosc nodded. 'Fera, can you show them where the spare rooms are?'

'Yes, Father,' Fera said, leaping to her feet.

'Tye, a word,' Carvosc said, as Fera reached the doorway.

'Please, follow me,' Fera said to the group. She lingered for a moment in the doorway and watched as Tye approached her father, then turned and led the way back through the house, pointing out rooms until only Zerren and Ehi remained.

'I can't believe that you're actually real, Ehi, but I'm a little relieved. I thought I was going crazy seeing the same dream again and again, and I'm so sorry about Tye.' Fera stopped outside the final spare room. 'He can be a bit brash and he's not used to living in a district.'

'Why, wasn't he born here in Narakae?' Zerren asked.

'No, we think Tye was part of the travelling groups which moved around Jheia. They never settled in one place, but they collected and made things to leave in our warehouses,' Fera said.

'So where is his family?' Zerren said.

'I don't know. Tye just turned up one day a few months ago. I don't know where he came from or what had happened to him. We asked him about his family, but he said they were all dead. He had nowhere to go so my father told him he could stay with us for as long as he liked. Ehi, do you know Tye?'

'No.'

'What did Tye mean before when he said catalyst?' Zerren asked.

'I'm not sure,' Fera said. 'I think it has something to do with his dreams of being invisible amongst the stars, though that's not entirely accurate. He said he had no body, just his mind, and that he felt the presence of twelve others around him. He said he would recognise them all instantly if he was near to them.' *Twelve?* Zerren thought. He had already done the maths.

'What do you think about it all, Ehi?' Fera asked.

'It's… troubling,' Ehi said.

'I guess it must be,' Fera said. 'Under these circumstances, I don't know what I would think or do if strangers told me that they had dreamt about me.' Fera gazed at Ehi's hair. 'Your hair colour is so strange and beautiful, and your eyes are incredible. I really didn't think it was possible to look this way.'

'I didn't always look like this,' Ehi said. 'The Usol Key changed me.' Zerren raised an eyebrow; this was a first.

'Usol Key?' Fera said.

'I'll explain later,' Zerren said.

'Alright, well, I hope you can get some rest; is there anything else you need?'

'No, thank you,' Zerren said. Fera flashed a quick smile and then hurried off down the corridor. Zerren pushed open the door to their room and let Ehi enter before him. He had a lot of questions, and this time he wanted straight answers.

# THIRTY-FOUR

She stood marvelling at the curved metal cylinder before her. It gleamed under the artificial lights and she peered inside at the shiny metal interior. It looked cold, she was certain it would feel cold, and she was glad that even though she would be inside it, she would be blissfully unaware. They had called it the Usol Key, and Hasree and Seffen had done a magnificent job; it was exactly like the picture from Arkeenell's page.

'Is this going to work?' Ehi asked.

'We don't know,' Hasree said. 'We hope so; we followed all of Arkeenell's instructions. It has taken us years to decipher their meaning.'

'How does it work?'

'A sweet-smelling gas will send you to sleep, and little sensors lining the inside of the cylinder will kick in and regulate your bodily functions for you. Once you're asleep, then the sensors will locate your usol, read its energy signature and then separate it from your body,' Hasree said.

'Separate it?'

'No, it won't really separate it,' Seffen said. 'It's more like a block, a wall if you will, between your usol and body; your usol will still be in your body but it won't have to adhere to the rules of the physical world.'

'We have monitors that will pick up the energy patterns from your usol so we will be able to tell if it is working, but we will have to wait until we wake you before we will know if you saw anything,' Hasree said.

'Arkeenell proved that the usol exists within different rules of time, otherwise it would have never been possible for him to achieve what he did. If that's the case, then the universe itself operates with different rules of time too. To know anything for certain, we must observe it or observe its effects. So the universe must observe itself somehow,' Seffen said.

'Seffen,' Ehi said with a smile. 'You know that stuff makes my brain ache.'

'Sorry.'

'Time will be at your fingertips,' Hasree said. 'If you can observe as the universe observes then you will know everything. We're running out of time and we need to find out how to save Iyeeka before it's too late.'

'I know,' Ehi said. 'Look for Iyeeka and find our future.'

'Precisely,' Seffen said. 'We just hope that there are solutions to find.' Ehi nodded, and the dream, the memory, vanished back into the depths of her slumber.

Ehi opened her eyes and sat up quietly in bed as the morning etansy-light streamed in through the windows. She clasped a hand to her head as she chased the details of her dream. *I was looking for Iyeeka's future? Did I succeed?* Zerren lay just a few feet away on another mattress, sound asleep, and Ehi slipped out of bed and dressed silently. She padded lightly down the stairs, slipped on her boots and stepped outside. She looked up at the sky. The brown dot was bigger now, much bigger. *Was I supposed to find a way to stop this?* A pang of sadness resonated outwards from her stomach. She felt as though her internal body was collapsing and falling into some deep dark recess of her mind. Someone would notice the brown dot, the planet, soon, even if they had been spared that awful detail from their shared dreams. *No, it can't be?* Tears spilled down her cheeks.

Ehi let her feet carry her aimlessly through Narakae. They

had talked and argued all evening at Carvosc's table. The copied pages from Arkeenell's work and the original Usol Key page were passed around and dissected, though no one really had any answers, just ideas and speculations, and Ehi sat wondering how much she should share from her mixed-up memories and dreams, if anything at all. Now she realised that something must have gone terribly wrong. Hasree and Seffen hadn't woken her up and she couldn't remember seeing anything that would be of use to them now. Did that mean she had failed?

Eventually the evening meal ended, and they retired to their rooms with no real plan of action for the next day. Once Zerren had got her alone again, he too had bombarded her with questions, but she hadn't been able to answer all of them or tell him how she felt. She harboured feelings of despair and dread, and she had her own questions. *Would the russet planet come?* Probably. *Would the storm occur?* Probably. *Would they be ok?* She had no idea. The thought made her queasy; all she had was hope, a slim hope at that. The answers had to be in Bosna; Arkeenell must have left something behind to help them. There was no way they could avoid a planetary collision; she knew somehow that their technology wasn't advanced enough. *Perhaps it will miss?* But even that thought gave her no comfort. *I should tell the others what I have seen. I should warn them.*

A sweet mournful sound echoed faintly to her ears. She turned towards the melodic tune and followed its fragmented harmony faintly dancing in the wind. She walked to the outskirts of the Narakae district the sound was enchanting, mesmeric. She stopped just before a deep gorge in the ground and gasped. Mounted on a wooden pole beside this gorge was a strangely shaped stone, nothing more than a large pebble with many holes drilled through it. A burst of wind picked up the ends of her hair and then the pebble emitted a long, single, pure note.

'It's the singing gorge,' Tye said, once the sweet sound had died. Ehi turned around; she hadn't even noticed or heard his arrival.

'Why does the pebble sing?'

'It was made that way; there's a sad story associated with this gorge,' Tye said. Ehi stared at the pebble, *stories*. Iyeeka had lots of stories, stories which would die if Iyeeka died.

'What is the story?' Ehi asked.

'Over two thousand years ago in the district of Narakae there was a woman who came from a long line of singers. It is said that her voice was so sweet and so pure, she could lull babies to sleep with just a couple of words. One day she was walking out of the district to meet a friend in the neighbouring district when a tremor occurred. This tremor was one of the strongest that Jheia had ever felt. It ripped open the ground beneath her feet and she fell into the gorge. When the Jheians of Narakae discovered what had happened, they looked into the gorge and saw her body caught perfectly between the rocks; it was as though she was just asleep. They were so saddened by their loss that they carved a pebble and placed it here so that when the wind blew in the right direction above the gorge, it would sing just like the woman had done, the gorge amplifies the tune, which can often be heard across Narakae. Of course, over the years they had to replace it, but it's always maintained and looked after, and the story is told to every Jheian.' Ehi gazed at the pebble and didn't speak for a long time.

'It is sad,' Ehi said finally.

'Yes, there are many sad tales from Iyeeka, but there are lots of happy ones too.'

'What was her name?' Ehi said.

'Galia,' Tye said. A gentle breeze brushed past Ehi's cheeks and the pebble sang several long, silvery notes. Ehi closed her eyes, and for a moment she could imagine Galia, singing amongst a field of laluta plants and eyeleetansy. The wind dropped and Ehi opened her eyes again.

'Do you know who I am?'

'No, not entirely.'

'Why were you waiting for me?'

'My ancestors have seen you for a while,' Tye said. 'And I felt it in my dreams; there is something about you, something important.' He looked up at the sky and pointed at the planet. 'It's coming.'

'You know about the planet?'

'Yes, but the others don't, do they?'

'They don't know. I didn't tell them. I didn't want it to be real,' Ehi said.

'It is real, but I don't know what it means for Iyeeka. I haven't told anyone either.'

'I hope it means nothing, but I feel terrible things.'

'Is that why you want to go to Bosna?' Tye asked.

Ehi nodded.

'If you feel like it's the right thing to do, then it probably is,' Tye said.

'We should tell the others about the planet.' Ehi pointed up at the sky.

'Why? There is nothing anyone can do about it now and they will see it soon enough.'

'They will worry and panic,' Ehi said.

'Yes,' Tye said. 'You won't be able to stop that.' Ehi's vision blurred and warm tears began to fall down her cheeks. She felt her mind fog up, her thoughts colliding with memories which didn't make any sense or appear to matter at all anymore. Humans, Earth, the girl and boy with the box, their scientists, artists, speakers and more; it all felt far removed from their troubles now. *So why am I seeing it? Why does my mind torment me so? I was supposed to see Iyeeka, I was supposed to fix this mess.*

'How old am I?' Ehi asked.

'I don't know the answer to that either,' Tye said. 'Older than you look.'

'How do you know that?'

'Your mind and usol are different.'

'You see usols too?'

'Yes, though no one knows that apart from you. It's not something you can just say to Iyeekans; they grow suspicious and wary,' Tye said.

'What does my usol look like? I can't see it.'

'No, of course you can't; you're not meant to see your own usol.' Tye laughed. 'Your usol is beautiful; it is full and bursting with amazing colours. It shines out around you like a rainbow and you have so much of the golden yellow colour, the most important colour.'

'Why is it important?'

'It's just good,' Tye said. 'Goodness in its purest form.'

'Zerren's usol… it's different.'

'You noticed that, did you?' Tye said, amusement dancing in his dark eyes. 'I'm not surprised, the way you look at him tells me enough. My family would have called him a sightless messenger.'

'Your family?'

'Yes, they had my abilities too. It's why we travelled and kept to ourselves for the most part,' Tye said. 'Zerren's usol is split; he has one foot in life and the other in death.'

Ehi frowned.

'It means he almost died at some point in his life and his usol tried to cross, only it didn't cross completely because he lived. My family were a rare kind; we can see usols, we feel things that others can't feel, we know things that we shouldn't know, and we hear the voices of the dead,' Tye said. 'They are all gifts or curses, depending on how you want to look at them. Most Iyeekans do not share our gifts, and it's hard to keep them hidden sometimes. So we travelled around, going wherever we felt was right to go.'

'The voices of the dead?' Ehi said. The pebble emitted another, long, sorrowful sound.

'You still don't understand, do you?' Tye said. 'The usol is and will always be who and what you are; when we die our usols cross over to another existence, somewhere up there, somewhere amongst the stars.' Tye looked up and reached his hands up as though he was trying to grab onto the sky and escape from Iyeeka. He lowered his gaze and dropped his arms. 'My family told me that our gifts were special, that the dead were trying to help us and that we should listen to their words. The only problem is, there are a lot of dead Iyeekans trying to make their voices heard; it can be pretty overwhelming at times.'

'Does Zerren hear the dead?'

'Yes, I'm sure of it,' Tye said. 'He might not realise it though. He probably thinks he's going crazy and pushes them away. I don't think he can see usols though, and he doesn't feel or know things like I do, that's why my family would have called him sightless.'

'I don't hear voices, but I do feel and I see… strange things,' Ehi said.

'Yes, it is another gift, though it is rarer. You see things in your dreams?'

'Yes, but I have seen things when awake too.'

'Usols?'

'No. Memories, and not memories, humans, Earth,' Ehi said.

'I do not know what these humans and Earth are.' Tye frowned.

Ehi sighed. She had hoped that finally someone would have been able to understand and answer her questions.

'But if you have seen these things, then I'm sure they are important,' Tye said.

'I don't know.'

'Your companions, I recognise them.'

'You do?'

'Yes, their minds are with us in my dreams of the stars,' Tye said.

'I have not dreamt that dream.'

'You might never dream it,' Tye said. Ehi looked back up at the sky and fixed her gaze on the growing planet; the pebble sang again.

'I volunteered to go into the Usol Key,' Ehi said. Tye didn't say anything. 'I was to find a solution, something to help Iyeeka. But I think I failed, I think it might be too late.'

'I know we will all die together eventually, but I don't know how long we have left. It could be days, months or years, but whatever happens, you shouldn't blame yourself for it. Iyeeka was set on a path of destruction way before you were born.' Ehi felt her tears dripping off the edges of her jaw. 'We should go back to Fera's house before the others start to wonder where we are,' Tye said. Ehi wiped her eyes with her sleeve and nodded. She cast one last look at the pebble and the singing gorge and then she followed Tye.

# THIRTY-FIVE

Varth lifted his water sack to his lips but not a drop of water came out. They had been walking for several days now, following Tye across the etansy-scorched land of northern Jheia, and so far, they had found no water.

'Here,' Fera said. She handed him her water sack and he gratefully drank. She had been the only member of their group to walk beside him; the rest still kept their distance and Roe, Roe wouldn't speak or even look at him.

'Thank you,' Varth said, handing the water sack back. He looked up and saw the red-brown planet growing in the sky; it seemed bigger than the etansy now. Ahrl had noticed it several days ago and pointed it out; now everyone periodically looked up at the sky and wondered why it was there and whether it would disappear.

'It's growing quickly,' Fera said. 'It could be heading towards Iyeeka.'

'That doesn't sound like a good thing,' Varth said. He thought of their dreams, the shadow across the land and the wind whipping around their faces. *It couldn't be?* He glanced upwards again and shuddered.

'So I've heard you're the troubled outcast,' Fera said.

'I suppose you could call it that,' Varth said. 'Yeah, I made some bad choices.'

'Does that include joining the N.I.L.?'

'Yeah,' Varth said. 'I mean Syvvak took me in when I left

Lazarack, but I don't think there was any real kindness to it, he just wanted my ability with lif. He made nice promises and made you feel like you really belonged to something greater than just yourself. It was easier to just go along with what Syvvak said because anyone who disagreed or upset him usually ended up seriously hurt or went missing. Syvvak told us they had left, but I don't think that's the truth, there were plenty of whispered rumours going around.' Varth sighed. 'The others are right, just being a part of the N.I.L. and knowing what they did, knowing what Syvvak ordered for Skidaroi and the other districts, is bad enough. Someone should have stopped him years ago when he joked about destroying districts, but I never thought he would actually do it. Everyone kept saying he had crossed wires because of his son.'

'Syvvak has a son?' Fera said.

'Oh yeah, Jhuka. He's sick, seriously sick. Syvvak makes sure he always has plenty of food and water; it's one of the reasons why he doesn't share resources. He believes that if our ancestors hadn't built the wall and hoarded their supplies, then Jhuka wouldn't have had a chance to survive,' Varth said. 'Jhuka is his whole world, he would give up everything in Iyeeka for him. It's a bit… odd. Sometimes I think it's just an excuse to make him look compassionate; if he loved Jhuka that much he would spend more time with him and not be away, causing such destruction.'

'What's wrong with his son?'

'The medics don't really know, they think he has some sort of degenerative condition. They haven't found a cure for it yet and Syvvak frequently shouts at them over it,' Varth said.

'I guess Syvvak is more complicated than I thought. Not that it makes any of it right, just complicated.'

'Complicated or not, Syvvak is crazy and cold, and I am guilty by association.'

'Perhaps, but you did protect everyone.'

Varth raised an eyebrow at her.

'Oh, I've heard about what you did on the laburnem with your lif and I've talked to the others. If you hadn't stepped in then it's quite likely that the rest of them would have failed to keep their hold and you would all be at the bottom of the cliffs. I'm also aware that you kept certain things from Syvvak.'

'I was just protecting myself,' Varth said. 'Don't mistake it as a selfless act of kindness; I'm not a good Iyeekan.'

'You're being too hard on yourself,' Fera said. 'I know the circumstances are not ideal, but if things have been different, then we might never have known one another.'

'We're stuck in Jheia though, whilst Syvvak plans to take over northern Eloran,' Varth said.

'Yes, but at least you and everyone here are still alive.'

'You have an optimistic outlook for someone still young.'

'Not always,' Fera said. 'I just try to see the whole picture, my whole life should be decades long, not just a year, a month or even a day. So I try to think about all of my life and not just the moment I'm in now. It's too easy to get caught up in everything bad that's happening to you when you only look at a small section of your life, and really, you decide how you will live the rest of your life.'

'Maybe, but I've done some terrible things,' Varth said.

'Yes and no,' Fera said, 'there are lines that Elorans should never cross, and Syvvak has already crossed them, but you, you haven't crossed those lines yet. It's not just about what you have done or what you do, but about how you think and feel about it too. If you truly believed that you were above others, then you would have told Syvvak everything, and Syvvak's methods would not unsettle you so, but you abandoned him and the N.I.L. instead. You put Ehi before yourself; you protected her even though Syvvak sent you to watch her and you unwittingly protected everyone here.'

Varth opened his mouth and then shut it again and frowned. He looked up at Roe and saw her chatting happily with Tye as they walked side by side. He watched as they laughed and then Tye reached up behind his neck, removed his necklace and placed it around Roe's neck.

'I'm glad Tye has found someone to be friends with,' Fera said. 'This is the first time I've seen him laugh.'

Varth nodded.

'You can let your mind berate you, it's good to feel uncomfortable about your bad decisions,' Fera said. 'Remember it, but don't torture yourself forever over it, we all make mistakes sometimes. You can't use that to excuse what you've done, and those who have crossed the line will feel the pain of their decisions for years to come. But you can use it to forgive yourself and then live with it afterwards by making sure you go above and beyond to do the right thing. It's not easy, but you will feel better for it.'

'You speak like someone who's a lot older,' said Varth.

Fera laughed. 'I had a lot of wise and deep-thinking family members, both young and old, even my stubborn father.'

Tye stopped and held up his hand and the rest of their group came to a halt. In front of them lay a small, abandoned district and, in the distance, Varth could make out the sharp peaks of the O'ekma Mountains.

'Is it safe?' Myaie asked. Tye didn't speak, he just watched and waited, and, when nothing happened, he led the way forwards into the district.

'What is this place?' Ruick asked as they passed the first few abandoned homes. Their windows and doors were broken or missing, and their walls were stained and cracked.

'It was the district of Perr,' Tye said. 'It was abandoned decades ago but that didn't stop other Jheians from coming here, looking for anything that might be useful.'

'Most of the ghost districts in Eloran look like this,' Zerren said.

'Is there a well here?' Roe asked.

'Yes, hopefully this one hasn't completely dried up like the others,' Tye said.

'I sure wish we had a yebon,' Shousukei said. 'How are you holding up, Ioel?'

'I'm ok, thank you, but I think Esroz would appreciate a break,' Ioel said. The ziree snorted beneath him.

'Hmm, yes, I agree we should rest for a bit,' Fera said. Esroz was the only ziree her father owned and the only one the district could spare for their group. 'Tye?'

'The well should be up ahead,' Tye said. 'We can stop and rest in one of the houses.' They continued onwards and Varth found himself walking beside Fera again.

'Thanks, Fera.'

'What for?'

'For being honest and talking to me. The other's don't really speak to me that much.'

'They'll come around, besides, no matter what you say about yourself, you're a good Iyeekan, the others will see that eventually.' She smiled at him, and as their group rounded the corner of one particular dwelling their conversations stopped, and every breath was hushed. It was as though all of Iyeeka's past, the good, the bad, the everythings and nothings, had come together in one single point in time and collapsed right at their feet.

The sight that lay before them was something none of them had ever wished to see, yet it was something which made unwelcome sense now in their dying Iyeeka.

'Is that what I think it is?' Myaie asked.

'Yes,' Ahrl said. 'A bellua.'

# THIRTY-SIX

Zerren's mind screamed at him to run but every muscle was locked into place. The creature before them was just a shadow of what it should have been. Every bone and hollow in its body lay stark and exaggerated underneath its skin. Its chest rose with effort and crashed back down as it fell. Its eyes drooped, and its mouth hung open, revealing a long, pointed tongue which lolled to the side. The bellua looked so pitiful and harmless in that moment, but it wasn't enough to stop the tide of Zerren's memories and emotions. He felt a tingle of energy race across his skull and explode behind his eyes, and a pressure rising around his head as though he was being squeezed from all sides. The voices rushed into his mind, forcing their way through like loud Iyeekans squeezing into a small room. *Death. It's time. Look what we've done. Mother, Mother.* The voices toppled over one another, young, old, male and female, there was no order and they didn't seem to care about smothering Zerren's mind. The broken bellua before him forced his mind back, compelling him to remember the one day he had tried so hard to supress…

'Zerren, don't, it's too dangerous,' Roarn said. Zerren glanced back at his brothers; Lucoe and Roarn had followed him into the wilderness, the forbidden land.

'I just want to see one,' Zerren said.

'We should go back, the sanitation group for our district will be wondering where we went,' Roarn said.

'Come on, Roarn, we didn't volunteer just to dump our waste

over the cliffs and see the ocean. I want to see a bellua too,' Lucoe said.

Roarn frowned.

'Keep your voices down,' Zerren said. 'We don't want to be found by a bokhanya.' They kept quiet and moved silently onwards, only the sounds of the waves crashing against the cliffs below could be heard. Zerren ran his fingers over a bush and watched as the dried leaves and twigs disintegrated in his hands. He carried on scanning the land in wide arcs and straining his ears. Minutes went by, then ten and then twenty, his feet began to ache, and his legs burned.

'Zerren, we should go back now,' Lucoe said. 'There's nothing out here.'

'Shh,' Zerren said, motioning with his hand. He crept forwards and up a small rise. He made a deal with himself then and there. If there was nothing on the other side of this rise, then they would turn back. He crested the top and held his breath as his brothers joined him. There, chewing on the grass before them was a small herd of bellua.

'Bellua,' Roarn whispered under his breath. 'I never thought I would ever see one up this close.' The bellua were huge beasts; the biggest were easily over a dozen feet tall and their hides were hard and scaly. Their faces were elongated and round, and the males had two tusks protruding from their jaws. They used two big teeth in their lower jaw to shovel food into their long mouths and they had two small, floppy ears.

'I can see seven; there are two males, four females and a baby,' Lucoe said. Zerren inched forward to get a better look. The bellua had the most amazing patterns on their bodies, their stomachs and jaw were lighter in colour, but their faces and backs were a dark grey with darker stippled and striped patches. They were all looking a bit thin, but then again, every creature in Iyeeka was struggling to feed themselves.

'Zerren,' Lucoe hissed. Zerren ignored him and crept down the slope. He could see the baby bellua just up ahead and he hid within the dried bushes and dead trees. Zerren didn't dare breathe as he drew closer to the baby; it was only five feet tall, barely the height of an Iyeekan child. He was a couple of feet away from it as it raked the ground with its teeth, searching for roots and grass to chew. Zerren reached out a hand and the baby froze suddenly. It stopped feeding, lifted its head and fixed a dark eye on Zerren. Its pupils dilated and then it let out a strangled cry. Zerren clasped his hands over his ears and the baby bellua reared back onto its hind legs and stomped on the ground. Its frantic calls were answered by the adults and the ground shook as they too stomped and rushed over to their baby. Zerren gritted his teeth and scrambled backwards as the baby bellua reared back again and then kicked him squarely in the chest with a large, flat foot. It felt like he'd been hit by a yebon as he crashed to the ground with a *whump*.

'Zerren!' Lucoe yelled. Zerren tilted his head back and saw Lucoe and Roarn at the top of the rise. He wanted to scream at them to run but the sounds wouldn't form, and his body wouldn't respond. His lungs burned. Lucoe started to run towards him and Zerren felt hot tears leaking from his eyes. *No, run away you fool, run away!* But Lucoe didn't. He reached his brother in seconds and threw himself over Zerren's body as the ground shook and trembled around them. The bellua charged and Zerren saw the undersides of the massive creatures tearing over them whilst Lucoe's body shook and beat against him. Lucoe did not let go; he held onto Zerren and Zerren heard his cries, and then it was over. Zerren gazed up at the pink sky with his brother's body crushing down on him. He heard footsteps crunching across the earth and then Roarn's face appeared. Roarn's eyes were huge and wide and his skin was pale and ashy; Zerren would not forget the look of sheer terror on Roarn's face for the rest of his life.

'Lucoe, Zerren.' Roarn's hands trembled and Zerren felt the

weight of Lucoe's body lift. Lucoe gasped and shuddered and Zerren just about managed to turn his face as Roarn rolled his brother onto his back beside him. Zerren felt the energy drain out of his body, his brothers slipped away from him and then everything was dark...

'It's dying,' Ehi said. Her voice hauled Zerren out of his memories. He blinked, felt the wetness on his cheeks and looked away to rub his eyes.

'Where's the rest of its herd? Bellua usually travel in groups,' Ruick said

'They're probably dead,' Tye said. He stepped forwards and around the bellua to get to the well. The bellua didn't move or make a sound.

'Shouldn't we do something?' Ashta said, gesturing helplessly at the bellua.

'There's nothing we can do for it now,' Tye said. 'You could put it out of its misery though; it's as good as dead anyways.'

'Tye! That's not very fair,' Fera said.

'These are the rules of life, they're never fair,' Tye said. He reached the well; it was little more than a hole in the ground. He took a length of rope from his rucksack, tied it around his open water sack and then lowered it into the well.

'I'll do it,' Ehi said.

'No,' Zerren said.

'But she is in pain,' Ehi said. She crouched down beside the bellua and placed a hand on its head.

Zerren gazed down at the bellua and looked straight into its eyes, eyes which seemed far too similar to his own.

'None of you have any lif anymore,' Tye said as he pulled the water sack back up. He grinned. 'We have water.'

'Good,' Varth said. He stepped round the bellua and handed his water sack to Tye to refill. Ehi stroked the bellua's head and made soft, soothing sounds; the bellua closed its eyes and its breathing seemed to become a little easier.

'She's one of the last of her kind. There are few bellua left now,' Tye said as he finished filling up the water sacks they had brought with them. Tye's words hit Zerren and lodged themselves deeply in his thoughts. *The last of her kind?* He thought back to the bokhanya that Ehi had dealt with and wondered if that too had been the last of its kind. He felt the tingling sensation prickling against the back of his skull again and rushing over the top of his head.

*There is a last of everything that has a beginning which does not act,* Lucoe's voice said. *Existing as though life will always continue into the future is sure to bring about its end.*

Fera emptied some water into a bowl and let Esroz drink his fill. Ehi tried to pour some water into the bellua's mouth, but the bellua couldn't lift its heavy head and could barely move its tongue to drink.

'She's so weak she can't even drink,' Tye said. 'Though by the looks of it she's starving to death too.'

'This is horrible,' Ashta said, turning away.

*The odds are against life, they always have been, but there is no reason to fear death. Even you, I, and all the Iyeekans in Iyeeka will become the last of something. Whether that is the last minute of our lives, or a last member of a family, or the last Iyeekan left on Iyeeka. Make your peace with this bellua, what happened was not your fault,* Lucoe said.

'We should find somewhere to rest,' Myaie said.

'What about the bellua?' Ahrl said.

'We will deal with it.' Tye walked over to Ehi.

'Are you sure?' Ahrl asked.

'Yes,' Tye said. 'Go on, find a place to rest. You too, Roe.' Roe stood fiddling with the necklace; she bit her lip and glanced between Tye and Ahrl.

*The only things we truly take with us when we die are our minds and emotions, but you already knew that, otherwise you wouldn't be listening to me. Tye's right, the best thing you could do now is put it out of its misery,* Lucoe's voice continued.

Roe's shoulders slumped and she nodded. One by one their group trailed away from the bellua, leaving only Ehi, Zerren and Tye behind.

'So what are we going to do?' Tye asked as he gazed down at the bellua.

'Let me borrow your lif, Tye,' Zerren said. Tye raised his eyebrows but didn't protest; he slipped the gauntlet off his wrist and handed it to Zerren.

'I will stay,' Ehi said.

'No, please, Ehi. Go with Tye,' Zerren said. Ehi locked onto Zerren's gaze and he stared back into those purple depths. Those eyes which seemed to be the birthplace of galaxies felt both timeless and omniscient, as though with just a single glance she knew everything about him. She released him and rose slowly to her feet.

'Ok.'

'Are you sure you want to do this?' Tye asked.

Zerren nodded; he feared that any spoken word would betray his jumbled emotions.

'Alright,' Tye said. 'You know where to find us.'

Ehi cupped the side of Zerren's cheek with her hand. He felt the tingling sensation murmuring through her fingertips, into his cheek and to somewhere deep inside his chest. She stared at him again, her irises holding all the chaos of the universe yet so much warmth and kindness. She lowered her hand, stepped away and walked with Tye back to the others. Zerren touched his cheek and stared at her back until she disappeared. He held the gauntlet in one hand and sat down beside the bellua, gently stroking the skin between her eyes down to the top of her nose with his other hand. Not once since Lucoe's death had he dreamed he would sit next to a bellua and feel nothing but pity and compassion.

*It's hard to hate when the thing that you hate is so close to death on its own.*

'Where are you, Lucoe?'

*I am everywhere.*

'You never make any sense.'

*For someone who has always been so curious, you never ask the right questions.*

The bellua snorted beside him and Zerren gazed down to see that it had cracked open a watchful eye.

'I'm sorry, Lucoe,' Zerren said, his eyes welling with tears once more.

*Don't be. You can't undo the past, and if I had the chance to relive that day again, I would still make the same choices.*

The tears fell freely from Zerren's eyes.

'I'm still sorry.'

*I know.*

Zerren rubbed his eyes with the back of his sleeve but the tears kept falling. He sat there for a long time as he cried; he tilted his head back and blinked at the sky. The planet, or whatever it was, loomed high above him in Iyeeka's skies.

*You need to go to Bosna.*

'Why?'

*It's where you will find the end and the beginning.*

A chuckle escaped Zerren's lips. 'See, you never make sense.' Zerren summoned the lif from Tye's gauntlet and with one quick thought he sent a razor sharp thin line of lif straight through the bellua's brainstem. The bellua died instantly and Zerren blinked back his tears. There was no time for ceremonies, no hole in the ground or statue for this creature. He was aware of the tingling sensation slipping away from his mind as Lucoe left him alone with his thoughts. After a while, Zerren opened his eyes and stood. He imagined this bellua in the flourishing Iyeeka he had been told about, the Iyeeka that neither of them had ever seen, and then he bowed his head and left to find the others.

# THIRTY-SEVEN

'How much further is it to Bosna?' Roe asked.

'We should get there by tomorrow morning,' Tye said as their group huddled around a fire out in the wilderness of Jheia. To the east, the O'ekma Mountains were black triangles against the starry sky. The fire crackled as a gust of wind threaded its way across the land. Ahrl held a page in his hands and read it by the firelight and the light of a glass cube.

'What are you looking at?' Myaie asked.

'It's just one of the pages Ruick's students managed to copy,' Ahrl said. 'I've been trying to understand how this Arkeenell thought and what he was trying to say.'

'Have you figured it out at all?'

'No.' Ahrl sighed. 'He talks about the stars, the universe and time.' He gestured up at the sky. 'I don't understand it, but he talks about the universe being an elastic band, something which can stretch and be twanged like the string of a musical instrument. It causes vibrations, which make up everything, but I can't see how we are vibrations.'

'Everything?'

'Yes, everything, Iyeeka, the planets, the moons, the stars, our etansy, everything.'

'I'm struggling to picture that.'

'Me too,' Ahrl said. 'Arkeenell says if we can stretch an elastic band, then time must stretch everything in the universe.'

'That doesn't make sense.'

'It doesn't make sense yet,' Ahrl said. 'I'm hoping we'll find more of Arkeenell's work which will explain this to me.' Another gust of wind buffered against them, stealing embers from their fire and carrying them out through the night.

'Is it just me or is the wind getting stronger?' Varth asked.

'It feels stronger,' Fera said.

No one spoke for a long time; there was a word on the tip of everyone's tongue, but no one wanted to speak it and the wind moaned quietly around them.

'Has anyone had any dreams lately?' Ruick asked, daring to break the silence.

'I've not dreamt anything since we left Narakae,' said Myaie.

'I think that's the same for all of us,' Ashta said.

'We should get some rest,' Tye said. The others murmured and nodded in agreement.

The group dispersed into tents but as Ahrl left the dying campfire, he noticed that Ehi had taken herself a little way away from their camp and sat staring up at the sky. He couldn't be certain, but he was sure her shoulders trembled. *Is she ok?* Ahrl wondered, but before he could decide to go to her, Ehi stood and headed back to her tent. Ahrl frowned as the wind howled and buffered the tents; he quickly climbed inside and sealed their tent from the elements. He lay down and listened to the wind; it was definitely growing stronger.

***

The next morning, they rose early, and the wind tugged at their tents, clothes and belongings. Every morning the planet above was bigger; big enough that Ahrl could make out the red lines running through its rocky body and its large craters similar to the ones on their moons as it trailed across the sky. They dismantled their tents and battled with the wind as they secured them to their rucksacks, then followed Tye in a south-easterly direction across the barren land.

The wind did not let up, and their hair became clogged with dust and sand. It pushed at them from all directions, stealing the strength from their muscles and the warmth from their skin. A few hours of trekking muted all conversations as they concentrated on putting one foot in front of the other. Ahrl hoped they would find Bosna or another district soon; it seemed pointless to try and travel through this growing storm. Myaie shielded her eyes and stared down at the ground as they walked. Just as Ahrl was beginning to think that they would never find Bosna, the first buildings of a district began to appear on the horizon, but his heart sank. The entire district was partly buried under sand. The odd roof poked out above the sandy dunes along with the upper stories of several larger homes and a former school.

'Bosna,' Tye yelled above the wind. He pointed at the buildings and paced on with renewed strength. They arrived in the district but the easiest door to reach was a balcony on the second storey of one of the larger homes. They forced the door open and stepped into one of the bedrooms before wedging the door shut with a small table. They dropped their rucksacks and leant over to catch their breath.

'Everything is buried in sand,' Arvita said as Shousukei handed her a water sack. 'How are we ever going to find where this Arkeenell lived? All the single-storey homes are completely covered.'

'How many houses are in this district?' Ahrl asked.

'There must have been over a thousand, though I could only see twenty or so,' Ruick said.

'There's no way we can go out there and try to dig our way into every house, that would be madness,' Arvita said. 'I think we should hunker down, wait for the storm to pass and hope that we don't get buried in here.'

'This… not right place,' Ehi said.

'How do you know that?' Ruick asked.

'I feel it.' Ehi clamped her hand into a fist and pressed it into her chest.

'Do you know where we need to go?' Ahrl said.

'Out there.' Ehi pointed outside. The group fell silent as they watched the growing storm.

'I guess we should get moving then,' Shousukei said as he picked up his bags.

'What if we can't find Arkeenell's home?' Ashta asked.

'Then we will come back here or take refuge in one of the other buildings,' Ahrl said. 'I don't think poor Esroz will take much more though.' The ziree skittered across the room as Fera tried to calm it.

'Let's go before this storm gets any worse,' Tye said. He heaved the table away from the balcony door and opened it. Esroz let out a deep snort and stamped the floor as a gust of sand blew in. They quickly hefted their packs and stepped back outside. Arvita helped Ioel to walk and Ashta and Ruick held onto Esroz. Ahrl shielded his eyes with his hand as he followed Ehi; he could see the others battling with the elements ahead of him. They passed several larger dwellings and they even walked across the gently sloped rooves of smaller homes. Ahrl glanced up and down the rough line their group had formed, counting every member in an attempt to keep them together. After several long minutes, Zerren shouted ahead.

'Ehi. Where are you going?'

She stopped only to glance back at them and point out into the wilderness.

'There's nothing out there,' Zerren said.

Ehi continued to point and Ahrl followed the direction of her finger and squinted. He thought that in the distance he could see the outline of a building. Ehi pressed onwards and as they drew nearer, they could see the building was a small house perched on top of a rocky outcrop with a slope of sand reaching up and over one side like a wave. Ehi headed straight for it; she climbed the slope and took shelter in the doorway.

'Clever,' Tye said, as Zerren and Ahrl reached them. 'Building your house on a rock. It's almost like he knew Bosna would be buried alive.'

'Strange, if you ask me,' Zerren said as he forced open the door. Ahrl ushered the group in, counting them as they entered. They dropped their belongings in the hallway and tied Esroz to a door handle inside. They quickly realised that the place had been ransacked of anything useful. Tables and chairs were overturned and even the battery which would have been in the front porch was missing.

'Is this the right house?' Ruick asked.

Ehi nodded.

'Well, it does fit with the deep thinking alone type, being this far away from the other homes,' Ashta said.

'It fits the mad type, being on top of a rock,' Shousukei said.

'I guess we should take a look around,' said Ahrl.

They wandered through the rooms of the house, which were simple but comfortable. Ahrl found himself immediately drawn to the one bookshelf in the front room which had been left untouched. He pulled down a book, opened it and frowned; it was not Arkeenell's handwriting. He tried another book and then another and was equally disappointed. They had spent so long travelling just to reach Arkeenell's home, he had hoped the place would be overflowing with words from the illusive genius. They searched for some time and then a few of them sat down to rest.

'I've found something,' Ruick said. He appeared from one of the rooms with a brown-tinged envelope in his hand.

'What is it?' Ashta asked.

'It's a letter, it's addressed to Ehi,' Ruick said.

'What? How can that be?' Myaie said. 'Arkeenell couldn't have known Ehi; he's way too old.'

'Ehi,' Tye called from the doorway. They heard footsteps descending the stairs and then Ehi and Zerren stepped into the room.

'Did you find something?' Zerren asked.

'Ruick found a letter addressed to Ehi,' Ahrl said. Ruick held out the letter to Ehi and she took it from him and stared down at her name written on the front of it.

'Where did you find this?'

'It was inside that little chest there and tucked inside a cupboard,' Ruick said. Her fingers trembled as she held the letter and Ahrl could see the cursive writing adorning the front; it looked like Arkeenell's handwriting.

'I…' Ehi glanced at the faces around her and then she strode past them and out towards a room at the back of the house. Zerren began to follow her but Tye grabbed hold of his sleeve.

'I think she wants to read it alone.'

# THIRTY-EIGHT

Ehi's hands shook as she stopped in what she supposed had been a kitchen. There wasn't very much in the room at all, a couple of wooden counters and cabinets, a sink and a large black round circle with an empty, cracked pot sitting on top of it. The cube light recessed into the ceiling above her head was off and, above the sink, a murky window looked out across the land behind the house. She could hear the others talking quietly in the front room. She bit her lip and blinked back tears as she opened the letter; if this was truly Arkeenell's hand, if he had known about her, then perhaps, perhaps this letter would have some answers. She pulled out the letter, opened it carefully and read.

Dear Ehi

If you are reading this letter, then I am truly sorry. My greatest fears will have already passed, and my deepest regret will be imminent. You will be looking for answers but I'm afraid the answers I have for you now will not be pleasant for you or your companions. Yes, I know you will come here with twelve others, for I designed it that way. I shall explain as best and as briefly as I can.

My name is Arkeenell of the district Bosna, Jheia, though originally I lived in the district Ilaria, Eloran. I am your many great grandfather, though I'm sure my name would not have been spoken often by your parents, if at all. I was born with a gift, a gift that everyone has but no one realises. It is connected with our control over lif, though I am sure you have probably figured that out for yourself by now. My gift is simple. I can separate my usol and mind from my body and, as a result, I can see into the future. I have seen a great many things, a great many terrible things.

I first noticed my gift when I was a child. I would fall asleep at night and dream about events that would occur the following day. It was little things at first, knowing when a minor accident would occur, knowing who would come from another district and visit our district, knowing a baby's gender before it was born and knowing which lands would produce the best harvests. My predictions were always accurate, and I quickly realised that I had great power. I began to tell of what I saw and soon many from my district came to trust my visions and seek my advice. As I grew, I found that when I slept I could see more of the future, not just a day ahead but weeks ahead. However, the more I saw the longer I slept; sometimes I would sleep for days and cause great worry for my family.

As with all powerful things, there are both good and bad sides and, after a number of accurate but unpleasant predictions, the Elorans from my district began to grow wary of me. Rumours quickly circulated around my district and many started to believe that I didn't only just predict the future, but I caused it to happen. Enraged and deeply upset by these accusations, I sought to prove my powers and innocence. I made a machine that would enable me to sleep for not just weeks, but months instead. This machine used little electrical charges to shock my muscles so that they would not become too weak and medical equipment for breathing and managing my fluids. I informed my family of my plans and gave them specific instructions on how to care for me whilst I slept. They were not happy with my plan, but they understood why I felt the need to go ahead with it.

The plan worked perfectly, too perfectly. I saw visions of Iyeeka, but I also saw visions of another place, a place that I think you will know about too, Earth. I saw many things, some that I did not understand at the time but have come to understand later in my life. I witnessed the salvation and destruction of Iyeeka and all the many possibilities which lay open for us in between. I saw the birth of these strange creatures called humans and I saw their destructive ways and their capacity for compassion. So many lives were made known to me, so many faces and voices. One moment my heart would be warm with hope and the next it would be frozen with dread. It was as though all the mysteries of the universe had opened their doors and I only had to think the questions and then I would know the answers. Yes, I saw many great and many terrible things. I even saw you and your companions. I knew you would eventually go to Kiri, because I made sure that the plans for my newest version of my machine would be there to find. You see, every life is connected, Ehi; what you do even by just waking up and going about your normal day will impact the lives around you and the rest of Iyeeka.

When I woke up I was no longer in Ilaria. I was weak, confused and unable to talk or walk. A family found me and took me in and cared for me; without their kindness, I would never have made it. Over the weeks I came to realise that I had been asleep longer than I had planned. I didn't sleep for months, I slept for years, one hundred and fifty-two years, thirty-five days and eighteen hours, to be precise. The realisation was crushing, I believed that everyone I had ever known and everyone I had ever cared about was gone. I woke up in a new Iyeeka with new faces and new lives. I also discovered that I was no longer in Ilaria, I was no longer in Eloran, for some reason I had ended up in the district of Viskieria, Jheia. My body had crossed without my knowledge or consent to an entirely separate continent.

I spent weeks in bed, thinking and mulling over everything I had seen and learnt whilst I had slept. I realised that the Iyeeka I knew and loved would not last much longer if Iyeekans did not change. We were taking everything for granted, we expected things to work just because they did, and we never thought about the way we affected our Iyeeka or what the consequences of our actions would be. We didn't understand anything, and our past problems and disasters had never been too great or lasted too long that we could not survive them, but this time it would be different. The vision I had seen for Iyeeka, the disaster heading for our Iyeeka, was not something we could wait out or even hope to ignore. I know you have seen this vision too; it is already here.

I regained my strength and my voice and the family who had taken care of me came to me one day with great news. They had found and made contact with my living relatives and they were coming to collect me. I was delighted to find that my daughter Suroneko was indeed alive and well, and I had a new grandson called Aeito too. When I finally made it back to Ilaria, I learnt that my wife had passed away and so had many of my friends. I also discovered that Suroneko had grown old, much older than me. I do not know why this happened but for some reason, whilst I slept my body hardly aged. The only thing that had changed visibly was my hair and eye colour. I had once had dark brown hair and eyes, now I had white hair with a tinge of purple, and bright purple irises, exactly like you, Ehi. Suroneko was glad to see me awake but she was visibly distressed. I learnt that my family had cared for me all this time and that after my planned months of slumber I just hadn't woken up. They had tried to wake me but I continued to sleep and then one day, the day I had been found in Viskieria, I had just simply vanished from Ilaria without a trace.

I grew stronger over the months and eventually I was able to travel. I went to every district and wrote many letters, warning everyone of what I had seen and pleading with everyone to change. We needed to work together, get out into space and far away from Iyeeka before it was too late, but no one listened. I was careful not so show my face or hair, I did not want to cause alarm, but I was ridiculed wherever I went. No one would take me seriously, no one would listen to me, no one wanted to believe that the Iyeeka we knew would be wiped out in the future in just one day. After months and months of laughter and rejection, I gave up and I began to write. I wrote everything that I thought would be useful to Iyeeka down in a book and I took that book to Kiri.

After that, I became a storyteller and travelled through the districts telling stories to the young Iyeekans. I hoped that the new and younger generations would pick up on the information and wisdom I had purposefully woven into my tales. I hoped that maybe it would spark the right questions, get our Iyeeka moving in the right direction, but I don't think it ever happened.

Now I sit in a little district called Bosna and write this letter to you, Ehi. I know that in the future Iyeekans will grow desperate, the temperatures will continue to rise and the oceans will become more toxic than they have ever been before. Plants will die, lakes and rivers will dry up and the eyeleetansy will fly further and further north and eventually they too will die.

Two Elorans, Hasree and Seffen will find the notes for my new and improved version of the machine I used to see into the future; I will call it The Usol Key. Hopefully this new version has had less side effects and treated your body better than my original machine treated mine. It is a machine that works on the same principles of lif control, only it amplifies the individual's talent and will isolate the usol and force the mind to separate itself from the body. Hasree and Seffen will most likely seek you out, Ehi, because of your relation to me. The Usol Key will not work for everyone, though the twelve you have with you now would have been suitable alternative candidates.

I'm sure you will have heard of the term "usol" by now, and you would have seen them too. It was another gift I became aware of after spending so much time asleep. They are the little spheres hidden within each Iyeekan that no one seems to be really aware of. You have also probably figured out that each usol has different colours and that some of these colours change depending on how the individual is feeling. No, your eyes do not deceive you, this is correct. The usol is in fact the true essence of what we are, our capacity for thought, our memories and our emotions. Our bodies are merely machines which house the usol and our lives enable the usol to grow and mature for an existence beyond life. I know that when you entered The Usol Key you only intended to be asleep for a year; however, you will have slept for nearly one hundred years. This won't be your fault and Hasree and Seffen did not deceive you; unfortunately some time after you fell asleep the district of Cenic descended into chaos. Hasree and Seffen both died and everyone else abandoned Cenic and moved north. This is why you slept for so long, and this is why you were found alone.

I'm also sure you have realised that the humans have usols too. You will probably think the same as I did - how could these violent creatures be anything like Iyeekans? Well, in the end we are not so dissimilar, but I agree, our beginnings and much of our history is vastly different. Unlike Iyeekans, humans will advance from a place of violence, anger and guilt - they will advance much faster than we have. It will take them a few thousand years to reach the same levels of advancement that took us hundreds of thousands of years. It could be their greatest gift or their greatest curse. Their technology will put them into a unique position, they may actually survive the demise of their planet and live comfortably in space, but greed, violence and apathy are some of the hurdles they will have to face. As much as humans will become superior in intelligence and technology in some ways, in others they will not. They will not have lif on their planet and they will not understand the power of their own minds or usols.

You are probably wondering why I speak of humans in the future tense and not the present or past? Humans have not even begun to evolve on the planet they will call Earth, they are the future, millions and millions of years into the future. Why am I telling you this? Because my dear many great granddaughter, there is a life beyond death. An eternal existence for the usol, I have seen it, I have seen it with humans and their Earth. They will call it the afterlife and they will call the usol, ironically, the soul. A few intelligent humans have the potential to fully understand time and how the mind is capable of things beyond the physical realms. People will laugh and think it is ridiculous at first but slowly they will see and learn. This afterlife and its souls are bound to life on Earth, just like our afterlife and usols are bound to life on Iyeeka. You cannot have one without the other and this is why I write this letter.

Within a couple of days all life on Iyeeka will come to an end, but you already know this, you have already seen it yourself and it's why you are here. You were hoping to find an answer, a solution which would stop Iyeeka from dying or at least save the remaining Iyeekans and I am sorry, but I cannot give you either of the answers you seek. It is not possible, because if you are reading this now then it is already too late. All life on Iyeeka will cease to be and our afterlife will disintegrate into many fractured pieces, scattering clusters of usols from since the beginning of Iyeeka across the universe.

Ehi, you and your twelve companions will make a special group of Iyeekans known as The Thirteen. When you cross to the afterlife you must hold onto each other and I will find you and give you all of my knowledge, everything I have seen and everything I have learnt. You and the others may exist for a long time yet, but it will not be here with Iyeeka. You will drift through space and time for millions of years until you come across Earth; there you will be able to endure by forming a connection with the first humans. I am hesitant to write more, but I know you have already seen humans and many of their possible pathways.

There is a problem with observing the future as we have done; I do not know if we make the future happen by observing it, or if the future will happen regardless. There lies the crux of my own guilt, though that is a discussion for another time. If there is one thing that I do know it is this; no life is greater than another's, every life is equal. This is something humans will understand but fail to adhere to countless times; they will take lives without a thought and blame it on ignorance, survival, or something else beyond their control. I have witnessed the lives of humanity and Iyeekans and I know that every life is tangled together; often the smallest decisions made by the most ordinary individuals lead to the biggest and most extraordinary changes.

Ehi, I believe that in order for humanity to survive, certain individuals will need guidance. Certain ideas, discoveries and technological advancements will have to be made at certain times by certain people, but you will know this already and I will pass on everything I know to you and The Thirteen. Humans are not like Iyeekans, the majority are not as kind or selfless as our ancestors were, but they are equally not as ignorant, and they can change and adapt with time. It will be an alien world for you and the others and I hope that I have done the right thing. I am sorry that I could not give you the answers that you seek. It will all end and begin soon.

Arkeenell.


Ehi clutched the pages to her chest, and blinked back the tears. Even though she was standing still she felt as though the world beneath her feet was turning too fast. She wanted to deny everything that Arkeenell had written but there was a part of her deep inside that knew that it was the truth. She let the tears fall and walked back to where the others stood waiting for her. Her lips trembled as she met their gazes.

'Ehi?' Zerren said, stepping forwards. 'What's wrong? Are you alright?' Ehi pushed the letter into his hands and walked away. She heard the rustling of the pages as she walked to the front door and stepped outside. She stopped at the edge of the rock and looked up to see the red and brown striped planet which was now so large that you could see clear details on its rocky surface. It looked as if it were casting cast a partial shadow over Iyeeka. The others had named it the red eye, Ehi simply knew it now as death. The wind kicked up dust around her and stung her eyes, but she did not care, there was nothing left to care about. They were going to die soon, she had known it all along, but she had been too afraid to admit it. *I failed,* she thought. *Hasree, Seffen, I'm so sorry.*

She let the wind throw blasts of air like punches at her body and she cursed the planet looming above her. It wasn't long before she heard the door open behind her and two arms wrapping around her waist.

'Ehi,' Zerren said. She felt the moisture from his tears soaking into her shoulder. He pulled her away, back into Arkeenell's home, and then he cradled her body by the door.

'I'm so sorry, Zerren, I'm so sorry.'

'I know, but you weren't to know,' Zerren said.

'I'm scared,' Ehi said. A crash sounded from the other room as someone screamed in frustration and something smashed against a wall. Zerren drew Ehi into a small room further down the hall and shut the door. 'Are you angry?' Ehi said.

'Yes and I'm sad,' Zerren said

'With me?'

'No, not with you. There's nothing you could do, there's nothing anyone can do. I'm just sad that I won't be able to see my family before…' His words died in his throat and tears escaped from his eyes. 'Sorry.' He turned away from her and rubbed his eyes but Ehi hugged him gently from behind.

'I'm sorry,' Ehi said. Zerren didn't say a word, but she felt him place his hand on top of hers.

# THIRTY-NINE

Ahrl gazed at the others. No one had said a word for what seemed like forever and Zerren and Ehi still hadn't returned. Ruick stood, leaning against the wall, his head down and his arms crossed. Roe sobbed quietly into her hands. Ashta sat on one of the chairs, bent over with her head in her hands. Shousukei paced up and down with a crackling kaelo. Arvita was seated and rubbed her arms. Myaie and Ioel stared at the ground. Varth seemed to be in a daze as though the wind had been knocked out of him, and Fera stared towards the window, biting her nails. Only Tye seemed completely unphased by what had just transpired, he had picked up a book and sat quietly reading. The silence stretched. Shousukei held the kaelo up to his mouth, pushed a button on the side and spoke.

'This is Council Member Shousukei from the Myrion district, can anyone hear me?' The kaelo crackled but no voices came through, he pushed the button again. 'If anyone can hear me please respond.' The kaelo continued to crackle. 'The kaelo isn't working,' Shousukei said.

'What do we do now?' Ruick said.

'There is nothing we can do, but wait…' Shousukei said.

'Surely there must be something we can do?' Myaie said lifting her face. Her voice was faint and tears fell down her cheeks.

'I don't want to die,' Roe said.

'We don't even know if it will truly happen,' Ruick said. Tye shut his book.

'It will happen,' Tye said.

'How do you know?' Ruick said.

'Because there's a huge planet growing in the sky outside.'

'But we don't know that it will definitely destroy Iyeeka, some may survive, we might be the lucky ones.' Ruick said.

'Are you really going to doubt Ehi now?' Tye said. 'You all saw her in your dreams, some of you even saw her before you met her. Not to mention the dream itself, there was a great storm raging in your dreams and now there is a storm outside.' No one said a word.

'Why are you being like this Tye?' Roe said eventually.

'Because I believe Ehi and I believe Arkeenell. I don't want to but we have to.' Tye said.

'But they could be wrong,' Ruick said.

'Maybe, maybe not, but if they are right, do you really want to spend your last moments angry and afraid?' Tye said

'Of course we're afraid. Why wouldn't we be afraid?' Shousukei said.

'Because there are two options,' Tye said. 'You either believe we will exist after death or you believe that we won't. If you believe that we won't exist then there is nothing to be afraid of, we won't exist, we won't have any thoughts or feelings, we won't even know about it, it will be like going to sleep only we will never ever dream.'

'What if we do exist?' Ashta said.

'Then great, we're not truly dead,' Tye said.

'Who would be in charge of this existence, this place we may go to after death?' Ruick said.

'Does someone have to be in charge?' Tye said.

'Who created it?' Arvita said

'Does someone have to create it in order for it to exist?' Tye said. 'Iyeeka exists, Orleetan and Ariyeetan and all the stars and planets out there exist. Did someone create them?'

'Who knows,' Ioel said.

'Exactly, who knows,' Tye said.

'What if there is someone that did create us and we meet them when we cross over?' Roe said.

'Who is to say that it is a someone, what if it is a something?' Tye said. 'Water and etansy-light turn seeds into flowers, what if the something that created us is different but similar to how water and etansy-light affect a seed?'

'But where would it be? There must be a place, a starting point,' Ruick said.

'Must there? Maybe it was always there, maybe it was in a different form,' Tye said. Ioel chuckled, startling them all.

'You would make a very good Moribi,' Ioel said. 'You would give some of our deep thinkers a headache.'

'My ancestors debated all of these questions. We didn't always agree on everything but there was one thing we could always agree on, and that was treating each other and every Iyeekan with respect and kindness,' Tye said. 'Ehi and I, we're different in some ways but we're more alike in others. I don't know whether or not Iyeeka will be wiped out like Arkeenell says, but I would say the evidence we have above us now is pretty compelling. I believe it is going to happen. My ancestors were not like other Iyeekans, we spoke freely about death all the time. It was sad, yes, but just like the rest of Iyeeka, we honoured our dead by remembering all the good times. If we are all going to be wiped from Iyeeka then there will be no one left to remember our good times, so I'm going to remember my good times now whilst we still have the chance. There's no use getting frustrated or upset, all we can do is wait.'

'Maybe that is how you feel but the rest of us may not be able to bury our fear so easily, we have familes and communities to worry about, we feel for their fear.' Ruick said.

'I'm not afraid,' Varth said. He blinked and straightened up slowly.

'You're not?' Roe said.

'No. It's not fear,' Varth shook his head. 'I've done some terrible things, I know that, but I hope that my recent actions have made up for it at least in part. I'm not afraid to die and if I'm honest, I'm a little relieved. If there is an existence beyond life then I will get to see Anorae again. If I had realised that sooner then maybe I would have…'

'No,' Tye said. 'Don't even think that. That is not the right way. Your time will come when it comes, you shouldn't try to or wish to shorten it. It's never right, it's bad for your usol.'

'You see usols too?' Ioel said.

'I do. If there is one thing I know, everyone here has a good usol, and that's important for crossing over. Certain thoughts and actions aren't so good for the usol,' Tye said glancing at Varth.

'Do you know what these humans are?' Ioel said.

'No, I haven't seen them like Ehi has,' Tye said.

'Why do we find such strange creatures?' Myaie said. 'Even Arkeenell said that they are not like us, they won't evolve like us.'

'Maybe that's a good thing,' Ashta said. 'We haven't exactly looked after Iyeeka.'

'He also said they would need guidance but I'm not sure how we could possibly give these humans any guidance,' Arvita said.

'Perhaps we use dreams? Or maybe we can speak to them?' Tye said.

'This all sounds ridiculous,' Shousukei said. 'Arvita you can't seriously believe all of that? We should be focussing on getting in contact with the other districts, we should leave here as soon as we can.'

'We can't go anywhere with this storm, and if Ehi and Arkeenell are telling the truth then there isn't enough time to change anything now,' Ahrl said.

'So we're just going to give up?' Shousukei said. 'We're just going to wait here and see if we will die?'

'Shousukei, there isn't much else we can do,' Ashta said.

'In any case, we should talk,' Ioel said. 'We should speak

about how we feel, what we will miss and what we will regret. We should talk about the good and the bad things about our lives, and we should make peace with ourselves. The Moribi practise self-examination on a regular basis, it helps to calm you down and expands your awareness. I will go first… I feel great sadness for everyone in this room, especially the young ones who haven't had a chance to live a full life, but death is not scary for me, I am old, I have lived a fulfilling life. I'm glad that I met you all and that I travelled here with you. I have no regrets, but I will miss Kiri.'

Ioel gazed at the others but nobody spoke immediately, after several minutes Ahrl decided to speak.

'I will regret never making peace with my father,' Ahrl said. Myaie caught his gaze and smiled sadly. 'I know he just wanted to protect my mother and I by moving to Loenya, and I know he was scared. I know he felt that teaching was a waste of my time with the current state of Iyeeka, and we disagreed on many things, but I regret not being able to make peace with him. I'm glad though, that my father took me to Orleetan as a young boy and showed me his mining operations there before he was forced to close it.'

'I regret not being able to talk to my parents one last time and I regret not being able to help rebuild Skidaroi,' Myaie said. 'I'm scared and sad, but I'm glad we went to Kiri and I really enjoyed the night where we danced outside by the fire. It was one of the few moments in my life where I felt relaxed and happy, despite everything that had happened.' The group fell silent and passed glances between one another.

'Ok who want's to go next?' Ioel said. Arvita raised her hand and then lowered it as she began to talk.

'It would have been nice if we had been able to refill all of our lakes again,' Arvita said as she looked at Shousukei and Ruick. 'I guess the damage was just too much and time has run out. I regret not being able to help Iyeeka and not being able to say goodbye to our friends and family.'

'My thoughts and feelings are the same Arvita's,' Ashta said. 'I just wish we had found Arkeenell's work sooner, but I don't think it would have given us enough time even if we had. I'm glad I went to Kiri and if this is truly the end then I'm glad that we all met and spent our last days travelling together with a purpose.'

'I regret a lot of things,' Varth said. 'I regret not being at two friend's funerals, I regret not talking to my parents for all these years. I sure regret joining the N.I.L. and threatening Roarn and Zerren and trying to kidnap Ehi. What was I thinking? I shouldn't have followed you all in secret, but mostly I regret betraying your trust, Roe, I'm truly sorry. I don't know if I will ever be at peace with all of my past, but I'm glad I did some things that I can be proud of.'

'I'm scared, really scared,' Roe said. 'But I had no one when I met Ahrl, and I'm so glad that I got to meet you all.' Roe rubbed her eyes and sniffled. 'I wish my parents were still here, but maybe, maybe I'll see them again soon. Varth, thanks for saving me in the pass and teaching me how to play obimna. I was angry and upset at first when I found out who you were but everyone makes mistakes and I forgive you.'

'I just wish I had met you all sooner and I regret not being able to talk to my father one last time. We didn't always see eye to eye but I know he loved me and I wish I could be there with him now. I'm glad I met you all and that we made some sense of our dreams, even though they weren't the answers we were hoping to find,' Fera said.

'I really wanted to see Eloran and Jheia flourish again, I really wanted to push our technology and resources in the right direction,' Ruick said. 'I'm sad that we can't do that. I hope that Ehi and Arkeenell are wrong, but if this is the end then I'm glad that I did everything I could to help Iyeeka. I'm glad I met Ashta and got to spend some time with you, and I'm glad that I met all of you too.' Ashta smiled, stood and hugged Ruick. All eyes in the room turned to Shousukei. Shousukei sighed and put the kaelo down on the side.

'If Ehi and Arkeenell are correct, then my thoughts and feelings mirror everyone here,' Shousukei said. 'I wish I was back in Myrion, but with the planet and the storm out there I don't think there would be much I could do other than to try and keep everyone calm. I'm angry that our ancestors damaged our planet, perhaps if we hadn't been dealing with the problems they had created then maybe we would have spent more time getting out into space and away from Iyeeka, maybe things could have been different. I don't know what to think about it all, I hope Ehi and Arkeenell are wrong but as Tye has said, the evidence is pretty compelling. I regret not being able to save Iyeeka but I also regret not being able to start a family with Arvita, it would have been nice to live a full life with you.' Arvita's eyes welled with tears and she smiled and nodded.

'Tye?' Ioel said.

'I can't say I have regrets,' Tye said. 'But I'll be honest with you all, I have dreams and visions of the future, I also hear the voices of the dead, this is why I believe Ehi and Arkeenell. I wish I could give you all better news, but I knew this day would come. I'm not scared but I am sad.'

'You knew? Why didn't you say anything before, Tye?' Fera said.

'It wouldn't have made any difference if I had. All it would have done would cause panic and frustration. Even if we were in Narakae now, the storm would still stop the kaelo from working,' Tye said. 'I guess you could have stayed with your father, but with Ehi here and our dreams, would you have really stayed behind?' Tye said.

'I don't know,' Fera said shaking her head.

'I'm sorry I didn't tell you all sooner, but I couldn't and I needed to be absolutely certain,' Tye said. 'My ancestors may have been able to predict the future, but we didn't see everything and sometimes the future turns out differently from what we expected.' Tye stood. 'I'm going to go and check on Ehi and Zerren.'

Ahrl looked at the others in turn but only Myaie and Roe returned his gaze, they all sat silently with their own thoughts and avoided looking at each other. Ahrl wanted to speak but there was nothing he could do and nothing he could say to make anything better. He thought about his parents and tried to remember everything he could about the life he had led.

# FORTY

The wind grew steadily louder, throwing sand and debris at Arkeenell's home, scratching and howling as though it were made from the ghosts of all the bokhanya who had ever roamed Iyeeka. It hadn't been easy trying to explain her many great grandfather's words, but with the planet looming above them and the wind growing ever stronger, there was little to contradict her. At first the weight of their silence had been just like the silence born in the few seconds after a relative passes away. Eventually, slow and uneasy conversations punctuated the silence. Some accepted, some denied, but they all sat, cried, laughed and then shared memories from their lives and the Iyeeka they had once known. Their meals were both delicious and tasteless, and their hours both tenuously short and impossibly long. Every word uttered was a precious shout into the void that was to come, a piece of Iyeeka and their lives together.

Ehi had spent her last few hours with Zerren, and now, The Thirteen opened the door of Arkeenell's home and stepped out into the storm waging war around them. The dust and dirt scratched their skin and eyes as they stood outside and formed a circle, holding hands. They knew it was a useless attempt at staying together, but every one of them had agreed that they did not wish to cower inside during their last moments. Their dreams had always shown them in the midst of the storm, so now they would stand within it. Ehi felt the wind clawing at them, and her feet struggled to stay rooted to the ground. She looked up at the sky and saw only the reddish-brown planet bearing down on them. This was it, it would be over soon. The wind howled and screeched, and she felt dirt and sand trying to force its way into her mouth. A gap broke through the clouds of dust around them, and in the distance she saw a wall of dirt ploughing straight for them. It ripped up the ground as though invisible nails clawed at Iyeeka. Ehi turned her attention back to the rest of The Thirteen standing before her.

'You must find me,' Ehi yelled. 'When you cross over, find me.'

She felt someone squeezing her hand and she turned to her left to see Zerren. He smiled at her and she wished she could save that smile and keep it safe forever, but now all she could do was hope, hope that whatever lay before them, she would still get to see Zerren's face. The air grew thick with dust and she felt rocks and larger objects hitting the sides of her body. Ehi closed her eyes and waited; it wouldn't be long now. Her feet began to feel too light as the wind picked up her body. She felt the hand on her right side ripped from her grasp and then she crashed into a body on her left. It was Zerren; she would know his scent anywhere. She grabbed hold of him and he wrapped his arms around her. The wind roared in her ears. Their bodies hit the ground, once, twice, and then something hard cracked. The sound of the wind disappeared. It was dark – and she felt nothing…

***

She felt warm and safe in the darkness. It was as though she had been asleep for a hundred years and her body had melted, no, evaporated. She didn't know who she was or why she was here, but neither of these questions seemed important right now. She had felt as though she had struggled for a very long time and now, now she was finally allowed to rest. It was nice here, peaceful in the nothingness, but her peace did not last long. Cries erupted in the darkness around her, shrill, deep, ugly, painful cries. One by one they came, crying out as though they had lost everything they held dear. They were torturous sounds, merging together into a symphonic orchestra of despair. She wanted to cover her ears, but she realised she had no hands or ears to cover.

The first wave of feeling hit her; it was cold, so cold it froze every part of her being, yet burned its way into her thoughts. She felt pain as she had never experienced it before, everywhere, deep inside everything that she had become. Another wave hit her, and then another, and another. She didn't know where these waves were coming from, but they seemed to ride on their own terrible energy, and every one knocked her, every one carried a little more of her being away from her. The cries felt eternal, the waves, endless. There were hundreds, thousands of waves and she screamed into the void. It was hopeless; whatever she had done to deserve this fate, it must have been hideous.

She was waning, ebbing away and diminishing into the darkness around her. Just as she felt that the next wave would surely consume her, the cries began to fade until there was nothing but silence. *Where am I?* She tried to turn and twist but there was no sense of up or down. She reached out into the darkness with her mind. A tiny light appeared, flickering in the dark, then another appeared, and another, until thousands appeared and stretched around her. She felt a sharp tug on her mind and the tiny flickering lights disappeared into a bright golden glow. She saw nothing but golden light and then it eased, and she found herself staring up at a blue sky.

'Ehi,' a male voice said. 'Do you know who you are?' Ehi turned to the sound of the voice and saw an Iyeekan standing beside a short, stone column.

'Who are you?'

'I am Arkeenell,' the Iyeekan said. Ehi got up and then marvelled at her body.

'Yes, you have a body here because I have willed it so,' Arkeenell said. Ehi turned her attention back to the Iyeekan before her. He had purple-tinged, white hair and deep purple eyes; he was older than she and wore smooth, white, crisp robes. She looked down at the ground and saw beautiful green grass dotted with tiny purple and golden flowers.

'What is this place?'

'This is my sanctuary,' Arkeenell said. 'Though I won't be staying here for much longer.'

'What do you mean?' Ehi said. 'Where am I?'

'You're dead, Ehi,' Arkeenell said. 'You've been dead for a few hours now.'

'Dead?'

'Yes, you will remember it soon,' Arkeenell said. She was about to speak but then she did remember, she remembered everything. She felt tears welling in her eyes and her vision blurred. 'Come here, Ehi, I have something important to show you,' Arkeenell said. She walked over to him more gracefully than she had ever walked in life. He turned to the stone column and she saw that on its surface was a pool of water in a bronzed bowl.

'What is this?'

'This is a fountain,' Arkeenell said. 'I have placed all of my memories and most of my energy into it.'

'Why?'

'Because I will not exist for much longer and I hope that this fountain will help you. It is the only thing I can do for you now. Take a look.' Ehi searched Arkeenell's face; he smiled and seemed kind, yet there was a deep sadness in his gaze. She stepped up to the fountain and peered down into the water. The pool began to glow around the edges, first gold then black, then gold again. Images appeared and vanished on the surface and Ehi felt her mind being pulled down into the fountain. She held onto the edges of the fountain and felt the cool stone under her fingers. Her mind slipped, diving straight into the water, and she saw time and the universe as if the universe and time could observe each other. She felt an energy in this time which seemed to encompass everything within itself as though it were the body of the universe. Every possibility was made known to her; even life itself was just a possibility out of a seemingly infinite amount of possibilities. In minutes she had learned everything that she needed to know, and she tore herself free from the fountain. She gazed at Arkeenell and wrapped her arms around him.

'Don't go,' Ehi said as tears streamed down her face. 'Please don't go.'

'I have to, Ehi,' Arkeenell said. He hugged her back as she cried.

'You didn't do anything wrong.'

'I saw too much and now my conscience will demand its price.'

'No.'

'Ehi, this sadness you feel is not sadness at all, it is love,' Arkeenell said. 'It is the strongest emotion, the strongest energy and force in the universe; do not forget that.'

'Don't go.'

'Goodbye, Ehi.' The garden and the fountain blurred around her and faded into nothing. She caught Arkeenell's last smile before he too disappeared. Her body vanished and the darkness with the twinkling lights returned around her. She realised that it was the universe which stretched around her in all its elegance and authority. A tender warmth of another's mind reached out and wrapped around her; the presence felt familiar.

'Ehi,' Zerren said.

'Zerren.' She reached out for him.

'Ehi, you were right,' Zerren said. 'You were right.' She couldn't see him, but she felt his mind, his energy, everything that defined his being in its purest form. She wanted to grab hold of him, tie their minds together so that she would never lose him again.

'Stay with me.'

'Are you sure, Ehi?'

'Yes.' A rush of energy overwhelmed her being; she felt him everywhere and nowhere all at once. She welcomed it and for a moment there was no beginning to them and no end. She learnt his every feeling, thought and memory and he learnt hers. They became two as one and never quite two again. The warm feeling subsided, but Ehi was overflowing with energy.

'The others,' Zerren said. She reached out to them with her thoughts and found them quickly amongst the stars. She pulled them to her, felt their energies and heard their minds.

'What do we do now?' Ruick asked.

'We stay strong and stick together,' Ioel said.

'What are we?' Myaie asked.

'Usols,' Ehi said. 'Positive usols.'

'What happens if you're the opposite of a positive usol?' Varth asked.

'You cease to exist,' Ehi said.

'How do you know this, Ehi?' asked Ashta. Ehi said nothing; she couldn't explain with words, so she pulled their minds to the fountain just as Arkeenell had pulled hers. The garden erupted around them in a flurry of colours; she pictured them all and imagined them in white robes. She found them there and watched as they stared and marvelled at their bodies as she had done just moments before. She turned her gaze across the garden, but she saw no sign of Arkeenell anywhere. The green grass and purple and gold flowers stretched out in soft rolling hills as far as the eye could see. On a small rise, the fountain stood silent and patient.

'Look into that fountain and you will know everything that I know,' Ehi said. They stood around it, peered into the pool and became lost within its timeless depths, but Zerren did not look, instead he turned to Ehi.

'I was worried for a moment,' Zerren said, as he placed his hands in hers.

'So was I.'

'There was so much pain, so much sadness and despair, so many graveyards of hopes and dreams, I didn't think I was ever going to escape. Do you think anyone else made it?'

'I hope so,' Ehi said. The others began to pull away from the fountain, changed from the knowledge that they now knew as their gazes held weights handed over to them from the universe. She waited until the last Iyeekan, Ahrl, had left the fountain and re-joined her.

'We understand now, Ehi,' Ioel said.

'Our ancestors were tied to life on Iyeeka because of their usols and the forces which govern all things,' Arvita said.

'Iyeeka is gone,' Roe said.

'Yes,' Ehi said.

'Now what?' asked Shousukei.

'We find Earth,' said Tye .

'Humans look like Iyeekans, but they are very different from Iyeekans,' Shousukei said.

'No, their world will be unlike ours and their ways hard for us to understand,' Ruick said.

'Their planet is beautiful,' Ashta said. 'They have a kinder world than ours.'

'If they respect it, then they will achieve much more than us,' said Ioel.

'They do not seem respectful on many of the pathways,' Arvita said.

'No, but there are important influencers among them,' said Ahrl.

'The boy and the girl,' Roe said.

'And others,' Ioel said.

'Ehi, how do we find Earth?' Ruick asked.

'I don't know, I just know that we will so long as we exist.'

'Then we will exist, and we will follow you, Ehi,' said Ahrl.

'You must not give into despair or lose hope; you must remember everything good about your lives, yourself and Iyeeka. Cherish those thoughts and memories, and make peace with those that unsettle you. The energy that will sustain your usol comes from the emotional energy of your best memories and thoughts. Love is the strongest.'

The others nodded.

'We must keep our minds connected,' Tye said.

'Yes, and search our usols and minds,' said Ruick.

'Wait, how do we control our new forms?' Roe asked.

'With your thoughts and imagination,' Ehi said with a smile.

'We will go now and learn a new way of existing,' Shousukei said.

Ehi nodded and watched as each member of The Thirteen faded out and disappeared from the garden until only she, Varth and Zerren remained. Ehi could feel the minds of the others lingering around her own, but they were gone for now, exploring their new existence and searching for anyone who may have survived the death of their world.

'Zerren,' Varth said, 'I know that what I did was wrong. I know that a lot of things I did were wrong, I can feel it.' He clasped his hand into a fist and pressed it against his chest. 'But I need to apologise again, properly, with full heart and conscience. I'm sorry Zerren.'

'It's ok,' Zerren said. 'I understand now, I understand everything. I'm sorry that I punched you.' Varth grinned and rubbed his jaw.

'It was a good punch.'

'What will you do now?' Zerren said.

'I'm going to find Anorae, though there is one thing that bothers me about the fountain. It didn't show anyone else, just the thirteen of us.'

'I hope you can find her,' Zerren said.

Varth inclined his head, and then he too faded out.

'I need to find my family and friends, Ehi, and I know you want to find your family too,' Zerren said.

'Yes,' Ehi said. 'Let's go.' She held out her hand and felt his fingers lace between hers. They closed their eyes and reached out with their minds to the universe. Arkeenell's visions were like fragments of a much larger picture, they showed future possibilities and many, if not all of them, were uncertain. Somewhere amongst the stars they felt the minds of other Iyeekans and they were drawn to the warm energy which seemed to radiate from these souls. They had much to learn about their new existence, the fountain, and when the time was right, humanity. Like Varth, Ehi was concerned by the visions she had seen in the fountain yet, she knew that they must go on and exist, and she wondered if any other life lay out there, and whether or not there were more planets with life, with souls? Did they too end up in an afterlife? Was there an after, afterlife? What were they now? How did they exist? There were still so many unknowns and so many secrets of the soul.

*** | ***

# ACKNOWLEDGMENTS

I am eternally grateful to Emma Pritchard, Steven Greening, James Stoddah and Bruce Nicholson at Outlet Publishing for your continued faith and investment in my work. I would also like to express a huge thank you to my assistant, Hannah Hudson and my wonderful editor, Alison Williams. Thank you too to Catherine Cousins and the team at 2QT for getting the book prepared for release.

Moreover, I'd like to thank all of my family and friends for being so encouraging and patient with my writing.

# CAITLIN LYNAGH
## ONLINE

www.caitlinlynagh.com
Facebook: https://facebook.com/caitlinlynaghauthor
Instagram: https://instagram.com/caitlinlynaghauthor
Twitter: https://twitter.com/caitlinlynagh
Tumblr: http://thesoulprophecies.tumblr.com
Pinterest: https://pinterest.com/caitlinlynagh
*ALSO find me on: Goodreads, Amazon and Booklaunch.io*

Feel free to send a photo of yourself with the book and I'll include it on my *Hall of Fame* across my social media.

# THE SOUL PROPHECIES SERIES

Book 1 and 2: **Anomaly** and prequel, **Hidden Variables** – collectively, *Another Path*

Book 3: **Lost Frequencies**    Book 4: **The Quantum Messenger**

*The Soul Prophecies* explores the evolution of the soul from planet Iyeeka, three-hundred million years ago, to the birth of human, and ultimately artificial intelligent souls, in the near future here on Earth. Throughout the series we discover how all events in the universe and everything that happens is connected. The series explores the science through the idea that time itself is another dimension containing information about all the possible states of existence at any given moment in the future. With guidance from the prophecies of an Iyeekan scientist all the old world souls have to guide humankind, and any wrong decision could have disastrous consequences for both life and what lies beyond.

Present day foundations are set in **Anomaly** and **Hidden Variables** (*collectively, Another Path*). We learn how everything is connected and decisions made by a few can affect so many – and ultimately the fate of mankind. Human souls, with guidance of ancient souls from another planet millions of years in the past, help steer the living to make the right choices and to evolve the conscience – and ultimately the soul. Mankind can learn from its mistakes and avoid the fate of the old world.

**Lost Frequencies** is set three-hundred million years in the past, on Planet Iyeeka, but is connected to Earth and humans culminating in the birth of the human soul. The book follows thirteen wise individuals struggling with the demise of their planet, riddled with climate issues which have been caused unknowingly by its inhabitants over the centuries. They come together and journey to a town, lost to the desert, home of a scientist who prophesised the end of their civilisation and the beginning of a new one.

**The Quantum Messenger** is set on Earth, forty years in the future, and culminates in the birth of the soul of artificial intelligence. It's not just the popular trope of evolving consciousness it's about the soul itself. Apollo is an AI Personal Assistant who attempts to understand human behaviour and emotional feelings. There are elements of profound existentialism and hope to avoid a dystopian future.

*All books, though connected, are independent and can work as stand-alone novels even though some characters crossover the series.*